TRAPPED

TRAPPED

Valerie Tagwira

Published by Weaver Press, Box A1922, Avondale,
Harare. Zimbabwe. 2020

<www.weaverpresszimbabwe.com>

© Valerie Tagwira, 2020

Typeset by Weaver Press
Cover Design: Farai Wallace
Photograph of the author by Paavo Shooya, Am Photography
Studio, Windhoek

This book is a work of fiction. References to real people, events, establishments, organisations, or locales are intended only to provide a sense of authenticity, and are used fictitiously. All other characters, and all incidents and dialogue, are drawn from the author's imagination and are not to be construed as real.

All rights reserved. No part of the publication may be reproduced, stored in a retrieval system or transmitted in any form by any means – electronic, mechanical, photocopying, recording, or otherwise – without the express written permission of the publisher.

ISBN: 978-1-77922-370-8 (p/b)
ISBN: 978-1-77922-371-5 (e-pub)
ISBN: 978-1-77922-372-2 (pdf)

Valerie Tagwira is a specialist obstetrician and gynaecologist who lives and works in Harare. *The Uncertainty of Hope* (Weaver Press, 2006, Jacana Media 2006), her first novel, won the National Arts Merit Award for Outstanding Fiction in 2008. Her short story 'The Journey' was published in the Caine Prize Anthology 2010. Her story 'Mainini Grace's Promise' was published in *Women Writing Zimbabwe* (Weaver Press, 2009) translated into Shona for the anthology *Mazambuko* (Weaver Press, 2011), included in the anthology, *New Daughters of Africa* (Myriad Editions 2018) and re-published in *Windows into Zimbabwe* (Weaver Press, 2019). 'The Way of Revenge', a short story, was published in *Writing Mystery and Mayhem* (Weaver Press, 2015).

For

Rudo Ellen

1

Unesu was ready to drop. Emergency on-call shifts at the hospital were not for the faint-hearted. The pace was intense and there was a relentless influx of patients arriving at all hours. Some presented profound clinical challenges after being referred *in extremis* from provincial and district hospitals. Without dexterity, speed, and attention to detail, a life could be lost in a heartbeat.

Despite being on duty with a competent team of nurses, his weekend on-call duty in the gynaecology unit felt unusually brutal, though having John as his counterpart in obstetrics did give him some small measure of relief. His colleague was a deeply religious young man with whom he shared a good professional rapport. It was a given that there'd be no disappearing acts or malingering, no matter how hectic the shift. John was always conscientious and considerate of his colleagues.

Throughout the weekend, both young doctors were constantly on their feet. They made spirited attempts at cross-covering each other for periodic breaks and the briefest of stolen power-naps. They needed to rest because without exception, and despite a forty-eight-hour weekend on call, Monday was considered a normal working day. They'd be expected to be fresh-eyed, clear-headed and coherent during the morning ward round.

Unesu knew that they had it better than their specialist registrar, Dr Muchaneta (secretly referred to as Doc Muchy), their immediate senior on cover for both obstetrics and gynaecology. She was inevitably busier than they were, but, as usual, she seemed to take everything in her stride.

Since Saturday morning, their on-call consultant, Professor Chaka, had already been to the hospital three times to assist with patients who had complications. While he was a good clinician and teacher, Unesu felt that he was strict and fastidious to the point of being irrational.

During the Sunday morning ward round, he made Unesu feel small and incompetent for not being able to recite a seriously ill patient's medical history and blood test results from memory. Unesu was verbally paralysed as he stood there, fuming inwardly, while the man berated him.

The patient's records were right in front of them. All the professor had had to do was allow him to refer to the case notes during his presentation. Unesu knew that he would've given an excellent presentation because he was always thorough in his clinical assessments and record-keeping. In consultation with Doc Muchy, he'd drawn up appropriate management plans for all patients. No errors had been made and nobody had deteriorated or died because of any act of commission or omission on his part.

It wasn't his fault that the urea and electrolytes machine hadn't been working for two days. Neither was it his fault that the two patients for whom he'd ordered urgent blood transfusions were still waiting while their relatives searched for money to pay the hospital for the blood. Intravenous drug stock-outs were not of his making. So why did the Prof have to be so obsessive?

Afterwards, it took John's good sense to mollify him. 'Don't take these things personally, Unesu. Prof doesn't mean any harm.'

'Listen, the man practically dissected me in front of patients! ... "He doesn't mean any harm"! You're joking, right? Get real, John! What's the chance that anyone receives excellent care in this dump?'

'Of course, it's possible. But it starts with us always giving our best and having the courage to change the things that we can change.' John defaulted to his motivational speaker mode.

Unesu couldn't help laughing. The absurdity of this little speech eased his emotional indignation. If not from a biblical verse, John was always sure to draw from an apparently limitless source of inspirational quotes. With the change in mood, they returned to their respective work stations.

Checking his mobile phone, Unesu found nothing on voicemail. He switched on mobile data, which had been off since Saturday. His phone pinged through a flood of WhatsApp messages that had been on hold.

MedSch Class of '14 group was at it again. There was a heated exchange about their worsening working conditions in government hospitals. What were their employer's obligations? Weren't such poor working conditions a violation of their constitutional rights as employees? Should they go on strike or not? What about their responsibility to patients?

Unesu noted that instead of group members providing decisive answers, even more questions had been raised. To what extent did working with inadequate resources put them and their patients at risk? By accepting the status quo, were they not being complicit in this perpetuation of poor service delivery? And for how long could they continue working for such laughable salaries? And on it went. But there was still no consensus regarding strike action.

He held back from posting a personal comment because most of the sentiments expressed in the thread echoed his own. Besides, he just wasn't sure what, if anything, could be achieved by going on strike.

He scrolled down to a 'hullo' message from Cashleen, a childhood friend. She had such a good heart that she'd surely be the right person with whom to discuss that delicate matter of his mother. She was a girl, so she'd know what to do. But this wasn't the moment to arrange to meet, so he replied with a thumbs-up emoji, and almost instantly received a smiley one in return.

And then of course there was Takunda with a cryptic text: *Got a ryl beauty this tym. U shld c this doc!* A real beauty? Was his friend talking about a woman, a car, a diamond or a gun? For someone who lived on the edge like Takunda, you never knew what to expect. He'd have to call him sometime.

There were several forwarded jokes, mostly from Delta, another friend. Couldn't she be serious for once? The girl was the antithesis of anyone's idea of an engineer. He chuckled, and decided to ignore the rest of the messages.

The brief interlude had given him a glimpse into the outside world, stirring up a sense of envy. He had to get back to work.

The rest of the day progressed as expected, but the evening was one of unrelenting pressure. There were many admissions, and he had to act as Doc Muchy's surgical assistant for two patients. They performed an oophorectomy on a young girl who'd presented in the late, necrotic stage of ovarian torsion. Their second procedure was a hysterectomy on a woman with a badly lacerated uterus. She'd come in haemorrhaging from a botched backstreet abortion.

During her surgery a deluge of memories overwhelmed Unesu. An emergency hysterectomy had failed to save his young sister's life under similar circumstances. Chipo had been only nineteen and in her first year as a pharmacy student.

Time had not done much to ease his pain and the guilt that he still felt for having failed to recognise that she'd been pregnant, until one day when their mother had found her lying on the floor of her bedroom, the carpet soaked in blood.

He took a deep breath. He had to focus on the operation. Ethics and professionalism demanded no less. As soon as the surgery was over, he was back in casualty where a long queue of patients had formed. John hadn't fared any better as he'd spent the night shuttling between the maternity wards and theatre for emergency caesarean sections.

Thankfully, there was an unexpected lull around 4.00 a.m., and John told Unesu that he was going for a break. True to character, after an hour of rest, he came to cover Unesu, so that he could also have an hour's rest before Prof Chaka's morning ward round.

Unesu dragged himself to the on-call room. He hadn't realised how exhausted he was until he stopped. Never had the promise of oblivion on a bumpy bed in the airless little room been so appealing. His last thoughts as he drifted off were of the rather attractive new student nurse he'd met in casualty. Then he was out like a light.

But it seemed that he'd hardly fallen asleep when his bleep wrenched him into wakefulness. He blinked, reached for the offending gadget and pressed the READ button. It was extension 2026, gynae casualty. He noted that the time was 5:28 a.m. Why would they be calling him back scarcely thirty minutes after John had come to relieve him?

He picked up the phone and dialled. It was John who answered. With a sinking heart, Unesu detected the urgency in his voice.

'Sorry *shaz*. We need you back here. I'm off to labour ward for a breech delivery. Doc Muchy's tied up with severe pre-eclampsia.'

'Oh! Is gynae casualty full again?' Unesu asked, hoping that John would say no, and he could rest a bit.

'No. Only two waiting, but you should come down a.s.a.p. and prep one of them for a laparotomy. Likely ruptured ectopic. I've clerked her, drawn bloods and secured IV access. Fluids running. She needs urgent blood transfusion and theatre booking. Prof's on the way!' John gave a succinct summary in a tone that reaffirmed the gravity of the situation.

Unesu sighed wearily. Ruptured ectopic? Prof coming? That was it then. His chance of a rest, let alone a snooze, had just vanished.

'Sure. Coming,' he replied, trying to sound both reliable and competent. From experience, he could well imagine what an uphill task it would be to find blood for the patient, or get her into theatre. The situation had the makings of another personal tragedy.

Slapping his face with cold water, he felt a moment of anger and resentment: he worked in a system that pushed people to the brink. But just as quickly, he checked himself. The woman had not made a conscious decision to present with an ectopic pregnancy at that particular moment just to inconvenience him. How could a doctor sleep when there was a patient with a life-threatening condition waiting?

First do no harm... The thought prompted him to action. He also had to make sure that Prof Chaka didn't beat him to it. He felt a rush of adrenaline, which was just what he needed to jolt him out of his exhaustion.

Half running across the quad, swept bare not only of litter but life, he moved as quickly as he could down the long drab corridors, his mind returning as if by default to the now-familiar, gnawing sense of dissatisfaction with his work as a doctor. It was ages since he'd felt in control of his time, or for that matter, his life.

Surely there had to be better jobs somewhere out there. Ones that paid well and allowed one to have a life with some semblance of normalcy. Not this constant running up and down. Day after day. Night after night. Riding on adrenaline. And for what ...?

But then again, being a doctor had been his dream. For as long as he could remember, he'd always wanted to be one. But after a short fifteen months on the job, he just wasn't sure anymore. Being a medical student had been a breeze. But this?

His disaffection wasn't anything that he could freely talk about. A recent argument that he'd had with Cashleen and Delta crossed his mind. They'd both thought that he was being petty or childish.

How could **having a job** ever be a problem? What did he mean when he said his experiences as a medic were traumatic? Surely, this is what he'd bought into? So what if there was a multitude of expectations or demands from all directions?

He'd given up trying to convince them, to make them see. They were obviously too shut into the martyrdom of joblessness to understand.

Takunda understood, though. His friend had left medicine after six months and was dealing diamonds with a Lebanese cartel across the border in Mozambique. Unesu envied his fearlessness. His rapid acquisition of wealth. His fast cars. His panache and success with women.

Unesu had been invited many times into that intrigue-filled world, but it embodied risks that he wouldn't ever dream of taking. It was a wonder they were still friends.

He remembered the gleam of Takunda's sleek pistol. A Smith & Wesson, he'd been told. His friend had been evasive about why he might need one in the first place. Guns were designed to inflict injury or to kill, and Unesu wondered if his friend could actually shoot someone. After all, he'd been brought up a Christian: 'Thou shalt not kill' had been drummed into them from the moment they began to attend church.

He shivered and shook his head as he crossed the car park with wide strides and turned towards the entrance to casualty. The unwelcome sight of Prof Chaka's BMW X6 next to the entrance propelled his feet. How could the man have arrived already? There'd definitely be some kind of scene.

He wove his way through a stuffy corridor congested with patients and their companions, trolleys and wheelchairs and charged into gynaecology, doing his best to look the part of a no-nonsense, committed and efficient doctor who didn't waste time, no matter the emergency.

The nurse-in-charge shot him a warning look, inclined his head and pointed towards a screened bed in the corner. That wasn't a good sign. Normally, this nurse-in-charge was as verbose as anyone could be, a person who liked the sound of his own voice.

Unesu poked his head tentatively through a slit in the curtain. Then he froze. There was definitely a scene but not the one he'd feared. The usually taciturn Prof was all smiles, staring with open interest at the new nurse, Julia, as she secured a second intravenous line on the patient's antecubital fossa.

What else could go wrong before this shift ended?

2

The weekend had stretched endlessly and the days ahead held little, if any, promise. There was yet another power cut. Cashleen stared sightlessly into the gloom. While she'd never expected to walk into a job soon after graduation, she'd believed that her 2.1 pass in Media and Journalism Studies would count for something. That was over a year ago. Then she'd immersed herself in job-hunting, eagerly watching out for opportunities, networking, and submitting applications. But she'd been disheartened as advertisements for both employment and graduate-trainee learnerships dwindled.

Across most sectors, companies had downsized, while others had simply closed. Several of those still in business had cut salaries and suspended workplace benefits such as medical aid, housing and other allowances. It was expected that this trend would continue, and even escalate, as the economic downturn remained unabated, plunging many into poverty.

None of the three interviews to which she'd been invited had been successful, and most of her applications had gone unacknowledged. She'd often wondered what this meant. Had someone given her applications a cursory glance and then promptly dumped the documents in the trash? Were companies just going through the motions of advertising jobs that had already been promised to relatives or friends?

She'd lost that warm sense of anticipation that she'd felt when she graduated. Instead, an insidious sense of uncertainty had taken over. The country was being described as having a failed economy and the job market was overrun with countless unemployed people just like her.

Every year, an average of 30,000 students graduated from universities and colleges. Most failed to get jobs or opportunities for further studies. She had to contend with this rapidly growing number of unemployed local graduates, as well as those returning home after studying outside the country.

She also couldn't ignore competition from the hundreds who'd lost their jobs on the strength of the 2015 amendments to the Labour Act. After the well-connected – who were always given priority – the recently unemployed had work experience when she had none.

Naturally, she'd considered postgraduate studies. With her good grades, securing a vacancy for a Master's degree at UZ had been effortless. But her sister Rufaro had told her in no uncertain terms that she couldn't afford to fund her studies, while continuing to carry her cost of living as well as that of their brother, Itai. Like Cashleen, Itai was jobless.

For weeks thereafter, Cashleen had been consumed by a toxic resentment against her sister. Then, with gradual reluctance, she'd conceded that Rufaro could well be facing genuine financial difficulties of her own in England.

Besides, she'd already borne so many of the family's responsibilities over the years. Their late parents' upkeep had been her sole responsibility. In addition to contributing towards Cashleen and Itai's education, she'd also allowed them to live in her apartment rent-free when the previous tenants had left. Cashleen knew that all this had required Rufaro to work long hours while juggling extra shifts as a nurse.

Not willing to give up, she'd tried, but failed to get a postgraduate scholarship. Meanwhile, she knew of a minister's son, an ex-classmate with average grades, whose state-sponsored Master's was well underway because he'd been offered a full scholarship soon after graduation. Just like that.

Her Class of '14 WhatsApp group frequently shared job-hunting tips, which hadn't yet done her any good. She'd found it bizarre when Tunga texted that it was better to submit applications by hand and then offer a bribe to guarantee making the short-list for interview.

Apparently, this first step required the incredible sum of $200 – occasionally more. The bribe would have to be followed by a hefty kickback after the interview in order to actually secure a job. Cashleen had been sceptical. Never mind the amount of money at stake; she just couldn't imagine how such a conversation with a prospective recruiter might be initiated in the first place.

Wouldn't that constitute breach of professional codes of conduct, which might well cost one the desired job anyway? And who'd get the job if many paying interviewees went on to proffer a second round of post-interview bribes? The highest bidder? How on earth had it become a norm to pay bribes just to get an interview?

She'd responded to Tunga's text with a long, measured query to that effect. The group's reaction had blindsided her. She'd been ridiculed for being Miss Prim and Proper, with hardly any street smarts.

Kufa's text had been acerbic: *U def lost wateva waz btn ur ears in college Smiley Cash. Get real !!!*

U preachin Pastor Cash? Psychology had quipped insolently. Farai, somewhat kinder than the others, had asked how she expected to survive in Harare with such a naïve, idealistic mentality.

The jibes had stung, but aware of social media pitfalls, she'd restrained herself from hitting back. Her contributions tended to be carefully thought out. Secretly, she'd surmised that those group members who were endorsing such malfeasance were morons. And they wondered why corruption was so rampant!

A sexist comment from Nhamo about how females were fortunate because they could always resort to Bottom Power had left a bad taste in her mouth, this time provoking an instant retort.

Learn ur stats! Mo men in jobs than women & mi bottom has nothin to do wit n-thin!

U tell 'em girl. Susie's text had been accompanied by a bulging biceps emoji.

Frivolous rejoinders from some girls in the group had annoyed Cashleen even further. To them, the idea and the exchanges had all been just another big joke. Were they still in comic mode?

This was one problem with the group. After initially abiding by agreed chat norms at inception, it had taken Class of '14 just a few weeks to slide into a cycle of regular jokes, social and political satire and whatever else took their fancy, instead of focusing on real issues that were affecting their lives.

Cashleen had thought of having a private word with the Group Admin, and then she'd decided against it. Outside their defined rules, the group had indeed shared several light-hearted posts and some videos by motivational speakers, which had seen her through some of her darkest days. There'd really been no need to upset that equilibrium.

And tonight, a couple of weeks after the bribes-for-jobs group chat, newly-employed Amos picked up the thread again, following it up with a personal testimony. He'd successfully paid his way through an interview, although his appointment required him to give ten per cent of his salary to someone in HR for the first three months.

After the sarcasm that she'd received in response to her own post, Cashleen was surprised by the group's combined outrage and flurry of messages urging Amos to report this. But he replied with a *LMAO* text, embellished with a row of no less than five laughing emojis for emphasis.

U guys hi on weed or wat? Report 2 who? Crooked cops et al? Gotta b kidn, he texted, blithe and irreverent while poking fun at them and the republic police force. He pointed out that such practices were common but one hardly ever heard of them in the context of crime.

Zenith concurred and added: *Y'all chill & big-up 2 u Amos!*

Pretty chuffed :), Amos texted, clearly triumphant. Further texts of approval followed, including a few from those who'd initially wanted Amos to make a police report.

Herd mentality? Cashleen thought, somewhat confused by this flip-flopping which in turn challenged the shrewdness of her own uncompromising values. It was a fact of life that in Harare, merit was increasingly inconsequential. It was also common knowledge that even in the highest of offices, nepotism opened doors and presented lucrative opportunities, sometimes to undeserving individuals.

So much depended on who you knew, and how influential that person was. She had no person wielding high levels of power in her acquaintance. From that fact stemmed deep insecurity and a need for reassurance about where her life was going.

She wondered again if she should have allowed her friend and ex-classmate, Sando, to persuade her to leave the country when he did. It was five months since he'd gone to Johannesburg on a job-hunting mission. Although he had started working illegally as a waiter, he always sounded upbeat and optimistic about professional opportunities across the border.

His move to South Africa had been a relief to Cashleen because his growing involvement in opposition politics had worried her. He'd been too loud and too candid about his perception of bad governance and corruption. Although his online posts from South Africa remained equally provocative, at least he was far away and supposedly out of harm's way.

Time and again, Cashleen had scoured newspapers, hoping that she'd come across confirmation that at least one of the frequently reported government's mega-deals with China, Russia, India and South Africa had eventually borne fruit, and jobs!

This promise of transnational mega-deals worth billions of US dollars had long been touted as a panacea for the country's persistent economic woes. The latest story to make headlines had been about the trail-blazing Nigerian multi-millionaire, Dangote, and a deal for him to invest millions of dollars locally and create thousands of jobs.

And now, as a member of the chronically unemployed, Cashleen forwent her journalistic training, the necessity of relying on facts, and allowed her imagination free rein on the basis of those promised deals: the resuscitation of industry, the restoration of high-quality healthcare and education, ZIMRA fairly collecting individual and corporate taxes to feed into a depleted Treasury. And best of all, jobs. Solid, well-paying and secure jobs.

But she also knew that if there ever were genuine deals, those who would shamelessly benefit would be the elite. They never seemed to have large enough allowances or big enough vehicles or large enough mansions. She recalled how an MP had once justified the ownership of a luxury four by four bought with public funds. In his view it was the best car with which to dodge the potholes on the bad roads that he was 'forced' to use when he drove out to his constituency. It was no wonder that elected leaders were untouchable, living large, without accountability, and loving it. Yet, all she wanted was a job.

And then one also had to listen to people like Unesu complaining about being a doctor in a government hospital! Why on earth couldn't he see just how lucky he was to be working in the first place? She shook her head.

Since sending out job applications had not yielded results, she realised that she'd have to be creative about adding value to her CV and close the gap that seemed to grow larger every day. Faced with a very real risk that her degree would soon become a meaningless piece of paper, she mulled over trying her luck by venturing out, going from one media company to the next, being seen and making her case.

If not a job, she wondered if some kind of unpaid volunteer work or attachment would be a good starting point. She accepted that most companies would probably turn her away, but still, she hoped that at least one or two would hear her out. She resolved to get going the following day. There was something energising about the idea of starting out on a Monday morning.

3

It was past midnight and Delta was unable to sleep. Restive, her mind once again rehearsed past events: Agri-Innov8's closure, along with her job loss in early February, had thrown her off balance.

While she'd been trained as a chemical engineer, her job as a receptionist had given her the means to track adverts efficiently and to network on job-search platforms. However, she'd been lulled by the comfort of living with Aunt Peace and Uncle Dondo in their Borrowdale home. With the company's closure, she'd realised how frighteningly fragile her uncle's business had been, despite his Big Man bravado, his show of wealth and limitless generosity. Only after the fall-out with his foreign business partner had she understood that he'd borrowed heavily for his initial investment, and that he still owed the company half of what he'd originally pledged to put in as payment for his 30 per cent shareholding.

She'd learnt how reliant he'd been on his partner, who at least for a while, had consistently provided US dollars to maintain imports when banks were habitually failing to honour international payments.

The company had also been owed a large amount by several clients who'd been in arrears with their payment plans for equipment bought on credit. She'd discovered that her uncle had concealed this for several months as the company hovered on the brink of liquidation.

Then, not surprisingly, his partner had called a halt and refused to inject more capital into the business after the Minister of Indigenisation had given all foreigners a deadline to cede a minimum 51 per cent of company shares to locals, under provisions of the law.

The ultimatum had come with sustained threats of forced company closures and confiscation of assets belonging to any foreigner who did not comply. International banks had not been spared these very public threats. For a while, Aunt Peace had feared that there would be a hostile take-over of the bank where she was employed as a manager, and that she'd lose her job too.

Uncle Dondo had no assets, except his house, with which to repay his partner for the additional shares in order to ratify the legal requirement. No interested local investors had been forthcoming. So, his partner had cut his losses and opted out, leaving him with no equipment to sell and no means to keep the business running.

The company had finally gone under administration when the legal processes, which had been on hold, took effect. Her aunt and uncle had been forced to downsize from their Borrowdale mansion to a smaller house in Houghton Park.

Delta had decided against going back to her parents' home in Gweru. She'd instead moved with her aunt and uncle, retaining the ridiculous hope that she still might find a job in Harare. The city was familiar territory and compared to the smaller town offered more opportunities.

While Aunt Peace had continued working as a bank manager, Uncle Dondo had become a recluse. He'd taken to spending long hours in front of the television, surfing channels, drinking Castle Lager and chain-smoking.

Delta had often wondered if he'd intentionally withdrawn from his friends out of shame and embarrassment, or if they'd abandoned him, now that he was no longer the big-spending Mr

Harare who'd attracted all manner of hangers-on. She knew how capricious friendship could be.

She'd directed her focus on following up job applications and labour export possibilities for which the government had invited applications. At the time, she'd been optimistic that there'd be a country somewhere that needed chemical engineers, even if they were not needed locally, but she'd not heard anything back.

She remembered that 14,000 graduates were said to have applied, but there was no information about which specific countries within the region the successful applicants would be sent to, or when they might go. The whole process had been frustratingly vague. Her enquiries had taken her unsuccessfully from one office to the next, until, finally, she'd given up.

Having to live through each day with the simmering tension between her aunt and uncle had not improved matters. For a while, her refuge had lain in exchanging mindless jokes and videos with her friends on Facebook and WhatsApp. There were no new tips being shared on social media chat groups about applying for jobs. Potential or rumoured opportunities had been exhausted, though just a few continued to recycle the same old hopeless information.

Increasingly impatient, she'd come up with a scheme to cheat her way into a job. The work itself wasn't a natural first choice. Not at all. It was just what was available when she'd grudgingly accepted that she'd have to do whatever was necessary to get through one day and face the next. But now, the enormity of what she'd done was a worry that would not let her go as she tossed and turned in bed. Finally, she fell asleep.

XOXOX

She was instantly awake when her mobile phone alarm buzzed at 5:00 a.m. Cautious not to wake everyone else, she prepared herself with noiseless efficiency, bracing for her first day at work.

Houghton Park was so close to town that a *kombi* ride would take no more than fifteen minutes, but she wanted to be very sure of arriving on time. Making a good first impression was important to her. She wanted her diligence to shine through – a smokescreen to her deception.

Still, she was anxious. What if they found out? Was this a situation that could be defined as theft through earning by deception? Possible dismissal was not so much of a worry as a criminal record. That, like the tail of a monkey, would follow her everywhere.

She ought to have looked at the Labour Act's Code of Conduct online, but internet connectivity on her mobile phone had been very poor. And this morning she had no data bundles left.

She tried to console herself with the feeblest justification. Why should she worry when there were so many people getting away with far worse? There were real thieves out there who were stealing amounts that could not be sniffed at.

Surely, her minor infractions paled in comparison with say, the President's allegation that a jaw-dropping $15 billion of state diamond money had been looted, for which not a single head had rolled.

Or maybe not. The reality was that of too many paradoxes. Her culpability could be that much greater simply because she was, after all, just Delta. Not some big-shot official, fat-cat politician or minister. Wasn't it true that whenever the state wanted to make a show of stamping out corruption, they picked on the smallest of small fry?

What could she possibly say in mitigation if it ever came to that? Anxiety had her mentally rehearsing an implausible defence in response to imagined charges. Could she say that she'd just been doing some social research? For a blog on topical issues, perhaps? Not that she ever intended to start a blog, but in that moment, the idea had a veneer of credibility, undoubtedly fragile, but better than nothing.

Or, she wondered, could she just stand by the truth and say that she'd been driven by desperation and a need to start earning a living? Any kind of living? Surely, they'd understand, since her means to an end had no potential to cause anyone any harm? She sighed. She knew that she was being ridiculous.

Cashleen would probably have an idea about the possible legal repercussions, but Delta was loath to ask her. She'd only told her in the vaguest of terms that she'd found a job before brushing her friend off, embarrassed by what she'd done, unwilling to answer the questions that would've certainly followed. Cashleen could be judgmental at times. Right now, she didn't need that.

She slipped into a green, loose-fitting dress and cinched the waist with a thick belt. Then she combed out her Afro and applied Vaseline to her face, while critically appraising herself in the mirror. She knew that she was beautiful and would be naturally presentable.

She left the house and walked as briskly as she could through the shadowy morning half-light, taking great care to avoid the potholes that scarred the road, in case she fell and sprained an ankle, or worse. The rainy season had taken its toll and, as usual, the city council showed no sense of urgency in repairing the roads in residential areas.

She turned left at Waterfalls Avenue, taking a longer but safer route which cut through the Houghton Park shopping complex. She was cautious and alert to her surroundings. The street lights had long ceased to function, but thankfully, shop exteriors lent some illumination to the adjacent area.

At least two men and a woman, early starters like herself, were hurrying towards the main road. A phalanx of security guards leaned in a leisurely manner against the wall at OK Supermarket, which was still to open. A Lobels van was delivering bread at Engen Service Station. She noted that fuel attendants were already serving customers under the brilliance of canopy lights.

To her right, outside the tyre-mending yard, three vagrants jostled with each other as they rifled through the garbage bins with concentrated energy. Their grime-covered clothes blended with the semi-darkness, their bodies casting weird shapes in the gloom.

Two stray dogs looked on from a distance. They held their heads high on scrawny necks, tails wagging eagerly. It was almost as if they were politely waiting for the vagrants to finish, so that they could have their turn. The day had indeed started.

She hastened her pace and flagged down a *kombi* that was coming from Mbudzi Roundabout. She ran across the main road, jumped on board and squeezed into an uncomfortable seat between two large boisterous women who were each supporting a tier of empty baskets on their laps. She gathered from their loud conversation that they were on their way to Mbare Market to buy vegetables to be sold later in town.

She paid her fare and withdrew into herself, shrinking from the conductor who, having no seat, was bent over her, his smelly armpit an affront in her face. She wondered how someone could give off such a strong body odour so early in the morning. Harare water might be polluted, but there was certainly enough of it for him to have taken even the most basic of dry washes! She scowled involuntarily.

The blaring car radio was belting out Jah-Prayzah's hit of the moment, **Mdhara Vachauya**. The tune was quite catchy but the radio volume was incongruously loud for the early hour. But then, one couldn't really expect less in a *kombi*.

The conductor shouted 'Last Stop!' as the vehicle slowed down and turned into the parking bay at Copa Cabana Terminus. Here she was, a fraudster, just about to dig herself into a deeper hole! She alighted gingerly, avoiding a rivulet of filthy water that meandered along the crooked camber.

Already, open-air second-hand clothing hawkers had started erecting rudimentary tables and arranging their wares on the perimeter of the terminus. Their movements were brisk and faintly aggressive.

Those with no tables were spreading black plastic sheets on the ground, organising their wares into neat piles, and transforming the pavement into the humorously named *Kotamai* Boutique. Customers would have to contort themselves and bend over, just to take a closer look at the wares.

She took a deep breath, steadied herself and headed towards Leopold Takawira Road, 'Whatever gets you through the day', she told herself.

4

Unesu's weekend on call ended on Monday, bringing relief in its wake. All the doctors in Prof Chaka's 'firm' attended the morning teaching ward round, including those who'd not been on weekend duty. They were joined by final year undergraduates, the ward's sister-in-charge and her three nursing students.

Being in this large group afforded him a welcome sense of invisibility and some reassurance that he wouldn't get picked on. A teaching ward round had its merit, but Unesu was exhausted and craved sleep.

The Prof was at his academic best and charming to patients. He pushed postgraduate registrars to make decisions about complex medical conditions, all the while giving constructive feedback. He wasn't a consultant to allow anecdotal evidence, but demanded opinions that were based on published scientific fact.

There was no grandstanding either: just a clear passion to impart knowledge and make excellent doctors out of his trainees. Despite undercurrents of resentment, Unesu was impressed by the man's show of expertise and charm.

Tired, his mind wandered. He thought with a concealed smile of Julia, the new student nurse. Would he make a bid for her? He wasn't sure yet. Other than that she was an attractive young woman, he didn't know anything about her. Besides, he'd been around hospitals long enough to be familiar with the dynamics. One could easily lose out to a senior colleague.

By 11.00 a.m., the ward round was over. Prof Chaka delegated him to mop up the firm's few outstanding tasks, while the rest of the group moved on to the out-patients' clinic.

Keen to leave, Unesu worked with mechanical efficiency. His last chore was to issue their deceased patient's husband with a BD12 Form detailing the cause of death. He'd faced relatives in such circumstances several times before, but he could never completely detach himself. The pain of their loss clawed at something deep inside him, lingering for days afterwards, sometimes longer.

It was ironic that their patient had been called Kundai, a name signifying perseverance and overcoming odds. But some were stacked too high to be defied. Unesu knew for certain that her death could have been prevented if only the hospital had been well-resourced. However, there was an unwritten rule that you never told this truth to grieving relatives.

A post-mortem had been called to ensure best practice, as well as for medico-legal reasons. However, he understood that the family had declined this. Their focus had been on how much money would be needed to feed the gathering mourners in the event of a burial delayed while awaiting post-mortem results.

Kundai's husband entered the ward office with a heavy step. He was by himself, which was unusual for someone so recently bereaved. His eyes were puffy and red-rimmed. He sat hunched in the chair opposite and rested his hands limply on the table. Unesu thought he could detect a fine tremor. Although it was a warm morning, the man wore an oversized coat, into which he appeared to shrink. He cut such a sad, lonely figure that Unesu was deeply unsettled.

'I'm sorry for your loss Mr Gutu...' His voice cracked as he searched for the right words, then he quickly composed himself. Doctors were supposed to be poised and in control when faced with challenging situations.

He leant back in his chair and made direct eye contact. 'The form is almost ready. I only need to verify identity particulars with you, but first, do you have anything that you wish to discuss?'

Although Prof Chaka had earlier had a debrief with Mr Gutu, it was immediately clear that the man wanted to tell his story to someone who would listen.

He wiped a film of sweat off his face and began. 'Yesterday... she... Kundai... she was not very sick, you know. In the afternoon, she sang in the church choir. She had a little stomach ache since Saturday, that's all. So, she was able to go to church yesterday. When we came here, it was only to get painkillers. Painkillers only. Our nearby pharmacy is closed after six.' The disjointed account was given in a low, disbelieving voice.

Unesu nodded and listened. It was all he could do.

'That other doctor said something about a pregnancy bursting in her tube and some bleeding inside? But I think he was mistaken. Kundai is not pregnant. She has an implant. It makes her skip periods. The family planning nurse had told her this could happen with the implants, but they still work. So how can she be pregnant? And I don't know if those things can cause pregnancy ... in a tube...' he continued uncertainly.

The reference to his wife in the present tense struck Unesu. He realised that the man was still in shock. And how could he not be, when he hadn't even been aware that his wife was pregnant, let alone known that there was something called ruptured ectopic pregnancy from which someone could die? It would take time for him to accept that she was gone; to understand how and why she'd died.

He shook his head gently, saying, 'Yes, implants can cause someone to have an irregular cycle, but there is no health risk with that. Though they are safe and effective, they are not infallible. There is still a tiny chance – less than a one per cent chance – of becoming pregnant with an implant *in situ*. But it didn't cause this. Risk factors for ectopic pregnancy are...'

Mr Gutu's head jerked up. Unesu fell silent, at once aware that he was bungling, even trivialising a tragedy. His weariness was no excuse. The man's wife was dead. He hadn't come to listen to an inept doctor giving a contraceptive lecture or expounding risk factors for ectopic pregnancy.

When Mr Gutu spoke again, Unesu couldn't help wondering if the man blamed himself. 'The money, I have some of it now, but I... I didn't find it on time. There was nobody to lend me any. You told me to look for money to buy blood so that she could go to theatre.'

Unesu nodded. He had indeed. In rapid sequence, his mind replayed events in the uncomfortable silence. A bedside urine test in casualty had established that Kundai was pregnant. Other clinical findings on examination had nailed the diagnosis of ruptured ectopic pregnancy. She'd been extremely pale from internal bleeding. Her blood pressure had been rock bottom, her pulse a barely palpable, racing thread.

They'd rushed her to theatre, hoping to start immediate surgery. However, the anaesthetist had been explicit about safety implications of general anaesthesia and surgery at that point. IV fluids were running, but their patient obviously needed an urgent blood transfusion to commence pre-operatively. They'd be setting themselves up for a certain table death if they rushed in. It had been clear to Unesu that they were damned if they did, and damned if they didn't.

The anaesthetist had exchanged words with Prof Chaka. In such situations, clotting factors and blood transfusion had no substitute. They all knew this, but faced with a rapidly deteriorating patient, tempers had flared while they waited for her husband to return to hospital with the required money.

Unesu recalled howABkundai had collapsed, how ineffectual their efforts to resuscitate her had been, right up to when Prof Chaka had certified her dead, his jaw clenched with suppressed emotion.

'I'm really sorry for your loss,' he repeated a perfunctory, hopelessly inadequate mantra.

The man's crushed look shifted. There was a flicker of accusation in his eyes.

'But why didn't you transfuse and ask for payment later? They phoned me only an hour after I'd left to say she was dead. One hour. Did something else happen?' It was a determined, reasonable demand for an answer.

Unesu remained mute in mental overdrive. Doctors didn't determine hospital policy and issues to do with payments. He considered his words carefully. It would be insensitive to tell Mr Gutu that in a dire emergency, even fifteen minutes could be too long.

While haemorrhage could be catastrophic, he also knew that an initial three units of blood as soon as Kundai had arrived, coupled with urgent transfer to theatre to ligate the bleeding vessels would have saved her. They'd missed a narrow window of opportunity. He recalled from her medical case notes that she had two children, both under the age of five. Now they were motherless.

Just three units of blood! How could a dysfunctional health system exist when leaders could be airlifted to South Africa for all manner of ailments, including ones that could be managed locally? Charter a whole plane for someone to go as far as Malaysia for a routine medical check-up or cataract operation? Or have their family members flown to the same Far East just to deliver a baby? And yet here, at home, it wasn't sophistication that was lacking. It was just the basics, that was all.

Clearly, even as the economy collapsed, some lives would be lived in extravagance, whatever the cost to everyone else. Unesu's growing conviction was that as far as the leadership was concerned, the povo didn't count. Except maybe at election time when their votes can be bought with little food packs, cups of crop fertiliser and empty promises! His thoughts were spiked with cynicism.

He felt a sudden urge to stop the charade and leave before he made more inappropriate comments but he pulled himself together and sat up in his chair.

'Mr Gutu, our team on call tried everything. Everything. We

really did. There was nothing else we could do to save your wife. What the other doctor told you is exactly what happened. I'm really sorry for your loss. We all are.'

Resigned acceptance doused the spark in the widower's eyes. He bowed his head and shrank further into his coat. There was another pause.

'Thank you, Doctor,' he finally murmured, which did nothing to make Unesu feel any better.

He asked for Kundai's national ID card and they verified her identity particulars together. Then he handed over the signed BD12 Form.

'If you need further clarification, please feel free to come back.'

It was all he could offer with certainty. They rose simultaneously from their chairs.

'Thank you,' Mr Gutu repeated wearily. He looked beaten and even more despondent than he'd been when he arrived. Unesu watched his stiff, retreating back and doubted that he'd ever return. Not to talk about his wife anyway.

🔻🔻🔻

As he prepared to leave, two of the Monday firm's postgraduate registrars entered the office. Their voices were raised in a heated conversation about the order of the emergency theatre list. He didn't envy them. Of all weekdays on call, Mondays were the busiest and their firm always ended up with the highest caseload. Trailing them was their senior resident medical officer, Mazwi, a bubbly ex-classmate with whom Unesu was on friendly terms.

From their conversation, he understood that the patient who'd arrived first and was ready for theatre had a pelvic abscess and signs of renal compromise. However, her sepsis meant that she couldn't be the first to be operated on because of infection control issues in theatre. The second patient who had a bleeding hydatidiform molar pregnancy and was also in urgent need of surgery was still waiting for confirmation of payment for blood.

Only one theatre was allocated for all emergencies, and lists had a way of filling up quickly. Before they knew it, they could have more gynaecology surgical emergencies on their hands, the neurosurgeons could come in with a head trauma patient, the general surgeons with strangulated inguinal hernias, or the paediatric surgeons with an acute appendicitis.

Time was therefore of the essence. Hence their dilemma. Considering that either of their two patients could deteriorate with further delays, Unesu had the most surreal feeling that they were casting lots to determine which of the two women they'd allow to die first.

Same old problems over and over again and guess who has to pick up the pieces! he thought bitterly.

Still in animated discussion, the two left the office in search of their consultant who was said to be in the labour ward.

Mazwi stayed behind. '*Eish*, I can't handle this kind of craziness so early in the day!' she exclaimed, a smile on her face.

Unesu shrugged. It came with the territory.

'I hear you had a mortality early this morning, and that the weekend was quite rough.' Mazwi looked at him sympathetically.

Unesu gave a short, humourless grunt.

'You look terrible. Go home and rest, Doc.' She moved from the door to let him through. He was grateful for her quiet solicitude.

'Thanks. Have fun on call and don't do what I wouldn't do,' he attempted an old joke to compensate for being so moody.

'As if I would! Let me walk with you to the car park. Got to get my phone before I start in gynae casualty.'

❦❦❦

Her car was parked right next to the entrance into the parking lot for junior staff; a fenced-off space overgrown with weeds. He stared at the late-model Mercedes Benz. It stood in stark contrast to the other cars parked in the yard. Mazwi had been driving a presentable car since their fifth year of medical school when she'd married a prominent accountant. But this?

He teased, 'I sure wouldn't mind owning these wheels, Doc! Wish I had a rich husband like yours!'

She gave a small smile, seemingly amused. 'Aah, but this has nothing to do with him. You know how bad things are these days with companies going bust. His work has dried up,' she opened up unexpectedly.

'Really? Sorry, I had no idea,' he was instantly ashamed for having been so presumptuous.

She didn't seem to mind and continued, 'I bought this car with my personal income.'

Unesu was puzzled. Nobody could afford this on a junior doctor's salary. Not even with locum top-ups.

'But how…?' He stopped, embarrassed by his own curiosity. She bit her lip, as if considering something.

'You really want to know?' she asked, a faint challenge in her eyes.

'Of course. Maybe you can give me some tips, 'cause I need to replace my ancient jalopy. It's now a proper hillmatic!' he joked, thinking about his fifteen-year-old Mazda 323.

'A what?' she asked, uncomprehending.

'A hillmatic. Starter doesn't always work. I have to park it on an incline, or else get a few hulks to give me a push-start!' he replied, and laughed for the first time since Friday.

'Uh uh, no way,' she remonstrated, 'you have to do better than that.'

'You tell me how – on the peanuts that I earn. Or inspire me with how you've done it. Maybe I can do the same.' Now he was openly fishing.

'Well… what I do is highly confidential, but I'm not exaggerating when I tell you that buying this car was easy.' She spoke in a matter-of-fact voice, but without giving anything away.

Her words penetrated his fog of exhaustion, but he hesitated because he didn't want to appear too eager. What sort of work could she be talking about? He allowed his imagination to run riot. Could she be a highly-paid intelligence operative? If the rumour mill was to be believed, almost every institution had its fair share of those planted strategically. They were supposed to be lethal and unrepentant about eliminating whoever was deemed to be a threat. Could she be someone like that?

'Do tell,' he asked anyway.

'Look, if you're serious, I'll need to think about this carefully and consult. I can't make a snap decision to get you involved. If I get the all-clear, I'll phone you later in the week for a meeting,' she continued in the same mysterious vein.

'Sure,' he replied, disappointed.

'Any news about the strike?' she suddenly changed the subject. A frown marred her pleasant features.

Unesu shook his head, remembering the weekend's flurry of WhatsApp group messages.

'Not yet. Want to know my own two cents? A strike would be pointless. Do you really think that the powers-that-be don't know how dreadful things are in our hospitals? If you ask me, a strike won't make them change anything!'

'I agree. It's not as if they care. They don't use these hospitals anyway, so why should they?' Mazwi was pragmatic.

Unesu shook his head. There was just too much to deal with. The weekend and its aftermath had drained him and taken him on an emotional rollercoaster. He'd best be getting home to sleep.

They parted cordially and he walked slowly through the grass to the rise at the far end where he'd reverse-parked. His mind strayed back into a fantasy about possibilities that might arise from his conversation with Mazwi. He could certainly do with some extra income. His net salary of $350 a month was a pittance. After-work locums provided some kind of relief but he had a dizzying list of things for which he needed money.

Top of the list was quality healthcare for his mother, if only that prophet, that self-styled healer could loosen the tentacles he'd sunk into her. One year on, the miracle that he'd proclaimed for her had not materialised, but her faith had remained obstinately steadfast and she'd declined all medical care. Unesu knew that one day, it would be too late. Even slow-growing tumours had a point at which they became deadly.

Thinking about Prophet Healer evoked bitterness. He wondered if there was indeed a God, and why He'd let these religious conmen prey on the vulnerable and the weak, all in His name? He knew that he was working himself up because he was so tired. And he reminded himself again to discuss the matter with Cashleen. She'd always got along well with his mother, so maybe she'd make her see sense where everyone else had failed. It was a long shot, but he had to hold on to some kind of hope.

He took a few deep breaths and allowed his frustration to ease. Sitting quietly in his car, he planned a route that would avoid the roadblocks manned by extortionist traffic officers. He didn't have money to pay bribes or the zeal to argue out The Highway Code and his constitutional rights with them. His best bet would be to take the long way home via Coventry Road, through to Belvedere and Kensington, onwards to Avondale and Pari Hospital doctors' residence on Mazowe Road.

5

An early morning text message from Sando wished Cashleen good luck with her day's mission. She appreciated how sensitive it was of him not to discourage her. He'd tried the same plan unsuccessfully in Jo'burg, but issues there were more complex because of the work permit requirements.

She took extra care with preparation. After a shower, she selected an azure Tahari suit, a cherished cast-off from Rufaro. Although the skirt was a little tight around the waist and the hemline a shade too short on her tall frame, the mirror told her that she looked just fine.

She combed out and parted her hair, then patted it down to give it a neat finish. She carefully dusted her face with crème-to-powder concealer, masking a crop of wayward pimples that had appeared overnight on her forehead.

Breakfast was a simple affair of sugarless black tea and plain bread. By 7.30 a.m., she was ready to leave. She knelt by her bed and said a prayer, as she often did when faced with a challenge. 'Ask and you will receive…'

She wondered if God would hear the prayers of a casual Christian like herself. Still, the prayer strengthened her. She promised herself to be more consistent, and even consider rejoining her old congregation at the city cathedral.

She stood up, remembering with a small smile her mother's mild admonitory humour, 'If you don't fellowship in church, you won't get a priest who'll be willing to perform your last rites and bury you; or a church choir to sing at your funeral.' How she still missed her!

There was no sound from Itai's room to suggest that he might be awake. She begrudged him the leisure of being indolent and without qualms. If he could no longer be bothered to get up and look for work, the least he could do was to clean up after himself and do his laundry.

He was two years older than she was and he was a man, so she expected him to be in charge, to be the strong one. She wanted to harden her heart against his apparent show of weakness, but on the other hand, she worried about him because she suspected that he was drinking alcohol and smoking marijuana.

On Saturday morning, she'd woken up to a distinctive whiff pervading the whole apartment. She'd knocked on his door, keen to confront him, but he'd ignored her. She could no longer keep up with his mood swings. Most times he was morose and withdrawn, but there were occasions when he came home in very high spirits and with an unsteady gait. Of late, he'd taken to spending an inordinate amount of time in bed. She wondered if joblessness was dragging him into a spiral of apathy and despair.

Another worry lingered. If he couldn't even afford to buy food, where was he getting money for alcohol and drugs? Did it have anything to do with that shifty policeman friend of his who always seemed to be loaded with money, despite being on a paltry salary like all civil servants? She sighed and hovered outside his door, resisting the urge to knock and order him to get up. They could end up quarrelling and she'd be late starting off. It was best to let sleeping dogs lie.

She left the apartment and set off to town on foot with single-minded purpose, knowing full well that her approach was rather unconventional. Normally, one would submit an application in response to an advert, and if successful be invited for an interview. But desperate times called for desperate measures.

There'd be no question of offering anyone a kickback today, because she didn't have the money. And even if she'd been able to afford it, bribery etiquette and its intricacies remained uncharted territory.

ﻞﻌﻠﻌﻠﻌ

Her first target, chosen for its prosperous ambience and its familiarity, was *The Daily Headliner* where she'd completed a year of workplace-based attachment as a student. The offices were in a tall, elegant building, the Eastgate Mall, along Sam Nujoma Street.

Mr Choto, the HR Manager, remembered her and expressed pleasure at seeing her again. He led her into his office and directed her to an armchair opposite his own. He was short and dapper, but his voice exuded authority.

He smiled and boomed, 'So, how can I help you, Cash?'

She cleared her throat and went straight into her practised speech. 'Well, Sir, I'm looking for work opportunities, and I'd be most grateful if I could work here. I haven't seen anything advertised, but I thought I'd ask, just in case you have openings coming up.' She spoke hurriedly, worried about saying too much, or saying too little and not getting a chance to say more.

He leant back in his chair, his face transformed by genuine surprise. 'Don't tell me you haven't been snapped up already. You were the best student we've ever had!'

The unexpected compliment gave her much-needed encouragement and she ploughed on. 'Not yet. But I'd be very happy to take up any position. Even for volunteer work'. She tried to filter desperation from her voice. Would mentioning unpaid work disqualify her even before an offer was tabled?

He patted his tie, and shook his head slowly, saying, '*Yah*, this is a difficult one. I'd be very happy to have you here Cash, but we're going through hard times. Very hard times indeed.'

Her hope wavered. *Hard times?* She'd not seen any overt signs of hardship. The place was clean with plush, modern furnishings

– and functional air-conditioning! Well, maybe hard times were relative. Doubtful, she leant forward and listened as he explained that they'd already laid off six people because the business was not performing well.

'So there isn't a chance…?' she let the question hang. Really, it was a plea.

He smiled ruefully and shook his head. 'I'm afraid not, but I'll tell you what? Why don't you return in August, after the current intern has gone back to university? Instead of taking on another student, we can tailor a graduate learnership position for you.'

With contrived enthusiasm, Cashleen accepted this provisional offer. He told her she'd still have to submit a formal application. Proposed terms of engagement would include a waiver exempting the company from paying her any allowance, since apparently, they had no capacity to do so.

She hid her disappointment and thanked him. She'd hoped that an offer would at least include allowances for transport and lunch. This was the widely accepted minimum provision for student placements.

She was also aware that she could easily end up falling into the same trap that many graduates were finding themselves in: providing free labour to companies that were letting go of full-time employees in favour of casual workers and unpaid graduates, ostensibly taken on for short-term work experience.

But these were hardly normal times and she couldn't afford to be selective. Her concerns would be a problem for another day. Besides, no commitment had been made just yet, and August was still a good five months away.

So she continued, moving doggedly from one place to the other, searching as the day wore on. As expected, most institutions told her quite bluntly that they didn't entertain unsolicited employment-related enquiries.

Others, accessible but more intransigent than *The Daily Headliner,* indicated in various terms that their workplace-based experience programmes were specifically designed for college students. Besides having enough students on attachment already, they had nothing to offer someone who'd already graduated.

It was a laborious process that took her the whole discouraging morning. She hadn't really bargained on how demoralising it would be.

※※※

By 2.00 p.m., she just had one more place to visit on her list, *Classic FM* on Simon Mazorodze Road. She walked towards Market Square, intending to catch a *kombi* that would take her there.

She was struck once again by how filthy and congested this part of the city appeared. Carelessly discarded litter had become a permanent feature of the landscape. A network of potholes disfigured the road and acted as receptacles for dirty water that was flowing freely from a burst pipe. She caught the whiff of an offensive odour and grimaced, hoping it wasn't sewage.

Vendors crowded pavements and street corners. They used forceful marketing tactics, raucously verbose in their determination to sell anything and everything. Whatever could be exchanged for money was game. While nothing seemed to be off-limits, roasted pig's testicles and aphrodisiacs left her faintly shocked.

Looking around, it was difficult for her to believe that these were the same streets where there'd been running battles between vendors and municipal police who'd tried to evict them just the previous Friday. This was vendors' paradise and they were definitely back in full force. Their persistence and tenacity could never be underestimated as the streets were their source of survival.

There were also street-kids, beggars and hordes of people just milling about, seemingly without purpose. Long queues snaked out of banks, reminding her of the developing cash crisis. She sensed a general air of despondency, which brought her own circumstances into sharp focus in a rather disconcerting way.

Downtown was denser, louder and more disorganised, with a pulsing mass of people and traffic. As usual, *kombis* were creating anarchy, with near-gridlock situations at most intersections.

As she walked, she began to feel hungry. She debated using the 50 cents *kombi* fare to buy a basic lunch and then walking to *Classic FM*. It'd probably take her almost an hour. She didn't really mind because she had time on her hands. The only problem was that her feet had begun to hurt.

She considered her meal-on-the-run options. For 50 cents the possibilities were: a bunch of five bananas, four standard-sized buns or a fruit scone. She settled on bananas. They were quite filling, and besides, she wouldn't have to wash them, or her hands. There were no sources of clean, tapped water on the street.

She quickly scanned her surroundings and realised how spoilt for choice she was. It seemed as if every third vendor or so was selling bananas, either from a conspicuous pile on the pavement, or from a pushcart.

She decided on a young man who was pushing an overladen *MaTanushka* cart on the opposite side of the road. His selection of the fruit looked quite big and their healthy colour hinted at freshness. She crossed the road and made a beeline for him.

'Excuse me. Bananas please!' she shouted, her voice carrying over the city din.

He swivelled and looked back, straight at her. She met his gaze and their eyes locked in a flash of recognition. Cashleen was stunned. *Zenith?* Could it be? This person was too thin, too dishevelled and *too cowed* to be her ex-classmate from university. Or even that cool dude who posted blasé WhatsApp texts on the Class of '14 Group.

She stood riveted, staring in disbelief at his clothes that were so out of character. **Threadbare overalls?** She took in his matted hair, the errant toes that peeped from carved-out holes in his shabby Nike trainers. Surely, this couldn't be Mr Bling! She'd not seen Zenith since graduation, but she still retained a vivid image of him as a self-confident, loud narcissist.

His dressing had been modelled on that of American R&B artistes: oversized baseball shirts, low-hanging, baggy jeans and heavy neck-chains. That was the Zenith she'd known. Not this shadow. Not this caricature. They stared at each other for that one frozen moment in time. It *really was* Zenith. There was no mistaking that distinctive scar on his forehead.

And what of his fairly recent posts on the Class of '14 WhatsApp group? Wasn't he supposed to be living somewhere in idyllic Mutare, doing some desk research work for an international client? What had that been all about?

She approached him hesitantly and stopped a few feet away, conflicted about invading his physical space. She intended to greet him and reminisce, the effect of his prior unpleasantness diminished by this explicit show of poverty.

He averted his eyes, made a swift-about turn and, pushing his cart recklessly through the crowds, disappeared, leaving her in open-mouthed bewilderment. Then her initial confusion gave way to a vague sense of understanding. She'd inadvertently outed his fictitious social media persona.

Cashleen felt a lump in her throat, sad about his visibly grim circumstances, and for being the one who'd exposed him. She'd have to send him a private message to reassure him. His secret was safe and would remain so.

Countless times she'd been engulfed in such a cloak of shame herself. Some people always seemed to assume that because she'd passed with good grades, by now she'd have a good job somewhere. Her explanations were often met with cynicism, almost as if not having a job defined a very personal innate flaw. She had an academic record that ought to have given her leverage compared to her contemporaries, but it just wasn't the case.

Of course, she'd heard that there were numerous graduates among the vendors who swarmed the streets of Harare, but she didn't personally know anyone in such a situation. Well, now there was Zenith, but she couldn't fathom being a vendor herself. She'd drawn the line at that. She was too educated, too smart. And she had her pride.

Granted, she did know some individuals from college who'd ventured into some sort of entrepreneurship, mostly unrelated to their field of study. And there were at least eight self-declared traders from Class of '14 who were selling a variety of goods from flea markets and little tuck-shops dotted around the city and in high-density residential areas.

Clothing, shoes and grocery items from South Africa, Mozambique and Tanzania were favourites. These could be sold at lower prices than locally-produced goods and hence their market base was wider.

She knew of others who were engaged in poultry or piggery projects. They claimed to be earning much more than some in formal employment, especially civil servants. Had she been able to source a start-up fund, she'd have considered that kind of entrepreneurship.

Entrepreneur. The word itself had a weighty, respectable ring to it. She could consider being an entrepreneur. But street vendor? And Zenith, of all people? She shook her head, still incredulous.

She wondered how many of her ex-classmates were hiding behind fictional lives projected on social media. One could choose to go incognito as an internet troll with licence to say the most outrageous things; or one could create an incredible fantasy, far removed from one's actual reality. And she knew all too well how seductive the gratification that came from creating beautiful illusions on those internet platforms was.

From a distance, you could concoct an image that made you appear more beautiful, more successful and happier than you really were. Virtual friends lapped it up and showered praise. Her face burned, as she recalled the time when she'd posted some unlabelled pictures of Rufaro at the Golden Eye in London on her Facebook page. They looked so alike that some of her online friends naturally assumed that she'd been the one there. For one glorious hour, she'd wallowed in the pleasure of flattering comments about her apparent holiday in London. Cold logic had soon kicked in. She'd deleted the pictures and comments, ashamed that Rufaro, Delta and others who knew that she'd never been to England would give her a hard time if they picked up her

Facebook deception. It was a wonder that they hadn't seen the posts before she deleted them.

Her thoughts returned to Delta. She wondered how her friend was faring. She'd received a brief message the previous night.

Got a job. Def. not wat u'd think.

It had been a surprise, but then again, Delta never ceased to surprise. She was a girl of constantly changing circumstances, always restless and searching for something.

While she'd wanted to be happy for her friend, Cashleen felt a spasm of envy. In all the time that she'd been looking for a job without success, Delta already appeared to be on course for a second one. It didn't matter that the first job had been as a receptionist at her uncle's company. It had been a real job with a regular salary and quite a few perks.

She'd tried to phone Delta to get more information, but her WhatsApp signal had been too weak to sustain a call. Their brief conversation had consisted of an exasperating string of broken sentences. So, she'd sent a text. The response had been in typical Delta-style, mistress of intrigue and drama.

Lol, g'frnd! Chill plz. Tyd up. Hectic. Upd8 2moro morn. X my heart. Nyt nyt! (:

Summarily dismissed, she'd gone to bed frustrated. Now she realised that morning had come and gone without the promised update. She'd been too engrossed in her own task to realise that Delta had been quiet, too quiet for a social media addict, queen of forwarded jokes, videos and all things scandalous. Not even a single absurd *Chinotimba* satire! It was all rather unusual. She wondered if she'd already started the new job, whatever it was.

Hunger and bananas momentarily forgotten, she decided to proceed to *Classic FM*. As she crossed Robert Mugabe Road, a battered **mshikashika** taxi hooted loudly and almost knocked her down. It sprayed her with muddy water that was flowing from yet another burst pipe into the road.

Hot in precarious pursuit were two police officers on a motorbike that was careening along the road at breakneck speed. The passenger officer was wielding a sinister-looking set of metal spikes. He looked very much like Itai's friend, Gerry.

Shaken, she ran to the safety of the pavement on the other side of the road and looked down at her suit in dismay. Most of her skirt front was covered in a patchwork of unsightly, dark-brown stains. A revolting liquid trickled down her legs and into her shoes.

There was no way she'd be going to *Classic FM* in that state. She drew in a deep breath. Defeated, she made a U-turn, turned left into Harare Street and set off in the direction of Northern Heights. She couldn't wait to get back home.

6

As she walked to her new workplace, Delta's sense of anticipation was tainted by anxiety. Despite having cheated her way into the job, she'd felt pleased that she'd broken free from the teeming ranks of the unemployed and the idle. Defining this job as a starting point for her bigger plan had given her a sense of purpose. However, an inner pragmatic voice told her there was no sanity or probity to this. She conveniently blocked it out, reminding herself once again that she shouldn't waste time dwelling on matters that she'd already considered. It was retrogressive. She would do what she had to do, even if it looked as if she was letting desperation eclipse good judgment – as Cashleen would say, if she ever got wind of what she'd done.

Anyway, she'd learnt that conforming to societal norms was overrated. If you wanted to get on in life, you had to set your own standards; ones that you could adjust at will to suit your specific situation at any given moment.

She now intended to 'eat a dog, preferably a big one, rather than a small one', as the wry and popular saying went. A small one wouldn't make her any less liable, because a dog was a dog! Of course, she would have to be discreet. She hadn't completely desensitised herself to criticism.

'Four months maximum', she promised herself. Anything in excess of that would only serve to increase her risk of exposure. Her home-based soap-making project would need one thousand dollars to start up. If she scrimped, saved and took extra shifts on this job, four months would be enough.

She increased her pace and neared Hunger Buster just as Mr Banga, the manager who'd been her sole interviewer on Saturday was opening up the restaurant. He was a young man with a conspicuous paunch and the beginnings of a double chin. She'd concluded that he was probably in his early to mid-thirties.

A blinding reflection of the early morning sun bounced off his watch. She supposed it might be the same jewel-encrusted Rolex that she remembered from her interview. His mien was representative of Harare's clique of wealthy young men who flaunted their opulence on social media, but were not known to be engaged in any type of honest work that could generate the largesse with which they were associated.

Most were flamboyant, with a penchant for fast cars and beautiful women. They were ostentatious in their conduct and obsessed with making exhibits of themselves. They boasted of defective moral compasses about which they were unapologetic.

Nothing was taboo. She knew of at least two who'd allegedly 'leaked' their own sex tapes online, just to increase their notoriety-ratings and gain column inches in the tabloids. They had certainly redefined what was trending and had a multitude of online devotees as validation of their success. Apparently, being a notorious bad-ass was a good thing, and worthy of praise. She suppressed a grin, wondering if Mr Banga could be one of those bad-asses.

He stooped over an external security bar and unravelled the reinforcement chain, freeing the door with a deft movement. He squatted, his back towards her, then began rolling the chain onto a holder mounted on the wall.

She slowed down and approached him warily, recalling the interview which had been held in his office. There'd been an awkward moment when his eyes had glazed over as they lingered on her bosom. 'Like a predator,' she'd thought at the time, feeling very uncomfortable and exposed.

Thankfully, the interview had been short and perfunctory. It had passed without real incident. Afterwards, he'd told her that she had interviewed well and the job was hers. The man was probably harmless, because, barring the complexities of setting herself up for the interview, getting the job had been fairly easy and there'd been no requests for any kind of favours.

'Good morning, Mr Banga.' She raised her voice to catch his attention. He stood up and swivelled round. His face lit up when he saw her.

'Aaah, you're here already? Good morning, Misi.'

For a split second, Delta was confused. Was he talking to someone behind her? She threw a backward glance, accidentally pulling a muscle. She pressed the side of her neck, remembering. How ridiculous for her to have forgotten so quickly! How would she last for a single day, let alone four months? She made a mental note to herself: I'm Misi Hurukuro, not Delta Choto.

Mr Banga didn't seem to notice her discomfort. Still smiling wolfishly, he gestured her to enter. She mumbled a self-conscious thank you and slipped past him into the restaurant's dining area.

She selected a chair near the cashier's till-point and sat down, observing that the plastic tables and chairs were in disarray, almost as if they'd been deliberately thrown about. What had happened here?

The restaurant looked somewhat shabbier than when she'd attended her interview. Maybe, on that day, anxiety had blunted her ability to critically appraise it. The place was clearly in need of repair with new tiling and new furniture.

Memories of her last year in college, when she'd associated with a man who'd wined and dined her in more expensive restaurants felt like something that her brain had contrived. Perhaps these standards were fine for the clientele on this side of town...

Mr Banga finished whatever he'd been doing by the door and walked in. 'Just wait there. The others are coming,' he said, entering his office.

As if on cue, the staff began to arrive, one by one. They cast openly curious glances in her direction, said their hullos and signed a register. They grabbed aprons and hairnets from under a counter, and then got on with their work, talking in low voices amongst themselves.

She counted two men and four women. One man came into the dining area and started rearranging the tables and chairs. She remained seated, quiet and observant, while waiting for someone to give her instructions.

Mr Banga emerged from his office and started an inspection, strutting from one area to another, criticising and barking orders. Delta felt as if she was watching a performance that had been put on especially for her. He took a quick call on his mobile phone, before shouting out that someone should attend to a chicken delivery at the back door. After some minutes he walked over to where she was sitting.

'You're going to love it here,' his tone was unexpectedly soft and very different from the way he'd spoken to everyone else.

'Thank you', she replied, unsure of what else she was expected to say.

'I'll introduce you before you start,' he clapped his hands loudly to summon the staff. He told them who she was and introduced everyone by name: Maruva, Norest, Chido, Sandra, Rutendo and Gabriel. She learnt that she was the replacement for someone called Talent.

She was assigned to work under instruction from Maruva, the supervisor. Maruva looked older than the others and Delta guessed she could be anything from thirty-five to forty-five. The woman was true to the stereotype of bubbly, well-fed restaurant workers who purportedly became fat gorging on left-over food. She had a motherly look, with an open, smiling face. Delta took an instant liking to her.

She was asked to hand over her mobile phone to the cashier for safekeeping, as private calls weren't allowed during working hours. While everyone continued with their tasks, Maruva handed her a plastic apron and a hairnet, then asked her to sit down for a chat. Sitting opposite her, and folding her plump arms on the table, Maruva leaned forward. Her gaze was direct.

'Mr Banga says not to waste any time on induction because you're very experienced. Is that right?'

'Yes'. Delta nodded vigorously. She wasn't about to give this woman any hint whatsoever that she'd never set foot in a restaurant kitchen. She'd googled for information about working in a restaurant and had some knowledge about safety and food handling. She hoped she wouldn't make any glaringly obvious mistakes.

'Good. Today you'll do only general work. From tomorrow I'll show you how to make our dishes,' Maruva added.

Here was Delta's biggest concern. You could invent a CV, fake your references and bluff your way through certain things, but no amount of googling could transform you into a chef. Neither could you master restaurant standards practising at home.

'Don't look so worried Misi. I'm sure things are not very different from where you worked previously. City Bakery and Restaurant wasn't it?'

'Yes,' she croaked, the lie choking her up.

'Except for the confectionery, our menu has similar items. Our top-sellers here are chicken and chips. You'll be fine,' Maruva reassured her.

'Thank you. But can you please treat me like someone who is learning from scratch? It's better that way for me', Delta said, thinking on her feet, and setting the stage to cover up any future failures She intended to watch, learn and put on a great act.

Maruva looked at her quizzically, but she was obliging. 'If you say so. But I'm sure you'll do fine. Come this way, please,' she led her through the kitchen to the back.

'This is where you're going to work today. We don't have a regular cleaner so we rotate duties.'

Delta scanned her surroundings, surprised. This display of chaos and grime was not what she'd imagined of a food-handling area. There was a clutter of utensils lying on a central table, and others on the floor. A large metal sink was filled with pots, pans and plates which were crusted with dirt and food residue.

Sacks of potatoes were in one corner. Red soil formed a fine dusty layer on the tiled floor around them. Adjacent was a pile of cabbages with yellowing outer leaves. A rank odour which she couldn't place pervaded the room.

Near the door were four drums filled with water, two small buckets and a couple of mops. Delta knew that availability of clean, running water was a must for restaurants, but this place seemed to have a certain lack of standards.

Maruva made a gesture encircling the room and its contents.

'It's not normally like this but there was a disturbance yesterday. We left in a hurry,' she did not elaborate further.

Delta resisted the urge to probe. Maybe it was related to the chaos that she'd observed in the dining room.

'Where should I start?' she asked instead.

'That's up to you. I have to see how you plan your work, but I want this place sorted quite quickly. Customers will be coming soon, so there'll be more stuff coming in here for cleaning from the servers and the chefs.'

Delta nodded. It looked like a lot, but she wouldn't let that dissuade her. Yes, the work would be physically demanding, but cleaning and washing up weren't exactly rocket science.

'There's no running water. Use what's in those containers and don't waste a drop. We'll replenish them when the water bowser arrives. Other cleaning materials are in here,' Maruva added, swinging open a cupboard door.

Delta squinted as she inspected the contents of the poorly-lit space. It was rather stuffy, with a smell of dampness and mildew.

'This back door leads to the alleyway. The big skip for all the rubbish is out there,' Maruva explained, and showed her how to release the door's security bar.

'We also receive our supplies through this entrance. I'll leave you to start then,' she said as she walked towards the cooking area.

She suddenly stopped at the connecting door and came back.

'Before you begin, I must warn you about something.' She dropped her voice to a secretive whisper. Delta listened expectantly.

'Just be careful around Mr Rich. He's a bit...' Maruva paused, then started again. 'He's not very straight but he's the business owner's young brother. So be careful.'

'Who's Mr Rich?' Delta asked, intrigued.

'Richard Banga, the manager... a bit of a show-off, calls himself Richie Rich. As I was saying, he's not straight and does a lot of deals in his office. You understand?'

Delta nodded, although she didn't. What was this woman trying to tell her?

Maruva continued. 'With him, you hear nothing and you see nothing. Don't ask him or the other staff any questions unless it's about your work.'

Delta's confusion escalated. 'What exactly...?'

Maruva interrupted with a chuckle. 'You don't listen, do you? No questions.' There was a pause before she continued. 'You're just here to do your work. Nothing else. And, oh, he likes girls... too much I think. But if he proposes something, be smart. Don't be foolish like that Talent girl.'

Delta stared at her. Was this a warning? Or was this woman telling her that she should let Mr Banga have his way with her? She needed clarity.

Fortunately, Maruva needed no prompting. She seemed to have forgotten that she'd implied limited disclosure.

She continued, 'Talent reported him to the police for sexual harassment, imagine! Obviously, nothing happened because the senior Mr Banga is well-known. And this one here has so much money he just pays off police officers, magistrates and ... and, well everyone! He's also friends with a minister's son, so...'

'I see,' Delta muttered downcast.

And it seemed Maruva wasn't quite finished. 'We later heard that Talent was a law graduate from UZ. A lawyer, imagine! That's probably why she was claiming compensation or something like that. Those silly graduates, I wonder what they teach them at that place? They know nothing about real life, but they think they're so clever!' She shook her head.

Surprised, Delta could only manage an, 'Oh!'

'Yes,' Maruva continued. 'But the funniest thing... for two full months I was boss to a lawyer. Myself, with my very basic O-Levels and a cookery course! And I never knew...'

Delta was floored. She could never let it slip that she too was a graduate, but this was not how she'd envisioned her first day at work. Things were getting more complex by the minute. She also couldn't understand Maruva's attitude either. She'd seemed such a good-hearted person, and yet...

'Anyway, about Mr Rich, just stay out of his business. Like yesterday, around closing, there was a scene with his friends who tried to con him out of a deal. He went mad, waving a gun... it was scary. We had to close in a hurry!'

All this and a mad, gun-toting sexual predator for a boss? Of all the jobs that she could've tricked her way into, how had she picked this one? Delta shook her head, now keen to change the conversation before she got second thoughts about being there at all.

'Thank you for the warning, but I'd better make a start now.'

'Of course. Keep checking that the tables are clean once we start serving.' At once, Maruva became brisk and business-like. She walked back into the cooking area with a firm step.

❋❋❋

Delta set about cleaning the dirty kitchenware and worktops. The lack of running water was a huge inconvenience but she put her head down and worked quickly.

Next was the floor. She lugged the potato bags to an area that she'd just cleaned and did the same with the cabbages after removing the yellowing outer leaves.

Just as she'd finished, Norest brought in more dirty dishes. 'How are you getting on?' he asked, looking around. He was very tall and cut an imposing figure.

'I'm managing fine, thanks,' Delta replied.

'Good,' he said, even as the shadow of a frown flitted across his face. Delta wondered if he might be Maruva's second-in-command, but he turned and retreated without further comment.

Under some thick plastic sheeting in the corner, she discovered the reason for the smell that filled the room. Two red containers were full of chicken pieces. A few were greenish-grey around the edges. She suppressed a wave of nausea. Maruva brought in more dirty utensils just as she was about to decant one container into a bin bag.

'*Misi!* What are you doing?' she exclaimed sharply.

Delta froze, startled. What had she done wrong?

'I'm... I'm going to throw these in the skip outside...'

'You're what? We received those chicken pieces just this morning. They're for the lunch menu!' It was more of an accusation than an explanation.

Delta was scandalised. Her face burned with indignation. How could they?

'You're cooking and selling decaying meat?' she challenged, forgetting herself, and realising too late that she shouldn't have. There was no sense in aggravating her only obvious ally so far.

Maruva shook her head in exasperation and raised her hand. 'Remember what I said? You don't question things around here.'

Delta drew a deep breath, still trying to assimilate the order. Now that the plastic sheeting had been removed, the smell was stronger. Another wave of nausea washed over her.

Maruva pointed at the containers and hissed in a terse voice, clearly trying to justify the unjustifiable. '**This is** the type of chicken that we use here. It's cheap; it's available. If we got fresh cuts, they'd be so expensive that our customers wouldn't afford them anyway.'

Delta opened her mouth and snapped it shut. What was there to say?

That she was revolted to discover that the secret to their top-selling chicken was a flagrant deception?

Maruva's features softened unexpectedly. She sighed and spoke in a calmer, kinder manner. 'Don't look at me like that. You'll get used to how we do things here. If you look closely, you'll see that it's just a few pieces that are really off. Most of these are good chicken pieces... we trim off the bad bits, wash the pieces thoroughly, season them, bread them and fry them until they are golden-brown and crispy. Our customers love them. I'll show you. In a few days you'll be an expert.'

Without another word, Maruva hefted one container and took it through to the kitchen.

Delta had sensed an implicit apology there, but she rejected the very notion that she would become an expert at frying rotten chicken. She decided there and then. While her contract included free lunch, she would never eat meat in this place. Chips or sadza and vegetables would do just fine.

A while back, she'd overheard a conversation about this in a *kombi*. Certain downtown canteens and restaurants were providing a thriving market for decaying off-cuts, which were supposed to be incinerated by big poultry producers. Some nefarious workers intercepted the waste and sold it off in town to selected restaurants. It had sounded like idle *kombi* gossip, the stuff of fiction, but here she was, right in the midst of it.

She shook her head and resumed work. The morning progressed in a cycle of mopping floors, washing dishes and emptying out rubbish in the alley skip. She found that she liked working in the privacy of that back room, alone with her thoughts, weaving elaborate plans for her soap-making business, whose likelihood of success grew the more she thought about it.

Periodically, she went out to clean the tables in the dining area. The restaurant sold budget meals, so it was no surprise that the place was quite busy. Here, she worked very quickly and avoided eye contact with customers, hoping that nobody that she knew would turn up. It was unlikely, but because Harare was a large metropolis, one couldn't be too careful.

Mr Banga appeared to have left the building, which was just as well because she had no particular desire to see him. Her intuition told her that he was very bad news.

But what stories she'd have to tell Cashleen! Of course, she'd leave out the bits that showed her in a bad light because Cashleen could be such a censorious what-not. But the rest of it? You just couldn't make such stuff up!

7

Always fastidious about timekeeping, Unesu arrived at Avondale shopping centre a little early for his meeting with Mazwi. There was the usual end of day bustle and the car park was congested. Some careless or selfish drivers had parked haphazardly, making driving difficult for everyone else.

Irritated, he navigated his way slowly, taking care to avoid gaping potholes. He still found it incredible that a relatively upmarket shopping centre could be degenerating into dirt and chaos. But then, everything appeared to be in free-fall.

Finally, he spotted an empty parking space next to Bon Marché Supermarket. He eased his car into the space, beating an oncoming driver, and this small victory secured, he experienced a frisson of childish delight.

As he made his way to Café Nush, a young girl approached him, leading a blind man by the hand. Both were barefoot and in dirty, tattered clothes. The two beggars were a familiar sight at the complex and Unesu had often wondered if the man was the girl's parent or brother. The relationship seemed positive so he didn't think it could be a relative exploiting an orphan, as sometimes happened, with no one willing to protect the child.

Whatever the connection was to Unesu, it seemed a form

of abuse: how could an obviously vulnerable child assume the implicit role of breadwinner? Maybe even a caregiver? Together with the man whose unseeing eyes were startlingly opaque, they could induce sympathy and even generosity from passers-by. More often, people turned away.

The girl held out a scarred metal plate, '*Chero* ten cents,' she asked plaintively. The man inclined his head and stared sightlessly into the distance.

The anxious look in the girl's eyes and her dry chapped lips, which indicated that she hadn't eaten, stirred Unesu. He pulled a $2 note from his pocket and placed it on the plate.

'Here,' he said.

The man grunted something unintelligible, while the girl singsonged, 'Thank you, thank you.'

It was a small thing to do, and Unesu was aware that $2 wouldn't even dent her numerous needs, but the gap-toothed smile which lit her face gratified him. With sudden understanding, he realised that he had offered her recognition, not the contempt or dismissiveness which came with the belief widespread among those committed to the gospel of wealth, that all beggars must logically be sinners.

Unesu shuddered. There seemed to be so much need around him and he knew it could drain him of empathy. He'd been asked for some form of help by strangers like this pair, his relatives, friends, hospital workers, patients, relatives of patients... Their needs were diverse, often desperate, and many. He'd been asked for money for food, rent, transport, medicine, school fees, diapers and bizarrely, a cousin had asked him for a bride price top-up.

Failure to respond had often placed him at the receiving end of overt disapproval and occasional, outright hostility. When dealing with those who weren't strangers begging on the street, he knew that perceptions stemmed from the affluence long associated with his profession. How could a doctor possibly not have money?

He'd been embarrassed when junior doctors' threatened to go on strike and their meagre salaries were published in the press, but he'd also been slightly relieved, hoping that people might now believe him when he said that he had no money to give them.

The Café Nush balcony seemed to have more smokers than usual. To avoid them, he went inside and chose a vacant, secluded table in the corner. He took a seat and accepted a menu from a waiter. Within minutes, Mazwi arrived, conveying energy and goodwill, her face wreathed in smiles.

'Sorry I'm late.' She settled quickly into the opposite chair.

'Not really. I'm the one who was early,' he smiled.

The waiter returned and took their order for a simple meal of chicken, chips and Coke.

'My treat, of course,' Mazwi said and Unesu murmured his thanks. It was late in the day and he hadn't had time to eat lunch.

She arched her eyebrows questioningly. 'So, were you moonlighting today? I didn't see you at the hospital.'

'Yes. I had a day off from work, so I took a GP locum in Highfields. Coughs, flu, rashes, the usual minor stuff, but my last patient had the most horrible groin abscess...'

Mazwi raised a hand and interjected with a laugh. 'Please. No gruesome details before we eat...'

'Sorry. Forgive my manners,' Unesu quickly changed the subject, 'So, how are you, Doc?'

'Great! In fact, I've got something to show you.' She tapped her iPhone screen with a finger and handed it to him. He stared at the image of a pristine Toyota Corolla and looked up at her curiously.

'Another new car?'

'Not for me. I imported it for re-sale. I believe it's just the car for you. We can't have you driving around in that ancient hillmatic of yours any longer.' She wagged an admonishing finger.

Unesu sighed. 'I do need a car, but I won't even bother to ask the price. I know I can't afford it.'

'Sure, you can. You have to learn to think big,'

'Aah, if thinking was all it took, I wouldn't be caught dead driving that hillmatic. I'd be soaring, Doc. Don't forget there's a helipad at the hospital.' They laughed.

The waiter arrived with their food and Mazwi broached the subject matter of their meeting.

'I've consulted my practice partner, Dr Reza. In fact, I did a bit of lobbying for you. There's an opening at his Orion Clinic in Belvedere if you're really interested in what we do. You know Dr Reza, don't you?'

'Yes, I do,' Unesu said. Dr Reza was a GP with multiple surgeries in Harare's high-density suburbs. He was well known for offering junior doctors locum work while he ran a practice in Belvedere. Unesu hadn't known though that Mazwi had joined him as a partner and he wondered what the connection was. The GP was one of the much older doctors in practice. He waited for her to explain what she meant by 'what we do.'

She continued slowly, 'You have to know that I'm not talking to you lightly. This is highly confidential, and whatever else you do, promise me that you won't repeat this conversation to anyone. Ever.'

'Of course. And thanks for trusting me.' Unesu set his fork and knife down, leaned forward and listened intently.

She started off in a roundabout manner. Unesu wondered why.

'The work isn't that difficult but the money is excellent. I can make up to five hundred dollars at a time. More at weekends, if I do longer hours.'

Unesu sat up. It was a staggering amount. No wonder Mazwi was always so classy! And why not, if she was earning that much?

'So, what's involved, Doc?' He hoped that he didn't appear too eager.

'You're sworn to secrecy, right?' The expression on her face was mild but he was in no doubt about how serious she was. He nodded, wondering if this cloud of mystery had something to do with her being a little territorial. Or was it something else?

She looked directly at him, lowered her voice and described the clinic in detail: a well-equipped and modern primary care facility offering excellent sexual and reproductive healthcare services, including termination of unplanned and unwanted pregnancies.

Unesu leant backwards, concealing his feeling of surprise. He hadn't expected this because termination of pregnancy was generally a taboo, even in medical circles. He'd become pro-choice because losing his sister had driven him into a deeper conversation with himself, a consideration about how and why women found themselves in such situations, and how lack of choice drove the despairing to risk their lives by taking chances with backstreet abortions, which were, in themselves, often a death warrant.

And like most doctors, he was also aware of the statistics on morbidity and mortality arising from unsafe abortions, and of how countries that had implemented legislation for access to safe abortion had reduced maternal mortality rates.

'What do you think?' Mazwi asked.

Unesu was honest. ' I'm definitely pro-choice and I can do the work. I'm just worried about breaking the law. You know how it is.' Legal terminations were restricted only to special circumstances with clearly defined indications.

She nodded and went on, 'I understand. I thought you might cite religious reasons, but if that's all you're concerned about, don't worry. The clinic operates with certain precautions. Can I make an appointment for you to see Dr Reza for further discussion?'

'Please do,' he accepted the invitation. If Mazwi had somehow found a way to work around the legalities, then why not him?

'Are you certain, Doc?' Mazwi had made the procedure and the commitment sound simple, but it was clear that she would not accept evasion.

'Yes, yes,' Unesu nodded quickly.

'Great! Are you available next Wednesday? Three o'clock?'

'Sure, I'll make myself available.'

'Let's meet at Orion Clinic then. We'll first have a meeting with Dr Reza, then I'll organise your induction, if the two of you reach an agreement.'

'Sounds good.' The more he thought about it, the more he warmed to Mazwi's proposal.

They finished their chicken as they chatted about this and

that, though Unesu's mind was spinning. But by the time he arrived home, he'd convinced himself that he'd join the clinic. The scheduled meeting with Dr Reza would only be a formality.

He knew that there was unmet need out there. If not him, there'd always be someone else willing to provide the service, and a professional medical facility with experienced doctors had to be safer than the clandestine route.

The money, of course, was excellent. He lay back on his bed and stared at the ceiling, suddenly daydreaming.

8

Cashleen found herself in a new state of apathy and solitude. Her hours were empty and endless. She'd read all the books, old magazines and newspapers that she could lay her hands on. For three consecutive days, she'd not had access to online news because her Econet mobile data bundle was down to the last few megabytes.

Watching television might have provided an alternative, but for the first time, Rufaro had not sent money for their DSTV subscription renewal. Much as she wanted to ask, caution held Cashleen back from mentioning television subs when there were more urgent matters like unpaid city council rates and electricity bills.

She missed the freedom of choice afforded by the diversity of DSTV. Like a true journalist, she wanted the varied international news channels hosted on the satellite service. The local television station, with its single channel, wasn't too bad if one could live with the monotony and the absence of basics such as time schedules, programming information, and episode summaries. However, having to play a game of wait and see annoyed her.

Maybe going to the City Library to read newspapers for free wasn't such a bad idea. It would also give her a chance to see if she could borrow from the Doris Lessing collection that had been donated from England by the late writer's estate. *The Grass is Singing* had long been on her list of books to read.

She missed getting together with her friends who seemed to be preoccupied with one thing or the other. Their communication through Facebook and WhatsApp had also become less frequent because she simply couldn't afford the expense, minimal as it was.

Delta was her biggest let-down. Apart from being uncharacteristically secretive about her new job, she'd become so reluctant to meet that Cashleen suspected she was hiding something. She dismissed the idea that her friend was pregnant, because as far as she knew she wasn't involved with anyone. So, what was it?

Itai was hardly at home. The frequency with which he was picked up and dropped by his friend, police constable Gerry, was worrying, but she could not bring herself to confront him, and so she just hoped for the best.

Unesu had often teased her about how obsessively she could fixate on something and worry about it, as if worrying was some kind of disease. But what did he know? She just happened to be someone who cared about others, when most people didn't seem to give a damn. They were living in a new age when the most important person was always me.

XOXOX

On Friday afternoon, she snapped out of her indolence and summoned the energy to walk all the way to Classic FM. She arrived at 2.30 p.m., only to find that Mrs Ndoro, the HR Manager, was in a meeting that was expected to last an hour or more.

She decided to wait. It might be worth it. Besides, she could sit in the air-conditioned reception area, relax and get some hard-earned rest. She was hungry, thirsty and tired from all the walking that she'd done. She gratefully accepted an offer of cold water from the receptionist who directed her to a water cooler in the corner of the room.

She was pleased to see a variety of newspapers on the table. *The*

Daily News, The Daily Headliner, The Herald and *The Financial Gazette*. With an hour to wait, she couldn't believe her luck.

She quickly checked the adverts and established that in all the papers, there wasn't a single job for which she could apply. Then she returned to the headlines and a report about the former Vice President who had just launched a political party, together with associates who were being referred to as her *putschist cabal*. Her initiative was said to be confirmation that she had indeed harboured intentions to overthrow the legitimate President.

Cashleen remembered covering a shadow story about the former Vice President for one of her final university assignments in 2014. The VP had been dismissed that same year. The term 'putschist cabal' had emerged, and no doubt someone was proud of it, given its prolific usage in the media with reference to the beleaguered VP and her co-accused.

Cashleen had visualised a sly group of men and women, sneaking stealthily to clandestine meetings, their collective whispers conspiring foul plots under cover of darkness in remote farmhouses. She'd had to look up the term online in order to understand its meaning.

She also remembered that the former VP had been publicly criticised by the First Lady for having the insolence to wear a mini-skirt that defied anatomical considerations at a meeting where she'd allegedly plotted treason. How dare she conspire to topple the President while wearing an indecent mini-skirt?

Cashleen suppressed a smile. A controversial figure, the First Lady was certainly making a name for herself through her very public ranting. At rallies, she'd habitually dress down internal and external political rivals in a manner that made for excellent entertainment, even though many shuddered at her language, which had the flavour of the gutter.

Her new nickname was Madame-Stop-It, after the phrase which laced her public outbursts, as if she was the chief nursery maid. Cashleen compulsively followed her public speeches. The entertainment value was irresistible.

And now the former VP had launched a party! From the opinion pieces in the various newspapers, it appeared doomed. There were vicious, gratuitous attacks on many fronts. And even those who were not partisan were asking what she, a woman, could possibly offer, when for over thirty years, she'd been a *bona fide* ally of the very people she now wanted to succeed?

It seemed unlikely that she could, or would, last the distance. Besides, Cashleen thought, even on a more level playing field, the country was very patriarchal, and not ready for a female leader. Of course, given the President's age, and that people were wary of a nonagenarian at the head of a kleptocracy of the entitled, it was no wonder that succession plots dominated the media.

However, her opinion was that openly talking of succession had become akin to having a death wish, something about which she'd argued with Sando. He'd been bold and outspoken to the point of recklessness, and he had not held back in South Africa. Candid as his social media posts were, she wished he'd exercise more caution, because one day he'd return home and then he could be held accountable.

She knew, verbatim, Section 33 (2) (b) of The Criminal Law (Codification and Reform) Act, under which one could be charged with undermining the authority of, or insulting the President. The rigour of this law meant that even a nickname used in jest could command a long sentence.

While Sando had been openly political for as long as she'd known him, her own interest had gradually developed in tandem with lectures related to essential components of her undergraduate curriculum. She was aware that journalists covering political stories that either inadvertently or deliberately showed the government in any controversial context were often made out to be enemies of the state. Theirs was a field liable to implicit censorship and control, although officially the law enshrined freedom of expression.

So it was that she had decided that she would focus on business, health and development, although she was now all too aware that one could not avoid politics entirely. Self-censorship offered a compromise, but one of her lecturers had hammered into their heads that self-censorship was a journalist's most effective way of killing off one's career. She'd have to take guidance from whichever organisation offered her a job, whenever that happened.

She gathered her thoughts. She had an opportunity to actually read the papers, but instead she was allowing her mind to wander. She turned her attention to a story in the *Daily News* headed: 'MPs Press for Pay Hike'. She was keen to see what their justification was – after all, the doctors, who'd been threatening all-out strike action, had been denied a pay rise and improved resources in hospitals on the basis that government was broke.

Just as she was getting into the story, she was drawn back to the present by the arrival of a self-assured, well-dressed young woman who breezed into the reception area with a rush of infectious energy. Cashleen instantly recognised her as JTL, her favourite radio personality, a character so magnified that her initials sufficed as a unique identity at national level.

JTL was only slightly older than herself, and Cashleen watched with envious admiration as she engaged effortlessly with the girl on the reception desk, then disappeared down a corridor. A whiff of expensive perfume trailed after her.

The receptionist interrupted her thoughts: the HR Manager was ready to see her. Astonished at how time had flown, Cashleen rearranged the newspapers into a neat pile and followed directions to the HR office.

※※※

Mrs Ndoro was a middle-aged woman with an inscrutable face. She wore an elegant black suit and square-rimmed glasses; her simple hairstyle of tight corn-rows was classic. Once again, Cashleen found herself on edge and hating the feeling.

The woman introduced herself and asked, 'How can I help you, young lady?' Her tone was surprisingly soft and courteous. Cashleen was briefly at a loss for words. She'd not expected kindness.

'My name's Cashleen Gumbo. I'm a journalism graduate, but I can't find a job. I've been looking for a long time. So, I was wondering if ... if your PR department could take me as an intern.' She made a mess of the pitch that she'd practised so often.

Mrs Ndoro narrowed her eyes and looked doubtful. 'May I have a look at your CV and your degree transcript?'

Her face taut with anxiety, Cashleen dug in her bag and gave the older woman her documents. She hoped Mrs Ndoro would be impressed by her three 'A' grades at A-level, and her 2.1 pass at university.

'I see you did quite well both in high school and varsity. But your majors are more suited for work in print and electronic media. You do realise that we're a radio station, don't you?' Her voice was patronising.

'Yes, yes, I do, but I just thought...' her voice caught in her throat. What had she thought? Exposing her desperation made her feel so small and vulnerable. Here was someone offering her a kind ear and a moment of hope, but she was falling to pieces. Perhaps sensing her disappointment, Mrs Ndoro's features relaxed.

'Look, I can mention your request at the next management committee meeting. I think we may be able to offer you something to occupy you, although it won't do justice to your qualifications. It wouldn't be a salaried position of course. Call me at least a week after Easter.' She gave Cashleen her business card.

Thanking her, Cashleen blurted, 'May I please give you my phone number as well?'

'Of course.' Mrs Ndoro wrote the number down in her diary. Leaving the room, Cashleen felt the now familiar sense of desolation.

With only $4 in her purse, and no idea if and when Rufaro would send more money, she debated walking back to town or paying for a *kombi* ride. How had the decision to spend only 50 cents become a major financial consideration? She felt an ineffectual rage well up in her chest.

Of late Rufaro had been rather cold. Cashleen was loath to keep sending messages that went largely unacknowledged. On the few occasions that Rufaro had initiated contact in recent months, it had been with brief, atypical one-liners to check if either Cashleen or Itai had found a job. Cashleen could sense a kind of impatience and resentment that was so unlike her sister.

She hated it that their communication had been reduced to that basic, functional level. She wanted and needed her sister back. Her new manner had caught her off guard, stirring fears of abandonment.

It was already after 5.00 p.m. and it would soon be dark. She decided against walking. She'd take a *kombi* to the city centre then take the shorter walk home. Her feet were now less painful. She'd be fine.

In just under ten minutes, two *kombis* arrived, almost running her over as the drivers tried to outrace each other. Their respective touts looked deranged, as they shouted and gesticulated for her to climb on board.

Shaken, she quickly decided against the mini-bus that was almost full and joined a woman on the one where the tout seemed less unhinged. She sat right at the back, handed over a 50 cent coin and tried to shut out the loud music thumping through the vehicle.

Her phone pinged to announce the arrival of a text message. It was Unesu asking if he could please see her sometime over the weekend. **Need ur advice.** Another message followed even before she'd replied to the first one. *Of coz,* she responded, curious. He sounded strangely formal. What type of advice was it that required him to make an appointment to see *her* of all people?

In the few weeks that she hadn't seen him, she'd understood that he'd been busy with what he called The Big Hustle… chasing locum shifts at general practitioners' surgeries in town. He often complained that his government salary was barely enough to meet the costs of living in the city. 'Modern-day slavery masquerading as a job,' he'd told her sarcastically.

She didn't take him seriously. She knew he loved being a doctor.

Thx. 7pm. Ur place on Sat, he suggested.

C u, she affirmed, wondering what it was all about.

Anyway, she'd hear from him when he came round. One thing she'd come to appreciate was that he never arrived empty-handed. She always made a show of protesting, but deep inside she knew that the groceries that he brought were crucial fillers for when they needed to stretch whatever money came through from Rufaro.

She hoped Itai was at home. With some luck he'd have started preparing the evening meal. He occasionally surprised her with moments of thoughtfulness.

For the remainder of the ride, she squeezed her eyes shut and tried not to think of anything. It was impossible.

9

Delta found that waking up in time to start work at 6 a.m. required a superhuman effort. Three consecutive early morning shifts had left her reeling from sleep-deprivation. Friday's 10 o'clock shift was a welcome change and she was in good spirits.

The rota took her to the back room where she'd first begun. She didn't mind being there, taking on multiple roles as the day's gofer. It was great being alone with her thoughts, scheming and daydreaming as she cleaned, peeled potatoes, trimmed necrotic bits from chicken cuts and did whatever else was ordered by Maruva who believed that every employee should be multi-skilled.

The back room was a refuge from Mr Banga's lecherous stares and risqué comments that were barely disguised as compliments. It also took her away from her rather inquisitive co-workers. She hated being constantly on edge, worrying that she might get mixed up about her fictitious persona and blow her cover.

To her dismay, Misi appeared to have on taken a life of her own. Her failure to craft a plausible back story was proving to be a real problem. She'd not bargained on her workmates being so nosy and she'd been caught off guard a few times.

She hoped that everything would simply boil down to mindless workplace tittle-tattle, where nobody would think twice about the finer details – specially how she'd morphed from being a twenty-two-year-old to a twenty-five-year-old within the space of a day. Mortified afresh, her face burned. What on earth had possessed her to lie about her age in the first instance?

The home front had presented yet another predicament. She'd had to do some mental gymnastics to solve that one. While Uncle Dondo in his usual detached manner had been happy that she'd found a job, Aunt Peace had been intrusive. She'd wanted to know exactly where she worked, what job she did, office contact details and the name of her manager.

Under normal circumstances, this would've been well and good, but Aunt Peace had turned into the type of officious person who'd probably do something absurd like turn up with her business card to introduce herself as Delta Choto's next-of-kin, 'just in case she caused any trouble' at work.

But here lay a tricky problem. There was nobody called Delta Choto working at Hunger Buster. For that reason, Delta had decided that her aunt should never know where she worked; let alone what she'd done. It would cause complications.

Without any qualms, she'd fed both her aunt and uncle a tenuous story about being a lab assistant in a very dirty and congested part of town. The area had such a firm reputation for petty crime that Aunt Peace would think twice before she dared to venture down there.

Delta had been confident that her aunt wouldn't discourage her from working because it had been tacitly agreed that she'd soon be contributing to household expenses. Full disclosure to her brother and her parents was out of the question. They'd surely have a collective seizure! She had to admit that perfecting the art of lying was no easy feat and she forced herself to rationalise her behaviour. After all, it wasn't as if she'd killed anyone.

As she worked, she smiled to herself. What a difference a few days could make! She'd been trained to prepare the restaurant's signature chicken dish and she was now competent at transforming near-decomposing pieces into delectable treats. Maruva had been right. She could fry the chicken so well that only an insider would have known the difference between fresh cuts and those that were slightly off, and even then, with some difficulty.

For the initial stage, one needed a good, discerning eye to be able to identify early rot and remove the flesh that was beyond salvage. Other than having to deal with unpleasant smells, Delta found the procedure surprisingly easy and the standard recipe simple enough to follow.

Prior to deep-frying, a special rescue marinade was used. It was concocted from lemon juice, soya oil, a dash of vinegar, a pinch of salt and Maruva's special in-house seasoning. For crumbed chicken, the cuts were glazed with beaten egg-white, then rolled in breading made from Gloria self-raising flour and a mixture of spices.

Although she'd initially vowed never to eat meat at the restaurant, Delta found herself looking forward to her scheduled break when she'd get her free piece of crispy chicken and a portion of chips. And the chicken did taste good. No wonder the restaurant was always packed, especially at lunchtime.

Around mid-day, she took delivery of two twenty-litre containers of oil under Maruva's victorious supervision.

'Finally, Mr Gonzo!' she gushed to the supplier, a small man who appeared intent on avoiding eye contact.

'You've really kept us waiting this time, but thank you so much. Cooking oil prices have shot up, and yet none of the brands last as long as this one,' she beamed with pleasure.

The man threw a suspicious look at Delta before responding in a low, conciliatory voice. 'I know, my sister. I'm sorry, but *eish*, the boys in town are hard to pin down. It's excuse after excuse. Things are getting harder, because those ZESA guys are like sniffer dogs. I have to be careful.' He gave a nervous laugh.

'I know,' Maruva replied. 'But please don't ever forget us. We'll take whatever quantity you can bring,' she added as she handed over the payment. The man pocketed the money and skulked out into the alley.

Delta's curiosity was piqued. She knew 'the boys in town' as any manner of dubious characters, from small-time crooks to hard-core criminals. And ZESA people? What did the electricity supply authority people have to do with cooking oil? This place was something else!

'What type of oil is this, *Sisi* Maruva?' she asked, against her better judgement. She'd been previously warned about asking questions.

Surprisingly, Maruva answered without hesitation. 'My dear, this stuff is like gold. It's transformer oil.'

'Transformer oil?' she echoed, puzzled, as she stared at the unlabelled containers. 'I thought it was some kind of *cooking* oil.'

'Of course, it is cooking oil!' Maruva asserted.

'But...' Delta gulped.

Maruva interrupted, 'You're not as smart as you look, are you? I might as well tell you, so that you won't ask silly questions later or dare to waste this wonderful product!' Smiling as usual, she spoke as if she was teasing, but Delta sensed a hint of disapproval. She listened, feeling put-out.

'This oil, my dear, is milked from electricity transformers around town, just a little bit at a time, of course. It can fry like no other oil. You don't have to change it as often, so it goes a very long way. It's the best for chips, chicken and whatever else you may want to deep-fry. We've definitely made a lot of savings on this.' Maruva patted one container, dropping nuggets of wisdom in the tone of a saleswoman pitching her prime product.

Delta felt herself go cold inside. She knew enough chemistry to conclude that Maruva had just identified this delivery as hydro-treated light naphthenic distillate or a similar compound. While she'd come to accept the chicken-cuts fraud as a matter of course, she was at a loss about what to say about this oil racket. With an effort, she maintained her composure and forced a response through a dry throat.

'Oh, I see,' she said, nodding, although she didn't see at all. She racked her brain, trying to remember if her chemistry modules and material data sheets had given any details about levels of toxicity associated with these compounds, or their risk of carcinogenesis.

Other than there being no harmful effects from ingestion, and no data to evaluate cancer hazards, she drew a blank. Maybe she was worrying without need, but this seemed wrong on so many levels. How did these people sleep at night? Milking electricity transformers indeed! Could there be a more sanitised manner of describing clear vandalism and theft? She wondered what percentage of Harare's chronic power outages were a direct result of such larceny.

'Any more questions, young lady?' Maruva asked playfully.

'No, *Sisi*,' Delta shook her head, hoping her expression had not been riddled with doubt.

'Good, good. See me in the office before you leave today. We need to finalise next week's rota. By the way, you don't have medical clearance, do you?'

'No. I told Mr Banga at the interview,' Delta replied before fabricating an explanation with a straight face. 'My previous one had expired.'

Maruva clicked her tongue and said, 'Chido's another one. We have to sort out both of you next week. Monday's too busy, so on Tuesday you should go to Beatrice Road infectious diseases hospital. First thing in the morning. They get long queues there.'

'Sure, thanks,' Delta replied.

'City council inspectors sometimes conduct raids. They can shut down a place if they find anyone working without clearance. Good thing Richie Rich has friends at the city council. But obviously, not everyone's a friend, so there's always a chance...'

'Thanks, *Sisi*. I get it,' Delta interrupted. Too many irregularities to handle. She needed a breather.

But Maruva went on, 'If they turn up before you're cleared, you vanish!'

'Vanish? How do you mean?'

Maruva rolled her eyes and sighed dramatically. 'You'll get a signal to leave the shop quickly. Easy enough if you're back here. Just walk into the alley and on to the main road. Stay out for thirty minutes or so and we'll be good. If you walk back in and an inspector is still around, you just act as if you're a customer.'

'Okay,' Delta replied slowly, trying to picture how she'd act in such a situation.

'Good, good. Don't forget to see me in the office later,' Maruva added with a little smile on her face and left.

Delta felt her respect for this woman collapsing. One didn't condone or aid and abet certain things without being compromised. But who was she to judge Maruva or anybody for that matter?

Not securing medical clearance had been a miscalculation. She'd been aware that industry standards for food-handlers required one to have an infectious disease screen before one could start work.

Of course, she could've made more effort to organise something through Kabias, her underworld contact who boasted that the only thing that he couldn't produce as a counterfeit was a human being, but if asked, he'd die trying. Even his generic reference sheet, modified for Misi, had sailed through with no further checks.

The problem was that he didn't come cheap. So, she'd taken a chance and Mr Banga had hired her without the medical clearance, saying dismissively, 'You can always get that sorted after you start working'. Now she just wasn't sure if the idea to use her fake Misi ID for the medical check wouldn't hit a snag. Maybe her plans weren't that well-laid after all.

She finished tidying up and went through to the eating area to relieve Norest for his lunch break. She moved quickly and efficiently, concentrating on her work. Out of the corner of her eye, she spotted Mr Banga standing near the end of the customer queue. He was engaged in an animated conversation with a tall man who had his back to her.

Gesticulating to stress a point, Mr Banga laughed in his usual self-important manner. Delta kept her head down as she picked up litter, cleaned tables, piled discarded plates into a metal dish and worked her way closer to the front of the room, nearer to where the two men stood. To her horror, as soon as she was within hearing, she heard her name spoken out loud.

'Isn't that Delta?' She heard a familiar voice. No way. It couldn't be! Surely not Dr Matinde?

'Who?' she heard Mr Banga ask.

'Delta. Former student of mine. Chemical engineering Class of 2013 or 2014, I think. She was one of the brightest I've ever tutored,' the man said slowly in his composed baritone. Delta remembered it so well from her varsity days. It had earned him the nickname 'Newsreader'.

'You're mistaken *Blaz*, that's Misi. As if we'd employ chemical engineers here, bright or otherwise!' Mr Banga emitted a hearty laugh.

Delta's heart thudded, as she stood frozen, trying to map an escape route for herself. The men were partly blocking her way to the kitchen and the back room. What was she to do?

To hell! She swore silently, picked up the bowl of empty plates and charged forward. Her eyes swept over Mr Banga, past the curious gaze of Dr Matinde and through him. She was counting on her blank look to give nothing away. All being well, inscrutability would sow seeds of doubt. After all, she could have had a twin.

And she had adopted a different look. At university, her hairstyle had been a racy, ginger S-curl and she'd been liberal with her make-up. Today, her face was devoid of cosmetics and she sported an overgrown Afro that was restrained in a Hunger Buster hairnet.

Behind her, she heard Dr Matinde say, 'I guess I'm seeing things. It can't be her,' much to Mr Banga's laughter.

'That girl's got swag, our Misi. She had you dazzled, didn't she?'

Delta blocked them out and walked through the bustling kitchen area to the back room. Putting the plates in the sink, she sat down on an upturned bucket as she tried to regain her self-control.

There was no letting up. Suddenly, Mr Banga burst into the

room hissing, 'CC is here. CC is here. Get out, will you?'

Alarmed, she stared up at him. She'd never seen him so flustered. He pointed at the door and pulled her upright. Pushing her, he repeated, 'I said the city council inspector is here. Are you *deaf*? Weren't you told that you must get out as soon as he arrives?'

What absolute bad luck that this should happen today! Stunned, she walked to the door. It wouldn't open.

'Sir, I think the door's locked. Maruva keeps the keys. She was in the kitchen earlier.'

'What the...!' he exclaimed furiously. Delta shrank back. It was disconcerting to see him so out of control.

'Then get in there,' he said roughly, and grabbing her arm again, he shoved her into a broom cupboard in the corner and slammed the door behind her. She was immediately sightless in the dark and so taken aback by this violation that she shook. Although it was spacious for a cupboard, the air was stuffy and dank with moisture and grease. She felt an urge to throw up. She groped for the handle and found it was missing. The door wouldn't open from inside. Someone would have to let her out. Panic gripped her. What if they forgot?

Her upper arm was throbbing as Mr Banga had yanked her so hard. She massaged herself and felt tears run down her face. After what seemed like an eternity, she heard voices through the closed door. It was Maruva, Mr Banga, and a third person whose voice she couldn't place. Most likely the dreaded inspector. A shadow flitted across the keyhole, temporarily blotting the sliver of light that shone into the cupboard. She could hear steps.

'Your cleaning schedule should be tighter, but it's not too bad,' the inspector was saying. He didn't sound pleased.

'Make sure that girl... what's her name? Make sure she has her ID at work all the time. We have to match health certificates with positive IDs, you understand?' he added.

'Oh, do you mean Talent?' Maruva asked in her sweetest voice.

'That's the one,' the man affirmed.

Talent? Mention of the unlikely law graduate who'd left

Hunger Buster had Delta suspecting that they might have passed off Chido as Talent, for whom they still probably had a valid certificate on record. Just her luck! Had she been in the kitchen or eating area when the man arrived, she could've been Talent, just for this inspection. She realised that being pushed into the broom cupboard hadn't been a personal attack.

'And what's in this cupboard?' the man asked. Delta stiffened.

'Nothing important. Just brooms and cleaning stuff,' Mr Banga said hurriedly.

'Open it,' the man ordered.

'Let me fetch the keys from the kitchen,' she heard Maruva say with exaggerated good cheer and she immediately knew that the older woman was putting on an act to buy time or totally distract the inspector.

Of course the door wasn't locked. Delta had been told that the key was lost long before she started working at Hunger Buster.

There was a moment of silence. She could imagine Mr Banga and the inspector sizing each other up as they waited for Maruva. She fought to suppress waves of nausea and took a deep gulp of putrid air which only made her feel worse. Her head began to ache.

'I locked this door a short while ago but I think I've misplaced the keys. I'm sorry I can't find them. So absent-minded...' she heard Maruva offering an apology.

'Next time make sure you are more organised,' the man said sternly.

'Sure. We'll do that.' Wonder of wonders, Mr Banga sounded meek.

She heard footfalls retreating. They were leaving. Then she heard another, softer tread approaching. The door was thrown open. It was Maruva.

'Hey Misi, Richie Rich couldn't take any chances. He panicked. It was a new inspector, you see, and those are always the worst. I'm sorry you ended up in there.'

She sounded sincerely apologetic. Delta had to give her that.

She squinted as her eyes adjusted from the darkness to the glare of sunlight streaming through the window and lurched out gasping for air. Her stomach heaved again. She covered her mouth and pointed at the door.

Maruva quickly unlocked the door and Delta staggered out into the alley. She vomited copiously into the skip until her stomach hurt.

Maruva stood by in concern, murmuring repeatedly, 'So sorry about this, Misi.'

Delta had had enough for one day. She was trembling so hard that she couldn't stand upright. She leaned against the skip. Maruva moved forward as if to assist her, but she raised a restraining hand, averse to any contact.

'Can I go home, please?' she wiped her mouth with the back of her hand.

'Sure. I'll let Richie know that you're not well.' Maruva smiled sympathetically.

Norest wandered out into the alley. He took one look at Delta and frowned. 'What's going on here? Are you okay?'

Maruva rushed to answer. 'She's unwell, so she's going home.'

'Oh! You just got the cupboard treatment, did you? I can see the cobwebs on your hairnet.'

'I told you, she's going home now', Maruva snapped in a tone quite unlike her usual self.

Norest shrugged his shoulders, saying, 'Good luck, Misi. Maybe you need to pass by the clinic. And get well, hey!'

'Thank you,' she replied perfunctorily.

Norest turned abruptly on his heel and went back inside. Delta couldn't stop shaking. She followed on unsteady legs, Maruva right behind her. Taking off her apron and hairnet, she washed her hands thoroughly. Then collecting her bag from the shared locker, she turned to Maruva, 'Can I sit down for a minute before I leave?'

'Yes, of course, take as long as you need. Here's some water,' she said, handing her a full tumbler.

Delta took a few sips and felt a bit better.

'I have to get back to work. Let me know early in the morning if you're still not feeling well tomorrow,' Maruva instructed.

Delta nodded a reply. She sat for about ten minutes then got up. Her co-workers threw curious looks at her as she crossed from the back room, through the kitchen and on to the eating area. Nobody said a word to her and she didn't attempt to say goodbye to anyone.

She walked out into Leopold Takawira Road and towards Copa Cabana terminus, thankful to be leaving.

The crowds in town were unsettling and there seemed to be several police officers and occasional soldiers idling on the streets. She wondered if the authorities were once again on alert for latent unrest.

She hastened, keen to get home and reflect on her new feelings of doubt and regret about pursuing a scheme that now seemed juvenile and poorly thought-out, with complications cropping up at every turn.

Real life didn't mirror novels or modify hare-brained plots. What had she been thinking? Hunger Buster was fast eroding what remained of her values, but with no obvious viable options, what on earth was she supposed to do if she left? She really had to talk to Cashleen, or she'd go stark raving mad.

10

Cashleen was jolted awake by the loud ringing of her mobile phone. Groggy, she sat up in bed. Her bedside clock told her that it was 2.30 a.m. Her pulse quickened. Unexpected calls in the middle of the night were always accompanied by a wave of anxiety. She groped about for her phone.

It was Rufaro. Why was she calling at such an hour? It definitely had to be bad news. She pressed 'Answer' and said hesitantly, 'Hullo, *Sisi*.'

'Cashleen? Is that you? Are you awake?' Rufaro's words fell over each other.

'Yes.' Of course she was awake. She'd answered the phone, hadn't she?

'How could you? Asking me for money to buy OBs! ***Tampons!*** For goodness sake, Cash!'

Cashleen was stumped. Was she really being woken up in the middle of the night to be accused of asking for money for such a small essential? Her offence, if it was one, hardly warranted such a reaction. She'd texted the request out of desperation. The two packs that she needed cost $8 and she only had $10 to her name.

'You have no disability, Cash. You have two whole arms and a set of legs. You have eyes too. A brain even. And a bloody degree that I helped to pay for. Both you and Itai. Why don't you get jobs or fucking do something instead of being such parasites?'

Across the vast distance that separated them, Cashleen was assailed by the strength of bitterness in her sister's voice, and it shocked her. She'd never sworn at her before.

So, this was what those terse messages had presaged? She should have paid attention to her premonition that Rufaro was running out of patience. She was at a loss. How could she explain?

'I'm so sorry. I didn't know you felt...'

Rufaro cut her short, 'It's got to stop! You must stop it now!' For a surreal moment, Cashleen could only think of how like the First Lady, **Madame-Stop-It,** her sister sounded. So imperious, so scornful.

'My psychiatrist says I'm enabling you...'

'Your psychiatrist?' Reflexively, Cashleen repeated the words in disbelief. Her sister was dependable, strong and capable. Not mentally ill. She shook her head vigorously. Was she fully awake?

'Yes, **my psychiatrist,** Cashleen. Think about it! I've got clinical depression. Six months on Prozac now. And I can't cope with your demands any more. Two grown-ass adults just sitting around waiting for me to feed you, clothe you and house you! And you've got the nerve to ask me for money to buy OBs! How can you?'

Those damned OBs! Cashleen couldn't think what had made her specify the sanitary-ware in her *SMS*. She should've simply asked for money.

'I'm sorry...'

'No, you're not. And I'm not doing this anymore. My psychiatrist says I have to break your cycle of dependence. You must get a job or get the hell out of my apartment!' Rufaro was shouting.

Cashleen couldn't let this pass. '*Sisi* Rufaro, it's not easy. I've been trying. There are no jobs. You need to come and see what's happening in Zimbabwe...'

'I'm doing no such thing. My psychiatrist says you're not trying hard enough. And I agree. Get off your backside and do something. *Anything!*'

'But...'

'But what? Don't tell me you can't find anything to do. I hear all the time that the streets of Harare are swarming with your fellow graduates. Why don't you join them? Sell bananas, cigarettes or whatever. Or go to Mbare Musika and start a vegetable stall! Then you'll be able to buy your own bloody OBs, Cash. Or, do you think that worthless degree of yours makes you too good to be a street vendor? If that's the case, you can tell me right now!'

The onslaught was unrelenting. Cashleen felt bewildered. She asked herself what entitled a faceless, nameless, psychiatrist in the UK to form opinions about her life in Zimbabwe?

An absurd image surfaced in her mind: a white man with a stethoscope around his neck hypnotising her sister, force-feeding her mind with tales of parasitic siblings as she lay on a leather couch in his softly-lit consultation room.

She shook her head and gathered her thoughts. 'I'm so sorry, *Sisi*. I'd no idea that you were unwell. I really didn't. Believe me.' The idea of any kind of mental illness frightened her, and for it to happen to her sister...

All of a sudden, Rufaro's rage appeared to have consumed itself. Cashleen could hear that she'd begun to cry. Tears stung her own eyes.

'I've tried my best for you, Cash. For Itai too. And for mother and father. You just don't know how hard it was for me all that time they were sick, and when they died... You just don't know what it did to me... I need a break, Cash. I really do. I have my own life, you know. Please.'

Cashleen felt miserable and out of her depth. She couldn't handle any of this.

'I swear, I had no idea that I was such a burden. I'm so sorry,' she repeated. Tears trickled down her face.

'I need... I need... oh, forget it. My head is splitting. I can't sleep. And I have to be at work at nine.' Rufaro's voice was still shaky, but she sounded calmer.

Cashleen didn't know what to say. How could she comfort her

sister when she needed reassurance herself?

Then, Rufaro blurted, 'Please help me, Cash. I can't do this anymore.' Before Cashleen could respond, the call was disconnected. She wasn't sure if Rufaro had ended the call or it had been a network problem. She had no calling credit to phone back. Neither did she have any real desire to resume what had been such a tense and painful exchange.

Sleep had deserted her. Her mind was in overdrive. How had things become so bad that Rufaro didn't care if she became a vendor? She, who'd always been so supportive of her dreams? How had they even reached a point where her sister was contemplating throwing her out of her apartment?

She didn't know what it felt like to be so depressed that you had to be on Prozac and under the care of a psychiatrist, but it had to be serious. How had she failed to recognise that Rufaro was unwell? Six whole months? Her mind went round and round in circles. The more she reflected, the easier it became to absolve herself. She really was trying her best. It wasn't her fault that Zimbabwe's economy had made finding a job almost impossible.

However, in as much as denial was tempting, she'd been presented with cold, hard facts. Her sister was clinically depressed. She and Itai were part of the problem and they'd have to be part of the solution. But how?

Troubled, she reached out for her little radio and switched it on. The sounds of Soul FM eased into the darkness. It was the station's so-called 'witching hour'. Two presenters were laughing as they shared trivialities about larger-than-life celebrities, who were so frequently in the media that they might as well have been locals.

'Beyonce's baby is called Blue Ivy. Dig that, dude? Maybe she took a cue from Gwyneth Paltrow. Hers is called Apple! Imagine!'

'Apple? The fruit or the computer?' There was loud laughter.

'Spare a thought for Kim and Kanye West's daughter. She's called North West! You've got to give it to them. It takes guts to give your children such names, but I feel for the kids. Imagine how they'll be teased at school!'

'Well, you never know. Don't underestimate the power of the celebrity X-factor. There might already be thousands of copycat Apples, Blue Ivies and North Wests by the time those kids go to school!'

There was more laughter before the light-hearted chat ended and one of the presenters initiated a discussion about corruption. Callers were invited to share their opinions. Cashleen listened with half an ear, her mind returning again and again to Rufaro's disclosure. And then a woman began to speak with such raw passion that Cashleen was left in no doubt about how deeply she felt.

'You're right. There're just too many greedy people out there. Look no further than the parastatals – Grain Marketing Board, National Railways, National Pensions, Public Medical Aid, National Roads Authority, the city councils! I could go on forever. Which one doesn't have corruption issues? And our ministers and MPs? Do you really think those guys are hungry? No, they're just greedy. If you want to see really hungry people, go to the streets! See the men, women and children who are vending and begging. See the people who are losing their jobs daily, and our unemployed graduates. See desperate men and women waiting in queues for healthcare at under-funded hospitals. The grandmother in the village who's looking after AIDS orphans. Then you'll know what real hunger is! Definitely not what you'd associate with *that* lot!'

More callers came through. Cashleen was struck by how the debate sounded more like a fight than a discussion: who owned the right to be called poor, while somehow being rich justified being corrupt.

Finding no relief, she switched stations to hear Chiwoniso's *Mai* lyrics come on air. Her voice was bold, clear and beautiful, in a tribute to a loving mother who'd passed on. Cashleen slid under the duvet, overwhelmed by memories of her own mother. Eventually, she fell asleep.

11

On Saturday morning, Delta called in sick. Her spell of nausea was over but she couldn't face going back to Hunger Buster. Not yet anyway.

Maruva and Mr Banga can stuff it, she thought, gleefully, although, with sudden sobriety she realised that she'd need a sick note. She did know of a downtown doctor who had a reputation for doling out sick notes for the right price, no questions asked. However, she didn't have any money.

Well, Monday was still a good two days away. She had time to think of a way round this. It was Tuesday that had potential to create real problems. She still had no idea if it would be possible to use her fake ID for the infectious diseases' clearance.

At home, she passed off her truancy as a day off. It turned out that Aunt Peace had a day off too, which was a surprise because she normally worked a half-day shift on Saturdays.

The prospect of spending the day with her aunt and uncle was daunting. She found it hard to deal with the growing tension between them: the former, all martyrdom and self-righteousness; the latter, withdrawn into wounded pride. Still, they'd always treated her kindly; she'd loved them and seen them as a strong couple. Now she worried that she might be witnessing the breakdown of their marriage.

At breakfast, they ignored each other, using Tarisai, their six-year-old daughter, as their medium of communication. The tension was palpable. Delta wished herself far away.

'Mama, Mama, Daddy wants some sugar.' Tarisai said in a small piping voice.

'Tari, can't you see the sugar? Give it to your daddy!'

The child leant across the table and pulled the basin towards her, spilling sugar in the process.

'Careful!' cautioned her mother.

'Please take it, Daddy,' Tarisai pleaded.

'Dee, how's the new job going at the lab?' Aunt Peace interjected with a tight little smile.

'All right, I guess.' Delta poured herself a cup of tea, feigning nonchalance, and quickly changed the subject. 'What's the cash situation Auntie? When I go through town in the morning I see long queues even before banks open.'

'You're telling me! Some of our clients now sleep in the queues. There's just no cash. We have to restrict withdrawals, so that everyone gets at least something. We're on twenty dollars a day max.' Aunt Peace shook her head.

'So, do you think it will get better anytime soon?'

'Not a chance. From next week we'll be on weekly withdrawal limits... possibly just fifty dollars to be withdrawn on one visit to the bank per week, imagine!'

Delta was surprised. Chronically broke, she'd long closed her bank account. 'That sounds bad. Do you think that they'll reintroduce the local currency?'

This was a worry for most people. Memories of the mid-2000s when inflation had been rampant and people had had to carry their cash in suitcases were still fresh. Delta remembered both the jokes and the euphoria when she'd acquired her first million-dollar note as a high school student. Disillusion had rapidly ensued. A loaf of bread cost $500,000.

Uncle Dondo stoically sipped his tea, silent in a brittle cocoon.

He'd often been animated at breakfast over his newspaper and the latest news.

'Well, things are happening behind the scenes, confidential discussions with the Reserve Bank.' Aunt Peace sounded a little smug. As a bank manager, she must have had some inside information and the expression on her face invited them to probe, but Delta knew better than to try.

Uncle Dondo flashed a warning glance, and cleared his throat. Tarisai whispered something in his ear, and he suddenly smiled and whispered in hers.

'Can I have some money for my school tuck, Mama?' she chirped.

'Ask your dad. And stop playing with your food!' Aunt Peace's voice was sharp.

'Daddy said he doesn't have any money, and I should ask you.' The little girl sounded close to tears.

'Your dad had better get a job, then he can give you the money himself. And if you don't stop playing with your food, I'll slap you, Tari.'

Delta was taken aback. Uncle Dondo stopped eating his unfinished breakfast and balled up his fists. Then, pushing back his chair with a sharp squeak, he stood up, his face taut. He opened his mouth as if to speak, then turning on his heel abruptly left the room. The door slammed violently behind him. Delta was certain that if she hadn't been present, he might have slapped Aunt Peace. In the awkward silence that followed, they heard him driving away.

Tarisai began to cry.

'Oh! Just shut up,' Aunt Peace snapped. Tarisai ran from the room in a flood of tears. Delta, taken aback by the sudden drama, was unsure whether to stay or leave the room. Her aunt quietly and deliberately added sugar to her tea and stirred it with unnecessary vigour.

'You see this, Dee? This is what I get for all the sacrifices that I've made. I shoulder every responsibility in this family but your uncle is *so* ungrateful. He just sits around smoking, watching television, and drinking beer. Am I supposed to accept this just because he's my husband?'

Delta smiled weakly. 'He might get a job soon, Auntie.'

'You're joking? What job can he find, when he spends his days indoors, moping?'

Delta stared at the remains of her breakfast. 'I don't know what to say, Auntie.'

'Don't say anything. Let me tell you. Real men are out there fending for their families. They make plans and follow them through. You tell me how sitting around the house will help your uncle to get a job! He has no initiative whatsoever!'

'I think he's depressed Auntie.' Delta grasped at straws.

Aunt Peace gave a cynical laugh. 'Depressed? Is he the first person to lose a job? Becoming depressed because you're out of work is a luxury that real men can't afford. They are fired up by hardship!'

There was really nothing more to say. Delta started clearing the table, taking dirty cups and plates through to the kitchen sink. She had a sudden longing to be out of the house and as far away as possible.

'Auntie, I'd like to go and see Cashleen now. Is there anything you'd like me to do before I leave?'

'No, no. You go ahead.' The woman waved her hand dismissively. Her rings glinted in the light. She looked suddenly small, deflated and contrite. Delta seemed to see her for the first time: a sad, disappointed, previously pampered woman who was trying to cope with the role reversal at home and all its attendant complications, but who still felt unappreciated and resentful.

On an impulse she said, 'Remember, Auntie, I promised I'd help when I get paid.'

The older woman looked up and sighed. 'I know, Delta, thank you. It's just that right now, we need so much more than you could ever give me. We have debts and our unpaid bills are mounting. I don't know what to do.'

Delta hovered, pretending to think, recognising that even this safe haven was built on sand.

'I've got a headache. I'm going to take a nap. Let me know when you go out, will you?' her aunt said.

Delta murmured. 'Sure. I'll just do the dishes and let you know.' The door closed. Delta leant against the wall and closed her eyes.

By the time she left, Aunt Peace was still in her bedroom and Uncle Dondo hadn't returned. Little Tarisai had recovered from her tears and was absorbed in a noisy Scooby-Doo episode on television.

On mi way, she WhatsApp'd Cashleen and embellished the message with three of her favourite smiley emojis. She was glad to be out of the house and away from the melodrama. One could only take so much.

She caught a *kombi* from Houghton Park to town, then wove her way through city crowds up Harare Street and towards Cashleen's. She'd taken care to avoid the Hunger Buster vicinity, just in case. Sick people weren't supposed to have merry jaunts in town, especially when they hadn't been officially signed off by a doctor. The idea of typing up her own sick note had fizzled away. Anyway, where would she get a doctor's stamp?

She dared not think about Tuesday's infectious disease clearance. Niggling regret swelled. Her situation was growing out of control. What had seemed like a great solution, now felt amateurish. The idea of letting the job go crossed her mind again, and with it came a transient sense of relief.

But what would become of her if she failed to raise money for her little project? Would she continue to send out unsuccessful job applications for months and even years? Maybe Cashleen would assure her and help her to work her way through this muddle that she'd created.

She shoved gloomy thoughts to the back of her mind, choosing instead to enjoy the moment. It was a sunny day with an ambience that was complemented by a gentle breeze. The walk cleared her head and refreshed her. A *kombi* drove recklessly up Harare Street.

She sprang to relative safety, her heart thudding as she stared in alarm at the tyre-tracks that the vehicle had left. It could have easily run her over.

Kombi drivers seemed oblivious of the distinction between roads and pedestrian pavements in the CBD or footpaths on the outskirts. They invented their own road rules as they drove, focused on competition to pick up and drop as many passengers as possible. Spotting a potential customer was more reason to stop than a red traffic light.

And as if on cue, one screeched to a halt near her, with catcalls and belligerent heckling to get on board from the touts.

'Dee Zed! Dee Zed!' they shouted out a truncated form of their final destination.

Delta ignored them. She hadn't flagged them down but trying to reason with an irascible tout could earn one some particularly vulgar insults from these young men who had a reputation for being uncouth and disorderly. With no alternative transport system available, the public were at their mercy.

As Delta approached Northern Heights, she noticed that Montagu shopping complex was quiet for a Saturday. On the complex's edge, several vendors had organised an assortment of goods for sale. Near the Harare Street intersection with Chinamano Road, newspaper placards displayed the day's headlines:

Chaos Fears as Zim Economy Burns
Unpaid for 14 months, Railway Workers Strike
Police Impounding Vehicles Illegally: Lawyers
War Vets Slam Looming Take-over of Foreign Companies
Mocking Mugabe, 150 Arrested to Date

No surprises there. It felt as if 'news' – if this was what it was – was simply recycled in the all too familiar depressing themes which now defined everyday life. Delta had long noted that politics dominated the news, general conversation, WhatsApp, Twitter and other social media platforms.

Those who saw themselves as patriots or nationalists slammed critics as sponsored western ideologues, friends of white people, enemies of the state and supporters of the opposition, all of which were not far removed from treasonous. If you were a true patriot, you supported the President and his government no matter what. Independent thinking was a threat that had to be shouted down.

'If you're not for us, you're against us.' Delta grimaced as she thought of an age-old slogan used repeatedly by nationalists in a time of war.

Newspaper vendors stood listlessly next to their piles of newspapers. It didn't look as if they were doing well.

A small shabby man with missing teeth lisped, 'My beautiful thithter! Pleathe come get thome newthpaperth! Eh! Jutht one dollar each!' He smiled gamely at her in earnest persuasion.

'Maybe tomorrow!' Delta replied, unable to resist his toothless smile, and the pity that he evoked.

'Tomorrow? Aayath, you're making fun of me, thihi!' he called out behind her, and shifted his attention to another potential customer.

The parking space between the apartment block and Montagu shopping centre was littered with rubbish. An incredible number of beer bottles lay strewn about, many broken. There were numerous cigarette butts and condom wrappers, all stark evidence of the previous night's decadence.

She recalled Cathleen's concerns about a nightclub that operated from the complex, unacceptably close to the residential blocks in that area. Friday nights were the worst. Excessive nocturnal noise, revellers' disorderly conduct in the car park and waking up to a littered neighbourhood were long-standing complaints.

At one point, Cashleen had motivated residents to sign a petition against the nightclub, but it had gone unacknowledged. It was rumoured that the club belonged to a powerful city council official. If this was true, then the issues would never be resolved.

Typical! Delta thought.

She turned left into Tongogara Street and stood at the padlocked Northern Heights gate. She could see the caretaker sweeping fallen leaves beyond a bed of wilting plants. He was a jovial, elderly man who doubled as a day-time security guard and he'd been at the apartment block for as long as Delta could remember.

She'd often said to Cashleen that such a benevolent grandfather-figure was hardly a deterrent to either small-time crooks or hardened robbers. She supposed he couldn't retire because like many elderly people his pension had been wiped out during the hyperinflation era, just like that of her own parents.

'Hullo, *Kule* Jojo' she shouted, knowing he was rather deaf.

His face broke into a smile. He set down his rake and approached the gate. She noticed that his step was slower than usual. His overalls were threadbare and his canvas shoes were tattered, but he opened the gate and greeted her cheerfully, as if he didn't have a care in the world.

Without being asked, he pointed upwards, 'Your friend, she's there in her flat. I didn't see her go out today.'

'Thanks, *Kule,*' Delta said as she turned a corner towards the staircase that led up to Cashleen's apartment on the third floor.

12

Cashleen opened the door to a firm knock and greeted Delta with a warm embrace. She stood back, appraising her, and then exclaimed, '*Yoh!* You look good, Delta!'

Delta twirled round playfully. 'I know. What's a girl to do if she has superior genes? But *iwe*, you look terrible. Why the swollen face and red eyes? And your voice? A frog's would be sweeter!' she said to her friend as she followed her into the sitting room.

Cashleen's eyes filled but she didn't want to tell Delta about her conversation with Rufaro. Not yet anyway. She forced herself to smile, offering Delta an armchair as she took the seat opposite.

'I'm recovering from a cold,' she picked on the first thought that came to mind, clearing her throat for good measure. Delta's face creased with concern. 'Are you taking anything for it?'

Cashleen shook her head. '*Aiwa*. These things usually go away by themselves. I have some Flu-Stop somewhere.'

'You need to look after yourself better.' Delta was solicitous and then asked, 'Is Itai around? I haven't seen him in a long time.'

Cashleen shrugged. 'He's fine, I think. He came in after I'd gone to sleep. Heard him leaving around six. Odd. I'm more used to him spending hours and hours in bed.'

'Maybe he's found a job.'

Cashleen shook her head. 'No. He'd have told me. He's now spending too much time with that police officer friend of his, Gerry.'

'*Aah,* Cashleen. You always worry. They're friends, aren't they?'

'Yes, but there's something suspicious about Gerry. He's too flashy, too slick… and he changes cars like bicycles! Yet he's only a junior police officer.'

Delta threw her head back and laughed. 'Cash!'

'Seriously. Don't laugh. You know those guys are poorly paid. Where does he get his money from?'

'*Inga, inga!* Is that a surprise? Aren't you journalists always telling us how police corruption has become the new normal? Anyway, I still think you worry too much. It's none of your business where he gets his money. Or what he does with it. He's only your brother's friend.'

'Exactly! My brother's friend,' Cashleen's voice had an edge to it. 'That's what bothers me. Come I'll show you something.'

She led Delta to the kitchen and opened a cupboard door.

'Look at these groceries!' She gestured towards two packed shelves, then opened the fridge and showed her more.

'I found all these this morning. Itai must have brought them in last night.'

Delta shrugged. 'So what's the problem?'

'Can't you see? Bacon, cheese, real fruit juice, imported biscuits but Itai is jobless. The last time we had these was over a year ago when Rufaro was here.'

She pointed under the table at some bottles of expensive wine and Castle-Lite six-packs. 'Where did he get all this from?'

Delta smiled and waved her hand dismissively. 'Take it as manna from heaven. He could have used the money to drink himself under the table, but he obviously thought of you. You're always broke. If I were you, I'd just be grateful and stuff myself!'

Cashleen was annoyed. Couldn't Delta be serious?

'Well, I can't. I'll wait for him to explain himself before I touch any of this.'

'*Aikazve*! I don't understand you, Cash. I give up.'

There was a brittle silence. Clearly, Cashleen thought, her friend was not going to provide any support.

Taking a deep breath, she changed the topic. 'Tea?' she asked.

'Maybe later,' Delta said, led the way back to the sitting room and they settled back into their armchairs.

'How's the new job?'

Delta bit her lip, hesitated, and said quietly, 'Hmm. My job? Where do I start?'

'*Ah iwe kani!* Go on.' Cashleen prodded.

Suddenly, Delta was overcome by a fit of giggles.

Cashleen stared at her nonplussed.

'Sorry, I just can't think where to start. You won't believe how much has happened.'

Cashleen was puzzled but curious. 'Tell me right this minute. Start at the beginning.' She leaned forward expectantly.

'Fine. This is how it started...'

Cashleen listened wide-eyed as her friend narrated a sordid little tale of counterfeit experts in downtown Harare, her fake ID as the unlikely Misi Hurukuro, her equally fake certificates and CV detailing just five O-Level passes. Squeezed in somewhere was a year's experience as a chef's assistant at City Bakery and Restaurant.

'*Misi Hurukuro?* Delta, you didn't!' Cashleen was shocked. She knew of such scams, but her best friend ...

Delta looked up, her face a caricature of defiance. 'Well, I did.' She sounded rebellious. 'Do you want me to finish or not?'

Cashleen nodded and bit back a reproof. Why hadn't she told her all this before? Delta had always been a fiercely loyal friend. It was this slowly evolving lack of morals which bothered Cashleen. They were too close to keep such secrets from each other.

She listened and willed herself not to interrupt as Delta described her exploits at Hunger Buster. Her dodgy boss who was also something of a sexual predator. The kindly supervisor who'd given her a crash course in creating tasty meals from decaying chicken cuts. The use of transformer oil for culinary purposes. Being almost discovered by Dr Matinde. And, lastly, her misadventure in the broom cupboard whilst evading a city council health inspector.

Cashleen couldn't decide which aspects of the narrative were the most shocking. No doubt, Delta had been candid, but while she spoke mischievously, as if this was a laughing matter, Cashleen felt that her friend was very unsettled.

'And don't tell anyone I'm here today. I'm supposed to be at home recovering from a bilious attack.' Her joke fell flat.

Cashleen hesitated, not wanting to sound sanctimonious, 'But why, Delta?' she finally asked.

'Why not?' Delta retorted with feeling. 'Please don't sit there and judge me. I had to do something. You can't tell me that you're not as fed up as I am. Trying to do things the right way and getting nowhere.'

'Yes, *I am* fed up. But a fake ID and fake educational certificates? Do you know how much trouble you can get into? Why didn't you just apply using your real name, your real certificates?'

'Do you think I didn't try? How many times since we left uni have I told you that I've applied for this, for that and even for all sorts of menial jobs. Nobody would take me on. A chemical engineer applying for a cleaning job! Give me a break. A manager at EuroZW told me straight to my face he suspected I was an intelligence operative who'd been sent to infiltrate foreign companies.' She clicked her tongue with feeling.

'Yes, but surely you could have tried to find something without having to...'

Delta laughed harshly. 'Not a chance. We'll grow old trying. And guess what? Nobody gives a damn. Did you hear what that minister said about unemployed graduates?'

Cashleen shook her head, unsure which of the numerous disparaging criticisms Delta was referring to. The industry and commerce minister, the education minister, the finance minister and even the President himself had all weighed in against graduates.

'He said, if varsity dropouts like Bill Gates could set up companies and create jobs, then we as Zimbabwean graduates should do better. *Better than Bill Gates?* Can you believe it? At least Bill Gates operated in a functioning economy. Not this!'

Cashleen remembered the admonition. It had been a mockery. She also recalled the ruling party's promise of two million jobs during the last election. What phony campaign rhetoric that had been!

Delta continued, 'Now, tell me. How does someone like me create a single job, let alone set up a company that can employ other people? Where would I start? *In this country*? And with no connections? Without a corrupt relative or two up there?'

Cashleen sat in silence. She'd had similar versions of the same discussion with many of her fellow graduates. A few got lucky breaks, others with connections made it, but for most of them the outlook was bleak. She rubbed her forehead, thinking.

She understood the plight that they all faced, but some deep moral instinct told her that this didn't justify Delta's actions. Her friend had been irresponsible. The consequences didn't bear thinking about.

'But this... this act of yours at Hunger Buster... Aren't you scared you'll be caught out? I mean not just over the job, but with what could follow an exposure of all the fake certificates!'

Delta threw her a cold, hostile look. 'I didn't tell you this so that you could condemn me. I thought you were my friend and you'd understand. I thought you'd help me.'

'I *am* your friend! Helping you starts with getting you to face the truth,' Cashleen protested.

'If that's how you're going to talk to me, then I'm leaving.' Delta stood up indignantly.

'Sit down, please,' said Cashleen gently, aware that in seconds the whole situation could get out of hand. Both of them were on edge; both had expected too much of each other. Since it was clear that Delta wouldn't back down, she had to be the one to serve a peace offering.

'Please stay, Delta. You've only just arrived. I'm sorry. Let's talk this through. We're friends, remember?' She bravely held Delta's furious gaze.

'No,' Delta waved the overture away. 'I'm going. What gives you the right to preach to me?'

Something that Cashleen couldn't quite define had broken and her friend had already disengaged. She picked up her handbag.

Delta turned and walked out without a backward glance. Only when the door closed with a thud did it really sink that her friend hadn't been bluffing. She **had** left.

A wave of intolerable loneliness came upon her. She felt bereft. First Rufaro, then Delta. What was happening to them all? Never in the many years of their friendship had Delta just walked out on her. Even when they'd argued, they'd always found a way through.

13

The mechanics who replaced Unesu's defective hillmatic starter plied their trade from under some trees near Avondale Post Office. In the makeshift workshop, business boomed with multiple repairs in progress, customers picking up and dropping their cars or waiting for completion of quick jobs.

Car washes thrived, the lack of easy access to running water being but a trifling inconvenience. Buckets were quickly filled and carried conveyor-belt style with remarkable efficiency from a solitary tap behind the supermarket.

Vehicles were polished until they sparkled in the sun. From one car came the thumping sounds of loud music to which several car-washers sang happily and out of tune. Who cared? It was a beautiful afternoon.

A cluster of vendors selling car accessories hung back at the post office boundary with affected indolence, well out of the mechanics' way. Unesu wasn't fooled. They had hawks' eyes and he knew how quickly they could spring into action at the slightest hint of interest from a possible customer.

And weren't they gifted and persuasive verbal craftsmen! He'd been coaxed into buying a generic Android car-phone-charger for $5. The seller had sworn on his dead mother's grave that it was durable and of superior quality, unlike most of the ubiquitous Chinese products which had flooded shops, flea markets and street corners.

Unesu scrutinised his new possession for evidence that it was really hot off the Friday night Emirates flight from Dubai, but of course there was no such proof. Well, it was his now. He whistled as he climbed into his newly-repaired car.

He'd been very pleased to pay $50 for a new, original Mazda-branded starter. Lacoste Autoparts had quoted him three times as much. At $50, he knew that the starter was sure to be of dubious origin, but after his many ignition problems, he couldn't care less. His car was fixed.

There'd be no more embarrassing episodes when his car sputtered and refused to start, even with the most energetic pushing. He'd no longer have to worry about finding the right incline on which to park, and be there'd no more haggling with street-hulks-for-hire over the amount he had to pay them to give him a push-start.

He did his weekend shopping, had a bite at Mugg and Bean, and then headed to Cashleen's, where he arrived at dusk. There was a power outage and she opened the door to him holding a fat Bigga candle. Its flame cast shadows on her face. Her smile lacked its customary vivacity and he had the impression that she'd either just woken up, or she'd been crying. He couldn't be sure. The lighting was so dim.

He handed her a bag of groceries and some old *Time* magazines that he'd found at the flea market. He knew that she was a news addict and he felt rewarded when her face came alive with interest.

With a grin, he waved away her thanks. '*Asi chii nhai!* Besides, the magazines are all out of date.' He settled into an armchair, 'So, no ZESA again? Any chance you'll have power today?'

'*Iwe-ka!* Not a chance. Maybe tomorrow or Monday.'

'That's too bad, Cash.'

'Not really. There was a time when I thought I'd never get used to this. But it's now so normal that I'd worry if there were power and clean running water every day. We now get water three days a week, so at least I can do the laundry and have some to drink. But I boil it first, just in case. Not that you can boil away the chemicals.' She laughed dryly.

Unesu clicked his tongue. The city fathers had once condemned their own water for lack of purity, and a Comic Hararian video that he'd received from Delta on WhatsApp came to mind. *The oppressed dancing up a storm, ululating and clapping wildly in praise of their oppressor for giving them non-potable water. Only to suffer from diarrhoea later.* It had been called The Fools Syndrome.

Well, he surmised, maybe blind adulation was much easier to express than dissent, which could be twisted into sinister proof of seditious political forces such as the manipulative imperial West.

He looked at Cashleen, somewhat unsettled by how accepting she sounded. It seemed time and unemployment had taken their toll. The verve that had defined her during their college years was absent. She'd been one of the most forthright people he'd known and she could have been counted on to advocate for one cause or another. Wasn't that why she had studied journalism?

Clearly, she was no longer the same person, or else she'd have been telling him about mobilising residents to sign a petition against ZESA for these power cuts. And against City of Harare for failing to provide a consistent supply of safe, clean water.

'I guess I'm one of the lucky ones. Don't like my bedsit at the hospital much, but at least we don't get frequent water and power cuts like you do here.'

'*Inga zvenyu!*' Cashleen sounded envious. 'How's Mama?' she asked.

Just thinking about his mother and the burden of being an only child pulled at the tension knotted within him.

'Not too good. I meant to tell you. *Mainini*, who's staying with her, has asked me to come home to see how she is,' he replied.

His mother's young sister was a permanently unhappy woman who liked making a fuss. She seemed to derive warped pleasure from exaggerating real and imaginary disasters. In this case, he worried that she was right to be concerned.

'Is she worse, then?' Cashleen asked.

'*Mainini* thinks so. I've tried talking to Mama on the phone but she goes off at a tangent. Sometimes it's like... she just switches off,' he said quietly.

'What about the operation? Can she still have it?'

'I don't know. Remember, her diagnosis caught the cancer very early. An operation would have cured her.'

'And now?' Cashleen ventured.

'Honestly, Cash? I don't know. I can't tell how much it's spread. She still refuses a medical check-up or any kind of treatment. She swears by an always imminent miracle promised by that conman.'

'Can't someone do something? Her sisters? Her brothers?'

He shook his head. 'They've all failed, like me. Many times. Clearly, that prophet has a hold over her. I can't understand it. She spends hours and hours at church. The house is littered with bottles of anointed water, anointed oil, anointed this, anointed that, healing bracelets and all sorts of other trinkets which are supposed to bestow miracles. To heal. To bless. To prosper. What rubbish! I thought she'd come to her senses. It's been a year, Cash. I am really angry with that man. And with Mama too!'

Cashleen gave him a worried look. '*Iwe,* disagreements happen in families all the time. I can tell you that. Just don't be angry with Mama please. She can't help it. She needs your support. Now more than ever'.

He peered at her in the half-light. 'Are you serious? Support her to what end? Or do you mean support her to dig her own grave? Voodoo makes no sense to me. No matter what religious gloss you put on it. Remember, I'm a medic. A scientist. That I am not a Christian is neither here nor there. Anyway,' he paused truculently, 'that these churches should call themselves Christian is a farce. Those prophets simply select biblical passages to suit their agenda. And, as you and I know, you can find anything to interpret whichever way you like in the Bible.'

Cashleen leaned forward. 'Don't misunderstand me. I only

meant that maybe you need to have a tactful discussion with her. Explain things again. Clearly and without the medical jargon that you guys use. Make her see she's running out of time. Make her understand that she's putting her life at risk.'

Unesu contemplated her words. It was all very well for her to make it sound so easy, to talk as if *she* was the voice of reason, when *he* was the trained health professional with the skills set to counsel patients. The only problem was that this was his mother, not his patient.

He shook his head, sighing. 'I did try.'

'Yes, but maybe you have to keep at it.' She paused. 'When are you going to visit her?'

'Next weekend. I think on Friday after work. Come with me? Please? I need to see how unwell she is. It might help having you there – you being a girl and…'

Cashleen nodded readily. 'Of course, anything I can do to help. But I doubt I'll be of much use when her own family has failed to convince her.'

'I think it's worth a try. We'll see. Thank you, Cash.'

While he could ask his mother or *mainini* about the severity of symptoms such as weight loss and appetite, it would be taboo to ask about uterine bleeding and so on. Cashleen could be his proxy. He knew that she could be persuasive while being sensitive and sensible at the same time.

And he also hadn't forgotten how, before they passed on, Cashleen's parents had been good friends with his mother, who'd often referred to Cashleen as her daughter. Who knew? Maybe she and Cashleen could ease back into that old, familiar space and she'd open up to the idea of seeking medical care.

In the companionable silence that followed, he stood up to stretch his legs and stared out through the window. The lights in the distance gave Harare an ephemeral beauty that it could never claim in the cold light of day. Not with countless buildings in disrepair, rubbish on every corner, crowds, traffic anarchy and makeshift markets mushrooming everywhere as people tried to eke out a living. He marvelled at the view, then glanced at his watch. It was already after 7 o'clock.

'*Ah!* I'm running late, Cash. Got to see Takunda.' His friend was back from the Chiadzwa diamond fields for the weekend and somehow Unesu had found himself being talked into a drink at Pariah State in Borrowdale.

'You still friends with Taku? *A diamond dealer*?' Cashleen frowned. Unesu shrugged. Surely she knew what strong bonds they'd had since childhood. They'd all grown up together.

'Why not? I like going on the wild side once in a while! Besides, some diamonds could sneak their way into my pockets,' he joked to mask his true feelings. In reality, he was conflicted about his friend's dubious activities.

'Be careful. I just don't trust him. Never have,' she said solemnly. Unesu laughed. Trust Cashleen to come up with something like that!

'I really should go. I'll call you about the trip to see Mama.'

'Sure. Please do.'

As Unesu ran down the stairs, he mentally planned his route to Borrowdale. His familiarity with the condition of the roads was compromised because he hadn't been for a few months. Certainly not since the pothole-spawning rainy season had ended. So he had no way of knowing which roads were in good condition.

With so many dysfunctional streetlights, he wouldn't see the potholes and he could easily damage his car. Driving past the Presidential State House would be a smooth, safe drive, but the 6 p.m. traffic curfew blotted that idea. So, it would have to be Sam Nujoma and Churchill, then up Churchill to Borrowdale Road.

Sitting in heavy traffic – it seemed the first thing everyone wanted to buy when they had money was a car – he acknowledged an ill-defined reluctance to meet Takunda that evening. Without saying or doing anything specific, his friend had begun to make him feel inferior and inadequate. They were of the same age, both trained as doctors, but Takunda was already living a life Unesu could only dream of.

He wondered if he was becoming too materialistic, but surely it wasn't a crime to desire the good things in life. He thought again about his decision to join Doctors Mazwi and Reza at Orion Clinic. As Takunda liked saying, everyone had to make their choices and live with them. He intended to live with this one and see it right through.

14

Delta sat in a crowded carriage and waited for her journey to begin. Her impatience grew. It was 7 o'clock. With no explanation, the scheduled departure time had been delayed by an hour. She tried to get answers. In a tone which suggested that she didn't want to be bothered, an irritable station officer told her that they'd be departing soon.

The air was thick with shouts of vendors competing to advertise their wares as they paced up and down the carriage. Delta's head ached from the din. The hustle involved men, women, boys and girls, all intent on making some final sales before their working day ended.

Each one declared that he or she had the best of bargains, and the best quality of whatever was on offer. Oranges, bananas, buns, sweets, bottled drinks and airtime were some of the items that were shoved in her face. She feigned sleep, just to put them off, so that they'd leave her alone. Too driven to be deterred, a few still strove to get her attention. The opportunity to sell anything was too precious to miss, even if it meant that they had to wake someone up.

Also going up and down the carriage were beggars – often a blind adult led by a child who held out a cup, calling out, 'We're asking for help. Please help us'. One particular little boy caught Delta's attention. He looked so thin and hungry that Delta wished she had something to offer him.

Others wandering aimlessly were perhaps opportunistic thieves, covertly studying potential targets, or just waiting for the right moment to pick a pocket, execute a con or grab something of value and make a dash for it.

Most of the passengers sat passively, uncomplaining and expectant as they waited for the train to leave. A few grumbled. One verbose man took a stab at humour. 'Who doesn't know that the train workers haven't been paid full salaries for over a year? I think the driver must have gone on strike. We'll get old before we leave this place, I tell you!'

He drew no laughter. Unfazed, he continued in comedian style. Politics of the day were his preferred subject. Slowly the compartment resonated with smiles, snickers and outright laughter, though one couple threw him hostile glances.

Delta tried to shut out the noise and focus on settling the tumult in her mind. Granted, her latest decision had been impulsive, but the more she thought about everything she'd said and done, the more she convinced herself that she wasn't just making excuses to mask her own mistakes. She'd been well and truly cornered.

Her thoughts went round and round, before settling on her argument with Cashleen, and then moved on to what had brought her here. She replayed events that were still as fresh in her memory as when they'd occurred.

From Cashleen's, she arrived home to another altercation between Uncle Dondo and Aunt Peace. She hung back in the kitchen, disinclined to show herself or to confront the fight unfolding in the sitting room. Uncle Dondo's words were slurred and Delta realised that he was drunk. This could only mean trouble.

The insults that the two were trading touched on such sensitive issues that she was sure both of them would be mortified to know that she'd overheard the argument. If she went in there, what would she say? What would she do? She stood transfixed by indecision and by the intensity of their acrimony towards each other. Tarisai's weeping mingled with their voices.

'This time you've gone too far. Who do you think you are? You're nothing!'

Aunt Peace retaliated, 'If I'm nothing, I can leave right now. Then we'll see who'll pay your living expenses, who'll babysit you and tolerate your failures... You impotent drunkard, I can...'

'How dare you insult me, you mad woman you?' Uncle Dondo shouted furiously.

Aunt Peace gave a hysterical laugh. 'Who's the mad one here? I dare say so because it's true. *Futi,* I've a better idea... Why don't *you* leave? And take *your* sister's daughter with you. Out of my house today the two of you! I can't be responsible for your whole clan. Do I look like a slave?'

Her words shocked Delta to her core. Did Aunt Peace really mean it? Had her presence in their home inadvertently contributed to their relationship problems? And to the extent that Aunt Peace felt *enslaved?*

Squeezing her eyes shut, Delta leant forward and laid her palms flat on the kitchen table. What was she going to do?

'Watch your mouth, Peace! Just watch it. Nobody's leaving this house. Today or any other day! I'm the man in this house and what I say goes. Point that stupid finger at me one more time and I'll break it. I'll beat you so thoroughly, you'll wish you'd never been born!'

Delta's head jerked up at her uncle's threats. The situation was growing out of control. Why couldn't Aunt Peace just shut up? Why was she continuing to provoke him when he was so obviously drunk and angry? Much as she didn't want to, she had to go in, if only to shield Tarisai from all this. She took a hesitant step forward.

Aunt Peace wouldn't be silenced. 'Call yourself "Man of the House?" You useless loafer. You'll beat me up... A real man doesn't use his fists!'

The sound of a forceful slap rang out, followed by sounds of a scuffle, swearing and grunting, things breaking and Tari's voice rising to a piercing scream.

Delta ran into the sitting room and joined in the mêlée, pulling her uncle away from Aunt Peace, as Tarisai huddled crying in the corner.

'Please stop fighting. Please. You're scaring me. You're scaring Tarisai,' she begged.

At the mention of his little daughter's name, Delta felt her uncle stiffen. He loosened his grip on Aunt Peace and shoved her aside. She landed violently on the sofa.

'Bitch!' he swore at her and spat. Delta stared at him in shocked disbelief.

'*Iwe!* What are you staring at?' he lashed out, pointing his finger at her, and clicking his tongue in an exaggerated manner as he strode off. She was confused by this onslaught which was surely misdirected. She wasn't the enemy here. Hadn't he just been defending her when Aunt Peace said she must leave?

Alcohol and rage was a toxic combination that played havoc with reason, but despite the anger in his reddened eyes, she had detected what she hoped might have been a hint of shame. She half-expected to hear him driving off as he'd done in the morning, but there was silence. Had he walked away?

Aunt Peace was a pitiful sight as she sat weeping silently, covering her face with both hands. Tarisai's screams had diminished to muted whimpering. She looked so bewildered that Delta's heart went out to her. She gathered her in her arms and they sat in an armchair facing Aunt Peace.

'*Shh. Shh*. It's all right Tari. It's all right. Please stop crying,' she murmured into the little girl's ear as she wiped her tears away.

She rocked the child until she was silent, knowing that the girl would probably never forget the scene she'd witnessed between her parents. She felt the child's body relax and mould itself into hers. Aunt Peace also stopped crying but she remained head down, her face covered.

The one thing that stuck in Delta's mind was the discovery that Aunt Peace didn't want her. She was certain though, that she'd have never said it to her face. She felt hurt and confused. What an afternoon it had been, first Cashleen's rejection, and now this horrible, physically violent squabble which had somehow involved her.

How could her aunt have been so two-faced? *Delta this, Delta that*, while all the time she'd wanted her out? Well, she could keep her house! An impulsive, rebellious thought rose and she spoke out loud before she could change her mind, considering that it was already 4 o'clock on a Saturday afternoon.

She arranged her face into a picture of calm. 'Auntie, I'd like to go to Gweru today. If I leave now, I can catch one of the last buses.'

Aunt Peace looked up. Her face was streaked with tears and her right eye and lower lip were swollen. It would have to be Monday off work, then, Delta thought. Her aunt opened her mouth as if to speak, but just managed an '*Aah!*' of apparent surprise.

In quick order, Delta's hurt turned to self-pity and then outrage. This gave her a kind of freedom from compassion and constraint. She felt no solidarity or sympathy for her aunt, but instead, she felt she held a kind of perverted power over her.

After a few moments Aunt Peace sighed, then asked, '*Ku*Gweru? What about work? Are you sure?'

Work, futi? She wondered if Aunt Peace was sincere or just aggrieved that she'd miss out on the part-salary that Delta had promised her. She obviously needed money and this had been the trigger to the resentment she felt towards her husband.

Without elaborating, Delta responded, 'Yes, I'm sure, Auntie.' In that moment of decision, she acknowledged that going back to work was a non-starter. After all, she still had her degree. She was done with Hunger Buster and all that it stood for; done with worrying over the risk of being outed and the potential consequences.

She hugged Tarisai close and told her that she had to pack.

The little girl's face crumpled. For a second, Delta feared that she might start crying again, but she got up quietly and went to sit on her mother's lap. Delta fetched a broom and swept up shards of the broken coffee table glass-top and two broken mugs. She threw them into the bin then went to pack.

She took her best clothes, shoes and educational certificates, stuffing the fake ones right at the bottom. She couldn't risk Aunt Peace going through her things in her absence and finding Misi Hurukuro's documents. Her little suitcase filled up quickly. She could always come back for the rest of her stuff later.

Next was a WhatsApp text message to Maruva. It was unprofessionalism at its worst, but what could she do? As a short-term contract worker, she was allowed to give twenty-four-hours' notice in the first week, but this was certainly not the best way to do it.

Serious family probs. Travlin 2 Gweru 2nite. May not cm bek. 4n u 2moro xx. There was no need to explain anything further. She didn't owe them anything. In fact, it was them who owed her five days' wages. She'd phone and ask for her payment soon.

She counted the money in her purse and was dismayed to find that it wasn't enough for a bus ticket to Gweru. She couldn't ask Aunt Peace or Uncle Dondo for a top-up. She briefly thought of staying overnight at Cashleen's while she figured out where she could get money for her journey home. Memories of their argument stopped her.

There was only one thing to do. She'd travel by train at a fraction of the bus fare. She didn't look forward to it though. She tried not to think of the infamous railway network's reputation: obsolete infrastructure worsened by theft-related vandalism, poorly-run services and reports of derailments. Today, she told herself, nothing would go wrong. She'd arrive safely, even if the journey took the whole night.

And here she was in the train with what she'd feared already playing out. She'd landed herself in this mess, but her mother's favourite proverb didn't always hold true: *He, who lays his mouse-traps in burnt grasslands, is not afraid of getting his buttocks soiled by soot...* Life wasn't that simple. It often wasn't easy to live with the consequences of one's actions. Then, at the sound of the whistle, several people who included the vendors and beggars scrambled for the exits. Delta was surprised when the verbose comedian also disembarked. She'd been certain that he too was a traveller. They were finally on their way.

15

Unesu parked at Sam Levy's Village and found his way to Pariah's. A popular haunt, the bar was full as usual. Conversation mingled with laughter and the clink of glasses. There was a live band and a few men and women were slow-dancing to the music. He caught a whiff of cigarette smoke, old brandy and what he thought of as the *macho* waft of superior quality liquor. Class was certainly what this bar was associated with.

He spotted Takunda at a small corner table and strolled over to join him. Surprisingly, he was alone. Normally, having a drink with Takunda was a social event with the usual suspects from medical school, a few suave dealers, and always a ridiculously beautiful girl clinging to him like an expensive ornament.

Because his generosity knew no bounds, the table would have been glinting with glasses, selections of the priciest beverages and a variety of snacks, *kutsvukisa*-table, as they called it. But tonight, Takunda was drinking straight from a lone bottle of *Windhoek* lager, an expensive import nevertheless.

'Hullo, *mdhara*!' Unesu greeted him with a pat on the shoulder. He looked up.

'*Mdhara!*' Takunda echoed as they high-fived.

Unesu took a seat as they exchanged small talk. He found that slipping into detached, diagnostic mode had become effortless. With an experienced eye, he appraised his friend. His beard was manicured, his shirt Polo-branded, and his watch gleamed gold in the overhead light.

But the signs of too much of a good life were also visible. His friend had put on a considerable amount of weight, and there was puffiness around his bloodshot eyes. He'd been drinking too much and was probably sleep-deprived. Did that mean he was bothered by something or was it simply a lifestyle issue?

Takunda raised a sluggish hand. A waitress came over and gave them a wide smile as she took their order.

'Mixed nuts? Biltong? 'she asked, her head inclined.

'Sure. One portion of each,' Takunda responded.

She brought their drinks and nibbles in no time at all. Takunda had another *Windhoek* lager while Unesu had a Castle Lite. He enjoyed a drink but preferred to remain sober and in control.

'So, what's up *mdhara*?'

'The usual, this and that. You know how it is,' Takunda replied slowly. Unesu certainly didn't know how it was and from the look on his friend's face, there had to be more. He waited for an explanation.

It was introduced in the form of an unexpected request. 'Can I crash at your place tonight?' Unesu raised his eyebrows slightly, surprised. Takunda owned a well-appointed townhouse on Tongogara Road, and he liked to say that if he couldn't sleep at home, he'd go to Meikles as the hotel had the best beds in Harare.

'But, *mdhara*, my place is tiny. What's up at yours?' Unesu wondered if maybe his friend had finally gotten himself into some serious woman trouble.

'Nothing much. I just have to disappear for a day or two,' Takunda said casually.

'Why? You can't say "it's nothing" and then talk of disappearing!' It didn't make sense.

Takunda hesitated, then said abruptly, 'I think I'm being followed.'

'By who?'

'I don't know… men in black suits and dark glasses.' Takunda shrugged and laughed without mirth.

Men in black suits. It was a euphemism for intelligence officers. Unesu looked about him as if expecting to see a spook hovering over him. 'But why?' He wasn't yet sure how seriously to take his friend.

'*Iwe*, I'm not playing!' Takunda said roughly. 'I upset some big guys, moved in on their turf and took a lucrative deal from right under their noses.'

'Takunda! What big guys?'

'Don't be so naïve! You can't tell me you don't know the big guys with diamond interests. Why do you think the army has been deployed in Marange? Which country do you live in?'

His friend's retort stung. Unesu, like everyone else, knew that diamonds had been looted and that money which should have gone to the state had disappeared. Fifteen billion dollars, the President had said. Corruption was endemic. It was best not to know too much.

'I'm talking of at least two hundred thousand USD, Unesu. The payment will be made offshore, so I have to lie low until I can fly out.'

The young doctor could only stare at his friend, trying to grasp the sum. Takunda had certainly moved a long way from sneaking into Mozambique to meet up with Lebanese dealers.

'So, can I come to your place or not?'

'Shouldn't you report to the police if somebody's threatening you?'

Takunda snorted. 'Are you serious, Unesu? You know what that lot… the police will do? First, they'll want in on the deal. Or, if the price is better, they'll sell me out.'

Unesu remained silent. He was on unfamiliar territory, and he felt very unsettled.

Takunda continued. 'Look, Unesu, you're the only person I can turn to. Remember we're friends! And you don't need to worry. Right now, nobody knows where I am. And, before you ask, yes

I've disabled "location" on both my cellphones.'

Ordering them both more drinks, he told Unesu how he'd left his car outside a hotel in Chipinge, and travelled to Harare in disguise and on a 'chicken bus'.

He grimaced, 'It was quite an experience! You should try it sometime.' This time his laugher was more natural. Arriving in Harare, he recounted, he'd changed his clothes in a public toilet and made his way to Pariah's by taxi, taking care to ensure that he wasn't followed.

Then he outlined a plan that Unesu thought was gratuitously complex. They should leave the bar separately by different exits, and meet at Unesu's car. Then Unesu would drop him off at Pari's Casualty Department, where Takunda would slip back into disguise. Then he'd walk to the safety of Unesu's bedsit at the doctors' residence.

Unesu felt as if he was being drawn into a rather surreal conspiracy, almost as if he'd become a reluctant performer in a badly scripted crime spoof. And while he wanted to help his friend, he also felt ashamed for being too weak to say no to all this.

As he walked to his car, he wondered if it was possible that Takunda was becoming delusional, that stress and heavy drinking had made him paranoid. But, no, much as he didn't want to believe this story, Takunda did seem to have his feet on the ground.

16

Days passed. Cashleen was sure that Rufaro hadn't phoned Itai about her mental health, or said anything about the two of them being parasites who should become vendors or else leave her apartment. Surely, she couldn't have done so – surely Itai would have said something. But he went on as before, disappearing for hours on end, presumably getting up to no good with Gerry and whoever else he was friends with. When he was at home, he'd mostly confine himself to his room, listening to loud Zim dancehall tracks. His pendulum of moods did, however, appear less extreme and he'd become slightly easier to live with.

Meanwhile, Cashleen was overwhelmed by guilt and anxiety. If she and Itai did not break their cycle of dependence, would her sister ever recover? Again and again, she rehearsed her situation. Even if she decided to become a vendor, as Rufaro had suggested so bluntly, she had no money to buy any initial stock. She didn't even know the first thing about where to buy what. Surely there was no point in either selling bananas, tomatoes, clothes or counterfeit CDs and DVDs when every second vendor seemed to be selling them?

What then? Were there any other options? One only had to go to a shopping centre to see the drawn, harassed faces of men, women and children padding the concourse, all trying to sell food, clothing, brooms, batteries, sieves, phone accessories and anything else the Chinese were offering at knock-down prices. If they managed to sell a couple of items a day, they were lucky.

Vending was also risky work. Who didn't know about the regular running battles between the vendors and the municipal or riot police? She'd been chased and tear-gassed enough times as a student. She didn't want a repeat of those experiences.

The more she thought about it, the more she convinced herself that Rufaro couldn't have been serious. It had to be her request for money to buy tampons that had triggered the outburst. Nothing else made sense.

She balked at the idea of discussing her sister's depression with Itai, Delta or even Unesu, who might have been able to help by giving a medical perspective. There was something about the stigma of mental illness which made everyone keep it very private. And when someone finally tipped over the brink and ran down the street stark naked or addressed a street light at the top of their voice, society distanced itself from the obviously 'mad'.

She prayed hard for Rufaro's recovery, but this only made her feel like a fraud. Would God listen to her prayers when she was partly responsible? She felt helplessly at sea.

Although she tried to reach out, her sister didn't respond to her WhatsApp or Facebook messages, so Cashleen remained trapped in a cycle of worry. Her new online obsession became clinical depression, its risk factors, diagnosis and treatment, which she googled and wikipedia'ed until her head spun. She acquired a new vocabulary with strange terms such as prognosis, biopsychosocial models and cognitive behavioural therapy.

What alarmed her most was discovering that serious depression was a suicide risk, and so she resorted to continuously checking her sister's online activity for any subtle clues it might give about her state of mind, as well as her 'last seen' time on WhatsApp. Anxiety rose whenever this went beyond twelve hours, which was equivalent to Rufaro's longest shift at work.

She felt a bit like an online stalker, but this was all she had to reassure herself that her sister wasn't hanging from a tree, or drowning in a bathtub after overdosing on a cocktail of drugs, or slashing her wrists. Fear had stoked her imagination and the emotional fluctuations were exhausting.

Then, Itai brought home some more groceries and, this time, a TV for his room. He multi-linked his new gadget with their old DSTV decoder and informed her that he'd paid the monthly subscription. There was a swagger and a new confidence about her brother, as if he knew that she wouldn't ask any questions.

She struggled with her feelings. For the first time in several months, she didn't have to worry about what she would eat. There was less pressure to stretch a little money over the longest possible time. She was back on track with the local and international news, as well as her favourite TV series. However, her relief was stitched through with an unshakeable sense that something was very wrong.

People without jobs didn't just magic up possessions. Money was a finite entity that could only be earned, stolen, borrowed or gifted and she didn't know of anyone who might give Itai money for nothing. He hadn't won the lottery either, and in her opinion, even those churches that promised miracle money were in the business of misleading gullible individuals into becoming their followers.

What made it harder to question him was that she'd compromised her principles on Day One when she'd found those unexplained groceries in the kitchen. Hunger had driven her to prepare supper with what she'd suspected to be stolen goods. How she'd eaten that evening and how good the food had tasted!

Then, she'd rationalised that not eating the food would have been self-defeating, like collapsing from dehydration whilst one's feet were immersed in a pool of water. Her initial resolve to demand answers had deserted her.

This, she was sure, she could have discussed with Delta. She missed her friend, as they hadn't been in touch since they'd argued. She was remorseful about upsetting her and wondered if she should apologise for the way in which she'd spoken. She was still convinced that she'd been right, but Delta could be stubborn.

She sent a text and was relieved when she had a response, but surprised to learn that Delta was in Gweru.

How long u ther 4? she asked.

+/- 3 mths. That was yet another surprise. If Delta planned on being away for that long, it meant that she'd either lost the job or left it. Secretly, Cashleen celebrated. That job had been bound to become a constant source of friction between them.

All good, g'frnd. XOXO & catch u l8r! Delta texted. That reassured her they were still friends but it hinted at Delta not being in a chatty mood at the time.

Thankfully, after the first contact, the frostiness eased. Exchange of regular WhatsApp messages and mindless jokes resumed, although they still skirted any issues that had the potential to cause tension.

※※※

On Friday morning Unesu phoned to say that they would have to postpone the visit to see his mother. She'd just gone to Victoria Falls for her prophet's week-long healing crusade.

Cashleen remembered seeing something about this crusade in a gaudy newspaper advert. It had been touted as the event of the year for Prophet Healer, the self-styled Midlands' Man of God who claimed that he regularly went to heaven for audiences with the Almighty.

The advert promised miracles of healing, deliverance from evil spirits, goblin creatures and generational curses that ruined lives by stealing prosperity. The prophet also claimed he would show his closeness to God by walking on water at the crusade.

A first since Jesus, Cashleen thought wryly.

Understandably, Unesu sounded very upset. 'Just watch! If anything happens to my mother, that fraudster is going to need God and all the angels in heaven to protect him.'

It was just his anger talking. Prophet Healer was such a

powerful man and there was no way Unesu could challenge him about anything. There wasn't much she could say or do to allay his anxiety about his mother.

She wandered aimlessly in the common garden area. It had lost its former splendour due to a lack of water and because most people didn't seem to care. Gardening meant growing maize not flowers; and as long as they didn't have to pick up the litter, they would drop it, even in what was 'their' garden.

Beyond the high durawall, she could hear the incessant traffic and boisterous *kombi* conductors shouting 'City centre! Copa-Cabana, Copa-Cabana!' and *'Dee Zed, Dee Zed!'*

She sat on a bench and tried to think how best she could occupy herself. She'd run out of institutions to which she could submit unsolicited job applications, she'd tried them all. She knew she could only watch so much TV, surf the internet and read the same news articles over and over again without starting to feel miserable. Visiting the City Library remained an option but somehow, she was apathetic and lacked motivation to walk out of the gate.

Restless, she drifted into a memory of her graduation, remembering the President's eloquent speech, and all the hope it had promised for the newly qualified graduates. Cashleen had known that getting a job wouldn't be easy, but she could see now how much she'd underestimated the difficulty.

And it seemed to her that the nonagenarian himself lived in a dream world, as most of the graduates he'd capped were unemployed. Well, there was one notable exception: the First Lady, whom he'd given a PhD on the same day. Not that she needed a job like the rest of them.

Cashleen reflected on the controversy surrounding the woman's doctorate, and the persistent allegations that it was fake. Most people, staff and students alike, had been stunned: how could someone write a doctoral thesis in three months, especially someone with no known higher education background?

There were some assertions that the PhD had caused the

university's international ratings to tumble, and that a students' pressure group intended to challenge the award in court. So far, nothing had happened.

Kule Jojo ambled by, breaking her train of thought. 'Are you okay, *vasikana*?' he asked.

Of late, his gait had slowed and she wondered if he had arthritis. He was pushing a wheelbarrow full of lush, succulent plants. As usual, he gave her a wide smile.

She forced a smile. 'Yes, *Kule*,' she answered as brightly as she could. 'What are all these?' She wasn't really interested but *Kule* Jojo was too pleasant to ignore, and too old to be working. She felt sorry for him. His face became animated. 'New plants for the garden. These are very good.'

He pointed at the wilting flower beds and a rockery depleted of plants, 'My other plants are dying with no water. But these plants, they don't need much water. Just look at how healthy they are.' He clearly wanted to talk, so she forced herself to engage.

'Nice! Where did you get them from?'

'From my friend, a gardener in Milton Park. His boss is changing the garden. They wanted to throw these away. I'll make this garden beautiful again. Just you wait and see.' He looked proudly at the plants.

'I'm sure you will,' Cashleen said, too polite to excuse herself. She just wanted to be alone with her thoughts.

The old man grinned then peered at her again, saying decisively, 'You don't look well.' He wasn't going to let her be.

'Just a small matter, *Kule*,' she said, even as she tried to suppress a frown.

'Why? Young girl like you? An old man like me with creaking bones and aching joints should do the worrying.' He burst into such infectious laughter that Cashleen couldn't help joining in.

Despite herself, she said, 'It's just that I can't find a job and I'm tired of looking.'

'*Ehe!* You young people! You're really in trouble. But you're lucky you have someone to look after you. You always have to be thankful for life's blessings. Others have nobody.'

Cashleen blurted, 'My sister, she can't manage anymore, **Kule**.'

'I'm sorry. But you'll get a job soon enough. Just try something else for now.'

'Like what, **Kule**? Tell me what? Maybe you have a good idea, because I don't.'

The old man sat down on the bench, next to her. 'It's not about what I think. It's about what you choose to do. Do you know the boy who comes to the gate every day to talk to me?'

She looked at him questioningly.

'The one who sells phone gadgets and airtime at the traffic intersection there?'

'Yes!' Cashleen nodded, recalling the reserved young man who often came to get drinking water from **Kule** Jojo. He'd been selling things from the intersection for the past month or so.

'That one is Nhamo. He's my grandson, a graduate like you. He finished last year. He studied Maths but he also can't find a job. That's why he's there at the intersection. He doesn't get much, but I tell you this, he can pay rent for his one room in Mbare. And he can buy food for himself. His sister, another graduate has a flea-market stall in town. She has a business degree. That's why I say, it's up to you. You can decide what to do until you get your big job. **Ziva zvauri**, being your own person. I have it. I enjoy it. Maybe you need that, especially now that your sister can't manage. Deal with today. I know your big job will come. When you have too much time to think, you can make yourself ill.' Again, his face broke into a smile.

It was the longest speech she'd ever heard from him. Not that she'd ever stopped to listen. And his advice made so much sense. Smiling at his wisdom, she thanked the old man as he picked up his plants, whistling happily. She wondered how one person could seem so content, so happy.

He was clearly a kind, unpretentious wise man. She'd never thought of him as anything more than the elderly caretaker-cum-security guard whose determined cheerfulness bordered on eccentricity. Subconscious stereotyping had blinded her to his humanity. A family man with two grandchildren who were university graduates. An individual who had opinions from which she'd learned something. She felt strangely empowered and she allowed herself to consider new possibilities.

She got up and turned the corner towards the staircase. There, she collided full on with a Chinese man who'd recently taken a lease on two adjacent apartments on the ground floor. The boxes he was carrying dropped. Red-faced, he threw her an angry look. 'You mad woman. You not looking where you going!' he shouted as he bent to retrieve the boxes.

'I'm so sorry,' Cashleen apologised, hoping nothing was damaged, and bent over to assist him. Her hands were quickly slapped away.

'Leave it now. *Now!*' he shouted.

She stepped back, her eyes wide. One box was labelled Aquamarine & Amethyst.

Precious stones! She couldn't see the labels on the other two.

The man straightened up and pointed an accusing finger at her, shouting, 'Don't look. Go, go!'

Shrugging, she turned and walked up the stairs, wondering why he'd been so upset and not just because she'd made him drop the boxes, but by her seeing the label.

He and his partner had been living at the block for about a month now. There were a lot of secretive comings and goings into their apartments which appeared to be in use for both business and residence purposes.

She wondered if they were engaged in dodgy dealing. It seemed likely. The Chinese had a reputation for being astute business people who went only where there was real money to be made.

Always follow the money! It appeared Zimbabwe was just such a place for them. She wished she knew what they knew.

17

Delta missed Cashleen, who seemed rather distant and preoccupied. She gathered that her friend was embroiled in some kind of family drama, of which scant details were provided. Somewhere along the line, sharing secrets had become a thing of the past. Their friendship was hanging by a thin thread of artificially cheerful greetings and superficial WhatsApp messages.

While she had no plans for the immediate future, her impulsive decision to leave Harare had been a form of flight. It didn't take long for her to realise that her move was like trying to run away from one's shadow. Problems might change in size, shape and colour, but they had a way of following you around. She now worried that being in a smaller city would leave her worse off, but there was nothing she could do about it now.

Gradually, she eased into Gweru life. As in Harare, she observed that conversations circled around the difficulties and the hustle involved in scratching a living. Many people whom she knew had lost their jobs with the ongoing company closures.

There was an incredible number of individuals trying to sell anything that could be sold from their homes and makeshift markets that had sprung up on city pavements and streets, at traffic intersections, under the trees and anywhere indeed that provided a bit of space.

In public toilets at the central bus terminus, she'd been hardly surprised to encounter women who sold aphrodisiacs, love charms, abortion pills and supposedly potent herbal mixtures for buttock and breast enlargement.

The abundance of subversive humour and grim laughter that prevailed in the midst of hardship struck her. Despite making political jokes being considered to be seditious – no matter how true or how funny – many clandestine witticisms were shared in ordinary conversation and on various social media platforms. If harsh truths could be reduced to dark comedy, maybe they could no longer hurt. Merciless satire of real life situations appeared to have become a panacea.

There were no taboo topics, from the President himself, to corrupt and self-important government officials, the police, the judiciary, as well as incompetent heads of parastatals and bungling council officials. The most surreal had to be the jibes directed at revelations of graft among the country's anti-corruption commission. Things couldn't get more bizarre than that, although there were reports, deemed to be true, that a few had been suspended, fired or arrested.

To Delta, it seemed unlikely, as many bigwigs who were openly corrupt were getting on with their usual skullduggery as free men and women. Perhaps for show, to be seen to be doing something, there was the occasional 'catch and release without consequence', as Sando, Cashleen's very outspoken friend had posted on Twitter.

However, small fry were almost consistently game, and were often made examples out of. Who was it who'd recently told her of a single mother from Redcliff who'd received a jail sentence of five years for possessing 0.22 grammes of gold without a permit?

The law is truly an ass, she thought. Or they make it so.

She also noticed how dereliction was slowly replacing the city that her parents often spoke of with nostalgia, a nineties' industrial powerhouse hosting giants such as Bata, National Railways and

ZimAlloys. She just couldn't identify with their memories. Evidence of the good times of which they spoke seemed only to exist in their minds.

They were barely surviving on their paltry, combined $120 monthly allowance from the national social security fund. Their lifestyle made a mockery of the years that they'd spent in diligent civil service as teachers. Perhaps she'd become paranoid, but she now suspected that glimpses of their disappointment had less to do with these devalued pensions, and a lot to do with the unfulfilled expectations that they'd had for her and her brother, Tendai. They'd invested so much in educating the two of them, and yet it all seemed to have come to naught.

Ownership of their modest home in Mkoba did provide some consolation. In rural Shurugwi, they also owned a small plot, which her father had inherited from his parents. It had three thatched huts, an unprotected well, a chicken run and a kraal where they kept six cattle. In return for looking after the home and livestock, their nephew had use of one of the huts and he was allowed to carry out subsistence farming on a piece of land adjacent to the cattle kraal.

While she could engage in interesting discussions with her parents, Delta found that she could barely relax enough to enjoy Tendai's company. She was constantly on edge, waiting for his long-drawn-out silences to become outright criticism. It was difficult for her to reconcile their relationship with the one they'd had as children.

Tendai was currently helping out with an erratic income earned from middleman activities for subsistence farmers from rural Lower Gweru. For a mark-up, he linked their horticultural produce to the markets in town. He worked very hard, or gave the impression of doing so, as he was rarely at home.

A psychology graduate, his mantra was that one had to do whatever was necessary to get through the day. This too had slowly grown on Delta, but one thing that she knew was that his philosophy wouldn't extend to dabbling in anything counterfeit as she'd done. So, she hugged her shameful secret to herself and spent her days in town, making enquiries about possible work, and occasional visits to the Internet café from where she attempted online applications.

※※※

One day, Tendai asked her if she could consider helping him out at the market in town. He suggested that instead of paying a runner, she could do the job and thus contribute to the household expenses.

Delta wavered between disbelief and a lofty sense of embarrassment. 'How can you even ask this of me?' she demanded, telling him that she couldn't and wouldn't reduce herself to the level of a common market gofer. She was aware of how supercilious she sounded, but she just couldn't help it.

He looked at her in open-mouthed surprise. 'Delta-*ka*!'

'What?' she shot back.

'You want to eat but you don't want to work!' His voice was loaded with meaning.

'Work, work, *njani, njani*! Who cleans up and cooks the meals that you eat?'

Tempers flared. 'And where does the money for your food and your upkeep come from. You talk of common market gofers. What are you saying about me? What's so special about you?'

Their mother intervened in what would have become a nasty argument.

'*Aiwa,* Tendai and Dee. Don't talk to each other like this,' she said, and added, 'Dee, you must think about what your brother has asked without being so emotional.'

So it was like that! This made her think the issue might have been discussed already. She was rather upset that the two of them might be conspiring against her.

Tendai walked out in a huff, but not before giving a rather condescending parting shot: 'You're so out of touch with reality, little sis. You better wake up, and very fast!'

'Don't mind him. He's going through a difficult time,' her

mother sounded conciliatory, then she asked, '*Nhai* Dee? I've been worried about you. Why exactly did you leave your job in Harare?'

Her concern was expected. The surprise was that her questions hadn't come sooner. Still miffed, Delta spoke at once. '*Eeh Amai!* That place was impossible.'

'But wasn't it what you wanted, Dee, an entry into your profession? Your uncle said it was a good start. He said it could lead to better opportunities.'

Then Delta realised her error. She'd forgotten that her mother wasn't aware of her having ever been at Hunger Buster. All she knew was that her daughter had worked as a lab assistant, the lie she'd fed Aunt Peace and Uncle Dondo.

Her mother sighed. 'Jobs are so hard to find. You only leave one when you have found another one. Not before, Dee.'

Tell me something I don't know, she thought irritably. Her mother was right, but she pursed her lips and remained silent. She didn't want a lecture.

Her mother went on. 'I'm thinking of joining your brother at the market. And your father is on the waiting list for manual work at the Chinese factory *kuma*industry.'

Delta realised there'd been no let-up about the market issue, indirect as it was. If her mother meant to fuel her feelings of guilt, she succeeded.

'But *Amai*, your blood pressure, your painful joints, how will you manage? *Baba* has a bad back and…'

'I always say, "never trust two women in a room together". Why are you two gossiping about me? What bad back?' her father teased them as he came in. To an outsider, he might have looked comical: a short, slightly overweight man with his white beard and shining bald head.

Her mother smiled indulgently, 'I was telling Delta that you want to go back to work.'

He chuckled, 'Yes! If they take me, no bad back is stopping me. We have a man who is almost thirty years older than me doing the hardest job in the country – **brilliantly** – without ever sleeping on the job,' he winked, 'and with few complaints, so who am I to complain about pushing a wheelbarrow or two?'

Despite herself, Delta giggled at the indirect reference to the President who was frequently the butt of jokes about how often he fell asleep at important meetings.

Her mother wagged a warning finger at him, 'Be careful.'

'*Aizve!* Careful about what? Am I not among friends? Unless something changed while I was out. If so, tell me now because I could be picked up by the police anytime.' He broke into laughter.

Delta knew that it was all an act. She shook her head, imagining the two of them back at work. A not-so-healthy sixty-eight-year-old man working as a labourer and a sixty-six-year-old woman competing with much younger, more aggressive women at the market. Women with street smarts.

But she also knew her mother's roundabout approach to weighty issues. She felt that old familiar pressure before it was expressed. The natural, expected thing would be for her to step in and protest, order them to stay at home and rest while she ventured out to take on such work. The discussion was inching into uncomfortable territory and she wasn't prepared for it. Not yet, anyway.

She'd already argued with her brother. Had they all forgotten that she was a chemical engineer? Why couldn't they just let her be? Yes, there'd been Hunger Buster but she'd been driven to it, and it had been a very personal, albeit misguided, choice.

Before her mother could continue, she got up decisively. '*Amai,* I'm going to buy paraffin for the Primus stove. It's getting dark outside.'

Her mother hesitated, frowning as a thought crossed her mind, then her face cleared. 'Yes, go before it's too late.'

Armed with a plastic container, she walked towards the small garage by the shops. On her way, she passed groups of young people standing about aimlessly, arguing about football, staring at passers-by, passing round what she thought was a cigarette until she caught a distinctive whiff of weed.

Further down the road, a congregation of white-gowned Apostolic Faith worshippers were gathering under some trees for an open-air evening service. She spotted three street kids crawling under a bridge with some cardboard and plastic sheets, possibly to stake out their territory for the night.

Near the community beer-hall was a debonair-looking man engrossed in hushed conversation with four scantily-dressed girls. He tweaked at his stylish trilby and drew one of the girls close. A pimp and his clients perhaps, she thought, although one of the girls looked hardly pubescent.

On the opposite side of the road, women carrying buckets and pots were making a beeline for the communal tap behind the clinic, which meant either a burst pipe or water cut somewhere in the area.

At the garage, there was a queue of cars at the petrol pump. A sign at the next dispenser read 'No Diesel'. In response to her query, an attendant brusquely told her, 'We no longer sell paraffin here.'

'Where can I find some?' she asked.

The attendant shrugged, 'Don't know'.

A vendor who was selling bananas and airtime to motorists on the forecourt laughed. 'She knows but she doesn't want to tell you. *Vakapinda* busy! A guy down the road is stealing their business.'

Delta wasn't really interested in local turf wars. She just wanted to buy paraffin so that she could go back home and cook the evening meal.

'Does the guy sell paraffin?' she asked.

The attendant ignored her, and the vendor laughed again, saying, '*Nhai Sisi*, are you new here? Paraffin, diesel, petrol, he has it all. Very good prices.'

The attendant threw him a warning look. Delta sensed mutual hostility. He probably wasn't supposed to be selling things on the forecourt and he certainly wasn't supposed to be advertising in favour of the competition while standing there.

'Go down the road and turn left at that big tree. You'll see a blue house on your left.'

'A house?' she asked, surprised. She'd thought maybe a new garage had opened in the area during the time that she'd been away.

'Yes. Just by the corner. You will find it easy easy.'

Delta nodded her thanks. She had to see this with her own eyes. Someone selling fuel from a house? What kind of person did that and how could he get away with it so openly?

She didn't have trouble locating the building. The gate was open. Just inside, under the glare of a floodlight, three men were offloading drums from a truck.

She approached slowly, noticing a big metal cage that was subdivided into three in the corner of the yard. Two partitions housed a number of drums and a third one held smaller plastic containers. A big sign demanded, 'Bring Own Container'.

'Hullo,' she said loudly.

'Can I help you?' one man asked, approaching her.

'I want to buy some paraffin.'

The man turned towards the truck and shouted, 'Farai! Customer for you. Paraffin.'

A man jumped off the truck with practiced agility. '*Aah*, Delta, *ndiwe*? What a surprise!' he exclaimed and moved forward to shake her hand. It was Farai, her old classmate from high school.

'Hullo, Farai,' she responded, equally surprised. She'd expected some sleazy, thug-like fuel dealer. Her indignation buckled.

The last time she'd seen Farai was several years before at the bustling Gweru Bus Terminus. He'd been holding a begging bowl, asking commuters for donations. She also recalled how he'd dropped out of high school in the fifth form when his father died. It had been said that he had no money for school fees.

He slapped one of his companions on the back saying, 'This girl, this girl, she was trouble at school. She shamed us all. Always top of class. She's now a *Biggaz* in Harare. *Handiti*, you studied engineering, Delta?'

Delta nodded, 'Yes.' The feeling of pride that she once had when she told people what she'd studied was a thing of the past.

Farai turned to the other two men. 'See, I know important people! Engineers!' he said, rubbing his hands together. They peered at her suspiciously and continued offloading the drums of fuel. She felt that they were neither impressed nor interested.

'So, you want paraffin, Delta?'

'Yes,' she replied fumbling for some money in her pocket. 'How much for two litres?'

'Let me get it for you. You don't have to pay anything.'

'*Aah!* I couldn't,' she protested.

'Don't worry. I'm now a big **dhara.** A proper fuel baron,' Farai laughed. 'And business is very good.' She didn't know if it was just banter, or an indication of how far he had come. He was like an excited child intent on showing off.

'I have a house, I have a truck and another smaller car. My wife drove to town with the kids, you could have met them otherwise,' he added, beaming with pride.

She accepted his offer and thanked him, saying, despite herself, 'You've done very well, Farai.' She supposed the transition from orphaned beggar to a self-styled, illegal fuel baron *was* a success.

On the other hand, surely he had no business selling flammable fuels from home, because it was very dangerous. Didn't he care about the risks he'd created for his wife, children and neighbours? It wouldn't take much to blow the place up or burn it to the ground. Just one match, indeed.

He took her container and went behind the truck to the metal cage where she supposed the paraffin was kept. She noted that his board by the cage showed diesel and petrol prices that were much lower than those she'd seen on display at the garage. How was that possible? Could he be selling contaminated, stolen or smuggled fuel?

In Harare, one heard of criminal fuel syndicates, which operated out of homes, as well as from both unlicensed and licensed places. Some dealerships were even said to involve smuggling rings controlled by politicians. For Farai's prices, she wondered how clean his fuel was. She had so many questions but she resisted asking him. He'd been so friendly, and what business was it of hers anyway?

He came back with her container. It was full. 'So where are you working now?' he asked. He looked astonished when she said she hadn't found a job. 'And you an engineer? That's bad, Delta. Let me know if you ever need anything'.

She nodded, seized by a sudden urge to get away. Who did he think he was, to be so presumptuous? What made him think he could do anything for her?

'Thanks. See you around,' she muttered, her mind conflicted.

'Anytime,' he said cheerfully and swung back onto the truck.

As she walked home, a conversation that she'd overheard between two men in a *kombi* came back to her. They'd been discussing a former academic high-flier who'd died in destitution, and the squalor they'd witnessed at his funeral.

'Zimbabwean life is a harsh equaliser, *mdhara!*' one had said.

The other had concurred. 'I think university degrees are a farce! Doesn't matter how educated or brainy you are. I'm not boasting, but with my Grade 7, I'm better than he ever was,' he'd said of their acquaintance.

She questioned herself. Despite running an illegal business, wasn't Farai, a high-school drop-out, much better off than her? A success, no less? He owned a house, two cars, and was a breadwinner, when she had nothing.

Biggaz from Harare, he'd called her. Her face burned with humiliation.

18

In the end, Takunda had stayed for longer than Unesu had expected. His phone had been switched off and he hadn't ventured outdoors, not even for a beer with Unesu. He'd borrowed Unesu's computer to make a flight booking, but he hadn't disclosed his destination.

'The less you know, the better for you,' he'd remarked cryptically.

Unesu had been very busy with work, and had decided that if Takunda didn't want to answer his questions, he wouldn't waste his time probing. He did worry, though, as he didn't know how much of his friend's story was true and how much had been embellished.

The vague sense of anxiety stalked him during Takunda's stay, only easing once he'd dropped his friend at the airport before returning to work.

As expected, there was gridlock at Coke Corner. Tempers were high as impatient motorists blared their hooters, shouted obscenities and waved their fists. Unesu had to concentrate as he inched his way through the traffic, while trying to dodge potholes.

But it turned out to be a good day. He'd been left in charge of the ward because Prof Chaka, Doc Muchy and all the trainee specialists had to attend a lecture by a visiting professor from Zambia. Unesu was by now very competent with standard patient care, and working without direct supervision always gave his confidence a lift.

He took the ward round with the sister-in-charge, a knowledgeable woman on whom junior doctors secretly relied as a sounding board for clinical care. Patient review was achieved quite quickly because most were stable, their treatment plans were clearly detailed in their case notes and there'd been no new admissions overnight.

Afterwards, he crossed over to obstetrics to help out John and two other colleagues in the antenatal clinic. They worked efficiently together and were finished by 2 p.m. He had half an hour before going to meet with Dr Reza, and he decided to return to the ward to check if their post-op patient's pathology results had been returned, which they had.

The woman had undergone laparotomy for removal of a large pelvic mass. Her histology had been expedited because she'd been considered to be high risk for malignancy. She cried tears of relief on getting confirmation that the mass was non-cancerous. It was moments like these which kept Unesu going, even when giving up would have been so much easier.

Cumulatively, the day-to-day challenges that he encountered made caring for patients difficult. Frequent shortages had become commonplace. If it wasn't drugs, it was gloves, blood for transfusion, intravenous fluids, and so on. For patients with financial resources, certain problems could be overcome if relatives could find supplies elsewhere. However, poverty and unemployment meant that sometimes patients simply deteriorated or died, as supplies could not be sourced, or were found too late.

In the past week, he'd been particularly concerned about theatre. Pre-operatively, they were using a cheap dishwashing liquid instead of proper surgical scrub solution, which was unavailable. Surgical procedures required high levels of infection control, and this could never be achieved with a simple dishwasher solution.

It bothered Unesu even more that for two days, there'd been no running water. Scrubbing up for operations involved an assistant pouring water onto his hands and arms using a jug that had been filled from the black plastic bins that someone had ingeniously converted into temporary water storage for theatre.

In general, he'd become used to working in this difficult environment and got on with the job like everyone else. As doctors and nurses, they'd grumble among themselves while trying to provide the best possible patient care. He could achieve cool, scientific distance as a buffer in most circumstances, but there were some events from which there was no immunity, such as the loss of patients' lives.

At times, he recalled those who'd died with disturbing clarity. Faces, names and events would come to mind during moments of silence, just before falling asleep, or sometimes in his dreams. The hardest part was living with the knowledge that some of those who'd died could have been saved, if only the hospital facilities had been up to standard. Days and nights merged into one long episodic stretch, a pattern which did not allow much of a social life. He hoped that this new lucrative locum at Orion Clinic would allow him to slow down, while still making enough money to build up some savings.

He was slightly nervous when he arrived for his appointment at Orion Clinic. Being pro-choice was one thing, service provision was a different ball game. To his relief, Dr Reza made things look and feel simple. The older doctor detailed all sexual and reproductive healthcare services offered by the clinic and took time to discuss ethical issues around patient care such as professionalism, confidentiality and being non-judgemental.

'Patients need to feel that their secrets are safe, and they aren't being judged or condemned for their choices, or for the unfortunate circumstances that led to those choices,' he said, with specific emphasis on termination of pregnancy.

'I understand.' Unesu nodded. Confidentiality and respect

underpinned good medical practice, whatever the circumstances. And this was medical practice, he told himself.

Dr Reza explained that for terminations, clinic records were kept to a bare minimum, and only for the duration of care. After that, they were shredded to destroy any evidence of contact because almost all such procedures performed at the clinic fell foul of the law.

Patients included women with unplanned or unwanted pregnancies, those where the paternity was disputed, or sex workers for whom pregnancy would have been an inconvenience at a given time. Occasionally, parents would bring their daughters, schoolgirls, who would have been unable to continue with their education because they had become pregnant. At other times, it might be married men bringing their girlfriends.

Dr Reza emphasised that it was important to provide an environment where women and girls felt supported, and that whatever adverse opinions Unesu might have, it would be inappropriate to project them onto the patients.

Unesu nodded, thinking briefly of the women he'd attended to, who had arrived at the hospital with an apparently spontaneous miscarriage. However, during assessment, it would be discovered that sticks or other objects were in the reproductive tract, and so it would become apparent that the girls or women had taken a chance with backyard abortion. He'd also known of a few who'd subsequently died from uterine perforation-related bleeding and severe infections. He tried not to think about his own sister.

Then, there were those flea markets and hair salons that sold Cytotec illegally, and some women would buy this and self-administer to initiate bleeding in pregnancy, and once at the hospital they'd pretend that they had had a spontaneous miscarriage. This would enable them to access safe surgical completion with no questions asked. *Very smart.*

Dr Reza asked him if he needed further information.

'Nope,' Unesu replied. 'I think everything is quite clear and I'm happy to come on board.' He meant it.

The man handed him two copies of a draft contract. 'Please go through these documents carefully. For obvious reasons, details only refer to hours of work and pay rates. If you're happy with the content, sign both documents and return one copy to Admin. One is yours to keep.'

'Thank you. I'll do that,' Unesu replied, then he made his way to the clinic's procedure room for his induction with Mazwi. She told him she'd spent most of the day at home.

'Day off?' he asked.

'No. I should have been assisting in theatre but our elective list was cancelled because the autoclave machine is down, so there was no sterile linen.... It was just as well. There's no running water in theatre either ... .' It was the same old story. Unesu shook his head, sympathetically.

He couldn't have imagined that his induction with Mazwi would be so perfunctory. 'I know what surgical skills you have and I know that you're a safe doctor, so there's no need to prolong this,' she told him, her smile ever-present. It was a compliment of sorts. He inspected the procedure tray and picked up a suction curette. Turning it over in his hand, he connected it to an aspirator syringe device. It was a perfect fit. All very familiar surgical instruments that he used at the hospital for post-miscarriage care.

Mazwi explained that in essence, the job entailed a simple transfer of practical skills from one standard procedure to another, but aimed at achieving a different outcome. That much he knew as a matter of course.

'Are there any additional checks that I should do?' he asked her.

Mazwi shrugged, 'Not at all. Of course, you understand that we can't send specimens for histology.'

'Sure,' he agreed. Under the circumstances, histology would always be out of the question. Scanty or zero information trails were key.

She added, 'You do laparotomies and caesarean sections, Unesu. You manage ectopic pregnancies and other gynae surgical emergencies independently. By comparison, this is child's play.'

'Well, Doc, I wouldn't exactly say that,' he said, reminding himself that these procedures were not risk-free, even under the best conditions.

She shrugged. 'Oh, you know what I mean.'

They looked at the rota and calendar together. He signed up for his first shift on Friday, and selected dates to the end of the month.

Driving home, he reasoned that a woman with an unwanted pregnancy would always find a way out. Surely it was better done by a medical professional than a non-medical person who used unhygienic sticks, reeds, bicycle spokes, knitting needles and herbal concoctions. By providing procedures in a safe, clinical setting, he would be saving lives. He knew a lot of people who wouldn't agree. He could imagine the small talk which he could never have with John, a devout Christian.

'I'm moonlighting at an abortion clinic. And by the way, the money's great!'

It was totally out of the question. Not with John. Not with anybody else in his professional or social circles for that matter. The risks were too high. Being judged for doing work that was generally frowned upon. Possible arrest. Loss of one's registration as a medical practitioner. He decided there and then that he'd keep this one close to his chest.

XOXOX

Unesu had strained conversations with his mother over the phone. She wouldn't agree to go for a check-up because as far as she was concerned, the cancer had left her body at Prophet Healer's crusade. He recalled his telephone conversation with her when she returned from Victoria Falls. He'd listened in disbelief to her description of how she collapsed when Prophet Healer laid his hands on her head, that glorious moment when she'd felt the demon of cancer escaping from her body in a blast of heat. She'd sounded excited in a manner that bordered on hysteria.

She'd told him that she was now well enough to tend to her vegetable garden and that he needn't worry about visiting her if he was busy at work. He certainly hadn't been busy to that extent, but he'd seen no point in going there just to argue with her in person.

Even *Mainini*, who was normally fixated on doom and gloom, had told him that his mother was now able to finish a plate of *sadza* without throwing up. Coming from *Mainini*, it had been as good as being told that his mother was bursting with good health. It had sounded like good news all round, but he hadn't been reassured. His mother was never far from his mind, but he'd run out of ideas. There was nothing to do except save money and prepare for what was sure to come.

Arriving early for work on Thursday, he decided to wait for his colleagues in the nurses' duty room. He found on the table an old copy of *The Daily Headliner* in which there was a long article about Prophet Healer's Victoria Falls crusade. And what a spread it was! The event was reported to have spanned an incredible week that had been packed with countless miracles.

Worshippers, who'd been interviewed, had given testimonies about how at the end of the crusade, the blind could see, the deaf could hear, and the physically disabled could walk. Cancers had been cured and HIV-positive people had become negative.

The Man of God himself had spoken about how he'd made hair sprout on bald heads and teeth erupt in toothless gums. His power of healing had melted large amounts of body fat in men and women who'd struggled for years with weight-loss issues.

During the penultimate evening service, showers of gold were reported to have rained upon the congregation. The prophet had challenged non-believers to come to his church to experience these miracles for themselves.

Asked by the reporter why he hadn't walked on water as promised in his advert, the prophet explained that God had instructed him to wait. Walking on water would be combined with resurrection of the dead at the next crusade.

The reporter had wanted to know how long one had to be dead in order to qualify for resurrection. For instance, would people who'd been dead for more than a year be given new life? The prophet had cautioned her against questioning or indeed limiting the divine. True believers didn't.

Unesu shook his head. Never mind the rest of it... but toothless gums toothed, bald heads hirsute and fat melting away? How could anyone make such a farce of people's faith? And now claiming he could raise the dead, and earn column inches in a credulous national newspaper while at it? How was it possible that people could actually believe his propaganda, and give testimony to it? And in such large numbers? Maybe one needed to be desperate to understand. It had little or nothing to do with Christianity, of that he was sure, even though he wasn't a believer.

He returned to the newspaper article, and inevitably his thoughts went to his mother. Guilt followed. There had to be something that he could do. He was, after all, surrounded by specialists, and maybe one of them could give him sound advice about how to manage his mother's refusal of medical care.

He decided that he'd start with Prof Chaka whom he knew to be a very good doctor, despite his cool arrogance. After the ward round, he sought the man out, certain that he'd be given some kind of assistance.

As expected, Prof Chaka was very blunt. '*Chiremba?* You're in the business of saving lives, so how can you fail to facilitate the same for your own mother? Unbelievable!'

The criticism stung. 'I really tried Prof. It's just that the prophet...'

'Forget the prophet. I expect better from you. How many terminally ill patients have come to us as a last resort after having had their time and money wasted by those prophets? How many? Is that what you want for your mother?'

'She's adamant, Prof. She won't see anyone,' he replied trying not to sound feeble. Did the man expect him to drag his mother kicking and screaming to see a doctor?

Prof Chaka raised his hand in a gesture of irritation. Then, unexpectedly, he said, 'Give me her name and phone number. I'll call her sometime soon and invite her to my private practice. I'll find a way of getting through to her.'

Unesu had no idea if his mother would give Prof Chaka the time of day, but he was both surprised and pleased by the offer. He wrote down his mother's details, wondering if Prof Chaka's abrasive manner shielded a soft heart.

There was just one more thing. 'Prof, what about the costs? She's on public medical aid and most specialists aren't accepting it. I don't have money for private care. Can I bring her here as a government patient instead?'

The Prof snorted disdainfully. 'Your real mother? And you want to bring her here? Be serious. And who said anything about money anyway? '

'I didn't want to assume…'

Prof interrupted. 'Young man, this is your mother. You don't want to live with regret for the rest of your life. My advice is save up as much as possible and get her the best care that you can. If she ends up needing surgery, you won't have to pay me or the anaesthetist, but there will be imaging costs, hospital shortfalls, and so forth.'

Overwhelmed with gratitude, Unesu thanked the consultant.

'Being in the profession has to have its perks, *Chiremba*; you'll learn that with time. Do favours for your colleagues and they'll have your back too. I expect you'll do the same for me one day.' And being Prof, he had to add, 'When you're a specialist of course.'

It figured. During bedside teaching when he'd failed to extract precise patient care plans from Unesu and John, he'd told them that he wouldn't trust them with his dog. Now Unesu could see that despite his austere manner, the Prof was human after all. He suppressed a smile as he watched him stride off in his uniquely self-confident manner.

He walked off the ward and headed for the outpatients' clinic. His phone vibrated. It was Cashleen, initiating what turned out to be an odd chat. Her use of full, grammatically correct sentences in the text conversation didn't intrigue him as much as the subject matter.

You free?
Sure.
I just need to ask something.
Go ahead.
Can depression really lead to suicide?
Depends.
Is it possible to tell if a depressed person is about to commit suicide?
Not always.
What's the commonest means of suicide for depressed people?
Can't say. Don't hav local stats.
Can someone with depression make a full recovery?
Yep!
Do mental health problems run in families?
+ve familial tendency for some. U ok Cash? He didn't like the way this was going.

Of course, I am. I'm just curious about things. You know me.
Wat u up 2?
Nothing much, except thinking and thinking.
Sounds deep. What about?
Life. Survival. How to get to tomorrow.
Really deep. Sure u ok? Want me 2 cum over?
She texted a row of crazy-laugh emoticons.
Kkkkkk! I'm fine. Seriously. Catch up later. Then she was offline.

The text conversation worried him. He'd been so preoccupied with his own life that he hadn't seen Cashleen recently or had any meaningful conversation with her. He knew that she was going through some difficulties with unemployment and family squabbles but he'd found it awkward to ask too many questions.

He thought of checking with Delta if she'd seen her recently, then remembered. Delta was still in Gweru. He'd have to find time to go and see her himself.

19

Cashleen's phone vibrated. It was a hullo message from Sando in Johannesburg.

Hi hi! She texted back, happy to hear from her friend. It had been a while. He'd been quieter on social media too, posting fewer and fewer of his usual, politically provocative sentiments. She'd wondered why, but hadn't asked because she preferred it that way. One day he'd have to come back home, but as a high profile subversive voice, this could be risky.

Howz u n work?

Nu job, was his surprise response.

4 real??? She wrote, fishing for possible good news about him having finally secured work at **Mail and Guardian, Business Day** or **The Times**, right in the heart of Johannesburg. She added: *Wow! Which paper plz?*

He he he! Paper??? Another café. Cleaner

He couldn't be serious. From waiting tables to a cleaning job? She had to hear this out. Her WhatsApp signal was strong, so she could phone him.

'Last month you said you'd had interviews with some newspapers? Did they finally get back to you?'

He laughed. She was familiar with his laughter's underlying

ring of sarcasm. 'Sure, but no luck there. Fact is, it's not easy for foreigners, especially if you need a work permit.'

This meant that even as a cleaner, he was still working illegally. Had he gone to university to end up as an illegal worker? An economic refugee in South Africa. What if he was caught? Was a cleaning job worth ruining prospects of his long-term plans for a future as an educated migrant? Despite its myriad challenges, home had to be better.

'Why not just come back, Sando?'

Again, that brittle laughter. 'For what? To what? Ours is a country for old men who'll stop at nothing to continue lining their pockets. No thanks, I'd rather fight it out here.'

He was adamant, and try as she might; she couldn't understand his logic. She bit her lip as he told her how when he'd lost his job as a waiter, his cousin had given him an ultimatum to find another job or leave his flat. His situation was so like hers that she backed off when he asked if she preferred that he become a criminal.

She knew that Sando was a proud man. Maybe it was being away from home that helped him cope with the humiliation of taking what he would have normally considered to be low-level employment, albeit often a starting point for people who went abroad to seek better opportunities.

She remembered something her mother had once told her: how the President had poked fun at people who left the country at the height of the hyperinflation-fuelled mass exodus, saying *'most are fools and cowards who'll end up cleaning old people's bottoms in England's care homes anyway'*. She wondered if that had been really true, or just the man having a shot at mocking his desperate citizens who were seeking relief elsewhere.

Sando interrupted her thoughts with, 'Look, I'll call you soon. I have to go.'

'Sure, thanks. Bye,' Cashleen replied. She turned things over in her mind, getting nowhere. Had Rufaro been right about her attitude? If Sando could be a waiter or a cleaner, and Delta could be a restaurant assistant, why couldn't she swallow her pride and look for similar work?

Her mother had instilled in her the idea that women should be strong and independent, and this had inspired her to work hard, and to be an achiever at university. But here she was today, a young, educated woman who couldn't even take care of her own basic day-to-day needs, one who still had to rely on somebody else for everything.

Her cheeks burned with shame. If her mother had been alive, what would she have said? She couldn't escape the feeling that she would have been very disappointed with her daughter.

Inexorably, time passed. Cashleen observed with increasing fascination as the winter of 2016 brought widespread discontent. She felt the ripples of defiance and fear, as well as excitement, as activists roused an unprecedented number of people into speaking out collectively and boldly in a way that she'd never seen before.

The drive for protests against corruption and bad governance was trending on Twitter, Facebook and WhatsApp as *#ZimShutDown2016*, *#Tajamuka* and *#ThisFlag*. The latter was led by a young minister of religion who'd attracted a following almost inadvertently when he spoke out about not being able to pay school fees for his children.

To Cashleen, the developments seemed surreal. Barring the heavy-handed crushing of dissent, she felt the protests had the potential to become a catalyst for 'change' – now a social buzzword and a political rallying cry.

Joining the fray were her fellow college and university graduates who mobilised each other to launch *#ThisGown* campaign under the Coalition for Unemployed Graduates. These, she joined without a second thought. Their cause resonated with her: to pressure the government into changing its socio-economic policies to those that would address rising rates of unemployment and poverty.

They'd attend protest marches in full regalia with graduation gowns and caps. Some would wear the same splendid outfits on regular days as vendors peddling their wares or acting out as idlers playing unconventional soccer on the streets of the CBD, ducking and diving from law enforcement.

Cashleen wondered if anyone was paying attention, or perhaps only when the police bearing teargas canisters would be unleashed upon them. It all seemed reminiscent of the protests when she'd been at university.

And, of course, police brutality was not a myth. Officers were known to be uncompromising. *Beat one person within an inch of his life, and you will scare a hundred others away.* One dreaded speciality involved hard blows to the soles of the feet. This caused such pain that the victim would readily confess to anything. Protest was always risky, but so far Cashleen had been fortunate and had not got caught during the skirmishes unlike some of her colleagues.

She marvelled at the increasing use of social media in raising awareness and co-ordinating events. It was a forum that provided an invisible, if somewhat inconsistent, protective barrier from the feared intelligence personnel, notorious for alleged disappearances and other acts of retribution.

Her journalistic curiosity stirred as she consumed the news and scrutinised tear-gas occluded protest videos. Something that one of her lecturers had reiterated was that objective, immediate recording of events was the key to good journalism – and history. And, here she was, an unemployed would-be journalist who should have been capturing these momentous events. She had nothing to lose by doing so, and the experience wouldn't be a wasted effort.

So, she took notes, pictures, and recorded video clips whenever she joined protest marches. At home, she'd download everything onto her laptop, then write reports and opinion pieces. Her voice had no real journalistic platform, but doing this challenged her mentally and awakened a sense that she was still grounded in her profession.

She carefully filed her reports and contemplated setting up a blog. The idea didn't go far because she felt that her work was still too raw. In the meantime, she decided, she'd settle for sharing a few selected articles and pictures on Facebook and WhatsApp. She was gratified when some of her posts received positive feedback or provoked analytical discussions.

Zenith was a surprise. After his sudden announcement to the Class of '14 group that his contract had ended, he slipped from the high perch of his imaginary research job to become one of the vendor contacts for #ThisGown. Cashleen assumed that the illusion of his fictional life had become too much of a burden.

She remembered how, in the aftermath of his flight with his banana cart, she'd texted to reassure him that she wouldn't tell anyone what he was really doing for a living.

We're good Cash, he'd texted back, adding a double thumbs-up sign. Thankfully, the awkwardness had passed.

Zenith was now actively circulating messages that incited everyone, including the few who had jobs, to go out and join various demonstrations, while giving a specific push for *#ThisGown*. Those who stayed away were ridiculed for cowardice, people who didn't care that the country's future was being shaped by old men with sclerotic ideas.

'Surely', Zenith asked rhetorically, 'We young people deserve a future in a modern society with real opportunities?'

His comments led to a very animated WhatsApp discussion about the First Lady's assertion that her nonagenarian husband was an irreplaceable President, so she'd push him to work in a wheelbarrow if need be. She'd declared that he'd even rule from beyond his grave.

In the ensuing social media storm, Cashleen became familiar with a suite of nicknames for the President, which she'd not heard of before, 'Fossil' and 'Goblin' among them.

The cruder monikers touched a nerve. She was an old-fashioned girl who'd been raised to respect her elders, no matter what. Besides, having lived with her ageing parents, she was particularly sensitive to the vulnerabilities of the elderly. Why did Class of '14 have to interact in such bad taste? She challenged them with a candid text message.

Susie jeered *Therz mirrors out there Cash. Of coz he knoz hez a fossil.*

Guyz. U sound lyk cyber-bullies! Way 2 abusive. Cashleen took a stand with a shaking head GIF visual that was synchronised with a wagging finger.

LMAO! Here we go with Preachy Cash. Tino mocked her with a line of laughing emoticons.

Ha ha! Define that. Talkmore challenged.

Define that wat? Cashleen countered.

Cyber-bully! Whoz bullied us 4 36 years?

But guyz... seriously??? &none of u r even 36! Cashleen couldn't believe her colleagues.

Country'z 36 Cash. Analyse that. Tino offered.

Don't defend people who trashed ur future. Talkmore was on a roll.

Bullyin'z about power-play. Who has power? Not us! Susie had another ready barb.

Cashleen knew that she was being trounced but she had to have the last word.

Y'all so wrong! she asserted with a text highlighted in bold red.

But quite quickly and illogically, the group chat had somehow moved on to some snow-graders which Harare council executives had once imported for use in a city where snow was unheard of.

Zim version of Dumb and Dumber! Kkkkkkkk. This came from Amos.

Not Scary Movie Part 5, u think? Talkmore mocked.

Cashleen put her phone away and reflected, feeling somewhat bruised by how she'd found herself at the receiving end of the group's derision. This was the downside of WhatsApp group chats, or was it free speech? One was disappointed by failure to influence opinion, or when no one agreed.

And she had to admit, her opinion was just that. An opinion. That the President might feel hurt by social media posts was hardly based on fact. That he deserved respect simply for being old was another of her opinions. However, she felt that boundaries of propriety had been crossed. At the same time, she'd sensed the combined force of mounting anger against the authorities. While she understood, she'd never allow herself to circulate derogatory messages, she told herself. Was she being priggish? She sighed, her thoughts going round in circles.

She'd been spending a lot of time alone in the apartment, brooding, and had observed with consternation how Itai was thriving: once moody and often drunk, a person who left dirt and clutter in his wake, he'd become a well-groomed, sober young man with money. And it was this that bothered her because her brother still hadn't found a job. She worried about being complicit in accepting groceries and even money for personal use from him. Surely, at the very least, she should have asked for an explanation.

Delta was one person that she could have reached out to, but her friend seemed absorbed by problems at home. The last time they'd spoken, she'd been distracted and irritable after failing to withdraw any cash for her father's medication, despite spending the whole day in a bank queue.

Cashleen had gathered that she was now working as a runner for her brother at the vegetable market. She seemed very busy, as she now spent little time on social media, and would go for days without responding to messages.

She couldn't decide which had been the bigger shock, the Hunger Buster debacle, or Delta reinventing herself as a market gofer. Menial jobs appeared to be in vogue. What was happening to everyone? Was she really supposed to accept these downward shifts in standards and ambition as the new normal?

Would her next logical step be to assume one herself as suggested by her sister? And by *Kule* Jojo? What the old man had said had been wise and realistic. Still she vacillated, obstinate in the belief that her degree had to be worth something more. With nobody to consult or confide in, she bottled up her feelings growing daily more introverted and miserable.

In the end, it was Itai who provided an indirect opening and inadvertently cleared her cloud of indecision. She was now aware that he'd received a call similar to hers, and that he'd also been given an ultimatum to find a job or leave the apartment. She suspected that this was the reason why he'd become so adept at circumventing any discussion to do with Rufaro.

They were having breakfast with bacon and eggs, a treat for which she'd recently acquired a taste.

'I'm leaving this weekend to crash with Gerry in Glen View,' he announced, smiling cheerfully.

She set her teacup down, 'Really? But why?' And with Gerry of all people?

'Yes. With Gerry. Rufaro doesn't want me to stay in the flat. Not while I'm unemployed anyway.' His voice was matter-of-fact.

'It's not true that she doesn't want you here. She's just unwell,' Cashleen rose to Rufaro's defence. If she agreed with her brother, logically she too would have to leave the apartment. She had nowhere to go.

Itai frowned. 'Yes, she's unwell, but she'd feel much better if she didn't have to look after me. Or you.'

'She didn't say that!' Cashleen was defensive.

'*Iwe!* Grow up, Cash. I'm sure she told you exactly what she told me'. He paused and took a mouthful of egg. 'You and me are making her worse. If we leave, she can let the flat, and actually earn an income from it.'

Cashleen bowed her head. His words might be harsh, but they were true.

'But how will you survive?' she asked, even as she became aware that her fear of abandonment was greater than any concern she might have about her brother's welfare out there.

'Cash, is that a real question?' His voice rose. 'How have *we* survived all these weeks? And not just survived!' He looked down at what remained of his plate of eggs and bacon.

'I know. It was you.' Cashleen answered quietly, 'but I'm worried about where the money comes from, and about you.'

To her surprise, Itai laughed. 'Me? Why? Because I don't have a job?'

She nodded miserably.

'You're very naïve, but anyways, I used to think like you. Now I know I don't need a formal job to survive Harare, I just need to be smart.' Her brother sounded almost smug.

'Smart?'

'Look, I'm a dealer, Cash. Anything that gives me money will do. And as you can see, it's working.' He spread his arms out in an expansive gesture. 'When did we last receive money from Rufaro?'

Cashleen didn't answer. It was close to two months. She also knew this: being a 'dealer' was a term that covered legitimate work and dishonest, even criminal, behaviour. She watched her brother stab at a piece of bacon as if he didn't have a care in the world. If Itai left, she'd be on her own as never before.

She had to do something, and fast. 'Itai, may I please borrow some money?' she blurted.

There was a look of surprise on his face. He'd probably expected more questions, maybe recrimination too. Cashleen added quickly, 'For my opening stock. I'd like to start a stall in town.'

Itai spluttered, 'You want to become a vendor?'

'Yes, I want to become a vendor,' she echoed his words as if to convince herself and strengthen her resolve.

'Interesting,' he said flippantly. Maybe he didn't believe her. Cashleen felt a flash of rage. Did he think so little of her that he automatically assumed that she couldn't do it? That she was some precious layabout who would not do the work because it was beneath her? At that moment it didn't matter that these had been her very thoughts.

'I have to start somewhere', she said in a quiet, determined voice. She had to do this.

He shrugged. 'Sure. At least we can try to make peace with Rufaro'.

She nodded. Despite being unresponsive to her text messages and phone calls, Rufaro hadn't unfriended her on Facebook, or blocked her on any of their shared social media platforms.

Cashleen held on to this as a positive sign. It had to mean that her sister still cared and it gave her some comfort.

'How much do you need?' Itai asked.

'Let me find out. I'll let you know,' she replied, somewhat relieved at having finally come to a decision. The rest would follow.

'Sharp!' Itai rose from the table and went to the sink to wash his cup, plate and cutlery. Another new side to his character.

In the doorway, he paused and turned to face her. 'I'm going out. See you later.'

Cashleen nodded without asking where he was going or when he'd be back. Sometimes it was better not to know. She finished her tea, washed the remaining dishes and tidied up the kitchen. The day stretched ahead of her, but she now had a mission.

She checked her phone for messages and found only a brief good morning voicemail from Sando. Rufaro's WhatsApp profile picture from the previous night had changed. In place of a puppy with incredibly large sad eyes, there was now a laughing girl, head thrown back, skipping in the rain. It had to be a good day in England. She felt her heart lift. She'd make hers a good day too with a decisive plan.

She headed downstairs to find *Kule* Jojo. He was weeding the rockery whose revival was still a work in progress. The dead and wilting plants were long gone and had been replaced by succulents which had already given the flower-bed new life.

She asked if she might have his granddaughter's contact details. 'The one with a market stall in town.'

The old man beamed. 'That's Tanaka!' he said as he looked for the girl's phone number. He was clearly so delighted to help that she was touched, and said,

'I'm planning to open a stall in town, *Kule*. So, I'll need some help from Tanaka.'

He nodded. 'I'm sure she'll be happy to explain how things work, especially if she knows you're a friend of mine.'

She smiled her thanks and left for town with a sense of anticipation and purpose.

20

Gweru winters were notoriously cold. Delta was freezing, despite her layers of clothing. It had been a long hard day. Residual marketplace ruckus still echoed in her head, and an ache was setting in just above her eyes. She craved a shower, a hot drink and some rest.

Thinking about it, she doubted that she'd ever get used to the work she was doing. There had to be something better. She only had to discover it, claim it for herself and own it. This was the kind of upbeat advice her newly acquired Life-Coach app had given her. But where and how? It certainly wasn't as simple as it was made out to be, and Zimbabwe was certainly not the U.S.A. where the app's developer lived.

She'd left Tendai to collect late payments from credit customers while she headed home from the market. Everyone else had alighted from the **kombi** and she was now the sole passenger, a relief. The vehicle had been packed and infused with a concentration of sweat, stale perfume and fried food.

The driver turned up the volume on his radio and sang tunelessly to Tocky Vibes' new hit, *Mari*. Money was indeed topical. For once, she didn't mind that the **kombi** was travelling at breakneck speed. She'd be home in less than fifteen minutes. The vehicle's precarious, meandering course dodged potholes, jaywalkers and stray dogs. Loud rattles and screeching brakes highlighted its need for repairs. None of this bothered her.

A few metres ahead, on the opposite side of the road, she spotted a large group of people. The conductor hollered, 'Last stop!' and the driver brought the *kombi* to a sudden screeching halt in the middle of the road. A hooter blasted long and loud behind them. Delta was thrust forward and she banged her head on the seat in front. Her Shangaan bag toppled over, scattering tomatoes and vegetables. A copy of *The Daily Headliner* which she'd bought specially for her father slid to the floor.

She was seized by a sudden, explosive rage. When she came on board, they'd told her that the last stop would be Mkoba Primary School which was beyond her home.

'*Imi!* What do you mean? And what kind of driving is this?' she yelled as she gathered up her vegetables from the dirty floor.

'*Sisi*,' the conductor was unfazed, used to the fury of passengers pushed beyond their limits, 'I said "we stop here", so get off now!'

Delta would have none of it. She couldn't stand bullies. She accused him of being a thief and demanded her fare back. Harsh words were exchanged over the raucous din of music played too loudly. She glared at him, refusing to budge. The conductor retaliated and called her a stubborn girl.

Not to be outdone, the driver joined in, all too aware that in his job every second counted. He didn't begin to earn until he'd completed many trips.

'You're very stupid if you think we'll give you your money back. And if you knew anything about cars, you'd be driving yours, not telling me how to drive mine,' he taunted.

Delta knew she didn't stand a chance, a lone young woman against two men hardened by the pressure of the jobs they were doing. In an experience that had an illusory quality, she found herself being shoved out of the vehicle by the conductor. Some of her vegetables fell out of her bag yet again. Passersby turned to stare but kept their distance. A small boy in school uniform pointed at her and laughed. He was frozen into silence by the icy look she shot at him.

The conductor slammed the door and the *kombi* was off in an instant. With a dangerous U-turn, the driver made a beeline for the group of potential passengers on the opposite side of the road. They surged out of the way as he pulled in, apparently regardless of life or limb.

Delta watched fuming. How dare they manhandle her, and after lying about the last stop? They'd as good as stolen her fare. She had to report this. She rummaged in her bag for her phone to take note of the registration plate before the *kombi* sped out of sight. But then, the futility of her action stopped her. This was exactly what one might expect from *kombi* crew. Anger fleetingly gave way to reason and she almost laughed at her own absurdity. How could she have even thought of making a report. To whom? When it came to such matters, the police force had a particular reputation which didn't inspire confidence.

She shook her head and sighed, then bent over to retrieve three tomatoes and an onion. The scattered *tsunga* leaves were caked with dust. She stared them in disgust. *The Daily Headliner* was soiled, but thankfully still legible.

Home was a good thirty or so minutes' walk away. She felt too exhausted to walk but the idea of catching another *kombi* piqued her. She'd still have to pay the full fare. As she stood indecisively on the edge of the road, a new Toyota Camry pulled up. Heavily-tinted windows prevented her from seeing who was inside. She hoped it wasn't a man trying to pick her up. She was in a foul mood and wouldn't entertain any nonsense.

The front passenger window slid open. The driver leaned over, and shouted, '*Ndeipi,* Delta? Need a ride?'

Mashura! It was Farai. She was mortified at being caught out looking so unpresentable and down on her luck, especially by this high school drop-out turned fuel dealer. She wished away the frumpy, polychromatic Shangaan bag clutched in her hand. But because there was no valid reason for her to decline his offer, she got in and sank into a comfortable leather seat.

After the noise in the kombi, *Stimela's* music from Farai's car radio was soothing. For a few short seconds, she was transported back to childhood when her father's records had frequently filled the house with Afro-jazz.

'So, where are you coming from?' Farai asked.

'Work,' she blurted without thinking.

'You finally got a job? That's good news!' he sounded genuinely pleased for her.

'Which company?'

She racked her brains. There was no way she could tell him the truth. A graduate in chemical engineering who spent her days haggling, pushing and shoving at the market? Definitely not.

She'd have to gloss this one up. *Fake it until you make it,* the Life-Coach app had instructed.

'A procurement agency for fresh produce – with my brother. We link rural farmers to companies in town and negotiate the best prices for them,' she said with as much confidence as she could muster. But, she was sure he could see straight through her. No successful agent could possibly look as scruffy as she did. Moreover, she knew that after he'd dropped out of high school, he had worked the market scene for many years. So he'd know exactly what she was: a glorified market vendor.

Still, when he spoke, he sounded impressed. Was it an act? 'You're so clever Delta. Those farmers are lucky to have you.'

They were definitely not. Her instinct was to say so and brush the compliment aside, but of course she couldn't. She nodded in agreement and silence fell. Other than her immediate family and inquisitive neighbours, only Cashleen and Unesu knew what she was doing for a living.

It had been both a relief and a surprise when Cashleen had told her that she was thinking of setting herself up as a vendor in Harare. It had made Delta feel less self-conscious. Admitting that she was doing something similar had eased their strained relationship, and she was happy to have her friend back. Tentative chats and phone calls had evolved into something warmer and more familiar.

Farai slowed down and sounded his hooter at a tall man who was wobbling across the road. He turned to face the car and swayed comically in the middle of the road like a reed caught in the wind. There was a huge, telling patch at the front of his trousers. He raised a sluggish but threatening fist and continued on his way regardless.

Farai sighed. 'Maybe drunk. The number of times I've almost run over somebody...' His voice trailed away.

'I wonder what he's on,' Delta said.

'Probably *Msombodia*,' he said, shaking his head. Cashleen agreed. The infamous *Msombodia* had a reputation for taking grown men from lucidity and intact sphincters to incoherence and incontinence within record time.

They were drawing nearer to her house. 'You can leave me by the tree over there,' she pointed straight ahead.

'No, no. I know where you live,' he said as he took a quick left turn. He dropped her off next to the lop-sided gate.

'Thanks Farai. See you soon,' she said, with no intention of seeing him again. He waved and took off in a cloud of dust. Throughout the short drive she'd expected him to say something to insinuate that *he* had the upper hand, despite her degree. She'd become hypersensitive in expecting criticism and disdain for how her life had turned out.

'Was that my future son-in-law?' her mother's disembodied voice asked, hoarse from a cold that had troubled her all week.

Startled, Delta turned to see her emerging from behind a bushy golden duranta which dominated their small garden.

'No *Amai*, he isn't,' she snapped. Couldn't her mother confine her disappointed expectations to employment issues? Did it have to be about her potential suitors as well?

'*Eh, iwe*! Can't I joke with my own daughter?'

Delta was immediately contrite. Irritation softened into compassion as she looked at her mother. Her lined face appeared constantly strained. Wisps of grey hair peeped from underneath her woollen hat. In her husband's tattered, oversized coat, she looked ridiculous. Delta made a mental note to buy her an extravagant coat one day when she had money.

'Sorry, Mama. I've had a rough day,' she apologised as she handed over her bag of vegetables.

Her mother peered at her and placed a hand on her shoulder in an affectionate gesture. 'You're working too hard. I know it's not easy,' she said, leading her inside.

It was a tender moment in which Delta knew without a doubt that she'd done the right thing by joining Tendai at the market in place of her mother. Whether her mother had really intended to join Tendai or not was neither here nor there. For now, she was simply glad to be fulfilling a purpose and supporting her elderly parents in her own small way.

'Come, I'll make some tea for you,' her mother said softly before a fit of coughing seized her again.

※※※

After she'd showered and changed, Delta felt clean and refreshed. Her headache had eased. She combed out her Afro and wrapped on a headscarf for warmth. Her ears were particularly sensitive to the cold.

Her phone vibrated. It was a surprise text message from Maruva.

Hey Misi. Howz u? Btw we r hirin. Richie askin bout u. U bek in Hre?

Delta couldn't imagine ever working for Hunger Buster again. Misi Hurukuro had died along with her fake ID and fake certificates which she had burned a few days after arriving in Gweru.

Hi. Not soon. Wil say wen m bek. She signed off with a smiley face.

Coolies. Maruva replied.

Delta walked into the sitting room. She liked this time of day when she could sit quietly chatting with her parents. Her mother came through from the kitchen with a cup of tea.

'Thank you, *Amai*.'

'Be careful,' her mother said, 'it's very hot.'

Delta placed her cup on the table and looked at her father. He was hunched forward in the only posture that his bad back could bear. His head was buried in *The Daily Headliner,* his face creased in concentration or annoyance, she couldn't tell.

'*Haa!* Are these people serious? *Asi chii nhai?*' he exclaimed.

'What is it?' her mother asked.

Her father looked up. 'All this time I thought it was a bad joke. They're confirming that they'll bring in the new money. Bond notes,' he said flatly.

It was a story that had been doing the rounds for months, difficult to believe, even as articles had appeared in the press and generated heated discussion. Most argued that it was probably a ploy to sneak back the dreaded Zim dollar. Others claimed it had to be fake news because the government wouldn't dare. Not after those bearer cheques of yesteryear that had resulted in hyperinflation and caused extreme poverty. The country had been the butt of jokes: home to the world's poorest millionaires, trillionaires, quadrillionaires and other tongue-twisting '...llionaires'.

While the US dollar was the main currency in use and had stabilised the economy, local bond coins, around for almost two years, were widely accepted – anything rather than boiled sweets that had been used for change. The idea of actual bond notes had triggered fears that history would repeat itself.

'And listen to this. It's not even real money. They're calling it surrogate money,' her father continued, frowning. 'Isn't that as good as saying "fake money"? What's the point?'

'To stop cash shortages?' Delta offered. That's what was being said anyway.

'Ha!' he snorted in disdain. 'Something more sinister, I think.'

'Don't get yourself upset, *Baba va*Tendai. Remember, the bearer cheques that made us trillionaires were not real money either. Maybe the cash shortages will stop like Delta says.'

The old man clicked his tongue. '*Nxa!* I have a right to be upset, Mai Tendai. What's with these people? Wasn't stealing my pension enough? I tell you, that miserable social security fund will be the next to go.' He threw the paper aside.

'It's not directed at you personally, *Baba*', Delta said. He looked so upset that she wanted to reassure him that he didn't have to worry; she'd get a proper job and look after him. But she couldn't say either of these things because like everyone else, she didn't know what the future held.

'Well, it feels personal. This is my life,' he replied shortly.

In the past, he'd often spoken of years when teachers were respected, well-paid professionals who retired on a good pension. Even the President himself was said to have been a highly respected teacher. Now everyone knew how badly paid they were and the profession had become a subject of ridicule. She'd seen teachers' jokes circulating on WhatsApp.

If you want to get rid of troublesome baboons raiding your fields, just threaten you'll force them to become teachers. They'll never come back.

On days when street-kids don't get any money begging on the streets, they refer to themselves as teachers!

Her father continued, 'This smells and looks like vodoo economics to me. Or plain propaganda. Since when has propaganda successfully run an economy? *Iwe* Delta, you're the one with a young educated mind. Tell us. If they bring in the bond note, can they really fix its value at one to one with the US dollar?'

That was easy. '*Aiwa Baba!*' She shook her head.

'And why not?' he demanded.

'Market forces of course. Supply and demand. Besides, we're not exporting much, and when we do, payments often go into private hands. And the bond will only work in this country. So, if people want or need the US dollar badly enough for imports or whatever reason, the bond will quickly devalue against the US dollar.'

Mr Choto looked triumphantly at his wife. 'See! Even the young ones can't be fooled. Where do these people get such crazy, no, reckless, ideas?'

Her mother was pragmatic. '*Imi!* They'll do whatever they want. Whether we like it or not. The bond notes will come if they say so.'

Delta frowned. This was the resignation with which her mother now accepted everything: power cuts, leaking water pipes, burst sewage pipes, uncollected refuse, disappearance of her pension. The feistiness which had always characterised her had disappeared. It was a kind of dying inside and it made Delta uneasy.

They were startled when Tendai suddenly spoke from the doorway. They'd been so engrossed that they hadn't heard him arriving.

'Don't worry too much. The Reserve Bank governor has promised he'll resign if the bond notes don't work. So, he'll make sure they work. Just watch.'

Delta burst out laughing. '*Iwe!* Of course they won't work, no matter what he says or does. And to believe the dude will resign ... That would be a first! The bond notes will definitely fail and the President will promote the man instead of firing him.'

Tendai shrugged and catching her eye, tilted his head meaningfully towards their father. Delta understood. They were not to upset him any further with this kind of talk.

Her mother sighed and suppressed a cough. 'Enough. Delta, start cooking, please. It's getting late.'

Delta went through to the kitchen and started preparing the evening meal on autopilot, lost in her thoughts. They were all at the mercy of a hopelessly broken system and they were headed for more difficult times. Maybe her mother's sentiments were right. There was nothing they could do about anything. The thought frightened her. What then would be the point in even trying?

She considered the wave of protests in Harare and wondered what it was exactly that people hoped to accomplish by risking their freedom and their lives. Cashleen had once said martyrdom rarely achieved results, although she guessed that they had all hoped the student protests would achieve something.

21

The city was on edge as protests and demonstrations intensified in tandem with growing dissent. The junior doctors remained divided about whether or not to strike. Those in favour accused their colleagues of lacking the willpower to face important matters head-on and force government to act. Those against argued that patients' lives could be lost. Meantime, the authorities remained indifferent to the crucial issues raised by the junior doctors.

Being against strike action, Unesu focused on doing his best under the prevailing conditions. He'd started his locum at Orion Clinic but he knew that by definition he'd become a criminal. The law was clear. Indeed, from a legal or ethical perspective, he was no different from the malefactors skulking in the underworld. An ever-present worry was that he'd be discovered and lose his registration with the medical council. Confiding in anyone was out of the question.

The clinic consultations were simple enough and the surgical procedures unchallenging. While he treated and discharged each patient without incident, time did little to ease the anxiety that burgeoned whenever he drove into the clinic's car park. He had to constantly remind himself that he had compelling reasons for being there.

And if Dr Mazwi could commit, then so could he. She was solicitous enough to check if he needed any assistance. His answer was always an emphatic, 'No, thanks'. His vulnerability was best kept to himself. There was nothing that she could do for him.

Just as he'd been promised, payments were regularly remitted, and it was good money. For the first time since he began working, he was able to save. He became obsessive about checking his bank balance, morbidly fascinated by its exponential growth. It gave him confidence and opened his eyes to fresh possibilities. With so much to accomplish, he only had to work harder at keeping his reservations in check.

Of all his colleagues, John was the first to observe that something had changed. During a break when they were on call together, he asked, 'How do you do it Unesu? You've bought chicken and chips for the team on call three times now. Are you competing with the Prof or what? Even Doc Muchy hasn't bought on-call meals for us in a while. At this rate, they'll soon be missing us at the hospital canteen.' He raised his eyebrows.

Unesu didn't explain that the meals were delivered on special discount from a fast food outlet owned by an old school friend who was now a dealer in town. And there was no way he could tell John about his additional income from Orion Clinic either.

Instead, he nudged him on the shoulder, saying, '*Ma*-locum *mdhara*, *ma*-locum! While you Bible bashers are preaching and singing sweet hymns in church, I'm out there working.' On the surface, it was a good enough reason, and he hoped that the answer would halt his friend's questions. It did, but being John, he had to say, 'But *iwe* Unesu? For what does it profit a man if he gains the whole world…'

Unesu protested, '*Aiwaka!* Not now. Let's go and chase patients' results before Doc Muchy asks.' And their conversation shifted back to safer, more familiar territory around patient issues and the hardships of being a government hospital doctor.

In time, Unesu became too busy at the clinic and offered John some of his regular locum shifts at 24/7 Emergency Rooms, for which his colleague was grateful.

Replacement of his old Mazda had happened sooner than he'd expected. On the last occasion that Takunda had surfaced, he'd offered him his Toyota Hilux double-cab for less than its market value. Without going into specifics, he'd told him that his last deal had gone well and he was upgrading to a Range Rover. For the Toyota, he'd proposed a generous payment plan spread over eight months.

Pleasantly surprised, Unesu had jumped at the opportunity. Nonetheless, he'd been a little envious at the thought of Takunda driving a Range Rover. He'd wondered what exactly could have given him such a windfall this time around.

Obviously, something shady. Otherwise, why the random disappearing acts and unexplained absences? And why the need to keep a gun in the glove compartment of his car? He'd sensed stonewalling, so held his questions back.

Proceeds of fraudulent dealing or not, the Toyota was robust and in pristine condition. Harare's roads were riddled with potholes, but the car was of a heavier build and could withstand them better than could his old hillmatic.

Unesu also knew that he wouldn't have been given such a liberal payment plan by any used-car dealership in Harare. Despite their complex relationship, Takunda was a good friend. Their shared history would continue to bind them together.

ཚོ་ཚོ་ཚོ་

After securing a start-up loan from Itai, Cashleen sought out *Kule* Jojo's granddaughter Tanaka. She pushed through city crowds and navigated her way across roads that were congested with traffic, moving briskly towards Inez Terrace from where Tanaka ran a stall on the periphery of the bustling market.

They'd spoken a couple of times on the phone and exchanged several WhatsApp texts, but she had no idea what the young woman looked like. Her photo on social media was of a wild-haired, female cartoon character flexing massive biceps below a Girl Power caption.

The real Tanaka was a surprise. She recognised her by her ginger braids and red dress which she'd given as identifiers. From their exchanges, she'd somehow expected a plump, cheerful, loud, market woman, but Tanaka was tall, slim and stylishly dressed. She looked like a model.

Cashleen was instantly drawn by her liveliness. She projected herself as a person who had a steady finger on the city's pulse and knew the latest about Harare's top money-spinners at any given time. She couldn't have been that much older than herself, but she came across as a confident woman whose free-spirited manner made everything look and sound easy. Having a business degree probably helped.

'So, you've decided on airtime and fruit and veg?' she asked of Cashleen. Her own stall was packed with good quality second-hand clothing, cosmetics and various items of gaudy jewellery.

'Yes. I've looked at other options, but I just don't have the capital to stock up with anything else.'

'I see. Airtime cards do sell well at road intersections. That's if you can run in and out of traffic. If not, you can try selling them from just about anywhere. My brother sells his near your block of flats and seems to be doing okay. You know Nhamo, don't you?'

'Yes, I've seen him,' Cashleen nodded. Nhamo was a near-permanent presence at the junction of Tongogara Road and Prince Edward Street. In her mind's eye, she could see his slight figure darting nimbly between cars at the intersection as he sold airtime to motorists. On occasion, she'd also spotted him at the gate, collecting a bottle of water from *Kule* Jojo or just chatting. She still couldn't believe he had a degree.

'Your idea of fruit and veg isn't a bad way to start either. You can pick any overcrowded part of the city,' Tanaka continued knowledgeably. 'That way, you can maximise on potential for sales and profits. Chat with your customers. Be attentive and make them feel special. If you show respect and serve them efficiently, you may end up with a loyal customer base.'

'Loyal customers on the street? Really?' Cashleen wasn't so

sure. Her own observations had left her feeling slightly defeated, even before she'd started. Boisterous and tireless, the city crowds moved with an impatient vitality that unnerved her. She couldn't imagine them as loyal customers.

Besides, there were seasoned, street-smart vendors everywhere, a good number of them being jobless graduates like herself. They could be quite territorial, and their competitiveness bordered on aggression.

'Really. Right here on the street,' Tanaka asserted with a smile. 'Whether you make money or not depends on you. The most important thing is to get started. I know things that you may not know about hustling. So, I'm here if you need me,' she added.

'Thank you.' Cashleen was truly grateful given her misgivings.

'You might have a few minor problems here and there,' Tanaka cautioned before she reeled off a number of issues that didn't sound trivial at all.

'Watch out for con artists. Street kids can be a menace too. Don't be fooled by the little ones... especially the ones with sweet, innocent faces. If you blink... they snatch whatever they can and speed off before you know it. And the municipal police raids, *yoh!* You can try and deal with some of the officers with a polite word.' Then she added with a wink, 'or a bribe.'

Cashleen could see how municipal police officers might accept or even solicit for bribes. City council workers had been in the news for threatening to go on strike over salary arrears dating back several months while their more senior managers were being paid huge salaries right on time. At one point, the government had stepped in with an order to cap council executives' salaries but it had not seemed to make any difference.

Ordinarily, the idea of bribing a police officer would have been inconceivable to Cashleen, but Tanaka possessed a decidedly candid street logic that lent credibility to what she said. So, Cashleen listened carefully, although she needed clarification.

'But isn't it a crime to offer a bribe?' she asked cautiously.

Tanaka threw her head back and laughed, seeming incredulous

that Cashleen could ask such a question.

'*Aah, askana!* If you think like that, you won't survive for a single day. Listen, there's the law. Then, there's street law. You'll learn quickly enough. Do you really think any officer in their right mind would arrest or fine you for offering a bribe?'

She frowned, confused. 'But I thought…'

Tanaka interrupted, 'Trust me. They'll even thank you for it. Much easier than having to sell your confiscated goods themselves later. These people need money. Just like you and me.'

'Do you mean that they take the goods for themselves for resale?' She'd always thought this to be no more than an urban myth.

'Most of them.' Again, Tanaka sounded convincing. 'And back to street law. If you get caught by these officers and they ask for information, never give your real home address. Or your real name. It can be tricky if you have your ID on you. I never do,' she added with a grin.

With this flippant talk of fake names and addresses, Cashleen's mind strayed to Delta. She wondered if she'd been too judgmental. After all, Tanaka was recommending something very similar without batting an eyelid. Where had morality gone? She felt harried by all the dos and don'ts, but she nodded quietly and listened, reminding herself again that Tanaka's tips, ethical or not, could well determine whether or not she'd survive as a vendor.

'There's a serious shortage of public toilets. Trust me, you don't want to have an accident on the street or get into a *dhuma-dhuma* situation with the homeless in a dark alley!' She laughed. 'Make sure you're always smartly-dressed, so that you can trick your way into customers-only toilets *kunana*-Chicken Inn and other fast food outlets. Just look confident and none of them will ask you for proof that you're customer.'

Cashleen nodded. It made sense.

'And lest we forget… there could be protests. Stay vigilant. If you hear there's going to be a march, don't bring out your stock because you might lose it all.' And then, almost as an afterthought,

'Have you been joining marches and protests by the way?'

'Of course, but mostly for *#ThisGown*,' was Cashleen's ready answer.

'Good girl. Can you believe that there are some young people like us who do nothing at all! Personally, I'm committed to doing my bit for the common good. Just imagine what would happen if we had enough people willing to drive change together. We pride ourselves with being an educated country, but just look at the mess that surrounds us. Just look at Harare, it's a shambles. The economy... it's in free fall. Who's going to fix this, if we young people just watch and do nothing?'

The words rolled so easily off her tongue that Cashleen felt this was not the first time they'd been uttered. She was left in no doubt that Tanaka was a true activist or even a budding politician, but this wasn't the time to explore such sensitive topics. They hardly knew each other.

She thanked Tanaka for her advice and left. It was time she got started. She ordered mobile phone airtime cards from Tel One and Econet. Getting fruits and vegetables from Mbare Market was also quite straightforward though she soon realised that she'd have to get there before the crack of dawn to secure good bargains directly from farmers. Middlemen were like sharks and were to be avoided at all costs.

The next day, she squeezed into a strategic selling point on the pavement along Robert Mugabe Road. This centrally-located thoroughfare resembled a giant, shambolic open-air market. Overpopulated with vendors, it was strewn with an array of goods that spilled from the pavement onto the main road, thus obstructing the free movement of cars. Nonetheless, Tanaka had assured her that dense foot traffic in the area promised brisk sales.

She chose a display rack designed to stock minimum quantities, just in case of raids and protests. Assistance with storage space from where she could replenish her rack as needed came from an unlikely source, none other than Zenith. He'd done well with his banana cart and was upwardly mobile on the ranks of street hawking. He now rented a small tuckshop at The Gulf.

Despite the air of competition on the street, she made acquaintances and tried her best to master tricks of the trade from relentless watching and eavesdropping. She became inured to the long hours, the noise, as well as the pushing and shoving. It was the pungent smell of stale urine which greeted her each morning near her spot which took some getting used to. Thankfully, the odour would lift during the day.

Sure enough, just as Tanaka had said, municipal police were often on the prowl. Like the other vendors, she became hyper-vigilant against possible assault, or tear-gassing and arrests by riot police. Such incidents tended to occur whenever vendors and *kombi* operators were ordered out of the city by government. Hardly any time would elapse before the vendors came back in their droves to reoccupy the same streets with their incongruous mix of goods. *Kombi* operators were equally and openly defiant.

She soon learnt that an essential aspect of being street-smart was being able to discern between when to offer a bribe, and when to pick up one's box or bag and make a run for it.

A twist to the dynamics was the First Lady's announcement at a 'Meet the People' rally. In the idiosyncratic style of her public *stop-it* commands, she ordered an immediate end to the harassment of vendors on the streets; they had to make a living because companies were closing everywhere, she told the cheering crowd.

Other than causing transient confusion about the legality of street hustling, and whether or not widespread company closures were a justification, the street market scene grew increasingly fast-paced, unpredictable and precarious. Despite threats of the army and police descending on demonstrators, there'd still be the odd protest.

Earning a living took precedence and Cashleen found that she was unable to attend most marches. On known demonstration days, she'd take her stock to the city's periphery where there was least likelihood of disruptions. Sales were less brisk, but certainly better than nothing.

With everything that was going on, she'd often feel as if she was in a big, disorderly mobile jungle. There were power games at play and she found herself in a compromised position, firmly at the losing end. But in the midst of everything, she developed a new respect for all vendors, who included her fellow graduates, as well as the children, men and women who toiled on the streets with enough dedication and tenacity to enable them to survive from one day to the next, and one month to the next. It was not work that anybody did out of choice. But for her and many others, it was a small step towards being self-reliant, while eking out a living.

22

On Thursday night, a phone call from Unesu brightened a week that had been otherwise dreary and gave Cashleen something to look forward to.

'*Ko*, how's the businesswoman doing?' he teased.

'Fine. And what of the Ministry of Health's slave?' she countered.

'Modern-day slavery masqueraded as a job', he liked to say of his government hospital posting.

'The slave bought a new car!' he laughed. She picked a trace of pride in his voice.

'*Inga!* I meant to call you. I thought you might have done, after I'd seen your latest profile pic.'

'It's Takunda's old truck though. The white one, if you remember?'

'Takunda's twin cab!?' No wonder it had looked familiar. 'Old truck?' she thought. Not by any standards.

'Yes, *ndiyoyo*. Do you want to come along on Saturday? I'm going to Redcliff to visit mother.'

'Of course, I'd be pleased.' She didn't have to think twice. The break would do her good.

'How is she these days?'

'When I last saw her, she looked well. And she sounded well

when we spoke on the phone yesterday. But you know what she has, Cash. It's just a matter of time.'

It was a sensitive issue. She hesitated, what could she say? 'You told me some time ago that your boss had offered to see her. Did she agree?'

'She promised to think about it.' Unesu sounded weary.

'Good. I'm sure all will be well. Just talk to her about it again,' she said with a confidence that she didn't feel at all.

'*Just?* So, you think I don't try? Maybe you can try for me then, Cash, you might do it better than me,' he spoke with unexpected intensity. Perhaps he'd mistaken her response for some kind of criticism. He'd asked her before, but he hadn't thrown the request at her this abruptly. Much as she doubted that whatever she said to his mother would make a difference, how could she refuse? There was no need to point out the obvious and dishearten him any further.

'Sure. I'll try,' she said readily. In the brief silence that followed, the awkward moment passed.

'Do you think Delta might be free and want to meet us on the way? We can pick her up at the Redcliff turn-off.'

The suggestion pleased her. If invited, Delta would most likely turn up because Redcliff was only a thirty minutes' bus ride from Gweru.

'I think so. Let me ask her.'

'Sharp. *Ko*, before I forget, when did Itai become a police officer?' he asked.

'*Aiwa*, he's not. You're confusing him with his friend, Gerry,' Cashleen replied.

'But I saw him at a roadblock along Simon Maz Road. He was holding a set of metal spikes... you know, the ones traffic cops throw at *kombis*.' He sounded sure of what he'd seen.

'Maybe it was someone who looks like him. I think you're mistaken.' Cashleen's heart sank. Unesu had to be wrong. *Itai, the dealer of Harare with a set of spikes at a police roadblock!* The idea was ridiculous. She wanted to laugh but felt a shiver of fear and quickly said goodbye to Unesu. 'See you Saturday, then.'

She shook herself. Why was life so hard? Every good moment seemed to be accompanied by another that was depressing; and Itai still hadn't given her his address, and was constantly evasive about her visiting him at his home. For the umpteenth time she wondered why.

❦❦❦

Unesu felt anxious about visiting his mother. Her refusal to listen to him had hurt him and strained their relationship. How could she take pride in having a son who'd become a doctor, if she refused his advice? Increasingly worried about disease progression, whenever he visited he could only make covert checks for what he'd been trained to look for in cancer patients: signs of pallor, jaundice, parotid swelling, hair texture, weight loss, how much she ate and the health of her nails.

Now, his main concern was how to convince her to see Prof Chaka for a proper assessment. Because Prophet Healer still had a hold over her, he suspected that she'd dismiss the idea. And yet any other woman in her position would have been grateful to have an expert offering his services at no charge. He worried that they could end up quarrelling. It gave him some relief that Delta and Cashleen would be present. They'd offer a buffer.

Lost in thought, he pushed a full shopping trolley from Pick n Pay supermarket into the car park. He was proud of how much he'd bought for his mother. He wanted her to be pleased, but he knew that she'd probably worry that he was overworking as a locum because she had an idea of what he earned from his regular job.

As he transferred groceries into his truck, he was interrupted by vendors who swarmed the car park, attracted by his conspicuous vehicle and its vague promise that anyone driving such a car would have money to spend. Although he felt somewhat guilty for having so much when they had so little, their persistence maddened him. He'd lost time in a bank queue and he was unwilling to waste more explaining that he didn't need or want whatever it was they were selling. Redcliff was more than a good two hours away and he didn't want to be late picking up Delta.

He pushed the empty trolley to the holding bay and made a phone call.

'You ready, Cash?' he asked.

'Yes, I'll go down to the gate.'

'Sharp. Ten minutes. I'm about to leave Avondale.' He got into his car and from the corner of his eye, saw a woman sidle up. He sighed wearily. *Yet another vendor.*

'Fruits for sale. I give you a good price, *mwanangu*.'

He shook his head without even looking at her. '*Aiwa!*' was his brusque response. He slammed the door shut and slid his key into the ignition.

'Please? See how fresh they are.' Her voice gave him pause. She held a bag of oranges in one hand, and apples in the other. How thin she looked in her threadbare dress! The expression on her lined face told a story, most likely one of struggle.

This woman, who was probably older than his mother, was in no condition to be hawking fruit in a car park.

He was immediately full of self-reproach at having been so insensitive. 'How much?' he asked, although he'd already bought some apples in Pick n Pay.

'Only two dollars.'

He pulled a five dollar note from his wallet and gave it to her, then accepted the apples, saying, 'Keep the change, please, *Amai*.'

To his surprise, she responded, 'Thank you, but I am not a beggar, *mwanangu*. What else can you take for your change?' She pointed to a box under a tree at the far end of the car park. 'I also have bananas.'

She obviously needed the money but he didn't want to offend her pride. He wondered again what her story was. 'I'll get more apples from you next time. Please keep the change.' He was polite but insistent.

She nodded and he thought the tension in her expression eased slightly with the ghost of a smile. 'Yes. Next time. Thank you.

Thank you and God bless you, *mwanangu*.'

He watched her walking away with a slight limp, her head held high despite the slight curve in her back. He felt a burst of admiration for this unknown woman, her unlikely dignity and that implicit show of resilience. Vendors were human. They were irrepressible and hard-working. With friends who'd become vendors too, he wondered how he could ever have forgotten.

As he turned left into King George , he spotted Julia waiting to cross the road, holding hands with a senior surgical registrar. She gave him a vivacious smile.

'Damn!' he swore under his breath, almost forgetting to flick his indicator as he switched lanes. A fellow motorist hooted angrily at him. Then he felt a strange wave of relief for having been wrong about Prof Chaka, and a sense of loss for what had never been his to begin with.

⚜⚜⚜

Unesu arrived not long after his phone call, and soon they were on their way. Cashleen didn't know much about cars, but she acknowledged that the Toyota had a somewhat ostentatious appeal. Outsized mag wheels, a massive bull-bar at the front, and something that Unesu called a snorkel on the driver's side. Shaded windows completed the vaguely sinister, pimped-up effect. It was Takunda's legacy of course.

After the persistent drama of breakdowns and starter problems with his old car, she was happy that he now had a reliable vehicle. She told him as much.

He grinned and asked, 'So, how's the market?'

She screwed up her face '*Eish!* The market is… the market! Every day is frenetic. You know what the city's like.'

'Yeah. *Saka ma*-one!' He shook his head and turned right, easing the car onto Samora Machel Avenue which would continue as the main highway.

'How are the applications going?'

'Rejection after rejection. You know, for months I've been waiting for news from **The Daily Headliner** and **Classic FM**. Both confirmed last week that they won't take me after all. And it was only unpaid work that I'd applied for!'

'I'm sorry.' He paused, then added, '*Zvichanaka.*' How often had she heard that optimistic expression, and always in defiance of the odds?

Unesu switched on some music and they fell into a comfortable silence. She could see that he was preoccupied. Other than the odd comment about yawning potholes, careless **kombi** drivers and too many police roadblocks, he made little effort at conversation. She didn't mind. The extended periods of silence allowed her some time to think, away from the noisy street crowds who'd become such an intimate part of her life.

Just past Kadoma, they were stopped at a police roadblock, their fifth since leaving Harare. This one was manned by no less than six officers, two of them holding sinister-looking spikes, while a third held a speed-trap device.

It was an open secret that the main purpose of roadblocks was fundraising for the police force, and a personal money-spinner for the officers involved. It didn't matter therefore whether one was in the right or not. As a group they backed each other up.

Unesu had his driver's licence on him, he carried a good spare wheel, his car had front and back reflector strips and was generally in prime functional condition. He had valid insurance and his radio licence was up to date.

Moreover, he'd stayed well within highway speed limits since leaving Harare. At the other four roadblocks, traffic officers had struggled to find anything which warranted a spot fine or extortion of a bribe. After routine checks, Unesu and Cashleen had been waved through with some expression of open hostility, possibly because the officers had gained nothing from them.

However, a particular officer at the Kadoma roadblock wasn't prepared to simply let them drive away. Without introducing himself, he ordered Unesu to show him his driver's licence. After inspecting it, he shoved it into his pocket and waved them off the road, while one of his spike-wielding colleagues signalled cars that had stopped behind them to proceed. The other officers moved on to the opposite side of the road to deal with motorists travelling towards Harare.

'What now?' Cashleen asked as she felt the tension in her body.

'These guys... *hameno*!' Unesu shook his head. He parked the car by the roadside and switched on his hazard lights. 'I can be fined for not having these on.'

Cashleen was surprised. '*Shuwa?*'

Unesu clicked his tongue. '*Shuwa*. You haven't seen anything yet. And now that he's got my licence, I can't leave. The fun and games are about to begin. Just watch,' he muttered under his breath as the officer approached.

'Unesu, be careful!' Cashleen whispered back. She knew how hard-headed her friend could be; while joining protests and working on the streets had shown her how vicious the police could be. She didn't want the day to be ruined.

The officer was a small, light-skinned man who seemed to puff himself up. He adjusted the cap on his head and gave Unesu a cold, hard stare. Unflinching, Unesu stared back.

The man opened his mouth as if to say something, then stopped. He walked slowly round the car then stood at the front, barking out orders. 'Key on. Indicator right. Indicator left. Headlights. Flash!' He walked round to the back and again shouted, 'Indicator right. Indicator left. Brake lights. Reverse lights!' There was a brief silence before he reappeared next to Unesu's window.

'Step out of the car and leave all doors open for inspection.' His tone was brusque, antagonistic. Cashleen and Unesu exchanged amused glances as they watched the little man strutting from one open door to the next. Squinting, he made a show of closely examining each door. And having reached the fourth door he straightened up triumphantly, '$100 spot fine. None of your doors have inside reflector strips.'

'What!' Unesu exclaimed in disbelief.

Cashleen was aghast. *One hundred US dollars for inside reflector strips! Protecting whom from what?* Then she remembered that spot fines for traffic offences had been increased from $20 to a maximum of $100 earlier in the year. This had been followed by a public outcry in which the Class of '14 WhatsApp group had eagerly participated on social media.

Cashleen wracked her brains trying to remember the outcome. Had the matter remained unresolved with some roadblock police demanding $100 fines, and others $20? Constitutional lawyers had challenged the legality of spot fines because the law allowed a seven-day provision for payment. However, because she didn't drive, Cashleen's interest in the issue had waned.

'You heard me right. Pay $100, or I impound your car right now.' The policeman's nostrils flared.

Cashleen placed a hand on Unesu's arm and said, 'We don't have $100 officer. This is a small offence. Please, allow us to go and look for some reflector strips in the next town.'

'*Iwe wati chii?* Something small? Who are you to teach me how to do my job?' He moved towards her, pointing at her with a threatening finger. Unesu pulled her back and took out his phone.

'What are you doing?' the officer shifted his attention. Unesu ignored him and began dialling.

The officer watched, undecided about whether to continue on the offensive. Concern on his face, he looked towards his colleagues but they all seemed preoccupied with other motorists.

Then he blurted, '*Blaz*. Let's talk about this. Just give me something small. Maybe $30 and we can forget the $100 fine.'

Cashleen gasped. Unesu shook his head and put his phone to his ear.

'Hullo. Assistant Commissioner, can you hear me?' A pause.

'I'm with one of your officers here, Ass. Com. Yes. I'm at a roadblock outside Kadoma. First of all, he didn't introduce himself. Then he put my licence in his pocket. Yes, yes. Very rude fellow. Right now, he's breaking the law. He's just asked me for a $30 bribe and I have a recording of the entire conversation.'

The officer motioned with his hand but Cashleen wasn't clear what the gesture meant. Unesu paused again, nodding his head vigorously as he listened, then continued in an angry voice, 'I'm trying to control myself here, but if you can't control these boys of yours on the roads, I'm taking away my business. I mean it.'

Cashleen was confused. What business did Unesu have with an Assistant Police Commissioner? She looked at the now very agitated officer. Looking helplessly towards his colleagues, he took out Unesu's licence.

'Fine!' Unesu said. 'Let me ask for his details and I'll call you back *now now*.'

He slid his phone back into his trousers pocket. Before he could say anything, the officer rushed to say, 'Here, take your licence *biggaz* and have a safe journey. Please. I'm sorry. Don't sink me. I can lose my job and my children will starve.'

Unesu snatched his licence back and said sternly, 'You're lucky I'm in a good mood today. Don't you ever do that again.'

'Thanks, *Biggaz*, thanks.' The officer couldn't escape quickly enough. He hurried in the direction of his spike-wielding colleague who was now gesticulating for a *kombi* to stop.

Still looking stern, Unesu said, 'Let's go.'

In the car, Cashleen looked at him wide-eyed, 'That was close. Aren't you lucky to know someone influential *ku*-Police! Which assistant commissioner was that?'

With a naughty grin he replied, 'That, my dear was someone very important. Assistant Commissioner Non-Existent, based at Nowhere Police Headquarters in Harare! I told you the fun and games were about to begin.'

So that's what he'd meant! Cashleen looked at him astonished. Their eyes met and they burst out laughing. At that moment, she noticed how attractive Unesu was and stopped the thought in its tracks. What had come over her? Still smiling, she quickly reined in the rush of inappropriate feelings and looked out of the window. A warm feeling settled over her as they continued on their way. Delta was waiting for them.

23

While the absence of congestion away from Harare was refreshing, Unesu observed again how Kwekwe seemed to be in accelerated decline: potholed roads, always a burst water pipe somewhere or another, buildings in disrepair and everything needing a coat of paint. It was as if no one cared that infrastructure needed maintenance.

But beyond the refrain about how difficult life was and how expensive, what could be interpreted as passivity was punctuated with humour. In scenes reminiscent of Harare, unemployed youths loitered jovially on pavements or engaged in hawking activities; beggars, street kids and the homeless blended seamlessly into the landscape. Considering that most companies that had been major employers in the area had either closed or were struggling to stay afloat, it was hardly surprising. Of all of the companies, his parents' previous employer, Redcliff's ZISCO, had been hardest hit.

The once dominant steelmaker had been reduced to a barely functional shell under care and maintenance. His mother had told him that the few part-time employees who'd been retained on a nominal wage hadn't been paid for several months.

They stopped at a roadside market stall to buy artificial flowers which Cashleen wanted to place on her parents' graves at the cemetery. Carefully, she selected two baskets, each with a colourful bouquet of synthetic blooms laid on a bed of impossibly lush, green leaves.

Unesu watched her interaction with the vendor, observing an intensity of character that he'd never witnessed before. It seemed she'd learnt a trick or two on the streets of Harare, and she was now applying those tactics in reverse. He wasn't averse to a good bargain but he couldn't help feeling sorry for the vendor.

Cashleen moved swiftly from unsuccessful sweet-talking to aggressive haggling. She gesticulated to make a point. The hapless young man appeared to wither into himself before he reluctantly agreed to reduce the price of each flower basket from $5 to $3.

'But *Sisi*, you killed my business today. Like so, I have to walk home. I can't even buy bread,' he muttered bitterly and pocketed the money that she'd paid him.

Unesu suppressed laughter as Cashleen came up with the most absurd of retorts. 'And *you* should learn that you don't milk a cow dry! You must leave me with enough money to buy from you next time I come by.'

Milk a cow dry! Where had such an expression come from? Besides, she was as likely to come back that way to buy this young man's flowers as she was likely to fly.

'Was that a show of girl power?' he teased.

Her face broke into a mischievous grin. 'Why?'

'You were too hard on him.'

'So, says the doc! Maybe *you* would pay more when you can pay less, but for some of us, it's dog-eat-dog. He should be happy he had a sale at all. If it had really been *that* bad, he would've refused. Anyway, we always factor in possible customer discounts into our prices.'

He noted the 'we' reference with a spasm of foreboding at the ease and acceptance with which she spoke. What if all she'd ever amount to, career-wise, was street vending? With the way things were going in the country, it was a real possibility. It felt so wrong.

But, as he'd overheard a colleague say, 'It suits the powers that be for people to remain poor and dependent. That way, they're more easily bought for a bag of maize meal, come election time.'

Delta stood at the Redcliff turn-off, slowly rethinking the previous night's events. With hindsight, Farai's home-based fuel retail set-up had been a disaster waiting to happen. But still, the fire and its magnitude had shocked her.

Farai and his two assistants had sustained severe burn injuries, while his house and part of the neighbour's had been damaged. It had taken something as apparently insignificant as a leaking petrol drum and an oblivious passer-by who'd lit a cigarette, to trigger the inferno.

When they'd discussed the tragedy that night, Delta's mother had choked with emotion. 'Today, God worked a miracle. Imagine if his wife and children had been home!'

'And I was surprised the fire brigade and ambulance came that quickly. You know what they're like,' her father had added. A fastidious man, he was disdainful of the day-to-day inefficiencies that had become the norm.

Tendai had weighed in with an opinion that underpinned ineffectual anger. 'I blame the authorities. It wasn't a secret that Farai was selling fuel from home. Why did they allow that to happen? Why didn't somebody put a stop to it? Maybe he bribed someone.'

Her father had concurred, 'Yes, he must have done.'

Still shocked by the accident, Delta had remained silent as their opinions swirled around her. Several times she'd bought paraffin for their Primus stove from Farai. On all occasions, it had bothered her that he was storing highly volatile and flammable fuels at home. Yet she'd never said anything to dissuade him.

Her mother had added thoughtfully, 'All these things would not happen if there wasn't so much corruption, so much poverty... if only these young people could get proper jobs...'

As she stood there waiting for Unesu and Cashleen, her thoughts went around in circles. She felt cheated by the American

Life-Coach app which didn't seem to have done her much good. She could feel the usual almost obsessive rigmarole of complaint, failure and misery ... and now she'd failed to use the very basics of her science education to advise Farai. Maybe he would have listened to her because she was a friend.

Or was she falling into a trap of stereotyping and condescension? Could he really have been that ignorant? She doubted it. One didn't need to have a degree to know that petroleum products were dangerously flammable. Something had driven him to take those risks. Supposing she had said something, would he have listened? His had been a success story, at least superficially.

She conceded that in these times of hardship, need would continue to drive the ever-present allure of illicit activity. People would continue to do whatever they had to do in order to make a living. And Farai had not only himself, but a wife and children to support and no doubt with his apparent success, there'd been other relatives all claiming hardship and wanting help.

She looked again at her watch. It was almost one o'clock. Unesu and Cashleen were running late. Since they intended to travel back to Harare that same day, this was bound to be a short visit. She hoped that Unesu's mother wouldn't take it amiss.

To her relief, her friends arrived just at that moment to pick her up. She was impressed by Unesu's new car. In real life, it certainly looked better than it did on Facebook. He shrugged off her congratulations, as if buying the car had been an effortless exercise. However, she could detect a hint of pride and a new air of confidence in his demeanour. Could it be that buying a car did more for one's ego than obtaining a degree? With concern, she noticed how thin Cashleen had become and wondered whether this was from deliberate efforts at weight loss, or from endless difficulties which seemed to plague her friend.

During the drive, Unesu made a request. 'Delta, I was just telling Cash that maybe the two of you can help me out with my mother.'

'How so?' she raised her eyebrows.

Cashleen threw her a backward glance, 'The doctor thinks you and I can persuade her to go for medical check-up,' she said with a smile.

Delta hesitated. She was surprised that after all this time, the impasse around Unesu's mother's refusal to get proper medical attention had not been broken. How could two young women manage, when close family members had failed? She'd only known Unesu's mother since their university years, although Cashleen had known her for most of her life.

'*Hameno,* Unesu. We can try, but it might be difficult. What do you think, Cash?'

Cashleen sounded slightly more optimistic than she felt. 'Sure, let's try. I don't think it can do any harm?'

'I'd really appreciate it,' Unesu said, before asking her, 'So Delta, what's up *ku*Gweru?'

'Quiet city, but you wouldn't believe what happened yesterday!'

'What?' Cashleen enquired.

Delta launched into a narration of the tragedy that had occurred at Farai's house.

Cashleen exclaimed, 'How terrible! The things that happen…'

'And will continue to happen…' Unesu added and let his thoughts hang.

In her mind's eye, Delta could still see the spectacular blaze and thick clouds of noxious smoke that had risen high into the still, night air.

She had an urge to change the topic and lighten the mood. 'Before I forget… Did either of you read *The Headliner* this morning?'

'Not me,' Cashleen answered with a glance at Unesu who shook his head.

'That prophet in Gweru, the one to whose church your mother goes, Unesu…' There was a brief silence in which she realised too late that her choice was unwise.

She needn't have worried though because Unesu prompted mildly, 'Yes?'

'He's being sued by a well-known businesswoman,' she answered.

'Really? Why?'

'A fake prophecy. It's said he promised that if she seeded one hundred grand at his church, the money would multiply threefold and her company's debts would vanish.'

'What is it with people and this craze about miracle money? And who ever heard of vanishing debts?' He clearly couldn't believe it. They all laughed.

'And now she's suing because…?' Cashleen asked, still chuckling.

'Obviously the money didn't multiply, her debt grew and her home is being repossessed.' Delta grinned. 'The report said the prophet's explanation is that his prophecy didn't work for her because she has no faith. He's also challenging having to appear in court. Apparently, heavenly matters cannot be heard in an earthly court!'

'So arrogant. I can just imagine him saying that. In private, he must think he's God. People worship that man and they'll defend him with their last breath. If she could earn a hundred grand, she should've stuck to working hard at whatever gave her that much money in the first place.' Cashleen's voice held disbelief.

Unesu said quietly, 'We can laugh… but there's something about these prophets that makes people believe the most ridiculous of things without question. They have a certain, unquestionable power. Take my mother, for example…'

Delta steered the conversation with an interruption. It was too awkward to have Unesu's mother as the focus. 'You forget what he did when he went to Israel.'

'What?'

'He asked his followers to write down prayer requests on pieces of paper and told them he was going to meet God in Israel to hand them over. They went along with his instructions and he stuffed bags full before he left.'

'Yes, I remember hearing something about that …' Cashleen

said, then asking, 'Could it be the power of pure faith?'

More like blind faith, Delta thought to herself. She'd been raised as a conventional Christian and had never really understood issues to do with divination and miracles which had fanned the mushrooming of prophetic churches everywhere.

To her, it seemed some of the churches had become cash cows for individuals who preyed on people's deepest fears as a basis for manipulating them into giving and giving until they had nothing left. Multitudes flocked to prophets, seeking divine intervention for all manner of problems in their lives. Desperation lay behind it all.

That and the concept of material wealth arising from faith, bolstered by seeding and donations to prophets' churches held an irresistible appeal. Who wouldn't want to get rich without actually having done any work? Who would not want to hope, when one's life was miserable?

She also knew of people who believed the most incredible prophetic pronouncements that defied all logic. She thought of the young self-styled Man of God in Harare who'd ordered his congregants to drink sewage water during a church service, claiming it had healing powers. Another had made waves on social media with claims that he regularly spoke with God on his mobile phone and sometimes went to heaven for lunch. His congregation had grown as his popularity surged.

In neighbouring South Africa, one had ordered his congregants to go on all fours like cattle and graze on grass in order to get closer to God, while an associate had convinced his followers of the miraculous healing power of the insecticide spray, Doom. Subsequently, the spray had flown off supermarket shelves as congregants sought to out-spray each other. They were indeed Doomed!

XOXOX

They passed by the cemetery. Unesu and Delta stayed back in the car to give Cashleen some privacy. She noted how the site was overgrown with weeds and how neglected or impoverished everything looked. A few graves had granite tombstones, while most were simple mounds of earth signposted with metal or wooden crosses.

She followed a footpath to her parents' graves, which lay next to each other. She positioned her flower arrangements and then forcefully pushed each basket hard into the earth, before sprinkling a handful of soil over the artificial petals because she knew that it was still possible for someone to try and steal the soiled flower baskets for resale.

She fought a sudden deep sense of loss, and wondered again, as she often did, what her parents would say, if they could see how her life had turned out. The cracks in her self-belief were widening. Shaking the feeling of sadness, she returned to the car and her friends. They proceeded on their way.

🔺🔺🔺

They were welcomed at the gate by Unesu's mother and *Mainini*. Amidst greetings, there was much surprise and admiration for the new car, which gleamed in the afternoon sun. Even *Mainini*, whose smiles were a rarity, managed to look pleased.

Cashleen was relieved to see that other than slight weight loss and a look of mild anxiety, Unesu's mother didn't appear to be as unwell as she'd expected. She'd also anticipated some degree of tension between the old woman and her son, but there appeared to be none. Unesu was very attentive, deferring appropriately to his mother as tradition required.

She told them that she'd attended a fellow church congregant's burial just that morning. Cashleen had a sense that she was about to say more about the dead man, but *Mainini* interrupted. Lunch was ready.

They sat down to a delicious meal of goat stew and peanut butter rice. Delta did most of the talking. She regaled them with hilarious tales from the farmers' market, infused with her particular sense for the dramatic. Cashleen was prompted to describe the protest marches and the incipient restlessness which seemed constantly on the verge of something more profound on the streets of Harare.

She brought to life a caricature of how she was always ready with a plan to take off with her Shangaan bag clutched in one hand and her fresh produce box balanced precariously on the head.

After they'd engaged in much laughter and bantering, Unesu's mother addressed Cashleen and Delta with an inevitable question, '*Nhai vasikana*, you can't be vendors for good … are you still looking for proper jobs?'

'Yes,' they chorused in unison, then Delta said, 'Mama, the problem is that the few jobs being advertised go to people with connections. Or people who can pay bribes.'

Cashleen, nodded.

Unesu's mother said wistfully, 'Corruption *futi*! *Mainini*, tell them... during our time, unemployed graduates were unheard of.'

Mainini cleared her throat and agreed with a severe look on her face. '*Chaizvo*.' She was clearly a woman of few words. She stood up and started clearing the table.

'What else can we do, Mama? We will keep applying,' Cashleen said to Unesu's mother.

'Indeed! Next time you see me, I might be a CEO at some big chemical engineering firm!' Delta added with a smile. Cashleen stared at her. Which fantasy land did she live in? Although she knew that her friend meant well and the remark had been intended to ease the older woman's concerns, she felt slightly irritated. She stood up and went to the kitchen to help *Mainini* wash the dishes.

When she returned, the atmosphere had changed. Delta was looking studiously at her hands in her lap. Unesu's mother was leaning forward, her arms resting on the table. There was an expression of anxiety on her face.

She listened to Unesu as he laid out a plan to book his mother on the City Link Coach to Harare. Arrangements would be made for her and *Mainini* to stay at their cousin's home. She'd be seen by the doctor within a day or two of arrival.

Cashleen was surprised. She looked questioningly at Delta. Had she managed to convince Unesu's mother in the short space of time that she'd been in the kitchen? *How?* She nudged Delta's foot under the table, at the same time wondering if they should leave the room to give Unesu and his mother some privacy. Delta raised a surreptitious index finger to her lips.

As the conversation went on, Cashleen gathered that Unesu's mother had been the one to volunteer for medical check-up.

'It's just to confirm that things are well, you understand?' she was at pains to explain. In her all-encompassing gaze was a plea.

'It's okay, Mama. I understand.' Cashleen could see the relief on Unesu's face. This had worked out to be much easier than they'd all expected.

When she went back to the kitchen with the remaining glasses and jug, she said casually, 'I hear you're coming to Harare soon, *Mainini*.'

'Yes. *Sisi* must have a medical check-up. The man who was buried today… he had AIDS.'

The connection escaped Cashleen. She stared questioningly at *Mainini*. The older woman gave her a mournful look and said, 'He was healed at the same time as *Sisi* at the crusade in Victoria Falls. Now he's dead.'

Cashleen nodded. She finally understood why Unesu's mother had changed her mind.

By the time they left, a clear plan was in place. On the drive back to Harare, she perceived the resurgence of Unesu's hope. It was in his voice, his smile and his laughter.

24

The bleak realities of trying to eke out a living on the streets of Harare couldn't be overstated. The city itself was unfeeling and aggressive, the hustle and bustle on its squalid streets dizzying. Cashleen's plan for marketing fruits and vegetables wasn't going well. Sales were disappointingly low and profits, at best, remained marginal. Occasionally, she made losses when she had to throw away or give street kids the fruit and vegetables that had begun to soften and rot.

To make matters worse, competition had become tighter as the number of vendors on the street increased. From the time she'd started, it seemed as if many more people had muscled their way into the territory. She realised that she'd have to think of more viable ideas, or else she'd lose the money she'd invested. There was no way she could continue as she was and still hope to make ends meet, let alone a profit.

She sold the last of her slow-moving stock and gave away everything to street kids that had lost freshness but seemed edible. With only a few airtime recharge cards remaining, she decided on a day off. She needed time to think and reconsider her options. Itai hadn't said when he'd want his money back, but it was better to be prepared. She was now more open to trying anything that promised a better return and carried little or no risk of losing shelf life so quickly.

Canned foods were a possible alternative, but she didn't know where she could get stock at a good bargain. Acquaintances who sold non-perishables on the street were not forthcoming. Although Tanaka sold different products, she was always a mine of information about the Harare street-hustle scene. Cashleen decided that it was better to consult her than to keep going round in circles, wasting time.

Qk qn Tanaka?
Yes?
Free 2 meet 2day?
No probs. Quiet morn. Tanaka's ready response was attached to an *'it's all good'* emoticon.
Tx. Nid 2 discuss s'thin wit u.
Sure. Come. @ flea mkt. Two thumbs up.
Comin. A smiley emoji.

She chose to walk all the way into town, enjoying the sunny, undeniably beautiful morning. Her serenity was abruptly broken when she crossed Samora Machel Avenue into the CBD. Here she had to be particularly alert and walk with extra care. There was always a risk of tripping on the broken pavement, or being run over by a *kombi*. And then there were pickpockets, strategising as couples, so that one diverted your attention, while the other made off with whatever they could purloin.

Inez Terrace Flea Market was unusually quiet, with few customers in sight. She spotted Tanaka standing by her stall, but she almost didn't recognise her because she was sporting a new, startlingly audacious look. Her clean-shaven head gleamed in the morning sun and she wore conspicuous *stop-and-look-at-me* earrings that hung so low they were almost resting on her shoulders. She was staring intently at the back cover of a book.

'Hi, Tanaka.' Cashleen raised her hand in greeting.

'Hullo, hullo!' Tanaka exclaimed, and placed the book on the table. Cashleen noted its title: *The 7 Habits of Highly Effective People*.

Tanaka pointed her towards a tall stool, and whispered sassily, 'You must be making real *moolah* in the city. You look good!'

Tanaka had such an infectious smile that Cashleen responded warmly, although she doubted that she looked good. Her hand-me-down dress from Rufaro hung loosely in all the wrong places because she'd lost weight. And Itai had once warned her that she'd soon develop permanent worry lines on her forehead if she didn't lighten up.

She perched on the stool. 'Real money *futi*? Not at all.'

'*Ko*, why not? Harare is full of money. You just have to refine the art of enticing it into your pocket. And I'm not talking about miracle money here!' She winked.

Cashleen shook her head. 'You know what? So far, the money hasn't been good, and being chased like animals by municipal police is not much fun. Then there are the protests! It all takes getting used to.'

'*Ayas, ma*-One! But what can we do? *Ndiyo* Zimbabwe *yacho*. Just don't fall into the trap of doing nothing except complain. If you can't beat them today, try harder, until you defeat them at their own game!'

'*Yowe* Tanaka! Really? Who and how?' There was an edge of sarcasm to Cashleen's voice, and she was aware that she was risking a budding friendship.

Tanaka didn't seem at all offended. She threw her head back and laughed, her big earrings swinging. 'I mean *whoever* gets in the way of what you want to achieve. Just throw it right back into their faces.'

Cashleen made a face. While Tanaka's carefree attitude was like a breath of fresh air, what she was saying wasn't practical.

Whoever gets in the way? The future that she'd dreamed of and worked hard towards had fizzled out due to governance issues and an economy that had nose-dived. Surely Tanaka wasn't implying that she could deal with all that, as well as the architects of a failing economy? *And how?* Such optimism bordered on foolishness and had its pitfalls.

She pointed out what really should have been obvious to Tanaka, 'But it's impossible...'

Tanaka raised an open palm, her smile giving way to a more thoughtful expression. 'You can't say that. Not without really trying. You ... a journalist, and you've been... what? Two years out of varsity, right?'

Cashleen nodded.

Tanaka continued, her voice now charged with such passion that, once more, Cashleen caught a glimpse of the activist she now knew her to be. 'Listen, it's almost five years since I left uni. I've forgotten most of what I studied, but I'm still hoping for a formal job. While I wait, I can't let what's happening in this country get me down. I'm taking control of my life, in spite and despite of them! I'll do anything – and I mean *anything* that I can – to chart my own destiny. Do you understand what I'm saying?'

Cashleen thought she did. She nodded again. It seemed Tanaka was just one more person who was quick to justify bending the rules to suit her perceived needs. What was happening to everyone? For a moment, she wondered how far this girl would go, and whether her stall was a front for something less mundane than second-hand clothing and cheap cosmetics.

She bit back the questions that were on the tip of her tongue and shook her head, saying, 'I still think it's really hard to make a success of... *anything*!'

Tanaka was insistent. 'Not entirely. Don't be so blinded by small difficulties. You must keep trying, no matter what. One day, something will give and change will come. Remember, there's also power in numbers, so don't underestimate our contribution at protest marches.'

Like most people, Cashleen was aware of the widely articulated desire for change. Truthfully, she said, 'Yes, protest marches... I've been feeling a bit disillusioned, though. We don't seem to have achieved anything. Many times I've skipped those to go vending instead, because my need for money is more urgent. And protests can be quite risky. People have been injured or arrested.'

'Sure, it's risky, and of course it's normal to feel the way you do, so when I speak, don't get me wrong. I'm not implying that I'm better than you, but I do make it a point to get involved as much as possible. I was in that march against police brutality. Some people were arrested and a policeman whacked me with his baton.' She turned her arm over to show scarring. Cashleen drew back.

Tanaka grinned and continued. 'What matters is that I was there with the others, driving our message home. Yes, you do need to sell your goods to make money, but there's so much happening that if I were you I'd choose at least one worthy cause and stick with it. Don't write yourself out of history, *askana*. If we all commit to something, we can make a difference. Life isn't a game with second chances, you know.'

Cashleen didn't care for clichés, but in a way, she understood that Tanaka was being honest. She also had to acknowledge that it was unfair for people to desire change and do nothing. She hoped she hadn't sounded weak, selfish and self-justificatory because that wasn't her nature at all. It was just that sometimes life's events had a way of taking their toll on one's willpower and sense of direction.

And it wasn't as if she'd completely detached herself from the struggle, or her profession either. At that point, she could've told Tanaka that she had a cache of articles and recordings about the protests, about graduates working on the street, and a few other topical issues, but she held back. The discussion could well take a new direction and she had to go. At some point, she would forward selected articles to her friend on WhatsApp

Tanaka's face softened and she inclined her head. 'Don't look so worried, Cash. It's gonna get better. Someday. By the way, you said you wanted to discuss something. What is it?'

'Oh yes, it's about where I can find reasonable prices for non-perishable foods. I need another line apart from fruit and veg. I've tried asking around but there seems to be a closed network of some sort.'

'*Ehe-ka*. Any competitor is a threat. But since you've asked me... I need to partner with someone on a very good deal ...'

Tanaka lowered her voice.

Cashleen was instantly alert. 'Yes?'

'You know about the statutory instrument banning certain imports, right?'

'Yes.' She certainly did. SI64 of 2016. A recent development, it had been in the news for a few months. Apparently, it had been introduced to protect local companies from competition with foreign firms. Some said it was to reduce outflows of the US dollar, of which there was now a critical shortage. Others said it had to do with politicians killing off any competition so they could create monopolies for their failing businesses.

'That ban has caused shortages of specific popular imports. Predictably! So here lies a solid business opportunity for us,' Tanaka beamed.

Opportunity in banned imports? She had to be referring to smuggling rings. Yes, those would be more lucrative than selling fruit and veg on a heaving, urine-reeking pavement along Robert Mugabe Road; but with that addition to the picture, she saw her future fast disappearing.

From an unemployed graduate to an unsuccessful street vendor, then an underworld purveyor of contraband, leading her straight to jail. Being a convict had never been part of the plan.

'Think about it,' Tanaka was saying. 'No pressure. If you're not interested, *haina hora,* I can always find someone else. It just crossed my mind that you and I would work well together.'

Cashleen made an effort to conceal her indecision and feelings of aversion. 'I'll think about it,' she said as positively as she could.

'*Coolies!* In the meantime, let me *app* you my good friend's number. Chuma. Phone him and say I've referred you. He works at Cut Price Foods in Ardbennie and has employee benefits. So, he can get you wholesale bargains.' Tanaka's earrings swayed and danced as she bent to retrieve her phone from her handbag that she'd hidden in a box.

Cashleen thanked her and slid from her perch on the stool.

'So what's up for the rest of your day?' Tanaka asked.

'Besides phoning your friend? Nothing much. I'm going to the City Library to return some novels and catch up with this week's newspapers. If they have wifi today, I might work on some online job applications.'

'Good, good. How have the applications been going?'

'Not a single response.'

'I'm sorry to hear that. Just don't give up, hey!' Tanaka placed an affectionate hand on her shoulder.

'I won't.' But at that moment, she'd never been less certain of anything.

)()()(

Cashleen pushed her way through seething masses of people as she headed towards the library. Just under the overpass at Joina City Complex was a cluster of newspaper hawkers, their advert boards lined up in a haphazard row.

One headline caught her eye: **$200m Power Tender Begs Investigation.** She was familiar with the power tender scandal that had surfaced intermittently over the past few months, a story that she thought was the perfect illustration of how unfair life could be, and how pointless it could be trying to be trustworthy and honest.

There'd been coverage of how a young executive with a criminal record had been awarded a $200 million power-generation tender under dubious circumstances. The reports had stated that he had no training or experience in power generation. No bank guarantees or any other form of security had been availed by the man's company as required by regulatory boards. A $5 million advance had already been paid to the young man, though no work had taken place.

Meantime, his affluent lifestyle and photographs of him drinking champagne with powerful members of the elite were regularly flaunted on social media, almost as if to say he could lavish the proceeds of the advance with impunity. Cashleen was reminded again of the anger that had been expressed on various social media groups about this matter. She wondered if there would really be an investigation. It was more likely there'd be cover-ups, she thought.

As she was about to cross the street, she heard someone calling her and turned around in surprise. It was Delta's aunt, Peace. She looked smart and professional in a blue tailored suit, the uniform of Prime Savings Bank. They exchanged greetings, raising their voices above those that swirled competitively around them. Cashleen asked after little Tari and Uncle Dondo, and was told that both were well and that the latter was now working as a cross-border trader. Cashleen couldn't imagine this. She'd retained a vivid image of him as a successful businessman.

Inevitably, the older woman asked if she'd found a job yet.

'Still looking, Auntie, but I now sell airtime, fruit and veg here in the city,' she replied with as much dignity as she could muster.

'*Shuwa?* That can't be easy.' Something akin to pity flitted across Aunt Peace's face.

'Yes. Not easy, but I couldn't just sit at home doing nothing.' Cashleen didn't flinch. Gone was that fierce pride and need to hide what she did for a living.

'That's good. At least you're keeping busy, which is better than moping at home. Delta told you she's at Gweru market, didn't she?'

'Yes. We actually met up in Redcliff some time ago.'

'I keep telling her that her chances of finding a job will be so much better in Harare, but she's still undecided about coming back. Anyway, things are sure to get better one day. Just don't give up.'

Then, seemingly as an afterthought she continued, 'I've got an idea. Why don't you come and find me at the bank, say in early December? I might have something that can help you earn a bit more, especially now that you spend so much time in the city centre.'

'Thanks. I'd like that.' Cashleen was touched by her kindness, and at the same time curious.

Aunt Peace smiled. '*Handiti* you see that long bank queue over there?' She pointed a manicured finger in the direction of a bank where hordes of people stood in a long disorderly queue that snaked out of the building and disappeared round the corner.

Cashleen nodded and moved closer so that she could to hear the woman who'd lowered her voice. 'Cash shortages are getting worse. It's the same at our branches, and at all the other banks. That's why bond notes are being introduced soon. Remember the black market from 2000 to 2009, and how some people got really wealthy changing money? So...' and she gave a determined smile, 'I want to go into money changing too. With the bond notes coming in, there'll be money to be made. I'll need an assistant because I'm not leaving my job.'

Cashleen had been young, but she did remember that long, stressful period of cash shortages, hyperinflation and empty supermarket shelves. One of her older cousins had been friends with a sophisticated money-changer who'd never dropped in to see them without bringing treats.

Aunt Peace continued, 'Even now, there's already a premium on cash. I'm selling US dollars hard cash against bank transfers for a small profit. When bond notes come in, the market will definitely improve.' The older woman spoke calmly and with authority, as if she was referring to an ordinary business idea.

Perhaps if the proposal had been put to her by someone her own age, Cashleen would have balked, but as it was coming from an older, otherwise conventional woman, the aunt of a close friend, someone she'd known for a long time, she experienced something of an epiphany, suddenly seeing Harare in a rather different light: a city with plenty of alternative opportunities if one was willing to reach out and grab them. Surely, under the circumstances, how could one refuse?

'I'll definitely come and see you,' she promised, and they continued on their separate ways.

❋❋❋

At the library entrance, her phone rang. She stepped back outside to answer. It was Unesu.

'Hullo,' she said.

'Cashleen? Hullo, can you hear me?' Poor connectivity caused initial background crackling.

'Yes. Now I can.' The static had cleared.

'*Iwe,* I'm positive I saw Itai again with two policemen at a roadblock last night on a back street off Arcturus Road. How come you told me he's not a police officer?'

'What are you talking about? Of course, he isn't!'

'I'm sure it was him, Cash... in uniform too, and carrying a set of spikes. He walked off too quickly before I could say anything. I think he was trying to avoid me. If you say he's not an officer, you really must find out what's going on.'

'Okay,' she said shortly. Her heart was beating too fast, and she felt a moment of panic. She didn't want to hear this. What if it really was Itai? But then, weren't a good number of people in Harare breaking the law in one way or the other, just to survive? And what of the discussion she'd just had with Aunt Peace? How could Unesu's phone call turn her newfound resolve on its head?

Rather unsettled. She changed the subject. 'How's your mum doing?'

He was silent for a moment, before he responded, 'She seems to have recovered well from surgery. It's the rest of it that's not going too well...' his voice faded with a sigh.

He sounded so dejected that Cashleen immediately felt sorry for having asked. Contrite, she said, 'I wish her a quick recovery. Listen, I'll find out what's going on with Itai. Thanks for letting me know.'

'Anytime, Cash. Bye.' He rang off.

She knew that Itai wouldn't take kindly to any prying, and would asking make any difference? If he was posing as a traffic cop in order to extort money from motorists, she was sure his police officer friend, Gerry, had set him on that path. She shook her head. Lawlessness was fast sinking its roots into society.

When she left the library, Cashleen phoned Chuma. He readily agreed to supply her with canned foods for resale. He suggested meeting up after work. Later that afternoon, he sent her a text message.

Car park behind OK Supmkt @ Hoton Pk. Blue Toyota Fun Cargo. 5 p.m.

It was an odd choice for a meeting place, but she decided not to read too much into it. After all, it was within the same locality as his workplace. She persuaded Zenith to drive her out to Houghton Park in his little Honda Fit.

The blue Toyota Fun Cargo was half-concealed behind a bushy purple hibiscus plant on the fringes of the supermarket car park. A short, muscular man was leaning against the car boot.

She approached cautiously and asked, 'Mr Chuma?'

'Yes. *Ndiwe* Cashleen?' the man responded, throwing a look at Zenith.

'Yes,' she replied.

'Here are your things,' he said, opening the car. He seemed to be in a hurry. She motioned for Zenith to come forward. Together they quickly transferred ten boxes of canned beef, fish and beans into the Honda.

A scruffy street kid hovered in the background, holding up his trousers with one hand and stretching out the other. 'Only a dollar. Just one please,' he begged.

'Get away,' Chuma snarled and the little boy ran off.

Cashleen paid one hundred dollars, which Chuma pocketed and drove away.

On their drive back into town, Zenith said, 'You know what you've just done, don't you?'

Surprised, Cashleen turned to him and asked, 'What?'

Zenith blasted his horn and dodged a **kombi** that had made a sudden stop in front of them.

He said matter-of-factly. '*Iwe* Cashleen? A hundred dollars only for all that? And no receipt? Did you see how nervous that man was? Those are obviously stolen goods.'

'You really think so?' None of that had crossed her mind.

'Of course!' Zenith said. 'I can't believe that you didn't suspect it. But don't lose any sleep over it. This is Harare. There are worse things.' He laughed, but Cashleen couldn't see the funny side.

Stolen goods? No wonder Chuma hadn't wanted her to collect from Cut Price Foods. And no wonder his prices were less than half the advertised wholesale prices that she'd seen in *The Sunday Mail*. Tanaka had said Chuma had employee discount benefits. Now she wasn't sure. How could she have been so naïve? And what did this make her? An inadvertent criminal was still a criminal.

She'd been brought up to believe in the transformative power of sheer determination, honesty and hard work. She could see now that such idealism was misplaced. A *'How to Survive Harare'* manual – if such a publication existed – would have been much more pragmatic. Anyway, the canned foods were now hers. She'd see how far this would take her.

25

His mother's visits to Harare for medical check-ups had made it necessary for Unesu to move from his bed-sit at the hospital sooner than he'd intended. However, thanks to the additional income from the Orion Clinic, he could afford to rent a spacious, two-bedroomed apartment at Trevi Gardens, a secure complex located conveniently close to the hospital.

He awoke at midnight when he heard his mother coughing. The oncologist had assured him that while chemotherapy was known to suppress immunity, she expected the cough to clear. The symptoms pointed more towards a common cold than something more serious, she'd said. Hearing the distressing sound, however, Unesu wondered if there was a chance that his mother was developing viral pneumonia.

Lying there in the dark, he reflected on how her treatment had gone. At first, he'd been concerned about medical costs under a multi-disciplinary team of specialists who included Prof Chaka as the gynaecology lead, plus an oncologist, a physician, a pathologist and a radiologist. However, the Professor had waived surgical fees and asked his colleagues to do the same for their consultations. So, the costs had been reduced to medical-aid shortfalls on tests, hospitalisation and medication.

'Your mother's a lucky woman, because endometrial cancer is a slow-growing tumour.' Prof Chaka had explained. 'A combination of surgery and adjuvant radiotherapy followed by chemotherapy should give her a good chance of a cure.'

As expected, surgery had gone well, as had radiotherapy. It was the chemotherapy that seemed to be draining her vitality, leaving her anaemic and listless. She often felt sick and she'd been struggling to eat. Unesu was grateful that *Mainini* was there to look after her.

It was a relief that his mother no longer made references to Prophet Healer's miracle, which she'd once so staunchly believed in. Her twice-weekly sojourns to his Gweru church had become history. Unesu wasn't sure if *Mainini*'s decision had been a personal choice or a means of supporting her older sister, but it certainly helped that she'd also quit.

He'd noticed the disappearance of his mother's jars of anointing oil and holy water, her wristbands and other religious paraphernalia which she'd bought from Prophet Healer's hugely popular shop in Gweru. Only her Bible had remained. She had not jettisoned her faith, just the prophet. Even though Unesu thought of himself as an atheist, the former would have worried him.

Controversies around the prophet continued nonetheless. In fact, his popularity had increased to rival that of any celebrity, if being nearly worshipped by congregants and hogging media limelight were anything to go by. Unesu thought the man was an insatiable narcissist with a real talent for wooing radio stations and tabloids, each of which vied to outdo the other in their coverage of his purported miracles. The sole national TV station wasn't immune to his charm either.

Every so often, there'd be a story about him, extraordinarily sensational in its weirdness. He was reported to have helped a woman with a longstanding history of infertility to conceive and give birth to a full-term baby within five days. He'd performed male organ enlargement during a church service. Women's fibroids had melted instantly at the laying of his hand on their abdomens. Many who'd been on their deathbeds had been cured of AIDS. Supposedly, they had valid HIV-negative test results and glowing health to prove it.

Unesu wondered how laws of science and logic could be so defied, how people could possibly believe such crackpot testimonies. For the moment, though, he was simply relieved that his mother had freed herself from thralldom to a man whose skills lay in unscrupulous manipulation of the fears of the poor and sick. She now seemed to be on the road to recovery, despite the occasional setback.

Cashleen had convinced him to buy a wig or two before his mother completely lost her hair to chemotherapy.

'Trust me, a bald look on your mum would be so *gwash*! What woman doesn't want to look good?' she'd challenged him, surprised that he hadn't thought of it in the first place. She'd taken it upon herself to help his mother choose the wigs the following morning.

He closed his eyes and willed himself to sleep. Tomorrow would be a busy day. He'd also agreed to meet up with Takunda who was briefly in Harare. Then, there'd be a trip to the bank before he put his mother and *Mainini* aboard the late afternoon coach.

He was leaving the ward for his lunch-break when Takunda arrived. They walked slowly towards the privately owned canteen just outside the hospital grounds.

'I haven't eaten since morning, so I hope they have *real food*. Not the guff they used to sell when we were in med school,' said Takunda.

'Ha, ha! Wishful thinking by the internship dropout who hasn't been to this canteen in ...what? Almost two years? Around here, things only change to get worse, *mdhara*.'

Unesu was cynical. He conceded, however, that the canteen had to be an improvement from back in the day when it had been nicknamed The Typhoid Centre by senior consultants who said when they were junior doctors, it had operated from a lopsided wooden shack.

'Still, I can think of much nicer places for lunch. Why don't we drive into town?' Takunda suggested.

'I can't. I still have some ward stuff to do before I go to the bank. And you know what the queues are like these days. Then I have to drop my mother off at the coach terminus before I go for my evening locum.'

'Juggling work and locums, how do you do it? I think I'll stick to my deals!'

Unesu shrugged. 'I do what I have to do.' He wondered if Takunda would ever consider returning to medical practice. He'd been a good student, getting excellent grades with seemingly minimal effort. It concerned Unesu that all that expensive training should go to waste, but Takunda hadn't completed his internship and he'd probably hate having to start afresh.

Besides, he seemed to be doing fine wheeling and dealing. One never knew half of what was going on with him. Recently, he'd been talking of new business possibilities, casually name-dropping. This minister. That MP. Some ruling party youth leaders who'd become rich overnight.

It sounded as if he intended to set himself on that path. And it worried Unesu. For him, anything to do with politicians was a no-go area. He hoped his friend wouldn't get involved in even shadier dealings than whatever had led him to flee a few months back.

Takunda interrupted his thoughts.'Talking of queues, I *never* queue for cash at the bank, and I get as much as I want. Whenever. No limits.'

'How come?' Unesu asked, raising his eyebrows.

'I've got a connection at my bank. Sorry, we don't have the same bankers, otherwise I'd have introduced you to her.'

The canteen was packed. They bought Coke and muffins and then found a free table in the corner, away from everyone.

'Internship's almost over, isn't it? Which district hospital are you being deployed to?'

Unesu leant forward. 'Nowhere. District vacancies have been frozen.'

'Why? When most district and provincial hospitals are short-staffed?'

'Exactly! It's said there's no money for salaries.'

'Un-*effing*-believable!' Takunda exploded, spluttering.

Unesu shrugged. 'Are you *that* surprised? I'm not.'

Takunda said, 'But it's tight! What are you going to do? You could always join me, you know.'

'Me?' Unesu cocked his head to one side. 'Become a dealer? No ways. I'll hang around Harare. Might open a surgery or join Psych.'

A rotation in Psychiatry hadn't been compulsory for internship, but his application to join the department as a senior house officer could be successfully made under the guise of one who intended to specialise in the near future. Concessions around staying on at teaching hospitals were sometimes made for aspiring specialists before they joined formal training.

'But why Psych? I thought you wanted to become a neurosurgeon.'

'Sure, I do. But Psych will have to do for now. Hopefully I'll get into the Pari Unit. I need a break. This hospital is too busy and *ObsGobs* here's been a killer.'

'Yeah. O and G. I can imagine. But Psych, **mdhara**... I'm dead!' Takunda burst out laughing. Unesu slowly bit into his muffin. He didn't respond, knowing exactly where this was going.

Doctors poked fun at each other across specialities all the time. Psychiatrists were bound to go off the rails. Male gynaecologists were twisted perverts, and in their obstetric role, they were glorified midwives. Orthopaedic surgeons were really carpenters who'd accidentally wandered into the medical profession. Urologists had the finesse of plumbers unclogging blocked pipes, while general surgeons were butchers masquerading as doctors... and so it went. In reality, the various specialities respected each other's different roles and valued the ethos of multi-disciplinary care for their patients when it mattered most.

'Good luck,' Takunda said before changing the topic. 'How's your mother doing?'

He sighed. 'Surgery went very well, and radiotherapy was okay. But she's been unwell since starting chemo.'

'I don't know much about endometrial cancer, but why both radio and chemo? Isn't that overkill, surely?'

'Not at all! It's what was recommended as standard care for her stage of cancer. Remember, she had a team of specialists looking after her.'

'I see. Is it possible for me to see her today?'

'Sure. She's leaving Harare around 6 p.m., but right now she's somewhere in town with Cashleen, buying wigs!'

'Good. I'll call them and find out where they are. How's Cash getting on? Is she still a vendor?'

'Yes. She was saying something about reducing fruit and veg in order to increase stock variety with canned foods. She's still operating from the street, though,' he said and raised his eyebrows, remembering how amazed he'd been by the versatility she'd shown since that week several months back when she'd started off along a pavement on Robert Mugabe Road.

'I see,' Takunda said, then he asked, 'Is that crazy boyfriend of hers still in Jo'burg? That one who was always posting controversial stuff on Facebook and Twitter?'

'You mean Sando? He isn't her boyfriend; they're just friends. And you know they were classmates. She doesn't really talk about him much, although some time ago she mentioned that he could be a missing person.'

'How so? He did go quiet on social media a while back. I wondered why.'

'I've no idea.' Unesu remembered Cashleen telling him that, like her, Sando's mother had been having trouble getting in touch with him. Then, Cashleen had said she was worried that he might have been killed or injured in one of the xenophobic attacks that sometimes broke out in South Africa. Unesu had dismissed that as a far-fetched idea. Whatever had happened, if indeed anything had, Sando would have to be accounted for. People didn't just drop off the face of the earth.

He'd often thought him rather reckless, secretly hoping that Cashleen wouldn't progress to his extremes when she started circulating articles about the protests in Harare. Thankfully, those seemed to have quietened down, which meant that she probably had less to write about. He didn't want her to endanger herself by placing herself under the spotlight.

Takunda was saying, 'But *iwe-ka*, there was a time when I thought you and Cashleen would be an item and...'

'You're mad. That girl is like a sister to me.' Unesu was taken aback. Besides, he was too preoccupied with important matters to be thinking of a relationship. His obsession with Julia had fizzled.

'Okay... no need to get upset. And it's not as if she's half bad,' Takunda said and laughed when Unesu scowled at him.

They finished their drinks and walked to the car park where they inspected Takunda's Range Rover. Unesu stared as Takunda drove off in a cloud of dust and a mighty roar befitting of the model's huge engine. Shrugging off a moment of jealousy, he hurried back to the lab to collect a patient's full blood count results.

Halfway there, he remembered that the haematology machine was down yet again. He'd have to re-bleed her and ask her relatives to take the sample to a lab in town. However, he knew that it was quite likely that they wouldn't be able to pay for the blood test at a private lab. At times he felt like a social worker or a counsellor, rather than a doctor. He shook his head and headed to the ward at a brisk pace. Time was flying.

His steadily increasing savings had earned him an invitation to join his bank's Premier branch in Borrowdale. Initially, the thought of being one of the bank's select clientele had made him feel like an impostor because he'd become so used to being an impoverished junior doctor.

Then he'd found himself enjoying the luxury of having a personal banker. Compared to what he'd been used to, the overall banking experience just stopped short of being pampered. In no time, however, worsening cash shortages had started to compromise the quality of service at the exclusive branch.

He entered the bank at three o'clock to find all eight armchairs in the waiting lounge occupied. The commissionaire directed him to a queue next to Enquiries. There were three people ahead of him. Adding those in the lounge made him number twelve. A couple soon joined the queue behind him. It was not what one would expect at this branch where immediate service had been the norm.

With general loss of confidence that money was safe in the bank, people were trying to withdraw as much cash as they could from their accounts. All banks had introduced daily cash withdrawal limits as a control measure, hence the queues. Unesu listened to snatches of conversation among people waiting patiently behind and in front of him.

It was Groundhog Day again. Fear of the country's economic collapse had created an instant camaraderie in the queue, as had indignation. There was general disbelief that the bond notes about to be introduced by government could be successfully pegged at a rate of 1:1 with the US dollar. Triggering an inflationary spiral was more likely.

If the US dollar had stopped inflation dead in its tracks for a few years, the greenback was a currency that everyone wanted, including black market dealers and smugglers. The dollars continued to haemorrhage out of the country.

Unesu rubbed the stubble on his chin, frowning. History did have an uncanny way of repeating itself. He wondered how long it would be before they were all poor trillionaires and quadrillionaires again. He didn't join in the conversations, but he smiled and occasionally nodded to show he was in agreement.

He grew impatient as time ticked away, but he knew that he couldn't leave without being served. Like many other places, the laboratory that would process his mother's post-chemotherapy blood tests in Redcliff only accepted cash as payment. There was no way his mother could endure hours of queuing for money at her own bank in Redcliff.

After about ten more minutes, the commissionaire directed him to a free seat in the lounge. Fidgeting with his car fob, he muttered irritably under his breath, 'Why are they so slow?'

The woman in the next seat looked up from *The Daily Headliner* and remarked with a smile, 'Actually, they're not slow at all. You're just not used to waiting here, are you?'

He grinned, admitting sheepishly, 'Yes, you're right. It's this waiting...'

'Just two days to go and *those* will make it better. Supposedly,' she said with cynical undertones, pointing a finger at an outsized **'Embrace Bond Notes'** poster on the wall. The garish notices had mushroomed everywhere as the introduction of bond notes loomed like a threat.

'To think that giving us an illusion of money is the best they could do after raiding the country's nostro accounts is effectively theft, no matter how elaborately they may want to gloss it up,' she said and shook her head.

'Tell me all about it,' was Unesu's oblique assent. It hadn't been reassuring at all when the reserve bank governor promised yet again that he'd resign if bond notes didn't work. His assertions that nobody would be forced to use the surrogate currency were met with general scepticism because his words were taken instead as implication that people would indeed be forced to use bond notes. Command-style praxis was certainly more familiar than choice and free will.

Public protests against bond notes in major cities, as well as an upcoming court challenge by the expelled former Vice President hadn't deterred the authorities. There was no indication that the matter would be up for further consultations with the concerned public or business entities either.

'This is shocking. Yet another armed robbery at a service station!' the woman exclaimed, directing him to an article that she'd been reading, *'Ten Armed Robbers Raid Union Petroleum'*.

'Ten!' Unesu was surprised.

'Thugs. They hunt in packs, armed and dangerous.' She raised her eyebrows. 'And this time a cool fifty thousand.'

'Really! Is that how much selling fuel can generate in a day?' Unesu asked, disbelieving.

'Not by a long shot. For that Union Petroleum Service Station, I'd say maybe the money was accumulated in a week or so. Thieves know that retailers aren't taking their cash to the bank because they won't be able to get it out when they need it. And, of course, we're all frightened that the banks will convert the USD into worthless bond notes.' She was voluble, her assuredness hinting that she was in her comfort zone with this topic.

Judging by her well-built frame and stylish clothes, she didn't seem to be someone who had suffered too much, and he found it refreshing that she should have such outspoken opinions. So many of the rich and well-to-do were sycophants.

All at once, it was her turn to be served. She got up and placed the newspaper on the table, saying with relief, 'At last!'

Unesu picked up the paper and flipped through what he thought were pages of opinion pieces passed off as factual reporting. Or propaganda by any other name. He lost interest and picked up a smaller tabloid, often accused of being sympathetic to the opposition. His eyes settled on *'Joke of the Day'* smiling wryly at the last line, 'That James Bond. He even gave the bond notes his name!' So said a putative minister.

The joke fell flat, but Unesu discerned the intent. Were their leaders in touch with reality? They apparently had doctorates but did they have a clue what they were doing?

'Sir?' the commissionaire summoned him with an inclination of the head. It was his turn. He stood up smiling. **Finally!**

26

Delta sighed. At this rate, she was at risk of forgetting even the most basic of chemical operations and formulae which she'd studied so diligently in college. It was one of those days when she longed to be cocooned in a state-of-the-art laboratory, working away at a scientific breakthrough. Or doing something stimulating. Not this. Not here. Her head was throbbing from haggling with farmers at Gweru's open market.

Still, she couldn't leave before securing enough produce for Tendai to deliver to the shops, fast-food outlets and street vendors who made up their inner-city customers. She'd come to appreciate that in this business, consistency was key to maintaining a loyal customer base.

She wondered how Cashleen was doing. The impression from her friend's regular text messages was that she was fine, but she also knew that texts couldn't accurately convey emotion. It had been a week since they'd actually spoken on the phone. Then, she'd detected a hint of contrived gaiety in her friend's voice, and in the feeble jokes that she told about her experiences as a vendor.

She suspected that Cashleen was disillusioned, but under the circumstances, who wouldn't be? She certainly didn't like the market, and she knew that she was never going to become a tycoon. It was only the steady trickle of income which made it more worthwhile than the alternative of idling her days away at home, waiting in vain for job adverts that were getting even fewer with continued company closures.

Cashleen had also mentioned that she was considering teaming up with Tanaka, who ran a smuggling ring between Harare and Jo'burg. Despite there being very little that astonished Delta these days, *that* had been a real surprise. Cashleen, of all people? It had to be this Tanaka girl who'd influenced her. She wouldn't have had such an idea on her own.

Delta felt a pang of jealousy. Would Tanaka become Cashleen's best friend and leave her on the sidelines?

※※※

The rainy season had begun, bringing intermittent relief from the summer heat. The downside was unsightly puddles and thick sludge everywhere. Swarms of flies swooped and buzzed over a growing mound of discarded fruit and vegetables behind the market. Heat and moisture accelerated decay.

Garbage removal trucks hadn't been seen for at least two weeks and nobody knew when they'd turn up, if at all. As if that wasn't enough, an overwhelming stench suffused the air. However, nobody else seemed to mind, so Delta gritted her teeth and got on with whatever had to be done. Clearly, hygiene standards were eclipsed by the need to make money.

She was thankful that a good number of rural farmers weren't familiar with inner city markets. Neither did they have the means or time to distribute their produce to every potential customer and then collect payments before catching the last bus back home. They had to rely on people like she and Tendai who bought from them in bulk.

Not only had the market taught her to be unsympathetic and inclined towards the use of con tactics; she'd also developed a keen eye for spotting vulnerable or desperate farmers. Older women, who were more likely to have children and compelling family responsibilities, were the softest targets.

She'd often defaulted to confidence trickery, convincing farmers that city customers were already oversupplied with fresh produce, before making an offer to buy from them at rock-bottom prices. Predictably, they'd beg her to reconsider. She'd counter their pleas with accusations that they were trying to impoverish her. Didn't they know that resale prices in the city were low?

Then she'd pretend to relent and increase her offer ever so slightly. There'd be more pleading, at which point she'd either move on to the next farmer with an exaggerated show of nonchalance, or offer another small increase which was usually accepted. Indeed, there'd been occasions when she'd bought fruit and veg for next to nothing. But one could only buy so much because of the short shelf life. City customers could be quite picky about freshness and quality.

By midday Tendai was almost done organising deliveries into the city, so Delta excused herself and headed home. In the Mkoba-bound *kombi*, she picked a week-old copy of *The Gweru Tabloid*, which a fellow passenger had left on the seat. It wasn't her brand of newspaper and she'd often thought it a waste of time and journalistic skill for grown adults to devote time to writing frivolous articles such as: *Man Enriched by Flesh-eating Goblin. Blackmail Hell for Nude Nun. Miracle Money Floods Bank Account.*

However, she needed something to distract her. There was too much noise from fellow passengers' loud conversations and incessant bond-note jingles from the car radio.

How many times could one listen to '*You must love the Bhondi Noti, Bhondi Noti*' sung like a nursery rhyme for adults, without feeling irritation or anger at being so patronised? As if a jingle could persuade citizens of the value of a pseudo-currency, when they knew otherwise?

Scanning the paper, she saw a job advert incongruously tucked between an article about a celebrity who'd been exposed as a love rat, and another about a woman who'd lost seven teeth in a street fight over witchcraft accusations.

Cleaning Agents, a detergent-making company that she'd

never heard of, was looking for a laboratory technician. Her pulse quickened as she read the job description. This could be the perfect job to launch her long-term career.

She had six days before the closing date for applications, but she decided to submit hers as soon as she could. Even better, she could hand-deliver her application to the company's offices at the listed Windsor Park address, which was just two *kombi* rides away from home.

※※※

When she arrived, home was eerily quiet. Her parents had travelled to their rural home in Shurugwi to assess their cattle when a suspected outbreak of foot and mouth disease had been reported. Losing their livestock would be a disaster because they'd pinned their hopes on a recent government announcement about proposed lending regulations.

Banks would be compelled to accept livestock, like cattle, as security against which individuals could borrow money. The announcement, improbable as it sounded, had been a lifeline for her parents who'd never recovered from losing their pensions. An ever-present concern was her inability to provide for them. Thinking of Unesu's mother and her diagnosis of cancer sometimes had her worrying about how she'd manage if either of her parents became really unwell.

She took a quick shower and dressed with care, choosing her favourite dress in an understated light blue. Anything to increase her likelihood of getting that job. Maybe some company executives would be on the premises when she arrived. It could be her chance to make a good first impression, which might well lead to an interview.

She smiled at the absurdity of her thoughts, a welcome snatch at optimism in trying times. She quickly hand-wrote an application, to which she attached a copy of her curriculum vitae and then she set off.

Two *kombi* rides and she was in Windsor Park. The company offices were housed in a nondescript building located on unkempt grounds. Somehow she'd expected better. It was only 4 p.m. but the place looked deserted. Wondering if they'd already closed, she followed a footpath which meandered through a garden full of weeds and knocked on a door signposted *Reception*.

In response to her knock, a female voice called out, 'Come in!'

Delta entered and stood uncertainly by the desk. A girl whom she assumed to be the receptionist was at the far end of the office, closing a window. She looked at her with barely concealed annoyance and teetered towards her on ungainly stilettos.

'Can I help you?' she asked, nostrils flaring and tapping an impossibly long fingernail on the glass-covered desk. Delta noted the name Settlement on her ID badge. Despite her instant dislike of the girl's manner, she forced herself to be pleasant. For all she knew, this girl could be influential in some obscure way. Appearances could be deceptive.

'Good afternoon Miss Settlement,' she said formally.

'I said can I help you?' Settlement responded rudely.

Bemused, Delta silently took an envelope from her satchel and held it out to her.

The girl snatched the envelope, snapping, 'What's this?'

'An application for lab tech. I saw an advert in *The Gweru Tabloid*,' she replied in a controlled voice.

The girl turned the envelope over and scrutinised it as one would something odd or highly suspect. She clicked her tongue and said, 'You're late. Applications closed yesterday.'

'Yesterday? *Ko sei?* The paper said next week. ' Delta was surprised.

'There were thousands of applications, so we closed the advert early.' There was an inflexion of triumph in her voice. The *'we'* didn't escape Delta. Could this girl be one of the managers?

Then, without preliminaries, she continued, 'But if you have $50, I can slip this into the manager's office.'

Not a manager then. Delta just stood there, caught off guard by her temerity in solicitation of a bribe. Wasn't there supposed to be an art to this? A kind of subtlety? Besides, the amount was an outrage. Did this girl think that money grew on trees? It wasn't as if she was actually securing the job for her.

Probably mistaking her hesitation for an invitation to negotiate, Settlement forged ahead. 'It's your lucky day. I can take $40 if you don't have $50.'

'I don't have any money on me. Please help me,' Delta replied, hating herself for sounding as if she was begging. But what could she do? Job adverts had become so rare, and this one had given her such a good feeling.

With an ungracious downturn of her lips, the girl returned the envelope to her saying scornfully, 'You're not my mother's child. You can't expect me to do this for nothing.'

Delta snatched the envelope back. Apoplectic with sudden anger, she turned on her heel and strode out. She stood for a moment by the gate, threw the envelope into a bin, then on second thoughts, she turned back and fished it out. Why waste a good copy of her CV? Reprints were expensive. And maybe, just maybe, other job adverts would come up. Resolutely, she picked a brisk pace and flagged down a *kombi* heading back to the city centre.

Past Gweru Hospital, the *kombi* picked up three young men who took the seat directly in front of her. From their rowdy conversation she gathered that two of them were lampooning their miserable-looking mate. Apparently, he'd just joined the civil service as a 'youth officer', a euphemism for youth militia, also commonly known as the Green Bombers. They were most active around election time, particularly in rural areas.

'*Shamaz*, a Green Bomber? With your degree? I'd rather sit at home and rot,' one young man laughed.

'But we'll be helping people and doing projects and...' The hapless youth didn't get a chance to finish before his friends broke into rowdy laughter.

One spluttered, 'You're mad. What projects? Beating up people to force them to vote *the right way*?'

'*Ehe*, beating up not just any people, *but old people!* Grandmothers and grandfathers. Imagine. If you're going to be a civil servant, at least be smart about it. Why not a CIO... or a traffic cop? Something that can help you line your pockets at least?' the other one teased, smirking.

Before their subject of ridicule could answer, they'd reached their stop. They disembarked noisily and left Delta reflecting on their conversation. If she ever had a chance to join the civil service, which of the suggested options would she consider?

Definitely not the CIO! To her hyperactive imagination, the intelligence service conjured images of extortion, torture and disappearing targets dropped into deep vats of acid. This was the type of reputation the agency had in some quarters, but who knew if it was true or melodramatic conjecture.

Maybe a traffic cop? It was a notoriously popular job, aided and abetted by numerous roadblocks at which officers wielded their weapons of mass extortion – handcuffs, baton sticks, wheel clamping devices and dangerous metal spikes which could perforate the most robust of tyres, forcing vehicles to stop in a manner which sometimes resulted in accidents.

She shook her head. Faking one's identity as Misi Hurukuro or playing smoke and mirrors with rural farmers was one thing. Extortion, issuing threats or indeed making people disappear constituted an altogether different type of malfeasance. No matter how thickly one's pockets could be lined, she wouldn't go there.

Back in town, she still felt rather bruised by her encounter with Settlement. She wandered aimlessly for a while, window-shopping for things that she couldn't afford. As she turned the corner at CABS Bank, she collided with a tall, heavily-built man. To her horror, she felt herself losing balance, then falling.

Mouth rounded in a silent scream, she squeezed her eyes shut, expecting immense pain on contact with the pavement. Suddenly, she felt strong hands steadying her, equally strong arms wrapping themselves tightly around her, and then she was upright. A bit unsteady, but definitely upright. Freezing cold liquid had splashed onto her chest, trickling between her breasts and down to her stomach.

It took a moment to focus. The man was looking down at her, apologizing, while she could only stare up at him, dumbfounded. What were the odds of an encounter with *him* on a street in Gweru? And in such a manner?

Mr Banga looked and sounded as surprised as she felt. '*Misi?* Are you all right? I wasn't looking where I was going. Sorry my milkshake has spoilt your dress.' She looked down. A dark liquid had made conspicuous stains, mainly around her bodice.

'Here, Misi, let me.' He fished a handkerchief out of his pocket and started dabbing with awkward futility at her chest, embarrassing her further. The liquid, which must have been a chocolate milkshake, had seeped right through the fabric, causing considerable discolouration. Her dress was ruined.

Passers-by turned to stare. She had to escape from this man. 'It's all right. I have to go,' she said, shaken, retreating from further physical contact.

'No, it's not all right, and you don't look all right. Come with me and sit down for a bit. We have some catching up to do,' he added authoritatively, taking her arm by the elbow. He steered her towards the nearby Chicken Inn, and she went along on heavy, reluctant feet. He found an empty table and they sat facing each other.

Looking at him, the word that came to mind was 'well-nourished'. He was overweight in the same way she remembered, and he cut an arresting figure in an expensive-looking suit. His hair was extremely short, almost to the point of baldness. This look, she didn't remember.

'I asked Maruva to call you about a job a while ago… What have you been up to in sleepy Gweru?' He stared at her with an intensity that only increased her discomfort.

'Umm, this and that.' Caught off guard by his question, she was instinctively vague. No way was she going to tell him about the market.

'I see. Can I get you something to eat, Misi?' he asked, his hands playing with a menu card. Why did he have to keep repeating *that* name? She had no idea how to end this conversation before it strayed to something personal about her fictional alter ego.

'No, thanks. I'm running late for an appointment.' It was a small lie, therefore in her mind, inconsequential.

'Really?' He looked and sounded genuinely disappointed. She wondered why. He slid a business card across the table, probably having concluded that 'this and that' meant she was unemployed. He said, 'Take this. I have a new business in Harare and we're recruiting. Give me a call tomorrow so that I can give you more information. Or better still, can I call you?'

With a measure of reluctance, she took the card and got up saying, ' I really have to go, but thanks for the card. I'll call you.'

'I look forward to that,' he said. She almost expected him to wink in that sleazy Richie Rich manner she remembered from Hunger Buster, but he didn't. Away from Harare, he was like a different man. Still, she couldn't get away quickly enough.

In the *kombi* she looked at his business card. There it was… Richard Banga, Managing Director, Silhouette Lodge and Conference Centre, 750 Enterprise Road, Harare. It was a place that she'd never heard of, but staring at the card, she felt a spasm of regret.

Forget chemical engineering. If only she hadn't faked being Misi Hurukuro, she'd have definitely taken a chance at this. What had she been thinking?

27

Cashleen was caught unawares by the onset of the rainy season. The archaic drainage systems in the CBD were in disrepair and choked with rubbish, plastic bags, bottles and tins. As a result, the drains overflowed whenever it rained. Dirty water tended to collect in puddles on the pavement, worsening unhygienic conditions where she and other vendors plied their trade.

Occasionally, the upside-down cardboard boxes which she used as display tables would collapse, leaving her stock at risk of sliding into the murky waters which ran along the pavements. Knowing how people used the streets as open toilets, especially at night, made her worry about selling contaminated food. Harare was no stranger to typhoid and the occasional cholera outbreak.

She castigated herself for not having invested in a fold-up plastic table like some of the other vendors. She had belatedly tried to find one, but there were none in town. Not even in the numerous Chinese shops that had a reputation for stocking such items.

She went over to Tanaka's stall to find out if she had a spare one. She waited in the background while the young woman attended to a customer. Always smart with an aura of efficiency, Tanaka seemed to exude even more confidence today, if that was possible.

How does she do it? Cashleen wondered.

Today, she boldly wore a bright red #*ThisFlag* protest T-shirt. Cashleen's keen eye took in her stylish Levi jeans and high-heeled leather sandals; no doubt quality steals from second-hand clothing bales. The sandals were of genuine leather, not the fake imitations from Chinese emporiums. Her outfit was complemented by large, intricately designed earrings, which could only be from South Africa, given their distinctive Zulu-style beading.

'Trust me, Magic Skin Toner is the best product ever. There's no skin problem it can't get rid of,' she was telling her customer as she held out a bright pink tube, which Cashleen identified as a potent, steroid-based skin lightener. She knew enough about its long-term adverse effects that she'd never recommend it to anyone.

She watched as Tanaka squeezed a tiny amount onto the back of the woman's hand and rubbed it in, saying, 'Here, smell this, and feel its gentle texture with your fingers'. The woman complied and nodded approvingly.

'I swear on my dead mother's grave. It's guaranteed to give you flawless skin in less than two weeks. Just look at my face,' Tanaka went a notch higher with her marketing pitch.

The woman who had a blotchy, pimple-infested face scrutinised her and said decisively, 'I'll take two!'

Cashleen seriously doubted that Tanaka's perfect skin had anything to do with skin lighteners, and she knew that her mother was very much alive. When the woman had walked off, happily clutching her purchase, she couldn't help giggling.

'Tanaka! *Your dead mother?*' she exclaimed. 'And since when did you start using skin lighteners?'

Tanaka laughed dismissively. '*Aiwa,* Cashleen! Leave me alone. I've got to make a living. I don't stock up on items so that I can spend the day admiring them. I have to sell. It's all about the money, *shaz.*'

Cashleen shook her head, saying, 'Aaah, Tanaka...' She held back a comment that could come across as criticism. There was no need to aggravate a friend from whom she needed more than just advice.

'So how are you getting on with the stuff you bought from Chuma? Any increase in sales?'

Cashleen sighed. 'Just a bit, but it's early days.' Then remembering, why she'd come, she enquired about the table.

'You mean these ones?' Tanaka asked pointing to hers. 'No, I don't have a spare one. They're now like gold, *wena*. You know they're imported, right? With these US dollar shortages, I doubt you'll get one anytime soon.'

Disappointed, Cashleen asked, 'Isn't there anything I can use instead?'

'Nothing I can think of. But let me get my runner to check for you in South Africa. But you'll have to pay me in hard cash USD or Rand. No small or dirty notes, no Ecocash or bank transfer either.'

Cashleen had no choice, so nodding, she accepted. She'd have to buy clean notes on the black market. Her customers bought from her using mainly Ecocash and dirty, small denomination US dollar notes, which people who needed to import always rejected. Crisp notes in bigger denominations were preferred. So she understood Tanaka's terms. The woman had set up an efficient cross-border smuggling network. Her customers were mostly downtown tuck-shop owners who appeared to be less regulated than formal businesses, as well as other individuals who traded under the taxman's radar.

She made no secret of how lucrative her business was, saying that she was overwhelmed by the number of customers. People generally preferred imports to locally produced goods which were often more expensive and not always of competitive quality.

The idea of joining Tanaka in this venture had grown on Cashleen. Before she told her, however, she'd tested the waters by revealing her intention to Delta. Not surprisingly, her friend had sounded sceptical, but Cashleen had decided she'd go ahead, with or without anyone's approval. It was all very well for Delta to take the moral high ground with her fake certificates and the fiasco at Hunger Buster.

Other than raising the required start-up amount in US dollars, she also needed more information from Tanaka about how to evade the law. It was best to be cautious. A glance at her watch told her that it was almost time for her appointment with Itai, so it would have to be another conversation. She thanked Tanaka and said her goodbyes.

※※※

Cashleen sat in Ocean City Restaurant along First Street and waited for Itai who was running late. Sipping at her Fanta, she lost herself in reverie.

Her thoughts danced here and there. What kind of future can I or my generation expect? she asked herself. She'd managed to pretend that everything was under control, doing what she had to do at that spot along Robert Mugabe Road. In reality, insidious erosion of self-belief stalked her most days. She wasn't sure how much Delta, Tanaka, or even Unesu, would empathise, because they seemed to be managing.

She'd considered talking to Rufaro. Communication with her sister had slowly improved. She could identify her slowly evolving financial independence as an important step towards healing their relationship. Recent conversations had led to tentative discussions around personal issues. Most importantly, Rufaro had spoken positively about her depression, about how her psychiatrist planned to wean her off Prozac and make cognitive behavioural therapy the mainstay of her treatment.

Indeed, it was in one of their recent, more intimate conversations that Rufaro had asked her to find out more about Itai. It was odd that after all this time neither of them knew where their brother lived, or what exactly he did for a living. She was hoping to get some answers now.

Itai arrived just as she was trying to dial his number again.

'Hullo, Cash,' he said with a grin and slid into the seat opposite hers. He shook her hand across the table, but there was no apology for being late.

'Hi,' she said, returning his smile, noting that he was well dressed and clean-shaven. He'd also gained weight and had a self-satisfied air about him. She searched his face for any signs that he was still smoking marijuana. There were none.

His deals must be going well, she thought.

'*Saka,* how's my little street-hustler sister doing?' he teased, his manner reminiscent of a time long gone, when life had been simpler and happiness hadn't been an illusion.

'Not that great.' She made a face.

'I can see that. And you're too thin.' He was candid in scrutiny but she chose to ignore the comments.

'What about you?' she asked, leaning back in her chair.

His phone rang just at that moment and he flipped it open to take the call. She watched a shadow flit cross his face as he listened.

'No, no, no!' he said emphatically, clenching a fist. He turned his head briefly and she saw an ugly scar at the back of his head. What had happened to him?

He was saying, 'The cheating bastard! He can't take it. Tell him I'm coming over right now.' Livid, he snapped the phone shut.

'What's wrong?' Cashleen asked, concerned.

'It's nothing,' he replied dismissively before saying, 'Listen, I have to go.'

'But you've just arrived,' she protested.

'Something has come up. I have to go!'

Cashleen felt hurt and discouraged. This, after all those times he'd failed to turn up? A weight settled on her heart.

'That scar on your head. What happened?' she asked abruptly.

'That? It's nothing.' Again, he was offhand. From a leather back-pack, he casually pulled out a wad of $100 notes. 'Here, take these. It's two thousand USD.'

Cashleen could hardly believe her eyes. She'd never handled so much money in her life. Besides, she still owed him money which he'd lent her to start off as a vendor. Had he forgotten?

'Thank you. But what's it for?' she asked warily.

Itai shrugged, as if it was a small thing. 'I don't know. Whatever you want. Get yourself some new clothes or something.' He'd slipped into the unexpected big brother role of a provider. A very generous one.

'Really? Thank you so much,' she repeated, overwhelmed but wondering how he could afford to do this for her.

He got up to leave, 'Cool. I'll call you later today.'

Cashleen nodded, although somehow she knew that he wouldn't. She sat there for a while, thinking about all the different things that she could do with her unexpected windfall. Taking it to the bank was certainly not one of them. Then a smile spread over her face as an idea dawned.

28

The New Year was well underway and Unesu wasn't doing badly. There was something liberating about being a medical practitioner with full registration. Completing his internship had not been easy, but for the first time since he graduated, he could explore options. It didn't matter that they were limited. He'd finally made it.

Some of his contemporaries had gone to work as medical officers at peripheral hospitals where government hadn't frozen recruitment. Others were in general practice like John, or they were working as casualty officers at private hospitals in town. At least seven had gone abroad for specialist training while a handful had secured postgraduate training posts at the medical school.

Unesu decided that he'd devote time to looking after his mother before taking on the demands of postgraduate studies. He stayed in Harare and joined psychiatry at the teaching hospital. This speciality was refreshingly different from obstetrics and gynaecology, which were always too busy, with life and death emergencies being almost a daily certainty. He didn't miss those adrenalin-fuelled days when he'd had to assist in management of women who arrived in such a bad state that poor clinical outcomes were inevitable.

His mother's cancer was now in remission. However, he had a residual, morbid fear of a possible relapse. He could never forget how, during his gynaecology rotation, he'd attended to a patient whose records showed that she'd been given the all clear just the year before. But she'd returned with her cancer so advanced that there'd been no alternative except palliation.

Such extreme recurrences not long after an apparently successful treatment were a statistical rarity, and his mother *had* been given a good prognosis. Still, that little 'what if' lurked in his mind and nagged him persistently.

All things considered, though, 2017 was turning out to be a good year. His mother was in better health. He'd paid off Takunda for the Toyota and he was planning to consult his bank about a mortgage. He'd also maintained his lucrative locum at Orion Clinic.

Although the clinic managed to keep its termination services discreet while offering excellent primary healthcare services for women, he'd give up the work in a heartbeat if he could. It was never far from his mind that being pro-choice wouldn't offer protection, should a medicolegal issue arise.

He managed his internal conflict and sustained himself with reminders about why he had to be there. While he was a clinically capable doctor, every shift required him to make a conscious decision to be circumspect and diligent, so as to avoid complications or any situation that could leave him exposed.

That Monday, after completing admission formalities for a known bipolar patient who'd presented to the unit with acute psychosis, he ran through the rain to his car and set off for a shift at Orion Clinic.

Irritated, he whistled under his breath. What could be worse than driving at snail's pace through a late afternoon thunderstorm on a congested, pot-hole-riddled road with hardly any discernible lane markings? Not only was general visibility compromised, but the rain had filled up potholes, concealing them, thus making them even more dangerous.

With a wry smile, he recalled Trevor Noah's quip: *'In Zimbabwe, they used to drive on the left side of the road. Now they drive on what's left of the road.'*

No wonder the President had declared Harare's roads a national disaster, and in the *Government Gazette*, no less! Sourly, Unesu asked himself if the man had been blind all these years. He was skeptical that any serious rehabilitation work would begin simply because the long-neglected roads had finally caught the attention of the highest authority in the land.

It would probably be said that sanctions were making it impossible to repair the roads. Or there was no money. And if there was any money, the roads to the elite's homes and farms would be repaired first. Elsewhere, there might be some half-hearted patch-work repairs, which would immediately revert back to holes the moment it rained.

Then, he thought, our MPs and ministers will each claim good reason to demand yet another fancy Landcruiser to help them dodge potholes. Nobody would be surprised.

As he approached his destination, the storm had begun to ease. Through the drizzle, he could just make out the green glow of Orion Clinic's neon signpost. He indicated left and drove through the entrance. He was just on time.

)0(0(

It was almost 7 p.m. Unesu had completed his list of consultations and procedures quickly, with no sense of time having passed. Dr Reza and the duty anaesthetist had already left the clinic. Walk-in patients hardly ever came this late in the day, so he could get ready to leave as well. He only needed to complete his last patient's post-procedure review.

Mazwi passed by to negotiate a roster amendment. A sprinkling of raindrops glittered on her braids, otherwise she was as well-turned-out as always. Agreeing to her request was easy. She'd always been accommodating and it was the least he could do to reciprocate.

'How's Psych so far?' she asked, smiling. He noticed that she'd put on a little weight, and thought there was something else subtly different about her, but he just couldn't put a finger on it.

'Psychiatry is,' he paused, 'good.' Then half-expecting her to respond with an all too familiar tongue-in-cheek comment about the speciality, he added defensively, 'I like it, actually.'

'Great! 'Cause there's no point in doing work that you hate. Would you consider specialising?' She sounded genuinely interested.

'Possibly.' He was being truthful. The experience, brief though it still was, had led him to reconsider an earlier idea about neurosurgery training, which he now thought to have been driven by nothing more than a craving for the prestige that came with being a neurosurgeon.

'What of you?'

'Preparing for USMLE exams. That's why I need you to cover some of my shifts.'

He looked at her, surprised. 'Really? You'd consider moving all the way to the US?'

'Of course. I'm not hanging around here like a sitting duck. With everything that's going on, where do you think this country is headed?'

Sitting duck? He was surprised that she'd have such an opinion. With her hallmark complacency, the latest model car, her tasteful dress sense and rumours of a mansion tucked away somewhere in Borrowdale, he didn't assume she was someone dissatisfied with her standard of living.

She hadn't even bothered to get involved when most interns had been advocating a strike for better salaries. Then he remembered her mentioning something about how her husband's work had dried up when companies that had been his major clients had gone bust. Maybe that's what had prompted her to take the US examinations.

'If you can't see that things here are bound to get worse, then you need to open your eyes, Doc. And your mind too.'

She'd never spoken to him in this way before and he wasn't

sure if she was serious. Of course, he was aware that things could be better, but not bad to the extent that he'd think of emigrating, or leaving his mother.

He shrugged. 'But is going away the answer? Why not stay and fix things?'

With a peal of laughter, she wagged a finger at him. 'Fixing things? Who can? You're the psych guy! Maybe you should be self-diagnosing a severe delusional state.'

Was she being patronising? He felt irritated but he smiled; she was entitled to her opinion. 'Let's wait and see,' he said and looked pointedly at his watch. He still had some work to do.

'Anyway, I have to go now. Thanks for this.' She waved a copy of the roster.

'Any time,' he replied.

As she turned to leave, he noticed, side profile, a gentle lower abdominal swelling That was it! She was pregnant. How had he missed it? He wondered how she could continue to work here, and what went through her mind when she performed terminations. It couldn't be that easy.

Sister Chenai walked into the consulting room with his patient's file. He enjoyed working with her. There was an infectious aura of happiness about her and she performed her work so well that her shifts invariably ran smoothly.

'Doc, your patient, Angelica…'

He interrupted her, his heart missing a beat. 'What about her? Is she okay?' The possibility of adverse outcomes was a genuine concern, especially uterine perforation. It was a known complication, which could occur during any procedure requiring uterine instrumentation, in any setting, and with whatever level of practitioner. Yet, it could mean a different kind of calamity here.

Sister Chenai smiled reassuringly. 'Of course she is, Doc. She's just having a cup of tea. I think she was too anxious during our pre-op chat to understand a word I said about contraception. Would you mind discussing that with her again when you do your post-procedure review? Please?'

'Sure. She can come through now.'

'You're a star, Doc. I've already given her an aftercare pack and antibiotics. It's just the contraception that needs sorting.' Sister Chenai handed him the file.

Unesu nodded. To remind himself of the patient's background once more, he read through her admission card, which would be shredded after she left the clinic. Angelica Gomo. She was nineteen years old, and a first-year law student at the university. She'd put down her home address as a mission school in rural Gokwe. There was no Harare address.

Her emergency contact person was a Mr Mbudzi. Unesu wondered who he was to her. She'd left the field for 'Relationship to emergency contact person' blank.

Anyway, it was clinic policy not to insist on potentially sensitive information, as well as other data that had no direct bearing on treatment. Confidentiality issues could be a barrier to accessing care. The record showed that she had no significant medical history, no known drug allergies and she was otherwise in good health.

His own treatment notes indicated that the procedure had been uncomplicated and there'd been no immediate post-operative concerns. The anaesthetist's notes confirmed full recovery from anaesthesia. So far so good. Idly, he contemplated what her back story might be, and how she'd ended up at Orion Clinic. Whatever the reasons, it was mandatory for the clinic to offer contraception and sexual health advice before a patient left.

There was a tentative knock on the door. He looked up to see Angelica in the doorway. Even though she had red-rimmed eyes and still looked subdued, he was stunned by the transformation in her appearance. When he'd treated her, she'd been make-up free, dressed in a plain hospital gown and her hair had been concealed in a theatre cap.

Now, the girl could pass for a model. Clearly, she had applied make-up after the procedure. Had she really brought a make-up kit to the clinic? Unesu wondered. She was impeccably dressed in expensive clothes. On her head was a weave with elaborate curls. The handbag that she carried was a designer label. A metal Coach insignia shimmered conspicuously. How could a young student from Gokwe afford that look, which he associated with older, well-to-do women?

He gestured for her to take a seat and called Sister Chenai to come and sit in during the consultation. It was clear that the girl was nervous. She sat awkwardly, leaning forward and hugging herself. She avoided his gaze and stared studiously at a spot on the desk.

He gave her a reassuring smile and asked, 'How are you feeling?'

'Fine,' she said, still staring at the desk.

'How's the bleeding?'

'It's a little,' she mumbled averting her gaze sideways, as if embarrassed by the question.

'Angelica, do you need more information about contraception?'

He deliberately avoided using the term family planning, which seemed to dismay young girls. She raised her head and gave him a furtive glance, then shook her head mutely. This wasn't going too well. He wanted eye contact. He wanted to engage her in a reciprocal discussion, but she clearly wouldn't be drawn.

He wondered if she was the victim of a lecherous older man, of which there were plenty who prowled the university, plying vulnerable young women with money, expensive gifts, or good pass rates in return for sexual favours.

Campus was fertile hunting ground because so many students couldn't afford the tuition fees or accommodation in Harare. Then there were other basics such as food, textbooks and clothing. 'Have you decided what you'll use?' he asked after a pause, making sure that his tone was cordial, as if they were talking about the most ordinary of subjects.

'I prefer Implanon.' Her voice was barely audible, but the fact that she'd actually decided on something was a step in the right direction.

After confirming that she did know enough about the implant, he offered to insert one right away. She accepted, her eyes finally lighting up with something akin to interest. He quickly performed the procedure with Sister Chenai's assistance, and then gave her a pack of condoms, stressing safe sex advice. Anything to prevent her from coming back with another unwanted pregnancy or an STI. She murmured her thanks and left.

Unesu felt a sense of having accomplished something that could well make a positive difference in her life. He imagined her completing her education without incident of another unplanned pregnancy.

Sister Chenai said, 'Thanks for doing that, Doc. I should be going. I really struggle with night driving. Thank goodness the rain has stopped.'

'Thanks to you too. Yes, it's time to go,' he replied, rising from his chair. Sister Chenai picked up Angelica's folder and left the room.

Leaving the security guards to lock up, Unesu exited the building through the back entrance and walked to the car park.

Not far from the gate, he spotted Angelica standing next to a black Mercedes Benz SUV under an incandescent floodlight. With her was a grey-haired, absurdly pot-bellied man.

He looks like a pregnant woman, Unesu thought, shaking his head. The man looked vaguely familiar, but Unesu wasn't sure where he might know him from, if at all. TV? The newspaper?

He certainly couldn't be Angelica's father from the way he was looking at her. They seemed to be either in intense conversation or having an argument.

For all her subdued demeanour in the clinic, Angelica was looking directly into the man's face, hands planted on her hips in a gesture of defiance. Then the man put his arms around her shoulders in an awkward embrace. One hand slid to the small of her back and rested on her posterior. She recoiled and got into the car. Then they drove off. Unesu shook his head, hoping that whatever was going on in her life, Angelica would be fine.

Before he took off, he cast a glance at his mobile phone, which had been on silent mode in the clinic. A number of messages had come through. His mother needed him to send money for groceries. He texted a confirmation that he'd do a bank transfer the following day. He made a mental note to add something extra for *Mainini* who'd become his dependent by tacit agreement. For her part in tending to his mother, he owed her that at the very least.

There was a message from John asking if he could please borrow his Oxford Handbook of Clinical Medicine. Apparently, he needed it *'lyk y'day'*. Unesu had two copies, so he could spare the older edition.

He replied. *Home @ 9. Come collect.*

Waving at the security guard, he drove out.

29

While adding canned foods to her variety had improved earnings slightly, once again Cashleen's sales dropped. She discovered that four other vendors within the area had begun selling identical brands of Cut Price canned foods, also at prices lower than those in supermarkets.

This was the exasperating thing about Harare's street-hustle scene. An idea was profitable only until another person pinched it. Why spend time cracking one's head when you could simply replicate someone else's ideas?

She'd given this venture everything she had. However, as she struggled to convince pedestrians who hurried past that she had the best on offer, she was aware of how much physical and emotional energy she was expending going nowhere.

The last straw came on Tuesday. It was a balmy day which started off unremarkably; other than for a few rumours on social media about a *#ThisFlag* demonstration. Because she hadn't seen the usual pre-demonstration posts on social media or heard anything from Tanaka, Cashleen dismissed the stories as the kind of melodramatic street gossip that kept everyone entertained and on their toes.

Besides, the government had imposed a ban on demonstrations

and public gatherings. Police clearance would be required in special circumstances, but she didn't think there was a chance of that being granted. To them, a *#ThisFlag* demonstration was likely to be taken more as subversion than special circumstances.

Around mid-morning, a woman turned up and took the spot next to hers. The vendor who'd once occupied that space had stopped coming due to injuries sustained in a beating by municipal police. Apparently, this woman was his cousin.

'I'm Maita, but you can call me May,' she told Cashleen brightly as she lugged a box of second-hand shoes and two cooler-boxes into position.

'Cashleen,' she replied, stretching out her hand to offer a handshake.

'Hullo. Sorry, no handshaking for me. I only do *cholera-shakes*.' She giggled and fisted her hand.

Cashleen reciprocated with a smile. Their fists made brief contact in the trending form of greeting which supposedly carried less risk of spreading diseases like cholera and typhoid in situations where there was little or no water for hand-washing. The streets were one such place.

May settled herself into position with much ceremony. She arranged the shoes in two neat little rows and half-opened one cooler-box to reveal bottles of frozen water.

Cashleen soon discovered that she was a relentlessly cheerful woman whose speech was peppered with jokes. Soon, she began to feel as if she was in the presence of a female version of *Gringo*. May's current subject of ridicule was bond notes. She found it riotously funny that government was insisting on parity with the US dollar, and joked with anyone who cared to listen, fellow vendors and customers alike.

'I'd be very stupid to believe something so laughable. Fortunately, I'm not. I don't think the government believe themselves either. If they did, I'd be very worried about them.' Her eyes danced with mischief.

May also had an inquisitiveness that matched her willingness to share very personal information. Unnecessarily, Cashleen thought. She didn't seem to care about how reserved Cashleen's responses were. In no time, she'd told her how she'd divorced an abusive husband and was raising two exceptionally bright children on her own.

'So clever, but I worry all the time about their future.' A frown flitted across her vivacious face. 'If things don't change, I can see them joining me on this street.' She spread her arms to encompass the broken pavement crowded with vendors.

'They'll be fine, don't worry,' Cashleen responded, automatically.

'I really hope so. I want them to go to university someday, but nowadays the streets are swarming with graduate vendors who can't get jobs. All that time spent teaching and studying gone to waste! And all that taxpayers' money…' She shook her head and widened her eyes, indicating that she couldn't believe anything so ludicrous.

Something stopped Cashleen from telling her that she too was one of those unfortunate beings to whom she was referring. Maybe it would be a story for another day, but she imagined May being so intrigued that she'd immediately tell everyone.

She changed the subject and pointed at the cooler-boxes. 'Where do you buy this bottled water?' May gestured for her to come nearer and whispered, 'It's boiled Harare city council water.'

Cashleen drew back, shocked that May could say this openly, and to someone she'd just met. For her to pass off boiled council water as purified water just to make money was beyond her imagination. The city authorities were on record as having condemned their own water, so people boiled it or used water treatment tablets and solutions. Commercially purified bottled water was too expensive for most people.

'How do you…?'

'Easy!' May said. Then in a low confidential voice, she went on to explain that she sent out her children to pick empty plastic bottles from bins, streets and rubbish dumps. They'd clean them thoroughly, taking care not to ruin the brand labels. They'd then fill them with boiled water, which they'd freeze – fortunately, May's sister had a freezer – and May would sell the water on the street. For this business, her only real expense was that of buying self-sealing bottle caps similar to those used by most water bottling companies.

Apparently, summertime sales were excellent, although they slumped on rainy or cloudy days. Cashleen searched May's face for any qualms, but the woman smiled widely, as if expecting a compliment for being so innovative.

While Cashleen was trying to think of a suitable response, all hell broke loose. With hindsight, she wondered how she, May and the other vendors around them could have been so oblivious. There had to have been some warning signs, such as an increase in the noise level, a sense of agitation, or just a word, quickly passed on, confirming the rumours of a protest. Had they been so deeply engrossed in conversation to the point of being so unaware?

In the style of an ambush, a rowdy crowd descended upon Robert Mugabe Road, heading down from Kaguvi Street, with the police in hot pursuit. There was much shouting and screaming.

Momentarily disoriented, Cashleen froze. And then something exploded as clouds of teargas rose into the air. The crowd surged forward and chaos spread to the pavement. In the mayhem, goods fell and scattered everywhere.

'*Maiwe!* Run!' Maita shouted, abandoning attempts to gather her things.

Instinctively, Cashleen grabbed her backpack and ran as fast as she could. Gathering speed, she turned left, trying to break free from the crowd, which was largely headed down Robert Mugabe Road.

She felt a heavy blow of what she thought was a police baton stick on her back. In a moment of acute pain, she felt herself losing balance. A woman stumbled and grabbed at her to stop herself from falling. Cashleen's skirt was ripped, she found herself suddenly exposed. A male voice shouted an obscenity and another voice joined in, hurling a graphic description of her anatomy.

Their shouts rang out, distorted and amplified in her ears by her fear.

How was it possible that anyone had time to be abusive while running away from the police? Were these hardened street thugs with nothing to lose? Or was it a reflection of mob psychology? Eyes smarting, she tried desperately to cover herself with the remains of her torn skirt.

A small *mshikashika* screeched to a halt in front of her. 'Get in, get in,' the elderly driver shouted. She pulled her torn skirt tighter and hesitated for a split second. Then she dove into the back seat, deciding that she was probably safer with him than on the street. Someone banged on the car roof and a man tried to yank open the door on her side.

The old man sped off in silence, heading away from the commotion. By then, Cashleen was in tears of fear and humiliation. From her backpack, she retrieved a cloth that she sometimes used to cover her goods. Her hands were shaking so badly that she could hardly tie it around her waist to cover herself.

The man stopped his taxi alongside Harare Gardens, well away from the pandemonium. With no reference to the incident or why he'd stopped to help her, he turned to her and said, 'I'm Mr Phiri. Where do you live? If it's not far, I can take you there.'

Cashleen wiped away her tears, choked with gratitude for the kindness shown to her by this total stranger. She cleared her throat. 'I'm Cashleen. Thank you very much. I'm at Northern Heights.'

'Tongogara Road?'

'Yes, thank you.'

'I know that place,' he responded, turning on the ignition.

He dropped her by the gate. 'Take care whenever you're in the city. Sometimes bad things happen out there.'

She nodded and again murmured her thanks, then rummaged in her backpack for some money. To her surprise, he refused payment for the taxi ride and drove off with a wave.

When she entered the gate, *Kule* Jojo shouted a greeting from the far end of the garden where he was watering a flowerbed. She waved back, ran up the stairs to her apartment and slumped into an armchair. Never before had she been so afraid and so humiliated.

She burst into fresh tears, and when those had ebbed, a wave of anger came over her. She rubbed her sore back, thinking. Once again, she'd lost her goods and there was no chance of recovery from that loss.

That evening, she wrote a deeply personal piece about the day's events. She made no attempt at objectivity; it was just an outpouring of raw, intense emotion. Putting down her thoughts gave her a chance to reflect once again, but this time from a very different angle. The feeling that life had her trapped firmly in a corner was unbearable. She realised she'd have to fight back. She couldn't allow herself to remain a victim of circumstances.

She had a new understanding of the frustrations that had driven Sando across the border, and the anger that had turned him into a fearless activist.

Where was he? She, and everyone in their mutual circles still hadn't heard from him. Thoughts of him and what could have happened to him were the last matters on her mind as she fell asleep.

The following morning, she woke up with renewed clarity of thought and purpose. It was time to team up with Tanaka, and without delay, she told herself. If it would take smuggling to get her on her feet, then so be it. Although in principle she'd made the decision weeks before, she'd procrastinated. She now decided that she'd deal with any consequences as and when they came up.

So much for trying to stay on the straight and narrow! In the grand scheme of things, it really was over-rated. Tanaka was thriving. She'd bought a neat Honda Fit and taken lease of a small apartment in The Avenues. A paid assistant now manned her flea-market stall.

'Can't do that anymore. I'm gunning for bigger bucks,' she'd told Cashleen in her customary sassy style. Apparently, she now spent more time networking, collecting orders and delivering goods.

They met outside Road Port bus terminus. Instead of her customary protest T-shirts, today she wore one whose front was emblazoned with: *Money may be evil but being broke isn't holy!* She told Cashleen that she was waiting for a parcel that her contact had sent on a bus from the DRC via Zambia.

'Viagra my friend! I've found a niche market. You can't imagine how fast those pills sell!' She gave a knowing smile.

Instinctively, Cashleen felt dismayed. The drug was potentially unsafe when peddled recklessly, and without a doctor's prescription. But just as quickly, she reined in the feeling, which was now at odds with what she intended to do herself. After all, Tanaka wouldn't be forcing anyone to buy the pills. It was about adults making their own choices.

For as long as she'd known her, Tanaka had been ready to listen and offer useful suggestions. This time around, Cashleen sensed that her friend's burgeoning success was making her impatient and abrasive. Tanaka replied sharply when she bemoaned how she'd been feeling as if she was trapped and unable to make anything meaningful out of her life.

'Honestly, Cash, must we talk about the same thing again and again? Sometimes you do *sooo* miss the point. Take the canned foods for instance. That was only to help counter your losses in the short term. You're a clever girl and I thought by now you'd have had enough insight to move on to something bolder, more enterprising. Tell me, how many tins of beans would I have had to sell in order to buy my Honda?'

'I don't know. Many thousands, maybe,' she replied, immediately on the defensive, stung by the criticism. This wasn't about Tanaka or her car. Besides she hadn't even given her a moment to say why she'd come.

'Exactly!' Tanaka said. 'What's the chance of something like that happening?'

Cashleen shook her head. 'Zero. Look, Tanaka. I think you misunderstand. I came to tell you that I've thought things over.

I'm ready for cross-border trading.' To her ears, trading sounded better than smuggling.

'Really?' Tanaka gave her an incredulous look, then her face split into a wide smile. 'Now we're talking! What took you so long?'

She was honest. 'Fear. I worried about breaking the law'.

Tanaka inclined her head and searched Cashleen's face. 'Hmm. And now...?'

'And now? Stuff the law!' Cashleen said and they laughed, conspirators united.

'Well, time is money my friend. My runner's going to Jo'burg on Saturday. If you can get five hundred US dollars for your stock and transport costs, and another hundred to sweeten up those customs fellows, I can lump your order with mine and get you started. I know what's selling, and at the moment I can't cope with demand. You can have some of my clients. How does that sound?' Clearly, Tanaka wasn't one to waste any time.

'Sounds great!' Cashleen was decisive.

There was no looking back and it was a relief to know that things could set off this quickly. Yes, she could certainly avail six hundred dollars. The surprise gift from Itai was still ensconced safely under her mattress.

Tanaka gave her a mock thumbs up gesture. 'You wait and see. I'm going to set you right. Once you start, you'll wonder why you've wasted all this time.'

'By the way,' she asked, 'do you have a bank account?'

'No. I used to have one, but I had to close it,' Cashleen replied.

'You'll definitely need a bank account for this. And didn't you say you and your friend's aunt will be selling cash soon?'

'Yes. We'll start at the end of the month.'

'Well, I'm surprised she didn't tell you about bank accounts.'

'I think we'll only be dealing in hard USD and bond currency only,' Cashleen explained.

Tanaka gave a short laugh. 'No, no, don't restrict yourself like that already. A savvy black market dealer runs several bank accounts and as many swipe cards. You'll have to transact on all platforms. Think ZIPIT, swipe, bank transfers and mobile money. Compared to cash-on-cash only, that's where you'll get bigger profits. I'm sure your friend's aunt knows all this.'

'Yes, I should think so,' Cashleen replied.

It was hardly a surprise that Tanaka was so well informed, her being a self-declared street-smart city girl.

'And another thing... At some point you'll need a driving licence. If I were you, I'd take the written test now'.

'But driving lessons are so expensive,' Cashleen replied. Anyway, what were the chances that she'd own a car in the foreseeable future?

'The written test is not expensive at all. Take that test to start off with. And you've got to stop making excuses for doing nothing. What do you have to lose?'

Realising that Tanaka was right. Cashleen thanked her, smiled and promised to see her on Friday about her first consignment from South Africa.

30

A sense of being trapped was now ever-present. Time had moved too quickly; each uncertain month blending into the next. Delta could project herself into the future, older, poorer, her years of education gone to waste. She hadn't bargained on becoming a phony market broker in the business of ripping off unsuspecting rural farmers.

Although they tried not to show it, she knew that her parents were bewildered at having two unemployed graduates at home. They'd grown up and begun their professions at a time when education had meant something; when at a minimum, successful completion of high school had been a foundation on which to construct prospects of a solid career.

She also heard disenchantment in their discussions. Now that 'bond notes' had been introduced, they spoke of how incredible it was that the government had gone ahead. 'If they succeed, they must write a handbook: *Principles of How to Con the Economy*. It would be a bestseller,' her father said. An educated man, he'd worked hard all his life, and ought to have retired in relative comfort. But here he was, old and impoverished, without a pension and without any indication that his life would improve.

'I doubt they'll succeed,' her mother responded. 'No matter

how loudly or frequently you proclaim that something you print is equal to the US dollar, it isn't and it will collapse. Exactly how or when, I don't know.'

Her father's laughter rang hollow. 'Yes, it won't work. But, of course, *they* won't feel the pain. *They* never do. It's always us. Over and over again.'

Years of adverse experiences had bred a profound cynicism. Economics and financial policy were not Delta's forté, so initially she didn't have strong sentiments about the bond notes. It was the pervasive sense of scepticism, futility and resignation about yet another government imposition that was beginning to get to her.

Planned protests and court petitions had fizzled out. People seemed to have accepted the situation with their customary volatile humour and cowed resilience, responses that never failed them. Jokes and satire were the only things to experience growth during a time of recession.

'Bond' took on a whole new meaning, which implied being counterfeit, or of inferior quality. So, one could have bond clothes from second-hand markets, bond wives with reference to prostitutes, and even bond degrees, as the running joke went about the First Lady's much-debated PhD being a 'bond-PhD'.

Delta commented to her father about how people were increasingly throwing caution to the wind. How did one now dare to say such things about the First Lady's PhD without fear of reprisal?

His response was, 'When people feel they no longer have anything to lose... that's when they're most reckless. And most dangerous.' She could see that he was right. But to what end?

She'd also noticed that the powers-that-be didn't seem to share a consensus about the objective behind the introduction of bond notes and she found the competing explanations confusing and conflicting.

Were bond notes real money or a surrogate currency? Something introduced to ease 'real cash' shortages? An incentive for exporters? Just some small denomination currency to provide change for transactions involving larger US dollar denominations? Or a type of Zim dollar being sneaked in through the back door to distort the economy while the elite dipped their hands into the country's dwindling forex reserves?

She could recall a video that had gone viral on WhatsApp. It showed an MP struggling with a very long and muddled explanation given to a reporter outside the parliament building.

His bald head glistened blindingly in the sun as he spluttered through a thick grey-speckled beard. 'People are not understanding the reserve bank governor. If you *rook*, the *bhondi-dhora* is not a currency. That money is not for *actuary* the money, which is to be used in this country. It is for the easiest change of the *dhora-dhora*, I mean the US-*dhora*. No, you can't say it's now money, proper money with one *dhora*, two *dhora* and five *dhoraz*. Are you going to be earned *onry* five *dhora*, five *dhora*, five *dhora* when you are being earned four hundred *dhoraz?* So, you see, it's not *reari* money.'

It had ended up being no explanation at all, but a convoluted and very revealing satire that had generated public ridicule. Delta's opinion was that if a legislator of note could fail to clarify policies, then they were well and truly doomed. It wasn't so much the MP himself, as an individual, or the video itself, but something to do with the wider, disconcerting implications which forced her to sit down and rethink her future.

More than ever, she realised that nobody and nothing was going to get her out of her predicament. Not even her Life-Coach app, which had been obviously designed by someone entirely out of touch with her reality.

She recalled the Minister of Education saying that graduates shouldn't expect the government to facilitate employment creation; that they ought to create employment for themselves and others.

At the time, she'd wondered if he actually believed his words, when his own children were educated abroad, and back home they had easy access to resources and work opportunities through multiple strategic connections in political circles.

How could she, Delta, set herself up in industry as a self-employed chemical engineer with no connections, no work experience and no financial resources?

It was clear. She'd have to fire herself up to be that girl who'd once believed that if you needed to eat a proverbial dog to carve a path for your life, it would be best to eat a large one. Nobody would give you concessions for having eaten a small one, especially if you then went on to fail. They'd just remember that you were that villain who ate a dog.

She'd have to wake up and do something. That phone call about which she'd been so ambivalent was long overdue.

▲▲▲

It had been a regular day at the market. At home, her father was taking a nap on a reed mat under the shade of a mango tree. He hadn't been sleeping well because his back pain kept him awake at night. He couldn't afford physiotherapy, but his continued treatment with Indocid painkiller was giving him gastric irritation.

A bottle of the antacid Relcer Gel was constantly at his side, and Delta worried that he might just overdose himself one day. She reminded herself to check the pharmacological constituents of the drug and any adverse effects it might have if taken in excess. She tip-toed quietly past without disturbing him and entered the house.

Her mother was sitting in an armchair, reading Charles Mungoshi's *Waiting For The Rain,* an all-time favourite of hers.

'*Amai*, how many times have you read that novel? Don't you ever get tired of it?' she asked, putting her bag down and kicking off her shoes. Contact with the cold cement floor brought instant relief to her aching feet.

Her mother looked up and smiled. It wasn't a smile that reached her eyes. There was sadness and weariness there. Delta knew how much she worried about her father, and about them all. Reading was a form of escape. She'd read anything and everything, from novels to magazines, newspapers and even old encyclopaedias that had been in the home since Delta's childhood. But there seemed to be something special about this novel.'

'You can never read a good book too many times,' she answered.

'You always say that, *Amai*,' Delta laughed.

'*It is* true, is it not? Can I make you a cup of tea, Dee?'

'Not now, thank you. It's too hot for tea, and I need to phone someone,' she replied and left the room.

Alone in her tiny bedroom, she rummaged through the wardrobe, looking in every nook and cranny, turning the drawers upside-down with frustrated urgency. Where was that damned business card?

She finally found it in a discarded wallet. Holding her phone with shaking hands, she tapped in Mr Banga's number. The call was answered almost immediately.

'Hullo, Misi. What a pleasant surprise!' Through the noise and music in the background, she could detect his exuberance. It was as if he was indeed pleased to hear from her. Still, she felt unnerved being called 'Misi'.

Hurrying to speak before she lost her nerve, she said. 'Hullo, Mr Banga. I'm calling to find out if you're still recruiting at the lodge.'

'We finished ages ago.'

'I see.' Disappointed, she knew that she only had herself to blame for having waited too long.

'When you didn't phone, I thought you weren't interested, but tell you what? One post in admin and two in catering just came up. We're expanding,' he said, a hint of pride discernible in his tone of voice. 'If you're interested, we'll be interviewing next week.'

A lift of hope, then her heart sank. Of course they'd have to hold interviews. What had made her think she could swan her way into a job at his lodge?

She swallowed, feeling as if she might choke on her lies. 'Actually, I have a job. I'm just asking on behalf of someone.' She tried to sound nonchalant. He wasn't supposed to know how desperate she was. And she had more to hide.

'And who is that?' he asked with less enthusiasm.

'My twin sister,' she replied cautiously.

'Didn't know you had a twin sister, Misi'. His voice held renewed curiosity. 'What's her name? Level of education?'

'Delta. Degree in chemical engineering, but she's willing to branch out,' she replied, hoping that her description hinted at a smart, potential employee.

'Yaah! Engineering jobs are hard to find these days. With her background, I don't think she'd be interested in a catering job. Maybe admin. Tell her to email a CV a.s.a.p. We might interview her.'

'Thank you.' Thinking on her feet, she added, 'If you decide to interview her... what about over the phone? Travelling to Harare may be impossible for her next week.' She had to pre-empt this. There was no need to waste time and money on travel if there was no guarantee of getting the job.

'I'll think about it.' He sounded doubtful. 'Tell her to call me tomorrow.'

'Thank you, Mr Banga.'

'Anytime, Misi.' He rang off.

Delta exhaled. That hadn't been too bad after all. She walked back into the living room to sit with her mother, who was still engrossed in *Waiting for the Rain*.

Getting a new phone number and emailing her CV could both be accomplished the next morning. If by some chance she was given the job, next up would be a re-invention mission, and what fun she'd have! It would be a bit like entering witness protection with a 'new' ID as Delta, complemented by a drastically new look. She smiled to herself.

❦❦❦

As it turned out, the telephone interview was a breeze. It was conducted by Mr Banga and a woman named Mrs Moyo who'd been introduced as a director. Before they proceeded, Mrs Moyo told her that she was on speakerphone.

Despite informal preliminaries and a passing comment from Mr Banga about how she sounded like her twin sister, the interview was more professional and better structured than the one she'd had at Hunger Buster.

They asked her various questions related to work plans, computer skills, office administration and organisational skills. Here, her previous experience working in Uncle Dondo's office definitely counted. She spoke confidently, giving clear, concise answers. For the first time, she felt that she was on track to getting a job based on merit.

It was therefore no surprise when Mr Banga called her the next day to say she'd got the job and was required to start as soon as possible. The offer of a seven hundred dollars monthly salary and an allowance of one hundred dollars was a pleasant surprise. She accepted and asked for a week's grace before starting.

Hearing the news, Tendai joked, 'After investing so much time and effort training you, where will I get a market gofer half as street-smart?' He laughed, and she knew that he was happy for her.

Their long days spent together had brought them closer together and they'd made a good team. Nevertheless, she'd been often concerned about the way he seemed to have resigned himself to the status quo. While she'd continued to yearn for something better, he seemed to have given up.

Although her father seemed pleased too, he said, ' Wherever you go, don't ever forget Perry's.'

'No, I won't,' Delta said, and she meant it. This was her father's subtle way of reminding her that she should hold on to their shared dream.

Perry's Chemical Engineers' Handbook was often casually referred to as the grandfather of engineering textbooks. She remembered how expensive her copy had been, and how proud her father had been when he managed to buy it for her.

Her mother embraced her saying quietly, 'You look after yourself in Harare, Dee.'

The words didn't dampen her heightened sense of anticipation and the lightness in her heart. '*Amai!* You're such a worrier. With me around, it's the Hararians who should watch out!'

She then called Cashleen to tell her the good news and ask if she could stay for a while with her. Next was a text to Unesu. He agreed to pick her up from the bus terminus on Friday night and drop her off at Cashleen's.

※※※

Delta had decided on a transformative hairstyle that would involve replacing her voluminous Afro with trendy bush locks. Combined with a new wardrobe of carefully selected second-hand clothing from flea markets, she could create a façade as far removed from Misi as possible.

She visited the hair salon at Mkoba shops on Thursday, where she had a haircut, then waited for her turn with the hairdresser who specialised in bush locks. The woman's reputation preceded her, and Delta had no second thoughts about paying for the expensive hairdo. She convinced herself that it was an investment.

It was while she was waiting that she heard two hairdressers discussing what had happened to Farai. At first, she couldn't believe it because just a week earlier she'd met him at the shops. Then, he'd been full of stories about his new enterprise in Kwekwe's disused gold mines.

She'd noted how the right side of his face had been scarred by his injuries, a horrible reminder of the petrol inferno at his house. There'd been a persistent trickle of tears from his right eye, which had blinked continually as if there was some irritation. There'd been extensive scarring on his right arm which was slightly bent at the elbow, with some contracture formation.

In spite of all this, he'd been his usual cheerful self and quite happy to see her. She'd been amazed by his show of resilience.

'I'm now an artisanal gold miner,' he'd informed her proudly. 'There's money to be made out there, Delta.'

'In that case, please get a job for me too,' she'd joked, even as her stomach tightened with apprehension for him. It was just like him to choose money-making enterprises that were known to be risky. The violence that rocked poorly-regulated mining circles in Kwekwe was an open secret which went largely unreported, possibly because of alleged involvement of senior politicians who controlled gangs of unskilled and semi-skilled labourers, *makorokoza*.

The mines had long been abandoned by mining corporates and were known to be unsafe. Over the years, there'd been incidents of shafts collapsing, people being trapped and often failing to be rescued. But the possibility of striking gold had an irresistible allure and Delta had heard true stories of people who got rich overnight.

'You won't like the hard labour that I do. It's not for a woman,' Farai had said to her. 'But if I hear anything to do with engineering at the next-door mine where the Chinese moved in, I'll tell you.'

He probably hadn't known the difference between chemical and mining engineering but she'd believed that if he heard of job openings, he'd really tell her. He'd always had a generous spirit.

Sitting in the salon, it was a shock to find out that what she'd feared had happened. Farai and five others had been killed when an underground shaft collapsed. Not surprisingly, rescue teams were said to have moved in too late.

She remembered Farai's young wife and children as she reflected on the risks that he'd taken in his short life, just to make a living. And how enforcement of order and regulations in his chosen enterprises would have saved his life. But who cared? Many more would die like him. They'd just be recorded as statistics. Or not.

31

Cashleen was excited about her friend's imminent arrival. Although Delta had been offered a room in the staff quarters at Silhouette Lodge, she'd opted to stay with her for the weekend. That was good enough for Cashleen. She'd missed her friend's easy liveliness and they had some catching up to do.

She was busy serving customers when Delta finally arrived at the apartment with Unesu. She thought the latter seemed self-absorbed and strained, but it was hardly the time to probe. He didn't stay, citing something vague about work, which was all he ever seemed to do these days.

She'd hoped to talk to him about Itai, especially now that a cousin had also spotted her brother at a police roadblock. When she'd asked Itai, he'd denied it, ridiculing their cousin for a wild imagination, adding that he might have been hallucinating on high-grade weed or some other psychedelic concoction. His flippancy hadn't reassured Cashleen at all.

Although she now knew that he lived in Avondale West, she still felt a sense of foreboding whenever she thought about him. It was one thing for him to have moved into a well-furnished bachelor's apartment, but quite another for him to afford a second-hand BMW sedan in good condition. Whatever his dealings were, it was all too much too quickly.

After her last customer had left, she hugged Delta and stepped back to appraise her friend, acknowledging how voguish she looked in a pretty summer dress. The short bush locks were more flattering than her previous big and bouncy Afro. Even the ginger highlights, which were a bit risqué for someone about to start an administrative job, suited her rather well.

She noted that her gait was a bit awkward in high-heeled pumps. Smart as they were, they appeared to be pinching her toes. They were probably a shade too small, a hazard often associated with buying from second-hand clothing markets where the right sizes were not always available. She suppressed a smile, thinking of Delta's experiments with extreme fashion at university when she'd often declared facetiously, 'You have to suffer a little to be beautiful.'

'I can't believe you're doing this!' Delta said with some astonishment, surprised to find Cashleen's apartment full of goods, customers coming and going, making payments and picking up orders.

'*Yowe,* Delta! Don't make me feel as if I've done something insane! It's much easier than being a street vendor; I can work privately in the safety and comfort of home.'

Delta shook her head and looked in awe at Cashleen's business card. 'You... an imports' procurement agent! A real pro, aren't you?' Somehow, she managed to make her expression of admiration sound like an accusation.

But Cashleen smiled. Laughingly, she told Delta that starting off under Tanaka's guidance had been a bit like taking a master class at a dodgy finishing school for smugglers and hustlers.

'She sounds like something else, this Tanaka of yours,' was her friend's comment and Cashleen thought she heard a hint of envy in Delta's voice. 'But how do *you* feel about work of this kind?' she went on, looking searchingly at her friend.

'Happy and proud,' Cashleen replied, although this wasn't entirely true. There'd been moments when she'd had to rationalise issues, telling herself that it wasn't as if she'd become an armed robber, or an axe-murderer. Besides, she wasn't the first cross-border smuggler, and she wouldn't be the last.

'*Saka*, how does it all work?'

Cashleen explained that while some traders dealt in listed products giving them the unenviable status of small-time crooks, playing cat-and-mouse games with customs officials at the border, she and Tanaka had worked out ways of co-ordinating their ring from Harare.

They pooled their resources so that they could benefit from lower-priced bulk purchases from South Africa. They stuck to goods which were unlikely to draw too much interest from the authorities. Their runners relied on selected cross-border buses and trans-national trucks for concealed shipping of consignments. They worked on the premise that large volumes of traffic crossing the border would leave Customs and Excise officials too overwhelmed to fully implement the necessary checks. Then, of course, there were those officers who couldn't resist a bribe in order to turn a blind eye on suspicious packages.

She concluded, 'Everyone has a price, my dear. And we can always negotiate.'

'*Inga, inga!* Seems you've mastered the art of all this.'

'To be honest, it's so much better than my gig along Robert Mugabe. I really don't miss that filthy pavement.'

Delta laughed. '*Aika*, that's what you say today. I remember your excitement when you sold your first fruit and veg!'

Cashleen prodded her playfully with an elbow, 'That was then. This is now. Life changes, *shaz*.'

'And journalism?' Delta wanted to know.

'Well, I'm still sending out applications, but you know how it is … And, I'm making more effort to write. One or two factual articles or an opinion piece now and then, circulating the odd one. Someday I'll put myself out there, maybe start a blog. It might be successful, who knows?'

Delta nodded. 'Well, you'll never know until you start. I like the few that you've already circulated. You might be on to something.'

'Sure. After establishing my business, that'll be next on my list.' *My business.* The words had a surreal ring to them, but she had to think of this as a business, otherwise what was the point? Leading the way to the kitchen, she said, 'Come, I'll cook something for us.'

Delta picked a tattered and faded handbook which lay on the kitchen table and scrutinised it, saying, 'Is this what I think it is?'

Cashleen grinned. 'Yes, *The Highway Code*. I passed my written test and I'm now on a driving crash course.'

'Really? How come you never told me?'

'It was meant to be a surprise, *shaz*,' Cashleen said. 'I wanted to tell you only after passing the road test. With those examiners… you never know. All they want are bribes.'

'So, will you pay?' Delta was curious.

'I didn't want to, but my instructor says I'll have to. It's just the way it is. And please don't look at me like that. For my deals to run smoothly, I need to drive. So, I'm not going to let something as trivial as a bribe stop me,' she explained matter-of-factly as she filled up an electric kettle and switched it on.

'*Yah!* This is Harare for sure. But you seem to be so busy. How do you even get time for money-changing with Aunt Peace?'

Before replying, Cashleen asked, '*Sadza* or rice?'

'Definitely *sadza*.'

Bending over to pull a small cooking pot from under the sink, she continued, 'It's only my first week with Aunt Peace, but it looks promising. Cash shortages are getting worse, and I'm no longer one to waste a good crisis, even though starting off was quite a challenge.'

'How so?'

'Opening bank accounts and mobile money accounts, getting the right cashier contacts at supermarkets and service stations …'

Delta frowned. 'Sounds hectic! But why all those contacts?'

'*Iwe*, nowadays shop cashiers and petrol attendants handle more cash than bank tellers. I give them my bank cards, which they use to swipe from my accounts against cash-paying customers' purchases. Then I collect cash from them at the end of the day and give them a small thank you. If I combine that cash with what I get from Aunt Peace, I have enough to trade with.'

'Really Cash, you're full of surprises. A smuggler and a cash baroness? Who'd have thought?' Delta still looked awed.

Smuggler and cash baroness indeed! Cashleen couldn't help but laugh. Not in her wildest dreams would she have thought of herself this way, but here she was. The seductive promise of financial independence had her firmly in its grasp.

32

Delta was tense with anticipation when she arrived at Silhouette Lodge on Monday morning. At the gate, a taciturn security guard checked her identity card and let her in. Despite its upmarket location along the Enterprise Road, she'd somehow expected the place to be of a poor standard, like the Hunger Buster. But so much for preconceived ideas – the two places couldn't have been more different.

The Lodge premises comprised a cluster of modern buildings on artistically landscaped grounds. The driveway was lined with golden durantas. She sensed class and order, a sentiment that she couldn't reconcile with her previous impression of Mr Banga and her experiences when she'd previously worked for him.

Although she'd been told that he had good connections, she hadn't imagined that he could own a complex like this. Then she pulled herself short; he might not 'own' it, but he could have taken out a huge loan or a mortgage. Too often, appearance was no more than a disguise.

At reception, she was welcomed by a man who introduced himself as Shoko, her line manager. With him was the catering administrator, a beautiful woman called Munotida. She had a smooth, strikingly dark complexion and strands of grey in her hair that was pulled into a tight bun.

Shuffling some papers, she looked suspiciously at Delta and said an abrupt, 'Hullo,' her manner cold and aloof. Delta wondered why. Shoko glanced at his watch. 'Take an hour to settle and then I'll see you back here for your induction.'

'Thank you, Sir', Delta replied demurely.

Munotida handed her a set of keys to the staff residence and told her that they'd be sharing quarters. Munotida was in Room 1A, while hers would be 1B. She walked to the staff quarters as directed.

She found her room was fit for purpose, furnished with a bed, a desk and a chair. It vaguely reminded her of her old room in Complex 4 at the university. There was a small sink next to the built-in cupboard. She liked the sight of a full-length mirror, which was mounted on the cupboard door. There was a shared bathroom and toilet between 1A and 1B.

When she drew the curtains, bright sunlight flooded the room. Her window overlooked a neighbouring property to which there was access through a small open gate, suggesting some connection between the two properties. However, she'd noticed that they had separate entrances on Enterprise Road.

She turned back to the room and unpacked her suitcase, arranging her belongings neatly in the cupboard. Perry's *Handbook of Chemical Engineering* took a prominent position on the desk. She'd keep it there as a reminder of greater things.

She made her bed using the branded linen, which had been laid at the foot of the bed. Then, she freshened her make-up and stood before the mirror, appraising herself. She was ready for work. Whatever lay ahead, she was determined to make a success of this job.

Before she returned to reception, she checked her phone. There was a missed call from her mother and a text message asking how she was getting on. She made a mental note to phone her as soon as she'd topped up on airtime. Then she opened her group chat to find that people had had a busy morning exchanging memes and parodies of the Minister of Education who was being lampooned for having suggested that cash-strapped parents could pay school fees for their children using goats instead of money.

Someone had shared a picture of the previous day's edition of *Sunday Mail* with the headline: 'Minister says School Fees Now Payable in Goats'. Delta couldn't help but laugh at the absurdity of the notion. A very creative individual had replicated a caricature of a MasterCard to one which read: *There are some things money can't buy. For everything else there's MASTERGOAT.* The Ecocash card hadn't been spared either. Another message stating, *Ditch the bond note,* was accompanied by an intricately-designed dollar note showing several goats plummeting down the Victoria Falls.

Delta laughed again, amazed at how creative people still were even as life became harder. Last, she read a message from Cashleen. *U ther yet? Izit O-some? Or zit gwash?*

Def O-some! she texted back.

Her friend's reply was almost instant. *Coolies. Xytd 4u. Off 2 collect stuff n stuff.* She shook her head. Based on what she now knew about Cashleen, she could imagine what manner of things might be referred to as stuff and stuff. It would take her time to get used to how her friend had changed.

Back at the office, Shoko informed her that he'd work with her for the first two weeks, after which he expected her to have mastered crucial front-office routines. He took her through basic induction, introducing her to her daily tasks.

Her main role would revolve around customer care. She'd be responsible for handling all phone and email enquiries, co-ordinating accommodation and events bookings, as well as issuing invoices and facilitating payments.

So far so good. It all appeared straightforward. Might be a stepping-stone to greater things, she thought, with a small, self-satisfied smile.

A staid-looking young man approached with a clipboard. He stood back, waiting for Shoko to finish speaking. Eventually he turned to him. 'All done?' he asked.

'Yes, Sir,' he handed over the clipboard.

Shoko inspected whatever was written on the sheet on the clipboard and nodded in approval. 'Good, good.' Turning to Delta, he said, 'This is Kudzai, our student attachée from university. When he's not busy elsewhere, he'll work with you. Kudzai, meet Delta.'

'Hullo, Kudzai,' Delta extended her hand.

Kudzai responded solemnly and they shook hands. He turned to Shoko. 'I'm just going over to the extension to make sure everything is ready for the MP. He has a booking at noon.'

'Good, good,' Shoko said again. It seemed to be a favourite expression of his. Delta wondered what the extension was, and whether Kudzai's reference to the MP meant an actual member of parliament.

Before she settled down to some work, Shoko took her round to the catering and housekeeping departments to introduce her to other staff members. Then he showed her the lodge's accommodation and conference facilities. Everything looked pristine and well-organised.

They walked round to the back where he wanted to show her the swimming pool and *braai* area. At the small gate leading to the adjoining property, he stopped and frowned, then he called out irritably, 'Security!' There was no response. Louder and impatiently, he shouted again.

'Coming, boss,' someone responded in a deep baritone. A tall, heavy-set security guard emerged from behind the bamboo thicket. His military-style salute was a surprise to Delta.

Shoko puffed himself up as if to match the guard's towering height. 'Why isn't this gate closed and padlocked? How many times have we spoken about this?' he demanded, startling Delta with the sharpness of his voice.

'Sorry, boss. It was the cleaners I think,' the guard said vaguely, a look of anxiety clouding his face.

'Forget the cleaners! It's your job to make sure it's always locked. The extension is private and it stays that way. All the time!

If I ever have to speak to you about this again…' He let the threat hang in the air.

For a moment, the man seemed to withdraw into himself, then he stepped forward and closed the gate. 'Thank you, boss. I'll go and look for the lock,' he said, beating a hasty retreat.

Delta's curiosity mounted. What was the real reason for such an impassioned show of displeasure? Why was the extension private and why was it important to keep the gate locked? If that's where Kudzai had gone, would she be required to work there sometimes?

She wondered if she could ask Shoko, but the tight expression on his face stopped her. Besides, she knew better than to show too much curiosity on her first day. Her questions would be answered sooner or later. They walked back to the front office in silence. It was time to start work. Filled with a sense of purpose, she settled at her desk.

33

Unesu had accepted Takunda's invitation to a boys' 'Friday night out' without a second thought. Takunda had chosen the aptly named Playaz Jazz Lounge, an upmarket bar and a popular haunt for those who could afford a fun night of drinking and dancing. Unesu had been there only twice before. It was a venue that could easily knock one off-budget, but he reasoned that because he'd worked so hard, a bit of indulgence wouldn't hurt.

He found Takunda in the company of a group of other young professionals, their girlfriends in tow. He was disappointed because the invitation had been issued as a 'boys' night out'. He'd have preferred that because there were certain things one couldn't say or do in the presence of women. At first, he felt awkward, being the only one without a partner, but soon decided that he'd enjoy himself anyway.

He'd arrived thirsty and hungry after an emotionally draining day at the psychiatric unit. Since joining the department, he'd begun to appreciate that beyond the necessary requisites of a doctor, psychiatry needed one to have a strong sense of empathy and understanding, as well as emotional fortitude.

In as much as he enjoyed his work, he was exhausted because he'd had to attend to two new patients who'd been brought in with manic psychotic episodes. One had been particularly verbose, hyperactive and aggressive. It had taken him a long time to get her settled down.

It was definitely time to unwind. He drank two bottles of cold Zambezi beer too fast on an empty stomach and soon felt light-headed. The night was still young, so he switched to mineral water and ordered a meat platter while everyone else ordered snacks and more alcohol.

Muted jazz, laughter and loud voices swirled around him. Still tipsy, he was content to listen and watch. He was struck again by how Takunda epitomised the quintessential man's man. Seemingly without effort, he drew attention to himself and dominated discussions.

He was a natural performer who loved an audience, and the presence of female company seemed to fire him up. Unesu felt a frisson of jealousy. He'd never enjoyed that kind of popularity or had that much luck with the ladies.

Most in the group were doctors and the conversation inevitably shifted to the deterioration in government hospitals. The general opinion was that policy makers had shown no will to act decisively and improve working conditions or service delivery. It was an old topic that never failed to arouse ineffectual anger as nothing ever changed for the better.

Michael, a junior resident, made the point that it was now almost guaranteed that there'd be a doctors' strike once or twice a year. Unesu nodded. In predictable cycles, the striking doctors would be threatened by government while being vilified in the press for being so unethical as to put their own welfare before that of their patients; and then they'd get fired.

They'd put up a spirited fight, insisting that by striking, they were also advocating for their patients. But eventually, they'd be cowed into returning to work, even as their working conditions worsened and patients continued receiving sub-standard care.

He heard someone say, 'Frankly, I don't know why we bother. When has this government ever listened to our concerns in good faith? They'll tell you they have no money, but there'll always be money for their luxury cars, limitless perks and all the fruitless but expensive foreign trips.'

'And then our one and only causes us international embarrassment by promptly falling asleep on arrival at meetings. Does he or his cohort ever bring anything of value back?' Jane asked rhetorically. Unesu knew her to be a lawyer who worked at a firm with a reputation for taking controversial cases to the constitutional court.

'Phantom mega deals and memoranda of agreement for imaginary billions of foreign direct investment!' Takunda said, and most in the group joined him in laughter. Promises of fictitious deals had become a national joke.

Unesu decided to redirect the discussion to fundamentals. 'Let's not digress. The strikes... we haven't been asking for anything more than the basics, have we? In the long term, I think we'll do more harm to our patients by accepting the status quo. Let's face it. Health services deteriorate every year and nobody gives a dog's shit.' The alcohol had lifted his inhibitions.

Jane laughed. 'You don't say! Tell us more. Give us some facts!'

Unesu was annoyed. 'You don't work in a government hospital so...'

She interjected, 'Of course I don't. Show me a lawyer who does.' There were sounds of general amusement.

'... so I don't expect you to understand,' Unesu rejoined, irritated.

'Then make me understand,' she ordered. Unesu stared into his glass of mineral water and scowled. Lawyers! Did she think she was in a courtroom?

Takunda patted him on the shoulder, saying, 'Well, **mdhara**, yes, help us to understand.'

Unesu ignored them both, reflecting. The list of hospital deficiencies was staggering. Where could one begin? Outdated and dysfunctional equipment, shortages of blood for transfusion, of IV fluids and essential drugs, the use of expired drugs (a rumour; but one he was sure was often true), lack of gloves and protective wear for staff, an inadequate, frequently interrupted, supply of running water...

Then there were their constant attempts to make do with whatever was feasible: patients bedded on the floor, the use of non-sterile gloves for aseptic procedures, cheap dishwashing liquid instead of proper surgical scrub in theatre, and so on and on.

A lump lodged itself in his throat when he thought of the resultant senseless loss of lives. Some would haunt him for life. He shook his head and forced himself to snap out of the cheerless mood that had descended upon him. This was meant to be a fun-filled Friday night out.

Givemore played with his glass, clinking ice. 'Well, for me, working in ICT is okayish. But I feel for you guys. If I ever get sick, I hope my hospital experience won't be like one of those awful stories I've seen on social media. But surely, the health minister knows all this…'

Chido, Takunda's new girl said flippantly, '*Iweka!* They and their families can afford to fly out to the finest hospitals in the world, if they so much as sneeze. Why would they bother with hospitals that are used by the povo?'

'Because we voted them into office, that's why!' Jane responded quickly.

Shingai rocked backwards and forwards in an exaggerated show of amusement. 'We did what? That's a fallacy. Elections are systematically stolen. Remember when the great man himself tripped up at a rally a couple of years ago… that time when he said the opposition had actually won an election by 73 per cent?'

'Oh yeah, I remember the President misfiring about the 2008 election, and at a public rally too, of all places!' interjected Takunda.

Kudzai, who'd been quiet for most of the evening, suddenly spoke up. 'You have to be wrong. They couldn't have rigged an election which they won so resoundingly. Check your figures.'

'Winning resoundingly? That's where you're wrong. Remember the violence against opposition parties, the murders, and how high-profile leaders were systematically beaten up in 2007 and

2008?' Takunda was emphatic. 'Of course there's no sophistication in violence, but beyond thug tactics, don't ever underestimate these guys. They're very, very smart in their own way.'

Then, switching tracks because it was obvious the conversation was encroaching into dangerous territory, he turned to Unesu. 'And you should've ditched medicine like me. Your monthly salary is a fraction of just one of my deals. Just one!'

And someone shouted to general laughter, 'So the next round is on Takunda! He can afford to treat us all!'

A loud announcement broke into the discussion. The live performance was about to begin. The group turned collectively to face the stage as the band began to play an upbeat rendition of Stimela's 'Shut Up and Listen'.

Takunda pulled Chido to her feet and onto the dance floor, swaying to the beat. More couples followed and soon, the atmosphere lightened as the dancing got seriously underway.

Just then, Unesu's phone vibrated. It was Cashleen. He answered and heard her hysterical voice. Although he couldn't hear most of what she was saying because of the loud music, the urgency in her tone was unmistakable. He gathered that she was in the casualty resuscitation room at Pari Hospital and she needed him right away. The call disconnected and he was dismayed to find that his battery had gone flat.

※※※

As usual, casualty was crowded with patients and their companions. The benches leading to the examination rooms were full and there were many people standing around in a disorderly queue. Some patients were in wheelchairs, others on stretchers.

Lying on the floor in the corner was a man in blood-soaked clothes. He was groaning loudly and seemed to be unaccompanied. Instinctively, Unesu stopped to check on him, then he realised that this would delay him finding Cashleen. Hurriedly, he made his way through to the resuscitation room where he found her with Delta. Cashleen was crying brokenly while Delta held her.

Without preliminaries, he asked, ' Cash? Delta? What's wrong?'

Delta shook her head mutely and stared up at him. She appeared shell-shocked. Cashleen, trying to say something through her sobs, pointed towards a stretcher on which a uniformed police officer lay at the far end of the room.

A doctor in scrubs was explaining something to two armed police officers as he disconnected a drip and pulled a white sheet over the one on the stretcher. That could only mean one thing. The officer on the stretcher was dead.

Unesu looked at Delta, who gave a very slight nod in the direction of the stretcher, and confused, Unesu made his way over to the group.

'Good evening, Doc. Good evening, officers.'

The doctor turned to face him and Unesu was relieved to see that it was Clement, an orthopaedic registrar under whose supervision he'd worked during his surgery internship rotation.

'Evening, Doc,' Clement replied, 'Can I help you?'

One officer grunted something inaudible and moved towards a desk with his colleague, paperwork in hand.

Those are my friends,' Unesu said and inclined his head towards Cashleen and Delta. 'They called me here but they're too distressed to speak.'

'Is that so?' Clement pursed his lips and shook his head. 'This dead man is the woman in red's brother. It's a real mess.'

'There has to be a mistake. Cashleen, my friend, only has one brother, and he's not a police officer.'

Clement shook his head. 'There's more than meets the eye going on here. Best you go and give what help you can to your friends.'

Unesu took a step forwards. 'May I?' he asked, as he drew the sheet back from the dead man's face. The shock was as instantaneous as the memory of seeing Itai at a roadblock somewhere in police uniform. He remembered telling Cashleen, and how she'd vehemently declared that this was impossible.

'What happened?' he asked Clement.

'Long story. Apparently, this one…' Clement inclined his head towards the stretcher, 'was in the business of masquerading as a traffic cop and mounting fake road blocks at night with a friend, a constable. This evening he threw a set of spikes at a runaway *kombi*. They ricocheted back and shattered his femur. His accomplice is on the run, but he was arrested on the spot by those two.'

Unesu swallowed, 'But how could he die from a fractured femur?'

Clement frowned, as if offended. 'My friend, you know as well as I do that it's possible to haemorrhage torrentially from this type of fracture. Yes, he was conscious and communicating when he arrived and I did my best to get him ready for theatre. But there was no blood for transfusion. The usual story.'

Unesu exhaled, still stunned. It was a familiar story indeed but he'd never thought it would hit so close.

'Thank you,' he said simply. 'I'll see to my friends.'

Clement nodded, 'Of course. I also have to do my paperwork. Then there's casualty. Have you seen the queues? It's a manic night.'

'It sure is,' Unesu acknowledged, and walked over to Delta and Cashleen. He offered his condolences, which sounded hopelessly insufficient. Cashleen had stopped crying, and she slowly filled the gaps in the story which he'd been told by Clement.

'Have you called Rufaro?' he asked.

Cashleen nodded and Delta said, 'She's arriving tomorrow on an evening flight. We expect other friends and relatives to arrive tomorrow as well.'

A third police officer had entered the room. He approached them, explained that he was the investigating officer and that he had a search warrant for Itai's apartment.

'You mean tonight?' Unesu exclaimed, dismayed. 'Couldn't you show some compassion? Surely the search can wait until morning!'

'No,' the officer said authoritatively, 'it has to be tonight. Remember, his accomplice is still on the run. We can't take a chance with possible evidence tampering.'

Unesu had to concede that the officer was probably right. And he was only doing his job.

'The keys…?' He turned to Cashleen.

'… have already been confiscated,' the officer confirmed.

Before they left, Cashleen was given the necessary paperwork which she'd use the next morning to process the burial order. Then they all left for Itai's apartment.

※※※

Cashleen was shaken to the core. The circumstances seemed like the stuff of melodrama. Part of her still felt it couldn't be true. She expected Itai to walk into his apartment at any moment.

Looking round, she caught a rare glimpse of her brother's secret life and understood what sort of activities he'd engaged in to make a living and amass wealth. It was worse than anything she could have imagined. Police officers found sachets of white powder which they suspected to be cocaine, a small metal trunk filled with gold, several Apple laptops and iPhones, three revolvers, two police uniforms and a fake police ID. Under his bed were two sets of metal spikes.

They confiscated it all and confirmed that they would also impound Itai's BMW which had been found near a service station on Glenara Road, not far from where the accident had occurred. They were polite, but Cashleen felt sure that at some point they'd also want to question her about what she knew.

In her shock and grief, she felt partly responsible. If only she'd taken time to talk to him. If only she'd asked him exactly what he meant when he'd talked of dealing. If only she'd probed after Unesu had told her that he thought he'd seen him in police uniform. Maybe, just maybe, things wouldn't have come to this.

She vividly remembered the day he'd given her two thousand US dollars in a wad of crisp, brand-new notes. Why had she accepted? Why had she not challenged him then?

'Get yourself some new clothes or something,' he'd said, almost roughly, as if he didn't want her gratitude. She blinked back tears.

By the time they left Itai's apartment, it was past midnight. Unesu dropped them at Northern Heights, promising to return the next morning. Fortunately, Delta had a weekend off work and could stay until after the burial.

Although Cashleen was exhausted, she couldn't sleep. To have her brother die was one thing, to understand that he had been a felon, was another, and she found both almost impossible to accept.

'All those officers could see was a criminal. Itai was really a good person,' she kept repeating to Delta. 'He was my brother and I loved him.'

'I know, Cash. I know,' was all that Delta could say repeatedly, sure that Cashleen hardly heard her.

'To hear them speak about him like that… so unfair, so unfair. Why couldn't we all have just gotten real jobs after graduating? Maybe my brother would be alive today.'

She felt an upsurge of the old helpless anger at a system that had stolen so many of their dreams and created vagrants, vendors and criminals instead. What was she herself, if not a criminal of some sort with her black-market money trading and cross-border smuggling activities?

34

Cashleen was overwhelmed by waves of grief. By Saturday morning, her tears were spent, but an ache had settled deep within her. In a daze, she went through the motions of what needed to be done. Thankfully, Delta, Unesu and Tanaka were there to support her, and they'd assumed the task of informing relatives, family and friends about Itai's death. Assisted by Cashleen's uncle, they also dealt with practical aspects of funeral arrangements and burial preparations as well as ensuring that mourners who'd gathered were fed.

The size of the gathering was restricted by lack of space. Moving boxes of Cashleen's contraband to Unesu's apartment hadn't helped very much. The funeral itself was a sombre affair, clouded by awareness of Itai's activities. Somewhat ashamed, but keen to protect the memory of her brother, Cashleen tried to keep the details private, but in vain. The mourners were obviously curious and she could overhear their murmured exchanges as they gossiped about the rumours they'd picked up.

It certainly wasn't a typical funeral. While there was plenty of coming and going, there was none of the customary singing and wailing which would have accompanied a good wake. Mourning was restrained in consideration of other households within the apartment block.

To Cashleen's fury and disbelief, three police officers came round to ask more questions. No matter what her brother had done, he deserved a respectable funeral. Couldn't they have waited? Unesu laid a cautionary hand on her arm, explaining that it was to be expected under the circumstances. Their investigation was ongoing and they still hadn't apprehended Gerry.

Her anger gave way to surprise when an officer told her that the BMW's registration book which they'd found in the car's glove compartment showed her as the owner. The car's registration in her name was dated just a week before Itai's death. The officer told her they'd release the car into her custody if they didn't find evidence of its use in commission of crimes.

In her ensuing confusion, it took Cashleen a moment to remember Itai casually promising that if she passed her road test, he'd give her the BMW because he intended to get a new car. She hadn't taken him seriously. How could she have? Besides, she didn't know if he'd finally bought the new car that he'd intended for himself. At that point, nothing seemed to make sense. And now that he was dead, it would remain a mystery. She didn't know what to say to the officers, and mercifully, they didn't ask any more questions before they left.

Later in the day, her uncle and two cousins went to Doves Funeral Parlour to where Itai's body had been transferred from the hospital mortuary. They took with them the suit in which he'd be buried and selected his casket. They also finalised the programme for his final service which was scheduled for Sunday morning at the funeral parlour.

By early evening, the apartment was very crowded, so most people left after paying their respects. They'd attend Itai's burial at Mbudzi Cemetery the following day. This was a relief to Cashleen, who'd begun to feel increasingly claustrophobic and irritable. She knew that she should be grateful to have so many people turning up to comfort her, but she also felt an invasion of her privacy and she resented the hum of gossip.

Rufaro arrived from London on the evening Emirates flight and was collected from the airport by Unesu. Cashleen hadn't seen her sister in over two years and she'd missed her. Their reunion, which ought to have been joyous, was anything but.

Rufaro wore a long, black dress and a headscarf. A grey shawl hung loosely from her sloping shoulders. Cashleen was struck by how drawn she looked, and how thin. The sight of her sister, so forlorn and lost, provoked her to a tide of fresh tears. They clung together as they wept for their brother. Tanaka and Delta hovered uncertainly in the background.

Rufaro was offered food, which she picked at listlessly and without real interest. Afterwards, she went through the list of funeral parlour charges and burial fees with Cashleen, then handed over enough money to cover almost everything, including what Cashleen had already paid for. She refused Cashleen's offer to take back some of the money.

'You might need it later,' she said simply.

It saddened Cashleen to learn that her sister intended to travel back on Monday morning. Surely, she needed more time to mourn and come to terms with Itai's death?

'But why so early, Rufaro? Couldn't they give you more leave days?'

'No, they couldn't. I maxed out on leave when I was sick and I'm very behind with my mortgage repayments. Can't afford more unpaid leave. And I've got some overtime booked as well.' Her sister's response was stiff.

These details distressed Cashleen more than ever. She remembered that Rufaro had blamed both her and Itai for contributing to her depression. Then, she'd neither thought of nor had any insight into what wider impact their requests might have had on her sister's life.

But if she was so financially straitened, Cashleen couldn't understand why she'd insisted on contributing all that money towards the funeral. Perhaps she also felt partly responsible for Itai's death, and Cashleen could imagine how. If they hadn't all fallen out, maybe Itai would have stayed at the apartment, away from Gerry's influence, and he might have been out of harm's way. But, it was always so much easier to know what might or should have been done after the event. Citing exhaustion, Rufaro went to sleep shortly afterwards.

A service for Itai was held at Doves Funeral Parlour early on Sunday morning. Thereafter, his body was transported to Mbudzi Cemetery in a black, limousine-like hearse. Other than brief confusion regarding the exact location of his final resting place, which appeared to have been allocated to another deceased person, they buried him without incident. The mourners dispersed soon afterwards.

Tanaka and Unesu offered to help Delta make lunch for the small group that returned to Northern Heights. They served food quickly and efficiently, then they both left after washing up the dishes.

35

It had been a long weekend and Delta had hardly slept since Friday night. She was tired but she decided to stay on. Despite Rufaro's presence, she felt that Cashleen needed her. Their emotions were still raw and it seemed they were making a conscious effort to avoid talking about Itai. So, they sat together in the lounge, mostly in silence, as they watched a travel show on DSTV, their minds elsewhere.

Delta thought about her work. Compared to the farmers' market in Gweru, her job at the Lodge was a dream. However, her contract had included an ironclad non-disclosure agreement, which made her uneasy because it read like a litany of threats.

She'd discovered that the extension housed a men's grooming spa and massage parlour, the perfect smokescreen for a high-end brothel and escort services. The discreetly managed 'extras' said it all. Their clientele included many prominent, well-dressed figures who arrived in expensive cars. Mr Banga certainly knew how to make money by indulging them and feeding their appetites.

He'd given an instruction for her to occasionally stand in at the extension as an evening receptionist, and sometimes during her weekends off regular work. His presumption that she would, of course, do the job had stung. What did he think she was?

It had taken her a few days to cool down, and she did when she told herself that his assurance couldn't have been personal. Like many people with money, he obviously had a sense of entitlement, sure in the knowledge that he could always get what he wanted. Her initial reluctance had disappeared when she realised how well-paid those extra hours were.

Workers at the extension were mostly young beautiful women. While they came from diverse backgrounds, a good number were graduates who'd previously struggled to find work in fields for which they'd been trained. While Delta couldn't imagine herself as an escort, or indeed a prostitute, she didn't judge them. She could identify with the kind of desperation that may have driven them to work for Richard Banga.

'I run a classy operation, *shaz*. Beauty *and* brains. When all's said and done, what man doesn't want some intelligent conversation? I certainly do.' Delta had overheard him saying during a phone conversation. His arrogance galled, but the service he provided was a reality of life, and harsh as that reality was, some people's livelihoods depended on it.

Of late, he'd been dropping hints that there'd be so much more to gain if she made herself available for escort services rather than just part-time reception work at the extension. She'd been tempted by his allusion to prospects of weekends in New York, Dubai, Johannesburg and other attractive destinations. She'd toyed with the idea of considering his proposition, if only there could be a guarantee that she wouldn't end up being groped, or worse, by a sleazy old man, but something always stopped her.

Cashleen broke into her reverie, saying, 'Let me find something interesting for us to watch.'

Only then did Delta realise that the travel programme had just ended. Her friend switched to Trevor Noah's comedy show on Channel 111. After just a few minutes, Rufaro was laughing. Cashleen followed suit and soon the mood in the room had lightened considerably. It was as if Trevor Noah had inadvertently given them permission to forget the funeral, to talk and to laugh.

When that show came to an end, they switched channels to audio and ate supper while listening to some music.

Delta made a deliberate effort to engage Rufaro. She asked her about her work, the London fashion scene and other lighter topics. She tried to orchestrate the conversation in such a way that Cashleen and Rufaro ended up talking more directly to one another. And it was with relief that she saw moments when the close, easy-going manner in which the two sisters had always related before Rufaro left for England resurfaced.

When Rufaro reciprocated by asking Delta about her job, she hesitated, wondering if she should tell it like it was, or offer a sanitised version. Deciding on the latter, she replied casually, 'Well, it's a no-brainer really, just routine office work, but I like it. The lodge is plush, up-market. My salary could be higher, I guess, but it's much better than what I made at the market.'

'Good for you,' Rufaro smiled. 'At least you girls have moved beyond vending. I can imagine how difficult that must have been, being degreed and all.'

'Well, needs must, *Sisi* Rufaro. We both had to forget about those degrees for a time. But you're right, I'm much better off now, even Cashleen here is doing really well with her...' Delta paused as she caught the warning look her friend shot at her.

Had Cashleen not told her sister how she was making a living? It was very likely. And, based in London, wrapped up in her own immediate challenges, Rufaro probably remained unaware of how so many people in Zimbabwe were having to engage in illicit activities in order to survive, so much so that a good number thought of the law as an ass.

'Let's check what's on the news,' Cashleen quickly changed the subject. She switched to e-NCA news and an intriguing story about the First Lady, detailing an incident that had occurred on Friday night. They'd missed most of it because of the funeral.

It was reported that the woman had assaulted a young South African model at an expensive hotel in Johannesburg where she'd been to visit her sons. She was said to have used an electric cable and had left the young woman with significant injuries. A warrant for her arrest had been issued by the South African police, but the question being debated was whether or not she was entitled to diplomatic immunity by virtue of her being married to a head of state.

It seemed a diplomatic stand-off had developed between the two countries because landing rights for flights had been mutually suspended, and hundreds of passengers had been stranded.

'Aah! Is this for real? Do such things happen? ' Rufaro sounded astonished.

'Well, they probably don't happen in London! But *eish*, the shame of it!' Delta said in wonder. 'Just imagine... we have a First Lady who can brawl like a woman at a beer hall' She paused. 'But it's not the first time, if my memory serves me right. Didn't she attack a security guard in Hong Kong? I seem to remember a joke about how the guard was badly injured by her large diamond rings!'

Both Delta and Cashleen switched to their social media accounts where the incident was trending. There were various cartoons of a maniacal First Lady wielding a sinister-looking electric cable, while a young woman cowered in the corner, eyes widened in a parody of amplified fear. There was also a lot of name-calling. From the moniker Dr Stop-it, she'd become Dr Electric Cables and Cable Warrior. As always, Zimbabweans were on a roll with their humour; laughter their unfailing salvation.

In this case, the First Lady had few friends, though those few were passionately on her side, saying that she'd only acted as any mother might have done to protect her sons from the model's bad influence, so laying themselves open to the retort, 'Oh yes! So this is what we can expect from the Mother of the Nation!' and 'Those young men are not babies!'

'Well, we have to give it to her.' Delta said in mock defense. 'Maybe she just represents an extreme of what we've all become. And why shouldn't she do as she pleases? After all, she's the ultimate rags-to-riches story. Look how she started. And now she's the most powerful woman in the land! Have you seen how meekly great big men kneel before her at public events? Didn't she say even the two Vice-Presidents take notes and advice from her? Tell me, what woman wouldn't want to live that story? I certainly would and I dare any woman to say otherwise!'

'*Unopenga! Unopenga!*' Cashleen giggled as she mimicked the First Lady's favourite insult to those whom she considered to be deranged.

They all laughed and set about getting ready for bed. It was getting late and Rufaro had to be at the airport early.

36

It was a typical late October afternoon. The weather was hot, the air dry. A scattering of clouds had gathered in the sky and Cashleen imagined they held the faint promise of rain, so desperate was she for relief from the heat. However, more rationally, she knew that it was very unlikely to rain in October.

Exasperated, she pushed her way through city crowds, navigating the piles of vendors' goods displayed on pavements. The months she'd spent on these streets felt like a lifetime ago. She couldn't imagine being part of this scene ever again. She wouldn't last a day.

At least the protests and demonstrations had quieted down, so maybe vendors were having a relatively easier time. The flip side of this relative calm was that it signalled a type of collective resignation and acceptance of perceived injustices that had driven people to take to the streets in protest in the first place. Change would probably remain an illusion.

Worried about her errand, she hurried on. While her commission from Aunt Peace was good, she was averse to city-centre cash drops and collections, especially those involving people whom she didn't know. Much could go wrong. The threat of being set up for arrest was very real, although getting away with a bribe was always an option. Being trailed home by undesirables was another risk. There'd been reports of money changers who'd been robbed, assaulted or shot at.

This time she had no choice but to go right into the city centre. Aunt Peace had insisted she do so because this transaction was urgent and she was busy. There was, however, some relief in knowing that she'd be dealing with a female. She considered men high-risk clients.

Going by the day's exchange rate, the US dollar as hard cash was trading on the black market at a twenty-five per cent premium against a bank transfer. Aunt Peace had somehow managed to negotiate a more profitable deal and she'd already transferred a substantial amount to the bank account of a woman called Jesca.

Cashleen had to collect US dollars in hard cash from her and give the dollars to Uncle Dondo. He would be leaving for South Africa that same afternoon to buy various goods for resale back in Harare. From being a company executive, he seemed to have adjusted rather well to being a cross-border dealer, which had initially surprised her.

Cashleen supposed that like most people, he'd come to accept that one had to adapt or sink. She knew that he operated under the taxman's radar and circumvented customs, just like the network she ran with Tanaka. Without a doubt, it was more profitable this way.

She wondered, though, if anyone ever stopped to think that by evading tax, they were doing a disservice to national interests. She shrugged. The law of the jungle and serving personal interests seemed to have become the order of the day; even right at the top with respect to elected leaders, who should have been setting an example. Wasn't that what drove corruption and lawlessness?

She turned the corner to the rising sound of music. 'Happy happy! *Mawoko mudenga, mawoko mudenga umo*! Happy happy…' Winky-D's lyrics blared from a pavement loudspeaker, his eternal optimism incongruous in the drab, teeming environs.

A group of street-kids danced and leapt in the air in tune to the music, seemingly oblivious to the grim realities around them. Cashleen stopped briefly to watch, amazed at the raw talent in their synchronised dance moves. She smiled and felt a sudden lift. Their spirit of cheer was contagious. Spurred by Winky-D, they danced on, *happy happy* indeed.

Next to them was a large puddle of dirty water, thanks to a burst pipe. A *kombi* swerved to avoid a pothole that spanned half the breadth of the road. As the children were splashed, they shouted out their collective disdain and made wild, threatening gestures at the *kombi* as it sped on its way.

'*Ma*-problem *ese* disappear… problem *ese* disappear… happy, happy!' Winky-D's voice continued, wooing the street-kids back into their energetic dance.

Still smiling, Cashleen entered the restaurant and identified Jesca as the woman in a white dress who sat at a table in a corner. They exchanged greetings and confirmed each other's names.

'We'll have some privacy in there,' Jesca said, pointing towards the toilet.

Cashleen got up and followed her. The stench was unbelievable and from the mess in there, it was obvious there was no running water. Regardless, she knew, the restaurant would continue to operate. Quickly and furtively, they counted out USD notes and agreed on the amount. Cashleen took out her small UV fake notes' detector and inspected the money.

Jesca laughed sarcastically. 'Don't you trust me?' she asked.

'It's not that, *Sisi*,' Cashleen replied. 'I do this all the time. Just to be sure.' The notes were indeed genuine. Jesca clicked her tongue and shook her head in an irritated manner as she led the way out of the toilet.

'Do you need a white gown for the Super Sunday Church Rally? I have a few for sale.' She asked suddenly, patting her bag.

Cashleen was taken aback. She'd heard about the First Lady's forthcoming rally with the apostolic religious sect. It had been so highly publicised that she knew the date and venue: 5 November at Rufaro Stadium. She'd never been one to attend rallies and she was bemused to think that this woman would imagine that she'd be attending *that* particular event.

'I'm not going,' she replied shortly.

Jesca shrugged. 'It will be the event of the year, my sister, the event to be seen at. Don't let things pass you by. If you change your mind, call me. My gowns are the best in town. The very best,' Jesca said with a smile as fake as the artificial weave-on hair on her head.

'No, thanks.'

'Suit yourself,' Jesca retorted, slinging her bag over her shoulder. 'See you around.' She waved, and was gone.

Cashleen walked out of Hunger Buster and crossed town at a brisk pace, all the way to Road Port, casting frequent glances over her shoulder, worried that someone could be following her. Who was to know if Jesca herself wouldn't tip off some felons to accost her and rob her of the US dollars? No honour among thieves, she thought irrelevantly.

It was with relief that she handed over the money to Uncle Dondo without incident. She sat with him for a while, chatting about the shrinking job market and how futile it felt to even bother applying. After his bus had left Road Port, she trudged back to town on aching feet. Now that she had a driver's licence, it would have been a good time to buy a used car, she thought, but she still needed to save more money.

She wondered if the police would finally hand over the impounded BMW. Several long weeks had elapsed and there had still been no word. She was too afraid to phone the investigating officer. She didn't want to draw attention to herself and have the police coming round to poke their noses into her business. She'd wait until the end of the year, then she'd consider buying an ex-Japanese used car if the BMW wasn't released.

❦❦❦

Supper would be last night's leftovers. She retrieved a portion of *sadza* and vegetables from the fridge and placed them in the microwave. Before she could switch it on, she thought she heard a tentative knock on the front door. She glanced at her watch. It was already after 7 p.m. Wondering who it could be, she walked slowly to the door and squinted through the glass peephole. Stunned, she caught her breath and stepped back. To be certain, she looked again.

Despite the visual distortion of an oversized head and a diminutive body through the peephole, she saw that it really was Sando. She opened the door and stared, taking in how thin and unkempt he looked in ill-fitting clothes. What had happened to him? She stared at him, shocked and pleased at the same time.

'Hullo, Cash,' he said, his voice hoarse. Almost immediately, he was seized by a fit of coughing.

'Sando? Is it really you?' she exclaimed, then, remembering her manners, she held out her hand to shake his, changing her mind to give him a hug instead. She stepped aside to let him in.

He placed his backpack on the floor and sat in what had once been his favourite armchair whenever he'd visit. Her mind full of questions, she took the opposite seat and faced him.

'You just disappeared. What happened? And when did you come back?'

'Got back last week. It's a long story...' He hesitated.

'And I have time,' she said simply and smiled to encourage him to open up, genuinely relieved that he was back. That he was alive. Time and again, she'd worried about him. With news of xenophobic attacks in South Africa, there'd been occasions when she'd feared the worst.

He scratched his head and sighed. In the past, conversation between them had been so easy. Now she sensed that things might have changed.

'You know, I couldn't get a job. I just got menial work. I hated it, Cash. And I still couldn't make ends meet, or pay my cousin for my upkeep. Jo'burg was more expensive than I imagined. We fought one day. He threw me out in the middle of the night.' He spoke in a rush of troubled words.

'Oh, I'm so sorry,' Cashleen said. She'd had no idea. He'd

always sounded so casual when he spoke of being a cleaner.

'I was mugged and assaulted that same night. They took my passport, my degree certificate, money, clothes... everything I owned. And then...'

There was a silence. She gave him another encouraging smile, sensing that he was about to drop a bombshell. And he did.

'There was a woman I knew. Someone from here in Harare. She was very good to me. She took me in when I had nowhere to go. And I... I guess I got careless, and ended up living like her. And with her. Drugs, men, women, it didn't matter. It was just about survival.' His voice was eerily dispassionate as he reduced one and a half years of adversity to a few brief sentences.

While Sando had always been candid, a real straight talker; these revelations were too detailed and too personal, but sensitivity held her real sentiments in check. What he was telling her couldn't have been easy. She wanted to reach out, hold his hand and close the gap in friendship that their time apart had created.

'Things got out of control and I lost my way. I was too ashamed to...' Another spasm of coughing interrupted his speech. He cleared his throat. 'And then I just had to keep a low profile.' It was an understatement.

'I'm sick, Cash. Very sick,' he said. She waited for him to explain exactly what he meant, but he didn't, so she had no choice but to imagine the worst. Her heart contracted. The emotional and physical pain that he was going through was right there for her to see.

She couldn't reconcile this broken Sando before her with the young man who'd been so full of vitality and dreams for a brighter future when he left for South Africa. She vividly recalled how well he'd done in college, getting the Book Prize for their graduation class. Now, here he was...

But if things had been that hard for him in Jo'burg, why hadn't he just come back home? He had his family and a tight network of friends with whom he could have shared mutual support and ideas for survival in Harare. She had so many questions for him but they all seemed inappropriate at that moment.

So she said instead, 'I'm so sorry, Sando. It's so good to have you back. Where are you staying?'

'With mother in DZ,' he replied slowly. 'And I think I had better get going.'

'No, please stay. I was just about to eat,' she insisted only to be disappointed when he said, 'I really must. Mother fusses. She'll be worried if I'm late. She still treats me like a little boy.' The ghost of his hallmark cheeky grin flashed across his face.

'Next time then,' she smiled back.

He declined her offer to accompany him to catch his *kombi* home. 'No thanks. You stay indoors. It's already dark outside.'

Long after he'd gone, she remained seated, her mind in turmoil, realising she'd forgotten to ask for his new phone number. Maybe he'd call her.

Several days later, Delta phoned. '*Iwe*, I've just seen Sando on First Street. He had one of those loudspeakers and was shouting unprintable things about the government. It gave me such a bad feeling, Cash. There was a crowd egging him on. He looked stoned.'

Cashleen sighed. Surely, Sando knew better. How could he? When he'd stopped by, he'd sounded reasonable. Could it be that he was at a point where he felt he no longer had anything to lose? Or was it simply the drugs?

'Thanks, Delta. I haven't seen him since that night when I told you he'd dropped in on me. But what you're saying is a worry...'

'Anyway, I thought you should know. I have to get back to work.'

'Thanks for letting me know.'

'Sure. Bye!' Delta disconnected.

Cashleen's mind fell into a vortex of the most extreme imaginings. How dare Sando go down that path? One heard of disappearances and state-sanctioned abductions of people who stepped out of line. Of men in black suits and dark glasses who plucked dissenters off the street into cars with tinted windows and no number plates. Spooks who snatched people from their homes in the middle of the night.

Such stories were told with conviction, but it was difficult to know what was true, and what was not. She couldn't help thinking that something like that could well happen to Sando. A weight settled in the pit of her stomach.

37

Unesu had a couple of days off work and he intended to get some proper rest. He was in very good spirits. After two months of going backwards and forwards, all the documentation for his mortgage application had finally been approved.

He'd be purchasing a modest town house within a newly-developed gated complex in Belgravia. The developer was pushing for a quick sale and he'd been told that he could move in as early as the end of November, which was just a few weeks away.

He'd also taken his mother to the oncologist for her scheduled review with test results that morning. The specialist had confirmed that all blood results were normal and imaging had shown no evidence of suspicious lesions. She was scheduled to return home with *Mainini* on the afternoon coach. Since they still had a bit of time before departure, he prepared a light meal, which they sat down to eat while watching the lunchtime show.

The breaking news was as unexpected as it was shocking. The Vice-President had been dismissed from office with immediate effect. Unesu found it inconceivable. For a man so powerful that he'd been dubbed The Crocodile, it was easy to conclude that his dismissal could foreshadow grave consequences.

His mother frowned, '*Yowe* ... but I could see this coming.'

Unesu began, 'You could? Really? I never thought...'.

She interrupted, '*Iwe*, just think about what the First Lady said at her rally yesterday.'

'*Ehe,* that Super Sunday rally,' *Mainini* joined in, her face alive with interest.

Unesu remembered. The First Lady had told the crowd in no uncertain terms that she could fell the Vice-President with one blow. So, was this what she'd meant? 'A snake whose head needs to be crushed,' she'd said of the man.

Unesu had no real interest, but he'd watched the television coverage because there'd been such a buzz prior to the event. What had struck him most was how much political content had found its way into the religious gathering. The First Lady had walked up and down the podium with enormous energy, as if on a stimulant, gesturing expansively during what amounted to a diatribe against the Vice-President.

He'd watched, fascinated as she alleged that the man was fanning factionalism in the ruling party and plotting to oust the legitimate President. And her laugh! Loud, and contemptuous, it had spoken volumes. Now, twenty-four hours later, the VP had been fired!

Unesu shook his head. This wouldn't be the last they'd hear of this matter. After more than thirty years of standing by as one of the President's most loyal aides, the Vice-President wouldn't be swept aside without repercussions. That he was sure of.

They finished lunch and he took his mother and *Mainini* to the City Coach pick-up point at Rainbow Towers. He helped them aboard and drove back home.

Still excited about his imminent move to Belgravia, he thought of boxing up his books and clearing out the chaos in his bedroom. There were piles of old newspapers, which he hadn't thrown away because he never finished reading a copy. His mother had often chastised him for this pointless hoarding.

He set aside copies of **The Times** and **The Economist** that he'd forgotten to pass on to Cashleen. Then, he decided to quickly scan some weeklies before he threw them in the trash. He glanced over the headlines, curious to see which reports had turned out to be authentic and informative, and which had been political spin or mere rumour.

He chuckled as he read an article about a youthful MP who'd claimed that the ruling party had created over three million jobs, far exceeding its 2013 election campaign promise. When challenged with facts, he'd explained that as an example, asking someone to wash your clothes contributed to job creation.

Unesu remembered how social media networks had had a field day mocking him, and suggesting other 'real alternatives' that had been inadvertently created in the declining economy: bribe-mongers, pot-hole fillers, spike-welders, bank queuers, bogus prophets, goblin catchers, cross-border smugglers, street vendors, armed robbers and thigh vendors in reference to prostitutes.

He laughed as he stuffed that paper into a disposal bag. As he lugged the bag out to the rubbish skip, his phone rang.

It was Dr Reza. 'Unesu, please come to the clinic immediately,' he said tersely.

Unesu felt a moment of alarm. 'Is everything all right, Doc?' he asked, already expecting bad news.

'Dr Reza, we need you back in theatre right now,' he overheard someone say in the background.

'Look, there's an emergency with a twenty-three-year-old nulliparous patient. I'll explain when you get here.' The phone disconnected.

As he drove to the clinic, Unesu was in a state of panic. He didn't need this, but there was no way he could have said no to Dr Reza. He pictured the possible scenarios: uterine perforation, uterine atony with haemorrhage, or sudden, unexplained collapse.

Although it wasn't his patient who'd complicated, being called out by Dr Reza could well also make him liable for whatever unhappy outcome eventually ensued. Such incidents were what he'd feared since he joined the clinic. He wished himself as far away as Dr Mazwi, who was now in the USA.

Arriving at the clinic, he went straight to theatre where he found the team resuscitating a haemorrhaging patient. There was blood on the floor and the scrub nurse was replacing blood-soaked linen with fresh drapes. The patient was moved from the surgical abortion's lithotomy position to the supine position for exploratory laparotomy.

'Get scrubbed,' Dr Reza said to him without preliminaries. Scrubbing up, Unesu could see into theatre through the glass partition as the anaesthetist put up an IV infusion, probably oxytocin, while the anaesthetic nurse was busy setting up a blood transfusion.

At the operating table, Dr Reza had already opened up the patient's abdomen. Together they inspected her internal organs, focusing on the uterus. There were no traumatic injuries or perforation. Of note was that the uterus was significantly atonic. That certainly explained the amount of bleeding.

As the anaesthetist stepped up with the uterotonic regimen in order to contract the uterus and stem bleeding, Unesu performed bimanual compression and massage on the flaccid organ, willing it to contract. They had to stop this bleeding, or they could well lose the patient. A life-saving hysterectomy, which he knew Dr Reza could perform, was an option but then again, the patient was only twenty-three years old and childless.

A riot of emotions swirled in his head, clouding his recollection of Prof Chaka teaching obstetric registrars how to perform the haemostatic B-Lynch suture. As a senior house officer, he'd only been an observer, so it was a procedure that he couldn't do anyway. He wasn't sure if Dr Reza could, and this wasn't the time for experiments. What were they going to do?

'Can't we transfer her to the central hospital, Doc?' he asked and looked pleadingly at the older doctor who was clearly as flustered and in as much of a panic as he was. They were facing a potential disaster that could destroy both their careers.

'Another ergometrine stat!' he heard the anaesthetist say to his nurse colleague.

'Transfer? You know what that means, don't you?' Dr Reza snapped testily.

Before Unesu could think of a suitable response, he felt the uterus in his hands miraculously contracting into a firm mass. It was such a reassuring sensation that he could have wept with relief. Contraction would definitely slow down the bleeding and eventually arrest it.

'BP and pulse stabilising,' the anaeasthetic nurse was saying.

'*Yes!*' the anesthetist exclaimed said and whooped in a rare show of emotion. There were general murmurs of relief. Dr Reza remained silent as they closed the abdomen but Unesu knew that he was as relieved as everyone else.

The stabilised patient was eventually taken to the clinic's observation ward where she'd be managed as an in-patient for three days until discharge. A transfer to hospital would have required explanations which none of them was prepared to give. What mattered most was that she was out of danger, and she still had her uterus.

Thereafter, Dr Reza thanked the whole team and said to Unesu, 'I suppose you can go now, Doc. I'll update you later. Once again, thank you for coming so quickly.'

Driving home, Unesu lost himself in reflection. The clinic provided safe abortion services and such emergencies were unpredictable and rare. But they could have lost the patient, and where would that have left them?

He thought of how, in recent weeks, women's health advocacy groups had once again raised concerns about the lack of access to safe abortion services in the country. National statistics for morbidity and mortality related to unsafe abortion were disturbing. And with a spasm of pain, he remembered how his young sister had died.

However, he once again acknowledged that if he was ever exposed because of complications at Orion Clinic, being an advocate for safe abortion wouldn't make him immune to losing his registration or to prosecution. And he'd barely started his career.

The incident had been a close shave. He felt shaken to the core. He certainly didn't need to go on living under a cloud of fear, always worrying that something might go wrong.

He decided that he'd give Dr Reza a standard three months notice to resign. Three months would be enough time for another doctor to be recruited, and for him to find a replacement locum. It would probably pay less than Orion Clinic, but at least he'd get his peace of mind back. Having made this decision, he felt calmer.

)O(O(

Two days later, he was back at work in the psychiatric unit for a night on call. Handover from the senior house officer who'd been on day shift was quick. There was nobody waiting to be assessed, so he could have some time to relax before patients started coming in.

It appeared, though, to have been a relatively quiet day, with just one new admission who'd been brought in by police officers. A plan of care for this particular patient had already been discussed with the consultant and Unesu was not required to do anything immediately.

He sat idly in the duty room, listening to his nursing colleagues chit-chatting. It seemed the news about the VP being fired from government was on everyone's lips. The matter was growing more intriguing by the day and most were of the opinion that the country was on the edge of something profound. No one knew exactly what, but incredible conspiracy theories were being tossed around. It was rumoured that the man had already fled the country in fear of his life and he'd sought asylum in South Africa.

Unesu switched his attention to the new patient's notes. The young man had been in such a state on arrival that he'd had to be sedated immediately. His history had been obtained partly from police officers and partly from his mother, who'd been directed to the psychiatric unit after reporting him missing.

The record stated that he was twenty-six years old. He'd been found stark naked, sitting on an anthill near Mukuvisi River. He'd been shouting obscenities and throwing stones at passers-by. Prior to this, he'd been missing from home for several days.

Other medical history obtained from his mother included HIV infection, ongoing treatment for tuberculosis and a bipolar disorder for which he'd defaulted treatment before he went missing.

On physical examination, he'd been found to have multiple bruises all over his body, which could have indicated a recent assault. He also had missing teeth, with swollen gums and on his buttocks were cigarette-type burns. Fortunately, the X-rays ordered on admission had not shown any fractures.

Unesu flipped back to the demographic information page. He looked at the patient's name and his heart missed a beat. Sandodzangu Chidhakwa. Could this patient really be Cashleen's friend who'd been presumed missing in South Africa? He hadn't spoken to Cashleen for a while and he hadn't heard anything about Sando being back in the country.

He got up and walked to the patient's bedside, afraid of what he might find. Sure enough, the man who stared back at him passively and without a flicker of recognition was Sando. When had he returned? Wondering if Cashleen knew, he dialled her number.

38

Delta had settled into an easy rhythm at Silhouette Lodge. She found that she didn't have to work very hard to impress clients, colleagues and the management team. Even Munotida had become something of an ally. Beneath her frosty exterior, she was a kind-hearted woman whose competitiveness arose from her determination to put her children through school.

Despite her relative success, Delta was feeling a now recurrent and familiar restlessness. She decided to take her lunch break in the garden, away from everyone. She needed solitude to help her clear her head and reflect.

As the country slipped downhill, she couldn't keep deluding herself that one day she'd just find work as a chemical engineer. Given this bleak, long-term view, she had no idea how to get back on track. Time and again, she would read through selected chapters in Perry's *Chemical Engineers' Handbook*, to check if she still knew fundamental facts and theorems. It worried her that, increasingly, she struggled with computations and calculations which she'd once enjoyed and found so easy.

She'd often thought of further studies as a way out. If she saved enough, she could do her Master's, maybe locally, maybe in South Africa. That would give her a break and an additional qualification, hopefully improving her chances on the job market. University of Cape Town, Stellenbosch and Wits were all highly-rated internationally, but for those, she'd need real money for tuition and living expenses, not bond notes. For now, it was increasingly difficult to access real USD.

For some reason, Mr Banga's proposition about escort work kept coming back to her as a possible way to earn real money. Still, she shuddered at the thought of what this might involve in reality. She had become wary of liaisons with older men. At university, she'd been first naïve and then foolish to have not just one, but two relationships with married men. The first one had claimed that he loved her and hated his wife whom he was trying to divorce; the second was with a man who was supposedly separated. Both relationships had ended badly.

Just that morning Mr Banga had spoken to her again, claiming, 'The governor has asked specifically for you. All he wants is your charming company on this business trip. Nothing else. And the US dollar fee he's offering is the highest we've ever been paid ...'

She hadn't known him to be so ingratiating, and she'd almost laughed. And of course she hadn't believed him. He was a man who took pride in being a savvy businessman, while in reality he was just a glorified pimp.

'I'll let you know,' she'd said politely, hoping that he wouldn't assume tacit acquiescence. Now sitting in the peaceful garden, she again examined her options.

While she'd compromised her values many times before, and she didn't judge other people for their choices, in this case crossing that line would be tantamount to throwing away the last vestiges of her morals. She felt this would leave her less grounded in life, and so she resolved that escort work, or indeed prostitution, were both no-go areas.

Instead, she'd keep working hard and settle for extra reception shifts during weekends and on her days off. Life didn't always give second chances, but this job had given her a lifeline of sorts. She'd make the most of it and save up to do her Master's degree.

Lunchtime was almost over. She snapped out of her reverie and switched on her mobile data to check phone messages before she went back to her work station. She was surprised to find social media abuzz with news of military tankers rolling on the streets of Harare. This was unheard of, but then again, it had been a suspense-filled week since the Vice-President's dismissal, with a wealth of rumours doing the rounds.

The messages on her group chats were rife with speculation. Someone mentioned the C word, throwing her into alarm. She phoned Cashleen. 'Have you heard about the army tankers? Is there really an ongoing coup?'

Cashleen laughed. 'Coup? What coup? This is Zimbabwe, not Nigeria or the DRC for goodness sake!'

'But the tankers...'

'Oh, those.' She sounded unimpressed. 'I wouldn't worry. I saw two. And I swear they looked like relics from a museum. Not sure why there's all this hullabaloo about them.'

'You actually saw them?'

'Yes, on my way in from Mount Hampden. I saw one that had broken down and another that was trundling slowly along Lomagundi Road. If the army wants to stage a coup, they won't get far in those ancient crocs!' Cashleen laughed.

Delta took a deep breath, relieved. A coup would mean suffering, blood on the streets and certain death for many. Cashleen was right. Coups didn't happen in slow motion. They didn't happen with archaic equipment either. And they certainly didn't happen in Zimbabwe.

'I hope you're right.'

'Of course I am.'

Delta switched to something that she'd meant to confirm all day. 'Did you manage to visit Sando?'

There was a moment of silence before Cashleen replied. 'Yes, I did. Yesterday.'

'How is he?' she asked, mindful of how shaken they'd all been when Unesu told them about him surfacing at the hospital in a bad state. By virtue of his friendship with Cashleen, he'd been a well-known acquaintance to all of them.

'He's like a zombie. He just sat there, staring into space. I don't think he recognises me. I met his mother and she said the same. The specialist said it's some kind of post-traumatic state. Like... something terrible happened to him during those days when he was missing,' Cashleen said slowly, her voice sounding rather impassive, but Delta knew better.

She felt a wave of compassion. Given his personality and his public, subversive utterances when she'd seen him on First Street, she had her suspicions about what might have happened to him. It was too unpleasant to think about, let alone speak out loud.

'So,' she said brightly, 'I hope he gets well soon. I can't get time off to go to the hospital. Can we go see him together *pa*-weekend?'

'Sure. Bye,' Cashleen replied.

Delta got up and returned to reception. Making a firm decision to save up for a another degree had renewed her. She had a goal, and it came with hope.

39

Cashleen went to bed late and then she overslept. She was woken up by a phone call from Rufaro, who sounded frantic. Apparently, there'd been a coup during the night.

'*Whaaat*? You're playing with me,' she mumbled, forcing herself awake. It was impossible. And, anyway, how could Rufaro in London know about a coup in Harare before she did?

'You're still sleeping, Cash? Check the news channels. *And* Facebook. *And* Twitter. It's true,' Rufaro asserted. 'Check it out, and I'll call you back in a few minutes.'

Cashleen wandered to the sitting room and switched on the television. The sole local channel was playing a triumphant revolutionary song to which a group of plump women in ruling party regalia were shaking their posteriors with much enthusiasm.

There was nothing unusual about revolutionary songs on the national TV channel. She scrolled through to SABC. And there it was. News of a coup in Zimbabwe!

Her phone rang. 'So,' said Rufaro, 'I'm right, aren't I?'

'It seems so,' Cashleen answered, still disbelieving, as she watched footage of what appeared to be a replay of an earlier announcement by the army.

'Of course, I'm right,' Rufaro retorted indignantly. 'Please stay safe, Cash. Don't go out until you know what's happening. And keep me posted. I have to get ready for work.'

'Sure. Bye,' Cashleen said, her eyes fixed on the screen.

A grim-faced, uniformed army general was saying, 'The President and his family are safe and their security is guaranteed. We are only targeting the criminals around him who are committing crimes that are causing social and economic suffering in order to bring them to justice. As soon as we have accomplished our mission, we expect the situation to return to normal.'

Whatever this was, the major-general certainly wasn't calling it a coup. It was referred to as Operation Restore Legacy. He sounded quite convincing, and benign. It was unlike anything she'd ever imagined of a coup.

Operation Restore Legacy! She felt a sudden lightness of spirit, an anticipation of change, and the possibility of a brighter future. After all those ineffective protests and countless efforts by civic society to engage government, who could've dreamed that this would happen?

The day progressed. It felt unreal, more like a film than real life. It seemed everyone was online; everyone had news, some of it very contradictory, but full of incident. Delta sent more regular updates than anyone else. Cashleen wondered if her friend was getting any work done at the lodge.

She learnt that the national broadcaster had been taken over by the army overnight. Soldiers had been deployed at the President's Blue Roof Mansion, Parliament, other government buildings, courthouses, and police headquarters. These were men on a mission.

Apparently, gunshots had been heard during the night. It was said that some ministers and intelligence personnel had been arrested in dramatic raids on their homes. She supposed those were the so-called 'criminals' who'd been targeted, though in reality they could have simply belonged to a different faction within the ruling party. There were reports that some people had already fled across the border.

By late afternoon, police duties had been visibly curtailed. Their roadblocks disappeared, much to the delight of motorists who'd long been at the mercy of corrupt traffic police. Soldiers, who were clearly not after extorting money, manned new roadblocks. They searched vehicles and gave road safety advice in a very polite and non-threatening manner.

In good Zimbabwean style, jokes and memes quickly flooded social media. Everyone found reason to laugh at the humorously named '*Coup-Not-A-Coup,*' as the generals continued to strenuously deny to the world that their action was any such thing.

It was as if the President and his wife being confined to their mansion had released a lid under which everyone had been slowly suffocating. Zimbabweans were on a roll, reaching what seemed to Cashleen to be new heights of recklessness and fearlessness in their euphoria.

In the midst of all the daring and irreverent jokes, the apprehension and the uncertainty, there was also hope and expectation that finally… finally, there'd be a chance for real socio-economic change to be ushered in by a new government. Soldiers were hailed as the people's saviours.

As the day went on, it became clearer that there'd most likely be no heads rolling in blood-soaked streets. Nor would there be public gunfights and violence. Nevertheless, Cashleen chose not to venture out all day. She felt safer that way.

As she watched the news coverage, there was again that stirring of professional envy. The reporters were doing what she'd always wanted to do. She wondered, if she'd forever remain a small-time Harare crook, or find her way into the profession for which she'd been trained. She had no idea, but for now, she supposed, her private writings would suffice. Her cache of current social commentaries had grown. Maybe one day she'd find use for it. Definitely a blog. And a novel perhaps? For the first time, she entertained the idea of writing fiction and found that she liked it.

The next day a criminal investigations officer phoned her. Her BMW was ready for collection from the facility for impounded vehicles in Southerton. To hear Itai's car being referred to as hers didn't feel real, but there it was. She asked Unesu to accompany her.

While the situation seemed peaceful enough, one could never be too careful. No matter how friendly the soldiers appeared, they were armed and one could never forget that they were also trained to kill.

They drove to Southerton police station, where Cashleen spotted Itai's car parked near the main office entrance. They were asked to wait in the reception area. After a few minutes, a burly officer in mufti came over. Cashleen couldn't help noticing that although clean and well ironed, his clothes were old and faded. Another poor civil servant, she thought.

'Miss Cashleen?' the officer asked.

'That's me,' she replied.

'Your ID please, Miss?'

She fished it out of her handbag, surprised at being addressed so respectfully. She was more used to being bullied by the police.

After examining it, he asked her to come through to his office. Then looking questioningly at Unesu he added, 'Are you together?'

'Yes,' Unesu replied.

The officer turned to Cashleen. 'He can come along too if you're okay with that.'

They got up and followed him. In his office, they sat on shabby chairs and faced him across an equally shabby table.

He pulled a folder from a drawer and at that moment, his phone rang. He answered it, saying, 'I'll call you back just now.'

As soon as he put the receiver back, it rang again. With a slight frown, he picked it up again, 'I said I'll call you back. Right now, I'm...' and then Cashleen saw a tremor in the hand that held the phone. His face caved in an expression of defeat.

'They can't expel her for school fees in the middle of exams!' he exclaimed tersely, then listened some more.

'*A hundred dollars*? How come it's so much?' There was a pause. 'Okay, tell the headmaster I'll find it. I'll find it and pay tomorrow morning,' he said and disconnected the call.

For a moment, he looked disoriented, as if he couldn't remember who they were or what they were there for. Then, silently, he handed Cashleen the car registration book.

'Please read this release form. Then sign and date at the bottom,' he said as he gave her another sheet of paper.

Cashleen did as she'd been asked.

'That's all,' the detective handed her the keys. 'The car's outside, near the entrance. Just check if everything is in order before you leave.'

'Thank you very much, Sir... Detective ...?' and then on impulse, 'Can I offer you something... as a thank you?'

'Aah, *Sisi!* Why? I'm just doing my job,' he said, but she thought his face lit up, if only for a second.

She insisted. 'Please, Detective. It's just a small token of my appreciation.'

There was absolute reproof in the look which Unesu gave her, but Cashleen was undeterred. She'd come expecting some kind of harassment, or a request for a bribe. None of that had happened and she was relieved and grateful. Surely there was no harm in her offering him a something? She took out her purse, counted out a hundred dollars and held the money out to him. The officer hesitated.

'Please,' she said, 'It's just a thank you for the help you gave me.'

'Thank you very much, Miss. You didn't have to, but thank you, thank you,' he said relief all over his face, as he accepted.

Outside, Unesu rebuked her. 'Are you out of your mind? What the hell did you do that for?'

Cashleen countered. 'Did you listen to his phone call? Someone, maybe his child, is going to be expelled from school in the middle of her exams ... And didn't you see how shabby he looked, how worn his clothes were. This is not a man who takes bribes, but a man who tries to do his job professionally.'

'And so ...what business is it of yours? Is he not on the government's payroll?' Unesu demanded.

'Listen, Unesu. I've acquired a car with no problems, and yet I came here expecting to pay a bribe. It's just the way things work and I've come to accept that. He didn't ask, and clearly he wasn't expecting anything from me. In a way, he was going to pay the price of honesty by having his child or relative expelled from school. Maybe, just maybe, I've made a real difference in someone's life today.'

Unesu snorted. 'Thank goodness I don't do sentimental!' He raised his hands in mock despair. 'Offering an unsolicited bribe. That's definitely a first!'

Cashleen was unabashed; indeed she felt a little irritated with her friend who seemed to not recognise the difference between honesty and dishonesty, compassion and self-righteousness. What planet did he exist on?

They parted ways and Unesu led the way back into town in his twin cab.

Cathleen pressed her foot ever so gently on the accelerator pedal and felt the BMW respond. After the driving school's Mazda 323 and ancient Datsun 120Y, it was the smoothest drive she'd ever experienced.

40

The days have sped by. The President remains under house arrest at his Blue Roof Mansion. The First Lady, who dominated the media, hasn't been seen since the army take-over. There's speculation that she and her sons have fled the country. No official statement has been made, so rumours abound.

The country is on the precipice of what everyone hopes is a new beginning. Today, Zimbabweans across the political divide and from all walks of life have chosen to march in solidarity against the nonagenarian President. Their shared resolution is trending as *#SolidarityMarch*. They are united in not wanting him to be returned to power by some external intervention. There have been mixed signals, especially from SADC.

Cashleen feels the excitement, knowing that she's in a position from which she can capture a crucial slice of history. The prospect of release from oppression has given her the confidence to employ her skills openly and without fear. This, after all, was what she was trained to do. Even as a self-funded blogger, there's potential, and with the country in the spotlight, she allows herself to imagine access to international news markets. Dreams can come true, she reminds herself.

While she's high on flights of fancy, an image of Sando pops into her mind out of nowhere: his bruised and battered body, his hurt and troubled mind, which seems to have frozen into a catatonic state. He *had* stepped out of line. It's a salutary reminder that she'll have to be cautious. Always.

She packs her camera, puts some bottled water into her backpack, then drives out to the meeting point at Belgravia shops. She's convinced that this is going to be an exciting day, despite the sentiments widely shared by the President's supporters who loudly proclaim that by staging a coup in the sacred month of November, the army will have provoked the ancestral spirits who will certainly bring a curse upon the nation. But let them say whatever, if it gets them through their catastrophe. After all, who in this day and age would believe such superstitions?

And could there be greater misfortune than what Zimbabweans have already experienced? Surely, the only thing that could jinx this historic day would be a surprise November thunderstorm!

She's first to arrive. Unesu and Delta had agreed to meet up with her at 8 a.m. but they're both running late. The car park at the shopping centre is almost full. She suspects that most cars don't belong to regular Saturday shoppers. At last, she finds an empty parking bay just opposite Zuva Service Station.

The crowds have already begun to gather, richly diverse in race and age. There's a festive atmosphere. Many people have complemented their outfits with multi-coloured national flags draped around the shoulders. Others are brandishing their flags in the air, high and proud. They spill into Second Street extension and head towards town. The march has begun. She can imagine similar scenes at all the designated assembly points in Harare.

While she's waiting for her friends, her phone pings, alerting her to a WhatsApp video from Tanaka who's at Robert Mugabe Square, where there's an even bigger and more exuberant gathering. Her friend's face fills the screen, before the recording swings over a sea of people, and into a blue shimmer of tinted glass windows on the high-rise Interpol building.

In a short while Delta arrives, followed by Unesu. They join the marching crowd. Their first stop will be State House, before they continue into the city centre. A feeling of release grips her. She snaps pictures and speaks into her recorder, reminding herself that she'll need some interviews for her blog before the day is over.

Looking around, she's struck by the forthrightness of people's placards. Just five days previously, some of them could've resulted in the arrest and imprisonment of the owner.

#MugabeMustFall, Mugabe Out, Gucci-Grace-Stop-It, Zimbabwe Army – The Voice of The People, and *South Africa, First Deal with This!*

The last placard carries the battered and bruised face of the young model who was assaulted in South Africa by Zimbabwe's First Lady.

Trying to stay true to journalism, Cashleen's own placard is a shameless steal from *The Washington Post's* tagline: *Democracy Dies in Darkness.* Delta's shows more humour: *Leadership Is Not Sexually Transmitted,* a jibe directed at the First Lady who had long been alleged to be eyeing the presidency after her husband's retirement. Unesu's is conservative and succinct: *Free Zim!*

Drivers in the few accompanying cars blow their horns intermittently, increasing the noisy exuberance. Some have radios that are blasting *Kutonga Kwaro* by Jah Prayzah, the song of the moment. For many, this song resonates with endorsement of the exiled former Vice-President as the incoming President.

There's a carnival atmosphere, with scenes of jubilation and camaraderie. Many are sharing hugs and exchanging high-fives. Cashleen captures as much as she can with her camera. She spots some young girls standing on a tanker, taking a selfie with a soldier whose smile stretches from ear to ear. She signals for permission to take a picture. They wave and give her a thumbs-up.

So far so good. How can the President possibly continue holding on to power in the face of such collective resistance? How can SADC, or indeed the international community, not see that people want change?

At the Josiah Tongogara Road intersection, they turn left towards State House. Cashleen spots several individuals perched high in the jacaranda trees that line the road, waving their flags and placards, cheering wildly.

Just past the corner is another tanker manned by a lone, armed soldier. Cashleen smiles up at him and he rewards her with a gap-toothed grin. He extends his arm and gestures for her to climb up. Instinctively, she grabs his hand and clambers onto the tanker. Unesu is right behind her, but there isn't enough room for Delta at the top. In that restricted space, the soldier moves closer and asks her to smile for a selfie.

Unesu comes between them, rather forcefully, she thinks.

Sorry Blaz, the soldier says to Unesu, *I didn't know that she's your girl.*

Unesu stares at her. With a sheepish grin on his face, he put his arm around her shoulder. She looks at him, surprised, then down at Delta who's giving them a thumbs-up sign.

She reciprocates and projects her imagination into a bright future. Today, like everyone else, she's sure of this.